LOVE AND MARRIAGE

www.transworldireland.ie

www.**rbooks**.co.uk

PATRICIA SCANLAN

LOVE AND MARRIAGE

TRANSWORLD IRELAND

TRANSWORLD IRELAND
an imprint of The Random House Group Limited
20 Vauxhall Bridge Road, London SW1V 2SA
www.rbooks.co.uk

First published in 2011 by Transworld Ireland,
a division of Transworld Publishers

A CIP catalogue record for this book
is available from the British Library.

ISBNs 9781848270701 (cased)
9781848270695 (tpb)

Addresses for Random House Group Ltd companies outside the UK
can be found at: www.randomhouse.co.uk
The Random House Group Ltd Reg. No. 954009

The Random House Group Ltd supports the Forest Stewardship
Council (FSC), the leading international forest-certification organization. All our
titles that are printed on Greenpeace-approved FSC-certified paper carry the FSC logo.
Our paper procurement policy can be found at
www.rbooks.co.uk/environment

Typeset in 11/15pt Palatino by
Falcon Oast Graphic Art Ltd.
Printed and bound in Great Britain by
Clays Ltd, Bungay, Suffolk

2 4 6 8 10 9 7 5 3 1

Mixed Sources
Product group from well-managed
forests and other controlled sources
www.fsc.org Cert no. TT-COC-2139
© 1996 Forest Stewardship Council
FSC

If you are lucky, there are friends in your life who know you inside out and who stick with you through thick and thin. Friends you can be absolutely yourself with, who share your joys and sorrows, who laugh and empathize with you, and who will understand your indignation when you have to start wearing glasses to read menus, write notes to yourself to stop you from forgetting what you're meant to be doing, and stop wearing skyscraper heels because they just aren't worth the toe-pinching pain!

So, how lucky am I to have three great pals? Pals who do all of the above and a lot more, as well as having hilarious holidays, lunches, spur-of-the-moment coffees, and many Cava, Prosecco and champers moments with me. To Mary, Yvonne and Breda: the Wick/Spain Gang. Ladies, this one's for you! Next lunch is on me. Roll on May!

'AUGUST IS A WICKED MONTH'

PROLOGUE

CONNIE AND DREW

'Morning.'

'Morning.'

'How did you sleep?'

'Really well.' Connie Adams yawned, curled herself in tight against Drew Sullivan and wrapped her arms around him. She couldn't believe how happy she felt. The joy of waking up in Drew's arms was exquisite. After years and years of loneliness and getting on with life, and being a single mother who had seen her only daughter safely up the aisle, who would have thought she would fall in love again? And in love she was, she thought happily. Heading for the big five-O and happier than she had ever been in her entire life. New job, new man: her life had changed drastically in the weeks since her daughter's wedding. Debbie and Bryan might be happy newly-weds, but she and Drew were like love's young dream. Connie smiled as she traced her finger down the length of his spine and then slid her hand around the front to the lean, flat plane of his stomach. Slowly she ran her fingers down the inside of his thigh.

'You are a wanton woman.' Drew grinned as he turned to face her and moulded her to him.

'You're fairly wanton yourself, mister.' She sighed blissfully as she felt him hard against her.

'What are you going to do about it?' he murmured against her mouth, his hand cupping her breast.

'This,' she said, kissing him and drawing him even closer. 'And this . . .'

'You are one sexy man, Drew Sullivan,' Connie said a while later, stretching languorously and slanting a teasing glance at him.

'I think you need glasses, woman.' He chuckled, twining his fingers with hers, his blue eyes glinting in amusement.

'Take your compliment and don't be bashful,' she retorted.

'You're pretty hot yourself, Ms Adams.'

'Well, that will get you breakfast, Mr Sullivan.' Connie leaned over and gave him a kiss. 'Fancy a fry-up?'

'No, I fancy you.' Drew grabbed her and kissed her again.

'We have to stop this,' she laughed when she came up for air. 'I bet we're having more sex than our children.'

'We're making up for lost time.' His arms tightened around her.

'I'm really, really happy.' She nestled in against him.

'Me too,' he said huskily. 'I never expected anything like this to happen to me. I think that's why I really appreciate it – I love being with you, Connie.'

'I love being with you too. I want to tell Debbie about us – is that OK?'

'Sure, I'd like to meet her. I'd like to tell my girls too. Pity they live in America. I'll phone them on Sunday.'

'How about I invite Debbie and Bryan to lunch some Sunday?'

'I can only come to lunch if your crispy roasties are on the menu.' Drew kissed her forehead and flung the duvet back. 'I have to get to work. I don't have the morning off like some people.'

'I know, it's great! I love this part-time work, I've so much time for myself.' Connie slipped on her dressing gown. 'You go shower and I'll put on brekkie.'

'Yes, boss.' Drew loped into the en suite and, moments later, she heard him whistling as he turned on the shower.

It was so deeply satisfying to know that she made him happy, she mused as she grilled some bacon and flipped the eggs in the pan. When her marriage to her ex-husband, Barry, had turned sour all those years ago she had lost her confidence completely. He had been so miserable at the end, and she'd blamed herself for being a bad wife, for not being sexy enough, for not being slim, or sufficiently interesting to keep him happy. It had taken her a long time to realize that much of the fault had lain with him and his immaturity. He hadn't wanted the responsibility of a wife and child, and nothing she could have done would have changed that.

But knowing that she had brought as much happiness to Drew as he'd brought to her gave her great joy. She set the table outside on the deck. It was a beautiful morning, and the sky was clear and cobalt blue. There was still heat in the sun, even though autumn's first tentative caress had come early. The berries were scarlet and ripe on the rowan tree, a sure sign that the summer was almost over. She used to dread the onset of winter, the shorter evenings and the lonely dark nights. Now she was looking forward to long walks with Drew on wild, windy days, to watching the sea surge on to the shore, drinking coffee in little seaside coffee shops and snuggling in front of blazing fires with candles flickering, sipping wine.

So different from all the other years, so much to look forward to, Connie thought joyfully as Drew clattered down the stairs. Her heart lifted at the sight of him, tall and rangy in his jeans and maroon shirt. Life had never been so good, she reflected, sending up a silent prayer of gratitude, as they brought their plates out to the table and sat companionably enjoying their breakfast in the flower-filled garden of her cottage.

BARRY, AIMEE AND MELISSA

Barry Adams lay beside his wife, waiting for the alarm to go off. Both of them had slept badly. Aimee had tossed and turned, crucified with heartburn. Eventually she'd ended up being sick. She'd fallen into a restless sleep, but he couldn't drift off. She was exceedingly stressed, between worrying about their daughter, Melissa, and wondering what the future held for her proposed new events and catering company. If she'd wanted the baby, it would be a hard enough load to carry, he thought dispiritedly, but being unwillingly pregnant was a burden too far for her. And he'd been no help. Guilt permeated his lethargic state – he'd really come the heavy on her about keeping the baby. He'd more or less told her it was either keep the baby, or the marriage was over. How supportive was that?

When he'd walked out on Connie and Debbie all those years ago, he'd been riddled with guilt, but not enough to go back. He'd ruined his relationship with his eldest daughter. Now he was ruining his relationship with his second wife. If their marriage broke up – and it would, under the weight of resentment and anger Aimee carried – he would be responsible. He'd issued an ultimatum. Aimee was right, he was as bad as her father, dictating and pontificating. Being compared to Ken Davenport was nothing to be proud of. And it was an accusation that stung.

But what about their child, he argued silently, an ache of

anguish constricting his heart. Aimee was carrying their baby, and even with all that was going on in their lives, he *wanted* this baby. Maybe it was to salve his conscience about being a crap father to Debbie, maybe it was about having someone to love him in a way that Aimee never would. Out of nowhere, the memory of a long-forgotten row he'd had with Connie surfaced. 'Me! Me! Me! That's all you think of: me, me, me. It always has to be about you, Barry, what *you* want, what *you* feel. You're not the only one on the planet . . .' she'd shouted at him in frustration. They'd separated shortly after that.

The first faint glimmers of dawn crept across the sky, and Aimee stirred beside him.

'Are you OK?' he asked.

'No, I feel grotty, and knackered,' she muttered.

'Aimee, if you want to have a termination, I won't stand in your way. Do what you think is best. I'll go with you if you want me to,' he said, his heart like lead. In offering Aimee his support, and by putting her first, he had betrayed their child. And that was something he'd have to live with for the rest of his life.

He heard his wife's sharp intake of breath. 'Do you mean that?' She was clearly stunned.

'Yes, Aimee, the choice is yours. I'll be there for you whatever you decide. I'm sorry I was so . . . so insensitive and domineering.' He tried to keep his tone neutral. He felt completely shattered, torn, bereft; myriad emotions were competing for dominance.

And then her hand slid down under the sheets and slipped into his. In an automatic reflex action, he squeezed it, and she squeezed back. They lay side by side, in silence, as the dawn chorus filled the sky and another day unfolded.

Aimee sat on the side of the bath taking some deep breaths. She'd just spent the last five minutes retching. She could hear the whine of the power shower in the en suite, where Barry was having his shower, and for a weird moment she wondered if she was dreaming. Had she *imagined* that she'd heard Barry tell her she could go for a termination and he would go with her if she wanted him to? What had caused this seismic shift? He'd been so adamant that she keep their baby, so angry with her that she'd contemplated having a termination without even telling him that she was expecting their child. She stood up and ran her hand over her stomach. Still flat; no hint of bulge or thickening waist yet. The only change was in her breasts: they were sore and tender, and her bra was tight, as her pert boobs were becoming fuller. For the second time in her life, she was developing a decent cleavage, she thought wryly, as the thin silk of her nightdress strained at the bust. It would be so easy to end the pregnancy. She could tell Melissa and her parents that she'd miscarried. No one would be any the wiser, and life would be so much easier. The unexpected opportunity of building up a new events company was already proving much more difficult than she'd anticipated now that the recession had come slashing like a scythe through the economy. Her potential client base was narrowing day by day as bankers, developers, builders and wealthy businessmen found their fortunes decimated – and the ones who had it stashed away were keeping it out of the country.

When she'd accepted businessman Roger O'Leary's invitation to set up Hibernian Dreams, the economy had been riding high, and she'd just overseen the wedding of his daughter, which had cost well in excess of a million smackers. Money had been no object to him or the other multimillionaire guests. Then the banking system had collapsed and Anglo had gone belly up, thanks to the greed, avarice and amoral behaviour of its senior bankers and the regulators and auditors who had not done their job properly. It paralleled the recession worldwide and it was a very different environment in which to be setting up a high-end business than the one she had anticipated when she had started out.

And then there was Melissa. Although her daughter did not yet know it, Aimee had made an appointment for her to see their GP to get a referral to an eating-disorders specialist. At least she and Barry had been able to put their differences behind them and put up a united front in the face of Melissa's determination to rush headlong into anorexia. Tears blurred Aimee's eyes. What warped thinking was in her child's head that could turn her from a fairly happy-go-lucky young teenager into a devious, lying, unreachable young girl who would not listen to reason?

She and Barry had given Melissa all she could want. Why had she taken this ruinous step, which was tearing their family apart? Maybe the doctors would be able to throw some light on it. Aimee sighed deeply; she could safely say this was one of the most difficult, unhappy times of her life. At least Barry had stepped up to the plate and *finally* recognized that she was in trouble. He'd given her back the space to make her own choices, as far as she could. He'd become once more the man she'd married. The one who had supported her, been there for her and treated her like an equal.

A burden lifted. Her marriage wasn't going to crumble, as she'd feared. They'd ploughed the depths and troughs and come through it, this time, and Aimee felt nothing but relief. Although she would have squared her shoulders and got on with being a separated or divorced wife, she was utterly relieved that that scenario, for now, had receded. She needed Barry. She needed her family around her. She had an uphill battle and hard choices ahead of her. She didn't want to make those difficult decisions on her own.

She walked back down the hall to their bedroom. Her husband was almost dressed, knotting his tie with his back to her, as she walked in. The early-morning sun streamed in through the voile curtains and she noted with a little dart of shock that Barry was getting very grey at the temples. He looked stressed, tired. Her heart softened. None of this was easy for him either and she'd been behaving like a complete bitch these past few weeks. 'Barry, thanks for what you've done for me. I just wanted to say that. You'll never know how much it means to me,' she said quietly.

'That's OK, Aimee. Do what you have to do. Let me know if you need me to come with you. I'll tell Stephanie to rearrange my schedule.' He slipped into his suit jacket and turned to look at her.

'OK,' she agreed. 'I'll call you.'

Their eyes met. 'Don't hate me, Barry,' she begged.

'I don't hate you, Aimee,' he said. 'If I hated you I wouldn't have said what I said this morning.' He held open his arms to her and she went into his embrace, and they stood together, arms around each other, and the comfort of his hug brought some balm to her frazzled spirit.

Melissa's mouth dropped in astonishment as she gazed at herself in her detested green and black school uniform. It was *hanging* off her. The skirt slid down to her hips; the blouse looked like a tent. 'Yes! Yes! Yes!' She punched the air ecstatically. Every single stomach-growling hunger pang, headache, feeling of faintness and tiredness was so worth it for this moment. For just this wonderful triumphant moment, she'd never felt so happy in her life. This horrible, horrible summer, the worst of her life, was over and she was two stone lighter.

She flung herself on the bed and began to squeeze a spot that had annoyingly erupted at the side of her nose. How typical when she was going back to school on Monday, having not seen most of her classmates for three months. So much had happened. Her half-sister Debbie had got married, and it was at her wedding that her life-changing moment had occurred: *Who is that little fat tart?* Even now, and twenty-eight pounds lighter, the words of that unkind, drunken slag had the power to wound. Still, at least it had been her wake-up call, and she had dieted *rigorously* for the whole summer. Now that she was on the way to being thin no one would ever call her names like that, and that disgusting boy, Thomas, would never do that horrible thing to her again. Melissa's eyes darkened at the memory and she banished it instantly. Being thin was the way to go, the way to happiness.

If only everything else in her life was as good. Melissa exhaled despondently. Her mom was pregnant, and she didn't want to be, and she was trying to set up a new company that was taking up all her time. Her dad was very worried about the recession and about some guy called Jeremy who wasn't taking phone calls about some investment he had with him, and there'd been an atmosphere of tension since they'd come back from their holidays in the south of France.

She never thought she'd say it, but in a way she was glad to be going back to school. But she couldn't go back to school in that uniform; she'd have to get a new one. What a pain. She grabbed her iPhone and dialled her mother's number, half-expecting it to go into voicemail, but Aimee answered almost immediately and Melissa knew from the background noise that she was in a hotel or somewhere public.

'Yes, Melissa, what's up?' Her mother sounded wary.

'Where are you?'

'The Merrion. I'm meeting someone in five minutes, so if I see him coming I'll have to go.'

'Mom, I was checking my uniform for school on Monday and it's, like, way too big for me. I'll have to get a new one.'

'Oh for goodness' sake!' Aimee couldn't hide her exasperation. 'Typical last-minute!'

'Sorry, Mom.'

'I'll be home around two – do you need me to go with you or can you go and get one yourself?'

'I'll get it myself, Mom. I'll ask Sarah to come with me.' Melissa raised her legs, parted them and stretched them as wide as she could before starting her bicycling exercise. It was no use losing lots of weight if she wasn't toned.

'Fine, there's some fifties in my black Prada bag – use them. See you later? Did you have breakfast?'

'Yep,' fibbed Melissa.

'And don't forget to have some lunch. There's organic smoked salmon in the fridge, and eat up some of that fruit.'

'Yes, Mother.' Melissa threw her eyes up to heaven.

'Right, have to go, I can see my business contact coming. See you later.'

'See ya, Mom. Hope your meeting goes well.'

'Thanks, darling. Bye.'

The phone went dead, and Melissa knew her mother had tuned her out, having far more important matters to deal with. Still, if her business turned out well, there was the prospect that Melissa might be getting a horse. How totally cool would that be? Ever since Connie, her dad's ex-wife, had brought her to Drew Sullivan's stables to see the adorable new foal, Frisky, she had *longed* to have a horse of her own to love and care for.

Her parents had said that if she ate proper, nutritious meals and did well at school, it was on the cards. She would have a tiny bit of smoked salmon and half a banana for lunch, she decided. After all, she'd skipped brekkie, so that was a few calories lost. A sudden weariness overcame her. The burst of adrenalin that had surged through her when she'd seen her uniform hanging off her had dissipated and she felt that familiar lassitude invade her body as it clamoured for food.

She hauled herself off the bed and went down to the gleaming chrome and white kitchen in their apartment. She boiled a kettle of water, squirted some lemon juice into a cup, filled it with the boiling water and went and sat at the round ceramic table on the wide wraparound balcony. She thought with immense pleasure of the expressions on the faces of Nerdy Nolan and Niamh Sampson, two of the bitchiest girls in her class, when they saw her on Monday morning, two stone lighter and the potential owner of her very own horse. This time last year, she'd been a bundle of nerves going to her new secondary school, and a fatso to boot. Things were on the up, definitely, Melissa decided, as she sipped her hot drink and watched a tug steaming out to rendezvous with a massive cargo ship heading across the sun-gilded sea towards Dublin Bay.

BRYAN AND DEBBIE

Mark Brody raised his hands for silence and Bryan felt a frisson of foreboding as he studied the stern countenance of his MD, who was standing at the podium ready to make a statement. The conference room was crowded, with practically the entire work-force waiting uneasily for what was to come. The buzz of edgy chatter quietened and silence descended.

'People, we've tried to postpone this moment for as long as we could but, in view of the current economic climate and the downturn in the commercial sector, we have to take radical steps to keep the company viable. Therefore I have to announce that, following a period of consultation, redundancies are being made. The statutory redundancy terms will apply. I'm also sorry to announce that, for a third of the remaining staff, a three-day week will commence in two weeks' time. HR will notify all those affected by these regrettable developments. As for the rest of us, a 10 per cent pay cut will take effect right across the board from the beginning of next month. I'm sorry to have to make this announcement, we tried hard to avoid it, but circumstances and current market conditions have made it unavoidable. Thank you for your attention.'

There was a stunned silence as the throng parted like the Red Sea to allow him to make his way out of the room.

'Bloody hell!'

'*I'm for the chop!*'

'*Christ Almighty, a three-day week! I'll never be able to afford the mortgage . . .*'

'*Ten per cent? I can hardly manage on what I'm getting. Why don't friggin' management take fifteen at least . . .*'

'*It's Friday – who's coming to the pub?*'

Bryan listened to the babble around him in a daze. Redundancies, three-day weeks, 10 per cent pay cuts. Any of these options was a disaster. He and Debbie were already in massive debt and struggling, barely keeping their heads above water. This was the killer blow.

Things were bad enough between them as it was after his little episode in A&E, when he'd had to have his stomach pumped after going on a drugs and drink binge at Kevin Devlin's party. Debbie was hardly talking to him. Sex was out of the question. So much for love and marriage. Newly wedded bliss had passed them by big-time. If they hadn't have got married and tied that boulder of a mortgage around their necks they'd be fine. Rents were at rock bottom – they could be living in a swish apartment with no responsibilities. This was all her mother's fault, Bryan thought savagely. Connie had harped on and on about getting a house. It was all her bloody damn fault. He couldn't stand the woman. He knew she looked down her nose at him. He *knew* she didn't think he was good enough for Debbie. Not that she ever said anything, she didn't have to, she just oozed attitude.

Oh, to go on a bender, he thought longingly. He could do with a hit of coke, but his ghastly experience in A&E was still fresh in his mind.

Jerry Fitzgerald, pale underneath his tan, grabbed his arm. 'I'd say I'm a goner, mate. You might get the three-day week, but I'm a goner. I came in after you. That's our house gone. Lisa will never be able to pay the mortgage on her salary; her salary's down the tubes with all these levies and pay cuts. Let's go and get pissed.' His colleague was nearly crying with shock and apprehension.

'Jeez, that's tough if it happens – you've got two kids.' Bryan looked at Jerry in dismay. Suddenly the reality of what was happening hit him like a hammer blow. His stomach lurched and he felt himself break out in a cold sweat. He'd seen the news, seen people in factories being interviewed after losing their jobs. Seen men his age, and more highly qualified than him, in dole queues. Now he could be one of these statistics that commentators droned on about. 'What are you going to do?' He heard his automatic response. His voice seemed strange, alien, a long way away.

'Have to go on a waiting list for social housing, or rent a kip somewhere, or emigrate . . . I don't know. Let's get out of here.' Jerry's face was ghost-white.

'I'm sick of this country and all those greedy bastards, with their dodgy banking and their brown envelopes, lining their pockets and getting away scot free. If Debbie agrees, I think we should get the hell out of here too, and start afresh,' Bryan fumed as he followed the other man out of the room, knowing that, one way or another, his lifestyle was going to change even more radically than it already had.

'So darling, I'd love you to meet Drew. How about if we try and arrange a date when you and Bryan are free, and I can cook us all lunch?' Connie suggested cheerily down the phone.

Debbie Kinsella's eyes widened as she absorbed her mother's news. Connie had just phoned her to tell her that she was dating a man – in fact, she'd used the word 'relationship' – and she was . . . *bubbling* . . . was the only word Debbie could think of to describe her mother's *joie de vivre*.

'Have you slept with him?' She couldn't contain her curiosity.

'Debbie!' Connie exclaimed, half-laughing. 'What a question to ask your mother!'

'Well, have you?' Debbie pressed.

'This is not something to discuss over the phone! Are you free for coffee tomorrow? I could hop on a Dart and meet you halfway. Dalkey or Killiney? You pick,' Connie said gaily.

'You're on. Dalkey then. How about lunch? One thirty?' Debbie agreed, agog to hear what her mother had to tell her about the new man in her life.

'Great, see you then, pet. Love ya.'

'Love you too, Mum. Bye.' Debbie put the phone down and, out of habit, glanced over to Judith Baxter's glass-fronted office. If her boss had been in work, there was no way Debbie would have been taking a personal call from her mother. Judith was a tyrant and ruled the wages and salaries section of the big multinational insurance company they worked for with a rod of iron.

Fortunately for Debbie, Judith was recovering from a car accident and was not expected back to work for several more weeks. Debbie had enough on her plate without worrying about her autocratic boss. Judith had bullied Debbie the entire year before her wedding, making her life a misery. Now that she had confronted her boss and actually used the 'Bullying' word, it would be interesting to see if Judith's attitude would have changed when she came back to work. Debbie sincerely hoped so: if Judith continued to pick on her, she'd have to bring it to HR, and that was the last thing she wanted. All Debbie wanted to do was keep her head down, do her work and get paid at the end of the week so she could try and reduce the mountain of debt they were in since acquiring a mortgage and splashing out on the wedding and honeymoon.

Her computer pinged, and she was surprised to see an email from Bryan. Her fingers hovered over the keyboard. Maybe he wanted to meet for dinner tonight. They should make some effort to try and put their bad feeling behind them and move on. But that was easier said than done, Debbie thought grimly, as she opened the message.

Ring me if you can, it's about work. B.

Her chest tightened as she read her husband's email. Something was obviously wrong if Bryan was emailing her on a

Friday afternoon about work. What was he going to tell her?

Things were so dire between them at the moment she didn't need bad news. She just couldn't face it. It *had* to be bad news, or he wouldn't have sent her an email. They weren't emailing, texting or phoning each other these days. Not since he'd let her down so badly the night of Kev Devlin's party. Her husband could have died, Debbie thought angrily, remembering the phone call from one of his friends telling her to get to the Mater A&E as quickly as she could. She'd never forget that nerveracking journey across town. And then the hurt and fury when she'd seen him lying on a trolley having had his stomach pumped because he'd taken a bad hit of coke. He'd spent a fortune on drink and drugs that night, even though he knew they were in debt up to their eyeballs.

She was still so angry with him, she acknowledged miserably. Angry because this was not the way things were supposed to be. They'd had a gorgeous wedding, all she'd ever dreamed of. A honeymoon in New York that had been the experience of a lifetime. She'd come home indescribably happy, and then it had all gone downhill. Real life had intruded as bills came in one after another, and they had to face up to the fact that serious cutbacks had to be made in their lifestyle. She'd been prepared to do it, but Bryan simply couldn't hack the fact that he was now a married man with a mortgage and responsibilities. Instead of being happy newly-weds they were utterly wretched. And now he had something to tell her about work.

No, Debbie decided, she would not ring her husband. She didn't want to know. She was fed up with gloom and doom. Some of the girls were going out for a meal; she hadn't been out in ages with the gang. Since before her wedding, actually, she thought with a jolt. She deserved a girls' night out. And she was not going to ruin a perfectly good Friday evening by ringing Bryan to hear whatever gloomy tale he had to tell her. She knew without the shadow of a doubt that something was up, probably with his job. The commercial sector was taking a big hit, and

Bryan's job in the office fit-out and supply company he worked for was not as safe as hers. There were talks of cutbacks; over-time, junkets and corporate entertaining had been slashed weeks ago, and something else had obviously happened now. She'd know soon enough. She just didn't want to know right now. If she were a good wife, she'd phone him, but she'd had it being the good wife. She'd given it her best shot and got nothing in return except moans and abuse. Typical of Bryan to come crying on her shoulder when he was in trouble. She'd put up with it for years, but the night of that party had been a turning point. She wasn't a doormat for her husband to wipe his size nines on any more.

She typed briskly:

Can't ring at the moment, staff meeting. Going out with the girls for a meal, will see you later. D.

The email whizzed into cyberspace and an unfamiliar sensation of freedom enveloped her. She was going to have fun tonight. She *deserved* to have fun, she thought wildly. If her life was going to fall apart even more than it had, she might as well go for it with all guns blazing. Hell, if her mother seemed to be having the time of her life, it was a poor lookout if Debbie, who was supposed to be living on cloud nine in newly wedded bliss, couldn't have a bit of fun in her life too. Today was payday, and she was going to do a Bryan on it. A last supper, so to speak, Debbie thought with rising giddiness as she logged out of her computer and went to join her friends in the locker room to change out of her work clothes and prepare for a night on the tiles.

JULIET AND KEN

'It's like this, Juliet, we're not broke or anything like it, but we've lost a hell of an amount of money. The shares in Anglo are gone. That money is *completely* lost to us. A hundred and fifty thousand. The same amount of shares each in AIB and BOI are on the floor. If we sell them we take a massive hit. Now, they may recover in years to come. Who knows? If those banks are nationalized like Anglo, as some people seem to think they will be, we've really had it. I'd invested in a commercial property portfolio with AIB: that's down 80k. The pensions are hammered. We're not going to be able to sell the villa in Spain; their property market is in as bad, if not worse, a state than ours is. I could go on, Juliet, if you want me to,' Ken Davenport said wearily to his wife, as they sat at the gleaming mahogany table in their formal dining room.

'So what you're telling me is I can't buy the apartment,' Juliet said quietly, her heart thumping in her chest.

'What I'm telling you is that, from having a very healthy nest egg and no money worries – we have that investment in An Post, which is the only one that hasn't been affected – we are now looking at a period of belt-tightening which does not include buying another property and me giving you an allowance to live in it. If you want to separate, we'll have to sell the house and buy two small apartments. And we certainly won't get anything like what this house is worth. That's if you'd get any buyer in this downturn. It's impossible to sell at the moment. Just look at the property supplements. I'm sorry, but that's the way it is. The accountant didn't sugarcoat it.'

He stood up and ran his hand through his thick white hair. 'I've a very ill patient I'm worried about. I didn't get to check in on him earlier because the meeting with the accountant overran, so I'm going to nip up to the clinic to check in on him. It will give you time to think. I know you wanted to move on that apartment in Blackrock, but our circumstances have changed and I can't be blamed for that, whatever else you want to blame me for.' He added his little dig as he turned on his heel and left the room.

Juliet sat, motionless, hearing his heavy tread on the stairs. Her chance for freedom was gone; her chance to live a life of her own had gone up in smoke. If what her husband told her was true, and she didn't think he'd lie to her about it, they had lost an awful lot of money. And they weren't the only ones. Paula Byron, who was married to a urologist, had bumped into her in Blackrock and told her that she and her husband had lost a fortune in some company or other that had gone to the wall. She wasn't driving her BMW soft-top any more either. She was driving a second-hand Golf.

The recession was affecting everyone, but it was just Juliet's luck that it had to hit when she'd made the decision to leave her husband. She rubbed her eyes wearily. She felt like crying. She had been on such a high since she'd come back from her few days in Spain, when she'd made her decision to walk away from her domineering husband and her marriage of forty-five years. She'd been the perfect wife and mother, the little doormat who'd suppressed her own needs and wants, standing in her husband's shadow as he built a very successful career as one of the country's top heart specialists.

In fairness to him, it wasn't his fault that the country was in the worst recession since the eighties. He'd worked hard for that damn money, and now a lot of it was gone and it looked as though they were going to have to count their pennies. Ken was right about selling the house. They wouldn't get a buyer. Large five-bedroom houses in sizeable grounds in Dublin 4 were simply not selling and, if the gloomy economic outlook was right, wouldn't be for years to come.

She was stuck where she was, and there was nothing she could do about it. Aimee would be so disappointed for her. Her daughter had encouraged her every step of the way, thrilled when Juliet had fallen in love with a bright, spacious apartment in Blackrock and commissioned a survey, which had been fine. She'd told Ken she wanted to put a deposit on it, hence the visit to the accountant.

Whether she liked it or not, she was stuck living with Ken, but if he thought she was going to go back to being the dutiful wife, he could think again. That Juliet was gone. She might have to live in the same house as her husband, but her days of being the perfect wife were well and truly over.

Ken Davenport felt weary to his bones. His life had turned into a nightmare. He scowled as he sat slumped over the wheel of his Merc, crawling through the traffic on Mount Merrion Avenue. This time last year, he'd had a happy marriage, a *very* comfortable nest egg for his retirement, a career that gave him *immense* satisfaction and not a care in the world.

Now he was beset by troubles. Juliet was looking for a separation and a place to live, and he'd had a meeting with his accountant that shook him to his core. His nest egg had been walloped, as the shares and investments he'd thought were blue chip and safer than houses were on the floor. His investment portfolio had lost two-thirds of its value; his shares in Anglo, 150k's worth wiped; his BOI and AIB down 90 per cent. Bonds and property portfolios he'd invested in were now practically worthless. All his years of hard graft – for what? True, he had property, but that too was a disaster: no one was buying and, even if he did find a buyer, the values had dropped like a stone. If Juliet persisted in her quest for this apartment she'd set her heart on, he'd practically have to give away their home. Two years ago, it would have fetched four to five million; now they'd be lucky to get two. It was just as well his children were doing well for themselves – their inheritance was dwindling rapidly, he thought despondently as the lights turned green and the traffic started to move.

Juliet had been so cold and unapproachable since she'd returned from her holiday in Spain. He'd had to move into the guest room again, and he couldn't believe how much he missed her comforting presence in the bed at night. He hated taking his meals alone in the kitchen. His whole routine was in uproar. No breakfast made for him before he went to work. No washing and ironing done if he didn't ask their housekeeper specifically to do it. No one to moan at if he'd had a hard day or sympathize if he lost a patient.

He was too old for all this upheaval and uncertainty, too old to face a lonely old age. His wife must have been utterly miserable if she was prepared to make that choice. And he hadn't even seen it coming. Had taken her so much for granted he hadn't even noticed her unhappiness. It didn't say a lot about him as a husband. He'd thought he'd been a great provider. He took pride in the luxurious and affluent lifestyle his wife enjoyed. He took pride watching her – elegant, well groomed, wearing expensive clothes and jewellery – when they were socializing with his colleagues. Juliet had never let him down . . . until now.

Women were strange creatures . . . there was neither rhyme nor reason to their thought processes. Juliet had him in a state of stress and high anxiety, and she didn't seem to care one bit. He almost felt she hated him. The thought was overwhelming. To his shock, a strangled sob escaped from his throat and then he was crying so much he had to pull in and wait until the wave of sadness and grief had subsided. He sat for ten minutes, taking deep breaths until he felt composed enough to start the engine and continue on to the clinic to check on his patient. Juliet might not need him, but his patients did, and for that small mercy Ken Davenport found himself unexpectedly grateful.

JUDITH AND LILY

'The asking price has dropped thirty thousand,' Judith Baxter murmured to her mother as they stood in the small galley kitchen of an apartment off Clonliffe Road.

'Well, every cloud has a silver lining – there might be a recession, but at least property prices have dropped dramatically. And rightly so, it was ridiculous the carry-on with those developers and builders, but of course the politicians couldn't be told. Or they were told and they didn't listen,' her mother, Lily, declared. 'The so-called intellectuals couldn't see what the dogs in the street knew. The property market was artificially inflated by greedy, greedy people,' Lily Baxter added tartly as she opened press doors and drawers with reckless abandon.

'Yes, Mother,' Judith said, a little dryly.

'Sorry, I was ranting. I just can't help it, I get *so* indignant about it all,' grumbled Lily. 'All our money frittered away, and none of that golden circle is paying for it, and none of the politicians are resigning.'

'Ma, stop fretting about it – you'll only give yourself an ulcer,' Judith advised, glancing out of the small window over the sink. The two-bedroom apartment was on the first floor, and the rectangular lounge overlooked the grounds of Clonliffe College. The view of the green mass of trees and the emerald sward of lawns, which was framed by PVC French doors that led out to a narrow balcony, made it feel almost rural and was soothing to the eye. But the kitchen and bedrooms were small and the low ceilings darkened the rooms.

'A bit disappointing, it sounded better in the ad. What do you think, Judith?' Lily whispered. Also looking at the apartment were a sharp-suited businesswoman in her late thirties and a middle-aged man with sad brown eyes, a frayed shirt and a shiny pinstriped suit that had seen better days.

'I like the view, but it needs a makeover and the communal areas are a bit shabby. The carpet is stained, and the place needs painting,' Judith observed. 'I don't think it's for me.'

'I'm glad you feel that way . . . not that it's any of my business now,' Lily said hastily. 'You must buy what you want to buy, but I wouldn't like to think of you here all by yourself. It's a bit gloomy. There are plenty of places out there for you to look at. You're in no rush, and it's a buyers' market.' Lily felt she was a bit of an expert on the property market now, having read dozens of articles in the various property supplements that came with the papers.

'Well, ladies, what do you think? Is there anything I can help you with? Any questions? There is a management company, which is responsible for maintaining the communal areas, grounds, building insurance, etc. The fee last year was €2,000,' the young estate agent who was showing them the property informed them chattily, leaning against the door jamb, his hand in his trouser pocket.

'It's not quite what I'm looking for,' Judith said firmly, edging past him.

'Bit too poky,' Lily added crisply, wishing she could tell him to stand up straight, stop lounging around and smarten up. Judith felt an uncharacteristic urge to giggle. She was seeing a whole new side to her mother since she'd come home from hospital. So different from the tense, edgy, nervy woman she'd lived with most of her life. Lily had a wry sense of humour that Judith was only discovering after all these years. Her mother, too, was very well up on current affairs and politics and had a view on everything. They were now having quite interesting conversations when, for years, they'd sniped at each other and could hardly bear to sit in the same room together for more than an hour or two.

And she too had changed, Judith reflected as they made their way out of the apartment. Her near brush with death, her passive suicide attempt, which had led to serious injuries, had made her take a hard, unflinching look at herself, and she hadn't liked what she'd seen. It had been easy to blame Lily for her loneliness, sadness and wasted life. But she had to accept the responsibility for the choices she'd made, and once she'd come to that realization it was as though a weight had lifted, and she'd stopped running away from herself. Judith felt a flicker of happiness. How wonderful was this, to be house-hunting for a place of her own with Lily and having fun at the same time?

'Let's go and have coffee and a big slice of chocolate cake in Anderson's to celebrate my first viewing,' she suggested impulsively, leading the way to the Ford Fiesta the insurance company had given her while she waited for the claim on her own car to be processed.

'Excellent idea, dear. We need to fortify ourselves for our next one. The bungalow in Fairview, wasn't it?'

'That's the one,' Judith said cheerfully. 'And then, tomorrow, there's the redbrick off Dorset Street.'

'And Sunday the apartment in Glasnevin. We could have lunch in the Botanics first, and you could do your walk.'

'Perfect idea, Ma,' agreed Judith, as she limped over to the car and held the passenger door open for her mother. Driving was still nerve-racking and she was just doing small journeys, keeping as local as possible to Drumcondra. Judith was determined to get her confidence back, but the new Judith was much less hard on herself than the old one had been, and today had been a triumph, even if she was beginning to feel tired. A viewing, coffee and cake with her mother in Anderson's, and cautious driving – she was making progress, slow but sure, and for now that was more than enough.

How pleasant it was to be having coffee and cake with Judith on a spur-of-the-moment whim, Lily observed as she took a sip of the cappuccino she'd ordered. It was very tasty. She'd never had one before. All the things she'd never done. All the time she'd wasted, succumbing to fear and anxiety, taking refuge in her home, afraid to face the outside world. She felt an ache of regret for a life not lived, for opportunities never availed of. She sighed. There was no point in looking back. What had she read somewhere . . . 'There's no future looking back' . . . It was too late for regrets; she had to make the most of what was left of her life, and she had to encourage Judith to do the same. Today was the start of a new life for Judith – freedom beckoned for her daughter, she thought sadly. Who would have thought they would be able to sit, relaxed in each other's company, *enjoying* each other's company. All the years of bickering and sniping and hostility when they'd made each other miserable, and all the time there had been a bond between them, that ran like an underground river, flowing steadily. How sad that it had taken her daughter's near-fatal car crash for that bond to be revealed, Lily acknowledged ruefully.

'Just going to the loo, Ma.' Judith got up stiffly from the chair, and Lily knew that her daughter's neck and shoulder ached. She watched her limp towards the toilets. The consultants had told her she would make a full recovery but it would take time for her broken bones to knit and heal.

Her daughter had been so nervous driving today. Lily had pitied her and tried hard not to be nervous herself. If Judith could be brave, so could she. But it was difficult. Lily's life had changed so drastically and was going to change even more so when Judith finally moved out. Even though she really wanted her daughter to buy a place of her own, it would be a wrench watching her move all her bits and pieces. The end of an era.

Moira Meadows, her great friend, had told her that she would get used to it. And there were worse things than living on your own. She'd managed very, very well when Judith was in hospital, Lily thought proudly. She would not slip into her old ways of fear and anxiety. She would not let her nerves get the better of her. St Michael, her great protector, had done a very good job of minding her thus far: he wouldn't let her down. She had great faith in him, and Judith wouldn't be a hundred miles away and Lily was very sure she wouldn't leave her to her own devices like her other two children. Tom and Cecily had never taken care of her the way Judith had. There were going to be ructions when the pair of them discovered that she had put Judith's name on the deeds of the house and left it to her in her will. Tom had his suspicions, he'd gone out of his way to try and get a gawk at her will, but she'd thwarted him, much to her satisfaction. It was too late now: there was nothing he could do. Judith would be rewarded for her sacrifice in giving up her own life to take care of Lily, and for that alone Lily would have peace of mind for the rest of her days.

'Can I get you anything?' A passing waitress smiled at her as she wiped an adjoining table.

'Yes, dear, could we have two more of those cappuccinos? They were very tasty, and when you bring the bill, bring it to me, please. I'm treating my daughter,' Lily instructed, feeling quite the lady about town, just like the ladies who lunch that she read about in the social diaries.

'EVERY CLOUD HAS A
SILVER LINING'

CHAPTER ONE

'Oh God, my head!' Debbie groaned as sunlight spilled through the curtains, causing her to wince and close her eyes rapidly. She was parched, her mouth sawdust-dry.

'I'm dying!' Carina moaned from the other side of the bed, burying her head under the pillow.

'What time is it?' Debbie struggled into a sitting position and tried to focus on her watch. 'Oh crap, it's after eleven. I'm meeting my mother for lunch – I'll have to go home and get changed.'

'Don't bother going home, hon, have a root in the wardrobe and grab something to wear. There're plenty of clean knickers in the bottom drawer.' Carina yawned and ran her fingers through the tawny mane that tumbled down in disarray over her shoulders.

'How come you look like a sex goddess and I look like a scarecrow?' Debbie demanded, catching sight of herself in the mirror. Her auburn hair stood up on end, and her mascara was smeared across the top of her cheeks.

'Sex goddess!' snorted Carina. 'You're still pissed.'

'I smell like a brewery. Never *ever* again!' Debbie grabbed a bottle of water from beside the bed, unscrewed the top and drank thirstily.

'Good night, though, wasn't it?' grinned her friend as she lay back against the pillows and closed her eyes against the unforgiving light.

'Yeah. I haven't been to Copper Face Jacks in years.'

'And you a married woman,' teased Carina.

'Don't remind me,' Debbie said dryly.

'Ah, you're entitled to a breakout now and again.' Carina broke a couple of squares of chocolate from a Cadbury's bar on her bedside locker and handed it across to Debbie. 'Have some breakfast.'

'Thanks.' Debbie's recovery began as she munched on the welcome treat. 'I might be heading towards being an alcoholic, but you're definitely a chocaholic.'

'I know. I have to stop, it's worse than smoking.' Carina licked her fingers. 'Do you want a grilled-rasher sanger?'

'Just one rasher and one slice of bread, to line my stomach so I don't barf on the Dart.' Debbie grimaced.

'You're so lucky you get on with your mother. If I was meeting mine for lunch, I can guarantee that we'd be fighting in ten minutes,' Carina remarked twenty minutes later, as Debbie, showered and wrapped in a towelling robe, buttered the bread for their sandwiches. The bacon was sizzling on the grill, coffee was brewing in the pot and both of them were beginning to feel human again. Most of the gang from their department had gone for a meal in Yamamori Noodles before moving on to Dakota for cocktails and then ending up in Copper Face Jacks, a well-known haunt for guards and detectives. She'd sent Bryan a text to say she was going out with the girls, and he'd sent one back to say he was with the guys from work, drowning their sorrows because there was bad news on the job front. She hadn't responded. She didn't want to know.

Debbie had embraced the evening's fun wholeheartedly, too wholeheartedly. She hadn't been so drunk in years. Around eleven, she'd sent Bryan another text to say she was spending the night at Carina's and then she'd turned off the phone. She didn't feel one iota of guilt. Bryan had pulled the same type of stunt on her over the years. It was her turn and, besides, it might be her last night of fun if her husband's text was anything to go by. That thought had spurred her on to down one vodka and Red Bull too many, and she'd spent the night flirting giddily with a detective from Galway until Carina had dragged her home, protesting, in the early hours of Saturday morning. She didn't remember undressing and falling into Carina's comfy double bed, where she'd slept her brains out alongside her friend.

Sitting in the kitchen, sipping scalding-hot sweet coffee and eating the crispy-bacon sandwich, she chided herself for behaving like a single nineteen-year-old and not a newly married woman in her mid-twenties who was up to her eyes in debt.

'You're so lucky to have a husband to go home to.' Carina wiped some tomato ketchup off her finger. 'I'd love to have someone who loves me, to share the rest of the weekend with, and someone to shag me senseless to boot.'

Me too, Debbie thought, but she said brightly, 'That Special Branch detective was very into you.'

'That Special Branch detective was *very* married. He had a red rash on his ring finger – you know, the rash you get from your rings sometimes.' Carina cut a slice of Maltana and offered it to Debbie, who shook her head.

'Oh! Well spotted. What a bummer.'

'I've been on the scene long enough to know the score.' Carina scowled.

'So that was why you bundled me into a taxi when I was starting to have fun,' Debbie retorted.

'Too much fun, for a very married woman.' Carina wagged her finger in jest.

'Sorry, I was pissed,' Debbie muttered. 'I haven't drunk like that in a long time.' The truth was, she'd enjoyed flirting with the Galway detective and hadn't objected when he'd leaned in and nuzzled her ear before giving her a long, lingering kiss. It was soon after that little interlude that Carina had stepped in and said they were leaving.

'No harm done.' Carina smiled at her. 'I won't be bringing you to AA just yet.'

'You're a great friend, Carina.' Debbie hugged her tightly. 'I enjoyed my mad night out, but I don't think I'll be having another one for a while to come. I think bad stuff is coming down the line about Bryan's job. I couldn't even afford to go out last night, to be honest. It was like a last fling before tightening the purse strings.'

'Ouch! That's tough. I know so many couples in the same boat. I guess I'm lucky I'm renting and don't have a mortgage. I was able to negotiate a rent reduction with my landlord. It's a renters' market at the moment.'

'Good for you. I think we're going to lose the house,' Debbie heard herself say, finally admitting her greatest fear was more than a possibility.

'That bad?' Carina was shocked.

'I'm trying not to think about it,' Debbie confessed. 'Don't say anything to any of the others. I haven't said anything to anyone, not even my mother.'

'Of course I won't. But look, it might not happen. Maybe you could renegotiate your mortgage. The friggin' banks owe it to us to lighten the load; we're bailing them out, for God's sake. It's all their fault, them and that friggin' muppet who was taking dig-outs from his cronies, them who wouldn't listen to the advice they were being given about the property bubble. Every Tom, Dick and Harry could see the bust coming, and those idiots who "run the country" couldn't?'

Carina's voice rose an octave she was so indignant. Her pay cuts had meant that she wouldn't be changing her car as she'd planned, and the one she had was on its last legs and was more trouble than it was worth. 'I feel really pissed off because I didn't vote for that shower in government. I never have, and I blame the people who kept voting them in, time after time,' she ranted, as she began filling the dishwasher. Her brother, an architect, had lost his job in the recession and been forced to emigrate, leaving Carina to keep an eye on their mother, who was a demanding woman at the best of times. And now she didn't have her sibling to share the burden with.

'I'd better get dressed and head off to get a Dart.' Debbie changed the subject. She felt too fragile to get into a discussion about the economy with Carina. Her friend was very into politics and extremely opinionated, but there was a time and a place for political argument, and this morning was not it.

'Help yourself to whatever you want. There're clean jeans and T-shirts in the wardrobe,' her friend offered generously.

'Perfect. You're a pal.' Debbie poured herself another cup of coffee and took it with her. She and Carina were of similar build, so she selected a pair of stonewashed jeans and a black T-shirt and dressed with haste, knowing that she had to catch a bus from Glasnevin to get into town to catch a Dart.

There was more than a hint of autumn in the air as she walked past the high, grey stone walls of the Botanic Gardens and felt a falling leaf brush her cheek. It was cold in the shade, and she crossed the street, hurrying past the Addison towards the bank on Mobhi Road. She'd spent a fortune last night and needed to withdraw funds from her current account.

She keyed in her PIN and her heart dropped like a stone when she saw the balance. She selected the €20 key. In the not too distant past she would have withdrawn a minimum of fifty without it costing her a thought. The repercussions of her night out would last until next payday, she thought gloomily. She saw a 19A bus heading for the lights, shoved her money in her purse and ran to the bus stop, trying to ignore the daggers of pain that pierced her temples. Paying in more ways than one, she thought, handing over her fare and lurching down the aisle to sink into an empty seat. She turned on her phone in case Connie was trying to get through to her and wondered would Bryan have sent her a text. Nothing, she noted flatly. It obviously hadn't bothered him that she hadn't come home. He'd probably gone partying with Kevin Devlin and that crowd and, if that was the case, he'd have spent a hell of a lot more than she had. She winced as the bus juddered to a halt at the next stop.

It was such an irony that she, who should be bubbly and happy, was going to meet her mother, who *was* bubbly and happy, and she was going to have to put on a façade to hide her general dreariness.

She clattered up the steps into Connolly twenty minutes later and raced across the concourse; there was a southbound Dart due in two minutes, and if she hurried she might make it. Crowds coming off a Maynooth train hampered her progress and she weaved in and out of the throng, cursing herself for drinking like a fish the previous night.

An elderly man going crablike down the stairs to the platform she was heading for brought a halt to her gallop, and she could hear the train trundling into the station and hoped there was a large crowd getting off as well as getting on. She was panting when she eventually leapt on to the train, just before the doors closed, and for one awful moment she felt bile rise in her throat and thought she was going to puke. She should have taken her time and not run like a maniac with the hangover she had. There was just something about making a train by the skin of your teeth. She hated coming into a station and seeing the last carriage of a train disappearing down the tracks.

She took some deep breaths, vowing never to drink again, and managed to locate a seat. A young Chinese man opposite was listening to his iPod and a teenager by the window was yakking away on his mobile. They took no notice of her taking deep breaths, willing her stomach to settle. If she didn't feel better she could always get off at Tara Street, which was just moments away, she comforted herself as they crossed Butt Bridge. The Liffey was glinting silver and gold in the midday sun and she could see Bryan's office building gleaming green and chrome in the sunlight. What was he going to tell her about work? Debbie wondered despairingly. They were in trouble, she knew it, and it frightened her. She wanted to lay her head on Connie's shoulder and pour out all her woes to her mother. But how mean would that be? Her mother had sounded on such a high the previous day. She hoped this Drew guy was a good bloke. Her mum deserved the best. And she would let him know that too, whenever she met him. Debbie started to relax as they glided into Tara Street and she felt the nausea ease, relieved that she wouldn't have to get off.

The teenager got off at Sydney Parade, and Debbie moved over to the window seat. She loved it when the train emerged from between the houses and ran beside the beach. The panorama of Dublin Bay spread out like a picture postcard for her delectation, and she could see the sun shining down on Dun Laoghaire a few miles away in the curve of the coastline. It was a very picturesque journey for the commuter, and such a pleasure compared to sitting in bumper-to-bumper traffic. It was one of those glorious early-autumn days, the light was less intense, opalescent almost, and Debbie realized with a start that September was almost upon them. She must text Melissa and wish her good luck in her new school term, she thought fondly, so glad of the growing closeness between her half-sister and herself.

What a year it had been, she reflected, as the sun warmed her face and the train curved along the track and increased speed. This time last year she'd been *adamant* that Barry would not be giving her away at her wedding and that Aimee and Melissa were definitely not welcome. The rapprochement with her father and half-sister was a very welcome outcome to what had been a very fraught lead-up to her wedding. It didn't particularly bother her that she and Aimee didn't get on. Her father's workaholic second wife was the least of her troubles, she mused, remembering a few of their frosty encounters. How Barry could have walked out on Connie and married someone like Aimee, who was so hard and ambitious, and the complete opposite of her mother, mystified Debbie. Even though it had happened years ago, it had taken a long time for the bitterness Debbie felt at his departure from their lives to heal. Had Barry felt as trapped as her own husband did now? she wondered. Would she and Bryan make it as a married couple if they were having such problems so soon into their marriage? Because her new husband did feel trapped, there was no denying it. Maybe her mother had been right all along, maybe they should have postponed the wedding and just continued living together. But she *had* given him a chance to bail out, Debbie argued silently as the train approached Dalkey. It wasn't fair for him to blame her and accept no responsibility for his decision to go ahead.

She wished she could talk to Jenna, her cousin and best friend. Jenna had been her bridesmaid and was like the sister she never had. But her cousin was working with a charity to help orphaned children in Bangkok and wouldn't be home until Christmas. Debbie didn't want to email. It was too impersonal, and she didn't want Jenna worrying about her, when she herself was so far from home.

Connie was waiting for her on the opposite platform, and Debbie caught sight of her as the train cruised into the station. Her mother was glowing, there was no other word to describe it, Debbie thought enviously. She was looking a million dollars in her white cut-offs and black vest top. A lilac sweater was draped across her shoulders and she looked happy and carefree with the breeze blowing her auburn hair off her face. Debbie had never seen her mother look so well, and she hurried across the pedestrian bridge and flung her arms around her, hugging her tightly.

'My God, Mum, you look fantastic!' she exclaimed as Connie's arms tightened around her. 'You *are* sleeping with him,' she declared, gazing into Connie's clear blue eyes.

Her mother blushed and laughed. 'Stop it, you brat. Don't be mortifying me.'

'I'm dying to hear all about it. Come on, let's go to Idle Wilde. You've got to tell me everything,' she urged, linking her arm with Connie's and putting her woes aside for the time being.

'Mum, you're glowing. What's going on? Tell me all,' she demanded ten minutes later as they sat ensconced in the popular eatery. The café was buzzing with lunchtime trade – even the courtyard was full – and they were lucky to get a table.

'Why don't we order first, and then we can settle down to talk?' Connie suggested, rooting in her bag for her glasses. 'It's such a bloody nuisance having to wear these things. I can't read small print now,' she moaned.

'Why don't you get laser treatment?' Debbie giggled as Connie perched the glasses on her nose. 'You look like a lawyer. They're very cool.'

'Thanks. I asked about the laser thing, but the optician said you can't do anything about it, it's an "age" thing. I hate being middle-aged, Debbie. Enjoy every second of your youth.' Her mother eyed her over the top of her new specs. 'You look a bit ropy,' she remarked. 'Late night?'

'Girls' night,' Debbie murmured, glancing at the menu. She wasn't that hungry.

'Aahh!' Connie smiled. 'Sometimes they're the worst. How's Bryan?'

'Great, in good form,' Debbie fibbed brightly. Under no circumstances was she going to let on that her life with Bryan was less than perfect, not today anyway. It would be so unfair to ruin Connie's day by selfishly unburdening herself.

'Well, I was hoping the two of you could come to lunch some Sunday soon and meet my . . . my friend.'

'Don't you mean your lover?' Debbie teased, noting Connie's heightened colour.

'Will you stop it?' Connie hissed, abashed.

'Only kidding. Is he, though?'

'Yes, we've slept together,' Connie admitted, putting down the menu, her mouth curving up in a smile.

'It's great, Mum. I'm *delighted* for you. It's about time you had someone special in your life. What's he like?' Debbie stretched her hand across the table and gave Connie's a squeeze.

'He's gorgeous.' Connie sighed happily. 'He's just a bit older than me. He owns a riding stables about five miles away, he's divorced, has two grown-up daughters, and we get on like a house on fire. He makes me laugh a lot, we can talk about anything and I fancy him like mad. That's it, in a nutshell.'

'What does he look like?' Debbie felt an unwelcome twinge of envy. It was so ironic: her mother was behaving like a love-struck teenager, and she felt weary and disillusioned.

'He's tall, over six foot, grey hair cut tight, real blue eyes, fit and rangy, and a strong face, great mouth . . .' Connie tailed off, embarrassed.

Debbie laughed. 'Who'd play him?'

Connie cocked her head to the side and stared dreamily into space as she thought for a moment. 'A mixture of Gary Cooper, and McSteamy in *Grey's Anatomy*,' she decided, grinning.

'Yum! I likeee,' Debbie approved.

'I likeee too,' laughed Connie. 'I can't believe I met someone at my age.'

'You look so happy, Mum. It suits you being with him. When did you meet him? Do you think it's more than a . . .' She had been going to say 'fling' but thought it wasn't appropriate '. . . an interlude?'

'I think he's someone I could be with for the rest of my life,' Connie said quietly.

'Oh wow!' Debbie was taken aback. 'Do you mean marriage?'

'I don't know if I necessarily want to get married again. Why would I? I did it once, and that was enough for me.' Connie shook her head. 'But I could see myself growing old with Drew, and having a hell of a good time doing it.' She smiled. 'Do you mind? I figured that, with you being married and having your own life to lead with Bryan, it wouldn't impact on you as much as it would have if you were younger and still living with me.'

'Of course I don't mind, Mum. Drew . . . nice name.' Debbie took a sip of the sparkling water they'd ordered.

'Drew Sullivan. It suits him. I have a photo on my phone.

Would you like to see it?' Connie scrolled down on her mobile and handed it to Debbie.

Debbie studied the image of the handsome man looking out from the screen. What a strong face, she thought. A face full of character, the hint of a smile softening the stern aura. Not the face of a man who would walk away, she felt, unable to stop herself from making a comparison with her dad.

'He's a hunk, Mum, and he's got kind eyes. Well done. Tell me all about him,' she approved, handing back the phone. 'Does Dad know about him?'

'He met him,' Connie said lightly, slipping the phone back into her bag.

'*Really!* What did he say?' Debbie couldn't hide her curiosity, and her mother laughed.

'Well, it was just a brief encounter, so to speak, and they shook hands and were polite when I made the introduction. I don't particularly care what Barry thinks, to be honest. He made a new life for himself long ago. It's my time now. I'm as free as a bird, answerable to no one. It's a great feeling, love. I'm really enjoying my life at the moment. Let's order, and I'll tell you from the beginning.' Connie sat back in her chair and smiled broadly.

Debbie sat looking at her mother, so happy, in love, completely carefree, and thought how incongruous it was that she, the newly-wed, was bowed down by pressure, financial and emotional, and by no stretch of the imagination could be considered happy, carefree or, most upsetting of all, in love. She swallowed down her despondency and listened as Connie told her how she'd met her tall, handsome man in Mrs Mansfield's kitchen.

Bryan let himself into the house and cocked his ear to see if he could hear any sounds to indicate that Debbie was home before him. The house had a dreary, silent air, and walking into the kitchen he could see the mugs in the sink from the previous morning's breakfast and knew that his wife wasn't there. Debbie hated mugs left in the sink.

He'd tried to get hammered the previous night, but for some reason he just hadn't been able to get drunk with the crowd from work. He felt too oppressed, too trapped to get into the zone. He'd been walking across the quays to Tara Street to get the Dart home when he'd bumped into his older brother and sister-in-law, who were heading for the northbound platform. He'd ended up going back with them to their neat bungalow in Killester, where they'd ordered a Chinese and opened a couple of bottles of beer. When he told them that Debbie was on a girls' night out, they'd insisted he stay the night. Falling into the double bed in the very Zen, eggshell-blue and cream guest room was a much more inviting prospect than getting a taxi to an empty house where an unmade bed awaited.

That morning, they'd all had a leisurely breakfast and read the papers in a small coffee shop five minutes away. As he'd sat in the Nuthouse, eating poached eggs and drinking hot, sweet coffee, watching his brother and sister-in-law sharing the week-end supplements and ordering more coffee, the hum of chat in the background, he knew this was the kind of domesticity Debbie craved, and he knew in equal measure that it was far, far from what he wanted. He'd sat on the Dart home and felt rage and bitterness as the train swayed across Butt Bridge. He'd looked up the quays and seen the office he was currently designing the fit-out for, and wondered how he could ever have got himself so trapped. The nearer he got to home, the worse he'd felt.

He filled the kettle and the tentacles of desperation and frustration that were tightening their grip around him squeezed tighter and tighter until he felt he was going to suffocate.

This was not how it was meant to be. He wasn't even thirty and he felt his life was over. And it was only going to get worse. He couldn't hack it any more. He felt as if he was swimming underwater against the tide. He took his coffee out to their small deck. The sun was just coming around the back of the house, and he lifted his face to it, ignoring the grass that needed a cut and the weeds that were like a miniature jungle around the tool shed. He could hear the drone of a lawnmower in the distance and the irritating *zizzzzz* of a hedge trimmer. Children in a nearby garden squealed as they jumped on a trampoline, and an alarm shrieked incessantly from a house at the rear of them. It was an alarm that went off frequently, in a house that was rented, and it would ring for hours on end, shrill and insistent, driving the neighbours mad. The owner couldn't care less. He didn't live in the area and so, with irritating regularity, it would go off, its shrill racket jangling Bryan's increasingly taut nerves. Today it was the last straw. God, it was so bloody *noisy*, and so bloody middle class, and so bloody *boring*! He had a sudden memory of himself around the age of six, out in the back garden playing. It was warm and sunny, there was the sound of lawn-mowers whining in other gardens and the smell of cut grass permeated the air. His father, having cut their grass, was slumped, snoring, in a deck chair, with his mouth open, a half-finished mug of cold coffee beside him. A fly had landed on his nose. Bryan had watched, fascinated, wondering would the fly go into his dad's mouth and would he choke.

He was turning into his father, Bryan thought in horror, grabbing his cup and slamming the back door behind him. He couldn't live this life. He *had* to get away. Debbie could come or stay, it was her choice, but he wasn't going to moulder away in the suburbs and get middle-aged before his time, buried under an avalanche of debt. Marriage or no marriage.

CHAPTER TWO

'Ma, I have to get out of Ireland, it's doing my head in. That house is costing me a fortune; we're in debt up to our eyes. Debbie and I aren't getting along. My life's a disaster, my marriage is in trouble, I'm at my wits' end.' Bryan ran his fingers through his long black hair and buried his head in his hands.

'Ah son, son, it can't be that bad,' Brona Kinsella protested in dismay as she put a comforting arm around her favourite child's shoulder.

'Oh it is, Ma, trust me,' he said mournfully. 'I sent Debbie an email yesterday to tell her I had bad news about work and she never even answered it, and she never came home last night either. I don't know where she stayed,' he fibbed, enjoying the sympathy his mother was oozing. It was a balm to his troubled spirit. His mother *never* let him down.

'You're not serious! You don't know where she stayed? Her place is at your side when you're in trouble, love. She's your wife. She took vows to be with you for better or worse. This is *dreadful*! And so soon after the wedding. I don't know what's wrong with young women these days; they're not prepared to put any work into marriage at all!' Brona exclaimed, bristling with indignation at the notion of her beloved son being abandoned in his hour of need.

'I know,' Bryan agreed sorrowfully, lapping it all up. 'We were better off just living together. I think she was meeting Connie for lunch today. I haven't seen her since yesterday morning.'

'Well, honestly, that's a bit rich.' Brona's lips thinned and her nostrils flared. 'She can meet her mother but she can't be with her husband in his hour of need. I don't like to say it, son, but Debbie's a mite thoughtless, I've always felt. I know she's your wife, but she lets Connie dictate too much. She's a bit under her mother's thumb, and nurses, I've found, are a bit on the bossy side.' Brona was delighted to be able to criticize her daughter-in-law and her son's mother-in-law and affirm her own place as the most important woman in Bryan's life.

'Well, Connie certainly is bossy,' Bryan concurred. 'I put up with her for Debbie's sake, but it's thanks to bloody Connie that we're in this mess,' he ranted, getting on to his favourite hobby horse. 'If it hadn't been for her going on and on about buying a house, we wouldn't be in this situation.' He didn't mention that it was he who had insisted they buy in Sandymount, because it was so upmarket. Debbie would have been happy to live in other parts of Dublin that were less expensive to purchase property in.

'She should have kept her nose out of things like I did,' Brona said self-righteously. 'I don't believe in interfering in my children's lives, and I've a good mind to tell her so the next time I see her. If you want to try and sell up and move back in with your father and me, the two of you are very welcome. We could do up the bedroom for you.'

'Thanks, Ma, but I want to emigrate—'

'Ah, son, don't do that, sure I'd miss you terribly.' Tears came to his mother's eyes.

'There's nothing here for me. If I don't lose my job, I'll be on a three-day week.' Bryan shook his head, enjoying his whinge and Brona's benevolent empathy.

'But Debbie has a good job – surely it can't be that bad?'

'Ma, it's worse than bad, I'm telling you. It's a disaster. If we sell the house we're in negative equity, so we'll still end up owing the bank money, and we won't have a home of our own. We just can't win.'

'So what will you do with the house if you're emigrating?'

'Try and let it, I suppose.'

'And will you get enough rent money to pay the mortgage?'

'Oh, I don't know, Ma. It's all a load of friggin' hassle.' He groaned and stretched out on the sofa.

'Have you eaten, love?' Brona jumped up from the sofa. 'Let me see. I have a lovely fillet of steak – I could serve it with pepper sauce – or I could do medallions of pork in creamy garlic and apple sauce. It won't take me a few minutes,' she tempted.

'Well, I suppose I could try and eat the pork, but I don't have much of an appetite lately.' He gave a deep, deep sigh and was rewarded with a comforting pat on the arm and a cushion placed tenderly under his head.

'You lie there, pet, and don't worry. We'll put our thinking caps on and come up with something. You have a little rest and I'll go and get you a bite to eat.'

'Thanks, Ma. You're the best in the world,' Bryan lauded as he picked up the remote control and began surfing channels. No one in the world understood him like Brona. She'd got him out of many a fix before, and she was always good for a few bob when he was stuck. He'd always have a roof over his head and food in his belly as long as his mother was alive, even if he hadn't a penny. It was a comfort of sorts.

Debbie heard her husband's key in the lock and felt her stomach tighten in knots. There was a time when she'd hear him arrive home and feel a surge of pleasure and anticipation. Would she ever feel that again? she wondered dolefully as she heard him drop the car keys on the hall table.

'Hi,' she said quietly as he walked into the sitting room.

'Hello,' Bryan answered stiffly, and she could see he was in a snit.

'Have you eaten?' It was after seven and she was a little peckish. She hadn't eaten much at lunch.

'Ma cooked me a dinner.'

The unspoken *'Seeing as you couldn't be bothered'* hung in the air between them.

'Oh, right.' No doubt her mother-in-law thought she was a bad wife. Brona Kinsella wasn't her greatest fan. Debbie had always found her mother-in-law very possessive of Bryan. She spoilt him rotten and treated him like a ten-year-old and felt that Debbie treated him far too casually.

'How is your mam?' she asked politely, thinking how awful it was that she was making small talk with her husband.

'Fine.' His eyes were cold. He sat on the sofa and picked up the remote control. 'Are you watching this?' He indicated the cookery programme that was on.

'Yes, I was,' she wanted to say, but she couldn't be bothered. She couldn't be bothered either sitting in the same room as Bryan and making polite conversation.

'Watch what you want,' she said heavily. 'I'm going to make something to eat. Do you want a cup of tea?'

'No thanks.' He didn't even look at her.

She felt sudden rage surge through her. How dare he act the martyr with her? How often had he spent the night with friends after going on a bender? She hadn't had a girls' night in months; she was as entitled as he was to the odd night out. If she'd gone all huffy on him every time he'd had one of his nights they'd never have been married.

'What was the bad news you have to tell me about work?' She stood up and planted herself in front of him. Might as well get it over and done with.

He threw a sullen look at her. 'Redundancy or a three-day week. I don't know yet.'

'Oh my God!' She felt as if she'd been kicked in the stomach.

'Let's hope He'll provide for you, because I won't be able to,' Bryan jeered nastily. 'Do you mind? I'm trying to watch the TV.'

'What?' She glared at him wrathfully.

'I'm trying to watch the TV. If you'd get out of the way,' he snapped.

Fury overwhelmed her and she grabbed the remote from him and turned off the flatscreen.

'Hey, what the fuck do you think you're doing?' His brown eyes glittered as he shot to his feet and grabbed the remote back from her.

'You tell me you're either going to lose your job or go on a three-day week and that's it? You want to watch *TV*?' she shrieked. 'We're in trouble here, Bryan, big trouble. We need to talk about it.'

'Well, you weren't here to talk about it, were you?' he spat. 'No, you were out on the piss with your friends.'

'And what about all the times you've been out with *your* poxy friends,' she shouted.

'You leave my friends out of this, Debbie. At least they're there when I need them.'

'Well, they weren't there for you when you ended up in A&E after overdosing, were they?' she shot back, her hands clenched by her side. She wanted to rake her nails down his face and kick him hard, she was so furious.

'Shut up, Debbie,' he snarled, brushing past her to walk out of the room.

'Ah yeah, run away, the way you always do when things get rough. Well, Bryan, things are going to get a lot worse, so we need to talk about our options, because we don't have many, *darling*!' she roared sarcastically up the stairs after him.

'Bitch,' he swore back, and slammed the door of the bedroom behind him.

'Bastard,' she muttered, stalking out to the kitchen. She was in such a temper she felt like hurling the contents of the crockery press on the floor. She was whisking eggs to make an omelette when she heard the front door bang. She heard the car engine start and hoped that Bryan wasn't going on the piss. He didn't usually drink and drive, but he was in such a bad humour he was capable of anything, especially with the news he'd got about work.

When it was made, she ate her omelette, hardly tasting it. What were they going to do? How were they going to get by? They were barely managing to keep afloat as it was.

She felt completely and utterly trapped. They had lived way beyond their means, blithely ratcheting up credit-card bills on top of a massive mortgage, and now they weren't going to have enough money to cover them. Who could help them? She couldn't ask Connie. Her mother was only working part-time now and, besides, she had given them a very generous cheque as a wedding present. In fairness to her parents-in-law, they too had been pretty generous. Brona was always slipping Bryan a few quid, Debbie knew, despite her mother-in-law's efforts to be discreet. Her in-laws were fairly comfortably off, they had no mortgage, but she wasn't too sure what their savings were like. It would be mortifying to have to ask them for a loan though. What would Bryan suggest? she fretted. Surely he must have some thoughts on the matter. But then, knowing her husband as she did, she knew one of his greatest flaws was his ability to hide his head in the sand.

Could she approach Barry for a long-term loan? As far as she could see, he and Aimee were fairly loaded. Would he be able to lend them twenty thousand, to clear their credit cards, at least? Was it time for her dad to finally step up to the plate? After all these years, was she going to go running to him because she couldn't depend on her husband? Was she going to have to abase herself before Aimee, her detested stepmother? Barry could hardly help her financially without telling his wife. Would it cause friction between them the way her wedding had? Aimee had stomped out of the church in a huff after a row with Connie on the steps, and things had not improved. She hadn't seen her stepmother since, nor did she want to, and she was sure the feeling was mutual. Would her stepmother nix the idea of a loan from Barry? She wouldn't know until she asked him about it.

It would be the first time in her life that she'd ever approached her father for help. That's how desperate things were, Debbie acknowledged, the tears rolling down her cheeks.

CHAPTER THREE

'OMG! Melissa Adams! You've lost *loads* of weight.' Tiffany Costello raked Melissa up and down with a look of undisguised envy.

'Thanks,' Melissa said with studied nonchalance. 'I guess I lost a few pounds over the summer.'

'A few pounds? Like, don't you mean a few stone?' Tiffany scoffed.

Evanna Nolan, who had been loitering around herself and Sarah like a nasty little virus, gave a smarmy smile, sycophantic as ever. 'It really suits you. It makes your eyes huge in your face.'

Melissa ignored her. Nerdy Nolan could lick all she liked: they would *never* be friends.

'Lucky cow,' Melinda Wright said coldly. She was on the chunky side and it grieved her sorely whenever someone lost weight.

'Did you try Atkins or the South Beach, or just stick your fingers down your neck?' Brenda Meyers eyed Melissa knowingly. She was stick thin and had been making herself sick for years.

'Don't be gross, Brenda,' Sarah exclaimed, standing up for Melissa. But as the words left her lips, Sarah felt a stomach-churning realization as Brenda's snide accusation struck home. That was *exactly* what her best friend had been doing over the summer. Making herself sick. It all fell into place now. The scurrying off to the loo in the middle of meals, the reluctance to meet up and go for something to eat in McDonald's or Real, the tiredness and lassitude her friend seemed constantly afflicted by. How could she have been so blind?

Sarah stood rooted to the spot as the rest of the group surged forward as the bell for assembly echoed through the school corridors. She'd have to do something, she thought in panic, noting how sharply Melissa's shoulderblades protruded through her uniform pullover. She'd have to tell Mrs Adams of her fears before it was too late. How could Melissa be so *stupid*? Sarah fretted, as the corridor filled with a tidal wave of laughing, chatting students and she trudged along with them, heavy-hearted and full of worry.

Melissa sat amidst her classmates feeling a triumphant delight that gave her more satisfaction than any other achievement of her entire life. She felt completely in control. It was such a high, she thought gleefully, catching Melinda scowling at her.

The only little hiccup had been Brenda's nasty little barb. Brenda Meyers was a lollipop head. Everyone knew she had an eating disorder: she looked like a peanut on pipe cleaners, Melissa thought dismissively. There was no way she'd ever end up like her classmate. Just because she was careful about what she ate and made herself sick occasionally, it didn't mean she had an eating problem. Far from it. She had actually acquired a sense of discipline and was eating much more healthily than she used to. She wasn't going down to Real, in the Pavilion, with Sarah, two or three times a week and gorging on burgers. She wasn't stuffing her face with chocolate the way she used to. She was eating lettuce and drinking loads of water, and using lemon juice instead of dressings – very, very healthy behaviour, she comforted herself, as the headmistress held up her hand for silence and began her speech of welcome to her students for the beginning of the new school year. Melissa let the words drift by as she sat on cloud nine, totally oblivious to the fact that her best friend was chewing her lip in the row behind her, working out the best approach to take when she broached the topic of Melissa's unhealthy method of losing weight to both Mrs Adams and Melissa herself.

Aimee Davenport took a deep breath, straightened her shoulders and smiled at the small, rotund, ruddy-faced man who was barrelling between tables and chairs to where she sat waiting for him in the lounge of the Merrion Hotel. Roger O'Leary, multimillionaire businessman and her new boss, was a whirlwind of energy as he waved at an acquaintance, stopped briefly to have a word with a well-known politician and caught the eye of a waiter, indicating to him to follow him to Aimee's table.

'Good morning, Roger.' She stood up and greeted him with a firm handshake.

'How's it going, Aimee? How are you feeling?' He returned her handshake equally firmly. 'Will you have another pot of tea or coffee?'

'Tea will be fine, Roger, although to tell you the truth, I'd murder a coffee,' she sighed. Being pregnant was such a pain. No coffee, no alcohol; just as well she wasn't a smoker, she thought gloomily as Roger ordered tea for her and coffee for himself. And then, with a jolt, she remembered Barry's declaration on Friday, and that she'd booked into a clinic in the UK for the end of the week. How could she have forgotten? Had she got so used to being pregnant it had become the norm? She banished the thought instantly, determined to be on top of her brief as she gave Roger her update on the new company.

Roger pulled up his chair and opened his bulging briefcase. 'Coffee's not good for you, and I should know – I drink gallons of the stuff,' he remarked, as he spread some papers on the table in front of them and put on a pair of glasses. 'Well, Aimee,' he gave a sigh, frowned and studied her intently for a moment. 'I don't have great news,' he said, in his usual direct manner.

'Oh? In relation to what?' Tension and apprehension

caught her in a vice grip and she struggled to keep her voice neutral and her facial expression from betraying the terror she felt.

'Well, as you know, setting up a new business in high-end events and catering isn't ideal now that we're very firmly in a recession – verging on a depression – we've agreed on that.' He fixed her with an uncompromising stare.

'I know,' she said quietly. 'It's all happened so fast it's scary.' Outwardly, she looked calm and composed but, inwardly, the fear tightened its grip on her and she had to struggle not to hyperventilate. She'd resigned from her extremely well-paid job with a top-class events and catering company when Roger and a business partner had invited her to set up a company for them and take the role of MD. She'd been thrilled. All her hard work had paid off at last. She was at the top of the corporate ladder, working with two of the country's most successful businessmen. She had been the happiest woman in the world, and then it had all gone downhill faster than Jenson Button off the grid. The recession had hit like a tsunami and her unexpected pregnancy had knocked her for six. Finding out that she was pregnant had been the most unwelcome shock of her life. Aimee would never forget that horrendous moment when Melissa had upended the contents of her handbag on the bedroom floor and Barry had seen the pregnancy test and *known* she was pregnant and hadn't been going to tell him. *Oh for God's sake! Stop thinking about that now. You're dealing with it.* She chided herself. *Roger's got bad news. Concentrate.*

Unemployed: that was what she was going to be, she just *knew* it, Aimee thought in panic, her eyes widening with dismay and her fingers curling into her palms, digging deep. She waited for Roger to continue, but the waiter arrived with their tea and coffee and her boss sat back to allow him to set the tray down. *Oh God, just hurry up,* she wanted to yell, but she stayed mute as the waiter replaced her china and napkins.

After what seemed like an eternity, when the tea and coffee

had been poured and Roger had taken a steaming gulp from his cup, he eyeballed her. Again. 'Myles is pulling out! He's taken a big hit on some property deals that have gone belly up. He was heavily involved with Anglo – who bloody well wasn't? I got burnt there myself,' he added grumpily. 'Anyway, this morning, a company he'd invested heavily in, and I mean *heavily* – millions – gone with the wind. I was blessed, Aimee. Was going to invest in it myself. A real blue-chip company set up by the cream of the banking business, *allegedly*, and it's gone under. I kept meaning to get around to it in the summer, and then I saw that the share price was starting to slide and didn't have a good feeling about it. I'm telling you, when I heard SCIP had gone bust this morning, I'd a feeling I'd be getting the call from Myles. He'd been telling me about what a sure thing it was.' He sighed again, a deep blast that came from his toes.

'So we're not going ahead.' Her voice remained admirably steady, but her palms were damp. Roger took another gulp of coffee. Today he was wearing a black pinstriped suit with a red tie. He looked like a Chicago gangster. All he needed was a fedora and spats, Aimee thought, a little wildly.

'Oh, it's going ahead all right, if you're still game,' he said, very firmly. 'Only we're going to have to re-evaluate our whole approach and take a fresh look at our plan, keeping in mind the economic climate.' He gave a wry grin. 'Half our prospective clients have scarpered with their ill-gotten gains, having brought the country to its knees. Just spend a bit of time in Marbella and Cape Cod and the likes, and you'll see 'em all quaffing Dom P., laughing at the bank bail-out, and the rest of us idiots who are going to have to pay for their greed. The other half are heading for bankruptcy. On the other hand, rents are down, wages are down, and the recession isn't going to last for ever. I think we should go more downmarket than we had planned for the time being, and quietly and slowly build our exclusive brand and be ready for action when the new millionaires and billionaires sur- face. Because, believe me, Aimee, money will be made out of all of this. Births, deaths and marriages will still be celebrated. Corporate spending on entertainment will come back, then the clients will be hollering for us, and we'll be waiting.' He sat up straight and rubbed his hands. 'What I'm thinking is . . .'

Oh thank God, thank God! Aimee thought fervently, beginning to relax as Roger continued enthusiastically with his new recession-buster game plan.

She was utterly drained by the time she eventually tidied up the papers she had brought to update him on her progress and snapped shut her briefcase.

'You look tired, Aimee.' Roger peered at her. 'Make sure to factor in the time you'll need off for the baby.'

'Oh! Oh! That won't be a problem,' she murmured.

'Aimee, I don't want you running yourself into the ground,' he said sternly. 'From what you've been telling me, you're going to have an excellent core staff in place. Factor in your maternity leave. If these people are as good as you say they are, we won't have a problem. You can liaise with them on the phone if you feel you have to.'

'Thanks, Roger,' she said gratefully, feeling an unexpected wave of affection and respect for the man she had looked down her nose at the first time she'd met him. Roger, despite his wealth and success, still had his feet firmly on the ground and still had the common touch, which ensured fierce loyalty from everyone who worked for him. Aimee was learning that her new boss had a lot of admirable qualities, even if his sartorial style left a lot to be desired.

'Good stuff. We're making excellent progress, Aimee. And we're agreed now that Myles is out of the picture we'll relocate our proposed office to my building on North Wall Quay. All that area is redeveloped. The new conference centre is there; the new theatre is across the river. You wouldn't even have to drive if you didn't want to. You could Dart and Luas it. Maybe this recession is a blessing in disguise for us,' he said energetically, his natural optimism coming to the fore. He looked at her, his eyes twinkling. 'Of course, it's on the Northside; you might need your passport, you being a posh Southsider and all.'

'I'll manage fine. It will be a challenge, of course.' She laughed, relieved beyond measure that she still had a job and that Roger was still gung-ho to get up and running despite Myles's unfortunate business difficulties.

'Right, I'm off. Let's meet for coffee here again on Friday morning, I have a client for you to meet. A buddy of mine who was at my daughter's wedding has a daughter who is getting married next Easter. He wants you to co-ordinate and organize it. He was very impressed with what you did for our bash. He's looking at Powerscourt House. Great venue, was at a wedding there myself recently. Excellent staff.'

'Friday?' she repeated, her heart sinking.

'Is that a problem? I hope not: this is important. Matthew and his wife are flying out to Russia for a couple of weeks next Monday; he has a lot of business interests out there. I'd like to get things moving for them, lock it down. You know what I'm saying?' He studied her closely, eyes a shade flinty, and she knew he wasn't asking her, he was telling her to be there.

'Friday's fine,' she said briskly. 'I'll juggle my other meetings.'

'Good woman. Priorities, priorities, only way to run a business,' he declared as he raised his hand in farewell, and then he was gone, nodding at someone to his left, pausing to say hello to an elderly couple on the right before disappearing into the foyer.

Aimee slumped back in her chair, relieved that the meeting was over. Roger's energy was boundless, but his intensity was hard going. Once Roger got into the swing of a meeting he was very focused and they had moved swiftly from one item to the next, he asking pertinent questions that surprised her, as she'd briefed him on her progress.

She could see how he had become so successful: his grasp of the minute details of everything they had discussed amazed her. He'd been the same when they were planning his daughter's wedding. She needed to be on her toes when she had meetings with her new boss. But he was invigorating to work with, even if she felt she'd been run over by a steamroller.

Just as well she hadn't booked the flight to London. That had been on her list of chores for today. Now she was going to have to ring the clinic and reschedule the termination. What a damn nuisance. She wanted it over and done with so she could close the door on it and move on. She'd arranged to have it on the Friday so she'd have the weekend to recover.

She signalled to the waiter. She hadn't had time to drink her tea, and it was now cold, having been ordered well over an hour and a half ago. It was after twelve fifteen, she noted in surprise, and people were coming in to have lunch. The morning had flown by.

'Could I have a fresh pot of tea and a scone, please?' she asked politely. She was ravenously hungry all of a sudden. It was only when the waiter was gone that Aimee realized she could have ordered that much longed-for coffee. She wasn't keeping the baby, so there was no need for her to be careful. She could have a glass of red wine this evening if she wanted, and some cream cheese and crackers to accompany it.

Her phone beeped. It was Melissa sending her a text:

Hi Mom, school went great. We're getting off for a half-day, yippee. Hope ur feeling ok.

A smiley face accompanied three kisses at the end of the text.

Aimee's heart softened. She'd been so sharp with Melissa lately, and so worried about her. Impulsively, she rang her daughter's number. 'Hey, why don't I play hooky for a while – we could go shopping. We could look at that new iPhone you have your eye on.'

'Mom!' Melissa squealed down the phone so loudly that Aimee had to hold it away from her ear.

'Don't shout. I'm not deaf,' she remonstrated.

'You're, like, so the best, Mom. Where will I meet you?'

'Hop on a Dart and ring me when you're coming into Pearse Street and I'll drive over and pick you up and we'll carry on to

Stephen's Green. I'm in the Merrion; I'll stay put until you ring me. I've a few calls to make and emails to send. OK?'

'Cool, Mom. See you soon.' Aimee could tell her daughter was grinning from ear to ear. She'd been pestering Barry and herself for the latest iPhone for weeks. Once they'd bought it, she and Melissa could have a browse in the shops and then she'd casually suggest a bite of lunch. That way she'd be sure her daughter would have eaten some proper food and had at least one substantial meal today. The sooner they had the appointment with the psychiatrist over and done with, to try and get a handle on this weight problem that had come out of the blue, the better.

Aimee picked up her BlackBerry and began to scroll down through her emails. It would take at least half an hour for her daughter to walk from school to the station and get a Dart to Pearse Street. She could get quite a lot of work done if she stayed focused. Aimee's fingers flew over the keys as she forgot her personal troubles and concentrated on the one thing in her life that gave her immense satisfaction: her work.

Two hours later, new iPhone successfully purchased, plus a new pair of Converses and a top from BT2, Aimee and Melissa were sitting outside in the afternoon sun, perusing the menu in GBK on South Anne Street. Aimee had suggested GBK because she knew Melissa had a great weakness for burgers. Before Melissa had got the bee in her bonnet about her weight, the three of them had often had lunch there. Barry adored the place; in his view, GBK's burgers were the best burgers in town.

'The avocado and bacon burger sounds rather tasty,' Aimee suggested.

'I think I might have the green salad and chicken,' Melissa demurred.

'Fine, I'm just ravenous, really hungry the last day or two,' Aimee remarked, determined not to push too hard.

'It's probably 'cos you're pregnant, Mom,' her daughter pointed out reasonably. 'You're eating for two.'

'I know, but I'm never *that* hungry,' Aimee retorted.

'Are you having cravings?'

'Umm, not really, but you know me, I'm usually the one having the chicken salad, and yet the sound of this avocado and bacon burger is getting my tastebuds going.' Aimee suddenly realized that she hadn't felt nauseous all day, apart from that morning when she'd got up, and she had a real desire for meat, which was unusual for her.

'Go for it, Mom. And enjoy it. Here's the waiter, let's order.'

'Isn't this nice, having some mother and daughter time?' Aimee remarked as they sat back after placing their orders and lifted their faces to the sun as shoppers strolled past and a busker played a haunting rendition of 'Stranger on the Shore' on his clarinet.

'Yeah, it's fun, Mom, and I just love my phone. I can't wait to show it to the girls. Nerdy Nolan will be, like, so totally jealous. She's, like, such a bitch, Mom – she told Karen Kennedy that she was talking total crap when she thought her computer might have run out of space because it wasn't saving documents. Like how rude is that?'

'Very,' agreed Aimee, wondering what was the point of paying a fortune for private education if displaying rudeness and using vulgar language like 'crap' was the end result.

'She thinks she knows everything about computers, that's one of the reasons she's called "Nerdy",' Melissa confided. 'She'd totally love this iPhone.'

'How's Sarah?'

'She's good. I didn't really get to talk to her today 'cos of meeting you for lunch, I'll meet her later. We didn't get any homework,' she added hastily, as their meals were placed in front of them.

'That was very, very tasty,' Aimee approved twenty minutes later as she took a sip of sparkling water and gave a discreet burp, and scanned her daughter's plate. Melissa had spent a lot of time pushing the salad and chicken around her plate, but she'd eaten some of it, and a few of the chips, and so far had not excused herself to go to the loo.

'Maybe the baby likes burgers,' Melissa teased, her face breaking into a grin. 'I wonder is it a boy or a girl? Are you going to find out? When are you going for a scan? Can I come? One of the girls at school went with her mom and dad last term, and she said it was really cool looking at the baby, she could see the hands and feet and everything.' Melissa chattered on, oblivious to the consternation her mother was experiencing.

'You seem very interested in the baby – I thought you didn't like the idea of me being pregnant?' Aimee murmured, taking another sip of water.

'It was a bit of a shock at the beginning for sure, but now I've got used to it. I think I'd like a little sister. I could bring her to the pictures, and baby-sit. I could be a good older sister, just like Debbie's a good older sister to me now. I like chilling with Debbie. We have a lot of fun. I'm really glad we're friends now.'

'What if it's a boy?' Aimee said weakly, ignoring the references to Debbie. She'd far prefer not to have anything to do with Barry's daughter from his first marriage.

'I'd prefer a girl, but if it's a boy it's OK. A brother would be cool, too.' Melissa said airily. She stood up. 'Excuse me, Mom, I need to pee.'

'Please don't, Melissa. Please don't go in there and throw up,' Aimee said quietly.

'Mom! I'm going for a pee,' her daughter protested, but a telltale flush rose to her cheeks and she couldn't look Aimee in the eye.

'You and I both know that's a lie,' Aimee persisted. 'Listen to me, Melissa, you keep going on the way you're going and this baby won't have an older sister.'

'Stop! Mom, stop saying things like that,' Melissa said heatedly.

'I will when you start eating properly and stop upchucking

your food. Your dad and I aren't fools, Melissa. We know you're not being honest with us about what you're eating. And that's why we've made an appointment with Dr Burke to get a letter of referral for you to speak to a professional about it. It's time to sort yourself out, Melissa, time to get to the bottom of what's behind all this.'

'What? I'm not going to no *professional*! There's nothing wrong with me,' Melissa exploded.

'Yes there is. Making yourself sick after you eat is *not* normal. Losing weight the way you're losing it is *not* normal. Behaving the way you're behaving is *not* normal. Your father and I would be very poor parents if we didn't step in and look for help, seeing as you won't help yourself. You should be grateful we care enough about you to try and get you sorted.' Aimee looked intently at her daughter.

'When have you made this *appointment* for?'

'Next week. I'll write a note for your form mistress.'

'No. I'm not going,' Melissa said truculently.

'Yes you are. We need to get you sorted, so let's leave it.'

'Mom, you're not listening. I—'

'Hush, Melissa, I'm not fighting with you in a restaurant,' Aimee said coldly.

'We're not *in* a restaurant, we're *outside* a restaurant, actually,' Melissa retorted sarcastically.

'Don't be smart. And don't ruin our lovely girly time, please,' Aimee said wearily.

'No, *you* ruined it. I was only going to pee, and I don't want to go and talk to anyone about being on a diet. There's nothing wrong with me at all,' she reiterated sullenly.

'Look, let's not fight. Let's go for a walk and feed the ducks on the Green – remember how you used to love doing that when you were small?' Aimee soothed.

'Oh Mom, that's for kids. Let's go home,' Melissa said dourly. Her triumphant, successful day had just turned into a complete disaster. She needed to get rid of the food she'd eaten to appease her mother, and she now had the worry of having to go and talk to a complete stranger about her weight loss and eating habits when there was absolutely nothing wrong with her. What a bummer.

They drove home in silence.

Barry frowned to see a mistake in the proofs of the latest issue of Weldon's *Christmas Craft and Cracker* magazine. Just as well he'd checked it thoroughly before signing off on it.

'Tell copy-editor to smarten up!' he wrote in red pen, circling the offending typo. It was hard enough to get new business in the current economic climate; it behoved them to keep the business they had, he thought irritably, placing the folder in his out tray.

His email pinged and he glanced at his computer screen and saw a mail from a golfing buddy, Alan Corry:

Sending you something I got from a colleague. Explains why we haven't been able to contact Jeremy Farrell. Al.

Barry felt a tinge of apprehension as he read the short email. Jeremy Farrell, a retired stockbroker with Crooks & Co. Stockbrokers, still worked as a consultant for the company. He'd given good advice in the past, which had netted a sizeable number of the members of the golf club, Barry included, a tasty profit on their investments. When, several weeks ago, he'd urged Barry, in his smarmy, smooth manner, to invest in a sure-fire hot prospect, SecureCo International Plus, headed by the cream of the country's financial whizz kids, with practically every high-rolling big name in the business world an investor, Barry had felt it was too good an opportunity to miss. He'd invested cautiously in Jeremy's previous hot tip and made a profit of 5k. Some of his less windy acquaintances had made 50k or 100k on the deal. This time, Barry, having read the sharehold register, seen who was involved in the running of the company and who'd invested, had agreed it *was* too good an opportunity to miss and it was time to up his game and not be a wimp, much to Jeremy's delight. Once he'd decided to throw caution to the winds, he had borrowed 100k, using his late grandmother's home as collateral.

He hadn't told Aimee, wanting to surprise her with his business acumen when he made his killing. Besides, they hadn't been on speaking terms because of her pregnancy. She didn't want to keep the baby and he did, and that had caused a terrible rift between them. Now that he had given her the choice of termination, the option she'd wanted all along, they were back on an even keel. He hoped to God nothing was going to rock their boat again. He didn't need any more problems. They had Melissa's eating difficulty to deal with, and that looked like it was going to be a long, rocky road, if the information Connie had given him was anything to go by.

The email pinged again and he opened it and read it with a sense of impending doom. Phrases leapt out:

Grey market . . . Serious setback . . . suspended trading . . . DBRS downgrades SCIP to junk status . . . Debt downgraded to a CCC rating . . . Debt is in danger of default on interest and principal . . .

Why did the word 'debt' keep coming up? What debt were they talking about?

What does all this mean?

He emailed back, hoping against hope it didn't look as serious as it appeared.

The terse reply came back.

It means we're fucked!

Barry felt the sweat break out across his forehead and bead his lip. What was Al saying? He couldn't mean that SCIP had gone down the tubes, surely? Barry took a deep breath and read the report again, and then Googled up the company. With mounting fear, he read and reread the material in front of him. SCIP was finished, kaput, the latest company to crash as a result of the international credit crisis. Investors stood to lose millions. He had just lost €100,000, plus the interest it would cost to repay the loan. When Aimee found out about this there would be hell to pay; he'd never be able to keep it from her.

What could he do? Who could he confide in? Connie – he'd have to ring Connie. His ex-wife was always very cool in a crisis, he thought in panic as he lifted the phone and dialled her number.

CHAPTER FOUR

'Calm down, Barry, and if Mrs Mansfield wakes up from her nap and rings the bell, I have to go pronto, so don't think I'm being rude.' Connie tried to hide her exasperation. She had just sat down for a quick cuppa and was about to ring Drew while Mrs Mansfield took a nap when Barry had phoned her, babbling so fast she couldn't hear what he was saying.

'Sorry,' her ex-husband said apologetically. 'It's just you're the only person I felt I could ring.'

You've got a wife, Connie wanted to say sniffily, but she restrained herself.

'Start from the beginning,' she instructed, sitting at the kitchen table and stretching her legs out in front of her. Five minutes later, she was sitting up straight saying very slowly, 'You're telling me that you *borrowed* €100,000 to buy shares in a company that's gone *bust*?' The last word came out as a squawk.

'Yes, that about sums it up. I used Granny Hooper's house as collateral.'

'You borrowed to buy shares?' repeated Connie, horrified.

'Don't rub it in, Connie,' Barry said wearily.

'Didn't Aimee mind?' she queried. If she had still been married to Barry, there was no way she would have allowed him to borrow a sum like that for such a speculative venture. Thirty-five thousand max would have been her

74

absolute limit. There was silence on the phone. 'Barry?'

'I didn't tell Aimee. We keep separate accounts as well as a joint one.'

'Oh!'

'I guess it's because we both have separate businesses – it wasn't like when you and I were married,' he said awkwardly.

'Of course, it's ... um ... different for you and Aimee. You have to tell her though – you can't hide a loss like that, surely?'

'This isn't a good time. She's going to have the termination. I told her to make her own decision, and she's going to go to London and have it.'

'Oh, Barry, I'm sorry to hear that. I know you wanted the baby.' She felt a pang of sadness for him.

'I'm gutted, Connie, to tell you the truth. I'll always regret it, but I had to let Aimee make her choice. It was driving a big wedge between us. She accused me of being a bully, like her father. So I had to back off.'

'Oh, that's rough. You're nothing like Ken Davenport,' Connie exclaimed. What a horrible position for her ex-husband to be in. He was nothing like that obnoxious man.

'I know that, but Aimee was in such a state she thought I was doing the same kind of thing to her that her father does: being authoritative and dictatorial. It brought up a lot of issues for her. Maybe it's her hormones. I don't know.'

'And how's Melissa?'

'No better. No matter how much we try and get her to eat properly, she's not listening, or eating. We told her we'd give her a few weeks to make an effort to get back on the straight and narrow or we would have to intervene. She hasn't done it. She's telling us lies, constantly. Aimee found laxatives hidden in her bedroom. So we've made an appointment with our GP to get a letter of referral to that specialist you suggested.' His dejection oozed down the line, as tangible as the air she was breathing, and she was heartily sorry he'd phoned her. She didn't want to be listening to Barry's problems. She wasn't his wife any more and hadn't been for a long time. Her life was good now; she and Drew were having a joyful time after years of loneliness for both of them. All the years Barry had been happy with Aimee, when everything was going fine with them, she'd rarely had a phone call from him. He hadn't been interested in her woes, and she'd had plenty. But she'd kept them to herself. She hadn't gone weeping and wailing to her ex, she thought crossly.

'Are you there?' he asked.

'I'm here.' She hid her irritation.

'What do you think I should do?'

'Well, you can't go paying interest on that loan for years to come with nothing to show for it.'

'I know,' he agreed miserably.

'Have you any assets you can flog? I don't mean to be nosy,' she added hastily, afraid he would think she was prying.

'I know that, Connie. I guess I could sell Granny's house and take the hit on it, or I've an investment I could cash in and make a loss there.'

His grandmother had left him her house in her will, soon after their marriage had broken up. Technically, Connie felt she could have gone after him for extra money for Debbie because of it, but she hadn't. 'Well, at least you have money to cover the debt,' she said robustly. 'Imagine if you hadn't.'

'I know, it doesn't bear thinking about. I know plenty of people who've borrowed who *don't* have anything to cover it. There's been quite a few people in our building downsizing their cars. A lot of the SUV wives are driving Micras and Fiestas now.'

'No harm for the environment. Listen, I have to go. Keep your chin up,' she said kindly, willing him to hang up. She was longing to talk to Drew.

'Thanks, Connie. It's such a relief to be able to talk to you. Maybe we could have coffee some day,' he said eagerly.

'Hmm, I'll call you next week and we'll see how we're fixed. Let me know how you get on with Melissa.'

'Will do, and thanks again, Connie, you're a brick,' Barry said warmly.

'You're welcome. Bye,' she said, and exhaled a sigh of relief when she heard the dial tone.

She made herself another mug of tea and stood staring out at the mighty oak trees that had been in the grounds of Mrs Mansfield's estate for hundreds of years. Crisp leaves wearing a light dressing of russet and gold down drifted on to the grass as the autumn breeze rustled through the branches and the afternoon sun slanted through the foliage casting long, dancing shadows on to the drive.

What sort of a marriage did Barry and Aimee have that he would borrow a huge sum to invest without discussing it with her? What did it say about their relationship that he was more comfortable discussing his problems with his ex-wife than his current one?

All those times she had looked enviously at what she thought was the perfect couple, the couple that had it all: affluence, good fortune, security and marital bliss. And all the time, it hadn't been what it seemed at all. No one ever really knew what went on in someone else's marriage, she reflected, dialling Drew's number.

'Hello, Connie.' She could tell he was smiling, and her heart lifted at the sound of his deep voice.

'Hi Drew, what's happening?' She sat down again and settled the phone snugly against her ear, wishing she were nestling into his arms.

'Nothing much. I went for a ride on Marino earlier, and it was a gift of a day, clear blue skies and just a hint of autumn. Magic. Caitriona and I are grooming the horses; Fiona and Rachel are giving riding lessons to a group of ten-year-olds. Same old, same old. What about you since I left you snoring in bed at the crack of dawn this morning?' he teased.

'I wasn't snoring,' she protested indignantly. 'And I heard you going out. I heard you leaving the cup of tea on my bedside locker.'

'You mean you opened one eye, closed it again, and when you woke up your tea was cold and the sun was over the yardarm.'

Connie laughed. 'You know me so well, and in such a short space of time.'

'Yeah, but don't forget what you always say: "We've known each other for lifetimes,"' he quoted her. 'So what's happening?'

'You'll never guess. I've loads to tell you. Just had a phone call from Barry, full of gloom and doom—' In the distance, she heard Mrs Mansfield's bell tinkle.

'It will have to wait, dearest, Mrs M. is ringing her bell.'

'How about I take you out after work for a bite to eat and you can tell me all then?'

'I'll look forward to it, Drew. Have to fly. Love ya,' she said gaily, and hung up.

How lucky was she? Connie thought gratefully, happiness whispering through her as she hurried upstairs to her employer's bedroom, a smile on her face and joy in her heart. How wonderful to have someone to share all the ups and downs and ins and outs of her life with. How lovely to be going out for a meal instead of eating on her own at her kitchen table, with the dusk drawing in and a long, lonely evening stretching out ahead of her and only the TV and her little black cat for company. It was her time for joy and happiness, and she wasn't going to let Barry's woes impinge on her precious time with her darling Drew.

The relief of talking to Connie and getting that burden off his chest was incredible. He wasn't carrying his worries alone any more, Barry thought appreciatively. And his ex-wife had been so sympathetic to his feelings of loss now that Aimee was going for the termination. And Connie was deeply concerned about Melissa too. It was very comforting. It was wonderful to have this closeness between them again. She was a real safety net for him. He hoped that this Drew guy didn't get *too* involved in Connie's life. He'd hate to lose her again, now that she was back in his life, so to speak.

He scrolled down his contacts, selected a number and dialled, and got the usual spiel about the customer not being available or having their phone turned off. The message facility had been taken off. He couldn't even leave a rant, much as he wanted to. That little rat, Farrell, had gone to ground and wasn't to be found. His landline rang and he picked it up. 'Aimee's on the phone for you,' his secretary said in her well-modulated tones.

'Put her through.' He didn't particularly want to talk to Aimee at the moment, but he supposed it was better that they were back talking again instead of being at each other's throats. She was something else, though – she'd obviously rung his mobile and found it engaged and hadn't the patience to wait, so she'd phoned the office number. If he did that to her when she was at work, she'd give him what for!

'Hi, Aimee, what's up?' Barry pretended to be cheery.

'Just to mark your card, I told Melissa we'd made that GP appointment for her, and she's in a strop, so be prepared for the cold shoulder when you get home,' his wife warned.

'OK,' he said heavily. 'How did your meeting go?' He asked more out of politeness than interest. He wanted to get Aimee off the phone so he could ring his financial advisor and see if there was any way out of his fiscal quandary.

'Oh God, Barry, I nearly had a heart attack. It seems Myles heard this morning that he's lost a shedload of money, a few million according to Roger, because some company called SCIP has gone bust, and now he's withdrawn from the project.'

'Good Lord,' Barry ejaculated, horrified. Was that bloody company going to be the total ruin of his family? What the hell was Aimee going to do? She'd resigned her previous job. What dark miasma had enveloped their lives? This couldn't have happened at a worse time.

'No. No,' Aimee hastened to reassure him. 'Hibernian Dreams is still going ahead with Roger, albeit a more toned-down version – unfortunately – but he still has great plans for it and, more importantly, the money to finance it. The only thing is, he wants me to meet a client, so I have to reschedule . . . er . . . Friday. I'll make the call when I'm sure Melissa won't walk in on me. I wouldn't like her to overhear me making arrangements like that. The sooner I get an office the better. I hate working from home.'

'No, not a good idea for Melissa to overhear anything like that,' he said feebly. 'She has enough issues to be dealing with at the moment. Look, I have to go, I've a meeting scheduled,' he lied. 'See you at home.'

He hung up and sat back in his chair, crossing his feet on his desk. Aimee had talked about nearly having a heart attack; he felt he was in the throes of one. His chest was tight, his heartbeat was erratic. He picked up his mobile again and tried Jeremy's home number. The phone rang and rang, echoing loudly in his ear.

'Bastard,' he muttered as he hung up. 'If I ever get my hands on you, I'll hang you from the nearest lamp post.'

Jeremy Farrell sat at his computer in his Portuguese villa and watched the *News at One* on the RTE player. The SCIP collapse was the main news item. He watched familiar faces speak to reporters, he saw the SCIP offices flash up on the screen: solid, imposing, impressive. The camera lingered on the highly polished gold plate: SecureCo International Plus. It had been the epitome of the Celtic Tiger. Not for the common or garden investor with their couple of thou to splurge. This was for the big boys, and he knew them all. This was to be his retirement plan. His chance to upgrade every aspect of his life. A new house in D4. A big new villa on a bigger, more exclusive golf course in the Algarve. A pad in NY. He damn well deserved it. He'd spent his entire life schmoozing for Crooks & Co., talking them and himself up. Name-dropping high-flying shaggers who didn't give him a second glance. To them he was just small fry. He'd sold high and made a killing on half his SCIP shares when they'd been up as high as €30. And then, a few months later, Jeremy had seen the writing on the wall and sold the rest as the share price began to drop gradually. He was just in time because the friggin' German banks had got windy and unexpectedly pulled the plug and then the whole thing had come tumbling down like a pack of cards.

He wasn't proud that he'd pushed half his buddies in the golf club to invest when he knew the company was on the slide. But he'd never thought that it was going bust, never to be traded on the stock exchange. There had been frantic behind-the-scenes efforts to save it. Crooks & Co. had put huge pressure on Jeremy to find new investors. And he had. He'd cajoled everyone he knew, even people who didn't have the money to invest, people who'd had to borrow, and he'd done a good job of it, he'd raised several million for the company – and for what? He couldn't quite believe himself that it was actually gone. He hadn't seen that coming. It was like a kick in the gonads.

He looked at his old mobile phone sitting on the desk; he'd got a new one and changed his number. He'd had so many messages left on the old one, frantic messages from people he'd advised to invest in SCIP trying to get hold of him once share dealing had been suspended.

Jeremy rubbed his eyes tiredly and closed the RTE player. The late-afternoon sun streamed in through the pristine fine-net curtains and a fresh breeze from the Atlantic tempered the heat of the sun. He certainly wouldn't be able to show his face at home for a while. His son-in-law had told him that Seanie Fitz was still playing golf in Druids Glen and eating out in the Troc. Jeremy didn't quite have the neck for it, he acknowledged, and he was a minnow compared to the ex-Anglo boss. He hadn't brought down the entire banking system, just encouraged a few punters to invest in what had started out as a blue-chip company, a sure thing, Jeremy thought irritably. It was all bloody Anglo's fault that he was in this mess. They'd been the rotten apple in the barrel.

He could hear his wife sobbing upstairs. She'd been crying since the news had broken this morning. She'd always hoped that some miracle would happen and SCIP would be rescued and she could go home and face their friends. That was never going to happen, Jeremy thought glumly. As of now they had no friends. They were social pariahs. It would be interesting to see how many Christmas cards they got this year. He walked out to the hall, his cream loafers soundless on the marble floor.

'Going for a game of golf,' he called up the curving wrought-iron stairs.

There was no answer. It seemed his wife wasn't talking to him either. She'd get over it, he thought unsympathetically. She hadn't objected to his business practices when everything was hunky-dory and he was providing her with a lifestyle most women could only dream of. She'd be crying a lot louder if they'd lost the sort of money a lot of their friends had, that was for sure.

With a grim set to his jaw, Jeremy Farrell hoisted his golf clubs on to his buggy and set off for the clubhouse, with the white breakers of the Atlantic pounding the golden curves of beach on one side and the rolling, emerald sward and knolls of the golf course on the other. Business was business, and if people couldn't look at their losses in that light, that was their tough luck. There was nothing personal in any of it. People took risks and that was their choice, and he would hold his head up high and not be bowed down by any of it.

But later, as he watched a playback of Bryan Dobson grilling the CEO of the defunct company and heard a selection of financial experts give their opinion on the cause of the collapse, his bravado faded. His wife was right to weep. They were now beyond the pale. His reputation was in tatters. No one would ever take advice from him again. His standing in society at home was gone. People had looked up to him, bought him drinks, wined and dined him and been anxious to be seen in his company because he had the inside track and they wanted to be kept in the loop. No more. Even when all the fuss died down, he would be known as someone who had sold his friends down the river, someone whose financial expertise and judgement was in question. He had lost all credibility, and *that*, Jeremy Farrell admitted, was the hardest blow of all.

Sarah Fleming scrolled down through her phone and found Mrs Adams' mobile-phone number. She had Melissa's mother's number on her phone, just as Melissa had Sarah's mum's number on hers. Aimee and Valerie Fleming had felt it was a good idea. Sarah had never used Mrs Adams' number before. She was a little in awe of Aimee, who was always so brisk and businesslike, and had hardly ever been at home until she'd left her job to take up a new one. She was an MD now, Melissa had told Sarah proudly. But it was a bit disconcerting that Aimee was working from home until she got her new offices, and that had certainly curtailed the fun she and Melissa had been having over the summer. But Sarah couldn't let her awe of Aimee Adams stop her from telling her that she had to do something about Melissa. Her friend hadn't had time to talk to her after school because she'd had to go into town to meet Aimee. Part of her was glad. She knew Melissa wouldn't want to be confronted about her weight loss. Melissa thought she was being really healthy, but Brenda Meyers had copped what she was up to, and that was because Brenda was anorexic herself. Sarah felt such a fool. And she was mad with her friend for not being honest with her. Having spent the afternoon thinking about it, Sarah knew *exactly* the moment that Melissa had turned. It was at Debbie's wedding, when that drunken slapper had said, when Melissa had accidentally bumped into her, 'Who is that little fat tart?'

Melissa had been *so* upset about it, even though Sarah had tried hard to get her to forget about it. Tears came to her eyes. Did that horrible girl know what a disastrous train of events she had triggered with her unkind, thoughtless remark? A thought struck Sarah. If she rang Mrs Adams, Melissa could be in the room with her, and she'd freak. She chewed the inside of her lip and came to a decision. She sent the text before she lost her nerve:

Hi Mrs Adams I need 2 talk 2 u about Melissa, can I ring u or will u ring me? Sarah.

She felt sick. This was serious stuff. Her first cousin had anorexia and had ended up being fed through a tube, and she was like a walking skeleton. Her whole family had gone through hell, and it was like a roller coaster for them. Her friend could end up the same way. 'Please, please, God, don't let anything bad happen to Melissa,' she prayed fervently, although she wasn't at all sure there was such a being as God. She had serious doubts about all of that stuff; especially with all the abuse scandals and the way the Pope and the bishops wouldn't apologize and resign for covering it all up and allowing it to happen. The Pope was supposed to be the stand-in for Jesus on earth, and he was letting these people get away with all that abuse when he should be kicking them out and reporting them to the police. He should even resign himself. They'd had a discussion about it in religion class, and that was the conclusion they had arrived at. If there was such a person as God, all this horrible stuff wouldn't be happening, and her cousin and her best friend wouldn't be trying to starve themselves to death, Sarah reasoned angrily. Her mobile rang and she jumped. She saw Mrs Adams' name flash up on the screen. She was very tempted not to answer it. She took a deep breath. 'Hello,' she quavered.

'Sarah, it's Aimee. I got your text, and I can talk privately. What did you need to speak to me about?' Mrs Adams sounded tired, she thought guiltily, remembering that her friend's mum was pregnant.

'I think Melissa's got anorexia,' she blurted.

'Why do you think that, Sarah? Please tell me everything. I know something's wrong, and Melissa's dad and I are trying to get to the bottom of it. What can you tell me? Please don't keep anything back, and just let me say I'm so glad you rang me. You're a true friend,' Mrs Adams said, and her voice sounded less brisk than usual; she sounded quite kind, Sarah thought with relief. Emboldened by her encouragement, Sarah went through her sorry tale, starting from the beginning, with the incident at Debbie's wedding.

When she put the phone down twenty minutes later, Sarah felt a huge sense of relief. Both of them had agreed that Melissa shouldn't be told about their phone call, or she wouldn't trust Sarah any more, and Mrs Adams said it was imperative that Melissa trusted Sarah. Mrs Adams was bringing Melissa to the doctor, and Sarah didn't have to carry the burden any longer. The adults had taken charge, and for that she was immensely grateful. She lay on her bed biting her nails. She just hoped it wasn't too late.

'Being called a little fat tart, that's what started all of this.' Aimee shook her head in disbelief as she told her husband of the conversation she'd just had with Sarah. 'If I could get my hands on the spiteful bitch who said that to Melissa, she'd rue the day she opened her big mouth. Can you find out who it was? It was one of the crowd that were at Debbie's wedding, because, really, Barry, that girl needs to face up to the havoc she's caused in our daughter's life. What a stupid, irresponsible thing to say.' Aimee was incandescent. 'I should never have allowed Melissa to go to that wedding reception. She was too young. And to have had an encounter with a truly obnoxious character who'd come out with something like that. Name-calling of the worst type!' Aimee continued her rant. 'What sort of people do Debbie and Bryan socialize with?'

'Didn't Sarah say that the girl was drunk?' Barry said tiredly. This was all he needed. It was bad enough that there was a rift between Aimee, Connie and Debbie without his other family slyly being blamed for being the cause of Melissa's eating problems.

'That's not the point, Barry,' Aimee snapped. 'That young woman needs to know what she's responsible for, and I've a good mind to ring Debbie and tell her what sort of friends she has.'

'Please don't do that, Aimee, things are bad enough without

another family row. Debbie and Melissa are getting on really well, and I'd like to keep it like that. Melissa's going to need all the help and support she can get, and she *will* get that from Debbie,' Barry warned sternly.

'But that bitch might say something similar to another young girl and cause the same kind of thing to happen, Barry. We have a responsibility to make sure she doesn't do it again,' Aimee retorted.

'We have a responsibility to Melissa. Let's just focus on her.'

'That wedding has caused us nothing but trouble—'

'Stop! Enough, Aimee, let's not go down that road again. We'll take her to the doctor and move on from there.' There was an uncharacteristic edge to his tone.

'All right,' Aimee said sourly.

'Let's not argue, Aimee. It's not good for any of us. Why don't you close your computer and put your feet up? Would you like a cup of tea?' Barry offered, changing the subject. His wife looked exhausted.

'Thanks, I'm bushed.' She yawned.

'Don't forget to let me know the date you reschedule your appointment for,' he reminded her.

'There's no need for you to come, honestly.' Aimee stretched out on the sofa and glanced up at him as he got up to go to the kitchen.

'You're not going through that on your own, Aimee.'

'Even though it's my choice and not yours?' she said wearily.

'We're in this marriage together, Aimee, with all the ups and downs it entails.' He stood looking down at her, and thoughtfully placed another cushion behind her head to make her more comfortable.

'I suppose we are,' she agreed, closing her eyes, grateful for his support in what, she admitted, was the roughest patch their relationship had ever encountered.

'Season of mists and mellow fruitfulness'

CHAPTER FIVE

'A three-day week starting on Monday?'

'That's right, Bryan, you were one of the lucky ones. You avoided redundancy because you were in six months longer than three other of your colleagues who came in the same year,' Gemma Reilly, the HR manager, said sombrely.

'If you call that lucky.' Bryan couldn't hide his disgust.

'Some people would think three days are better than none,' Gemma said quietly. 'You'll be taking over Jim Doherty's assignments.' She slid a file across the desk to him.

'So let me get this right. I'll be doing my own assignments plus Jim's and taking a huge reduction in pay. That sounds about right for this banana republic,' said Bryan bitterly, taking the file and getting to his feet.

Gemma rubbed her temples. She had a splitting headache. She'd been getting flak all morning. The CEO had told her she could email the news, good or bad, to the various employees affected by the new circumstances. She'd thought email was a cold, impersonal, cowardly way to tell an employee about something so important to them and had opted for the face-to-face option. Right now, she was sorry she'd taken the hard route.

'I'm sorry, Bryan, we're all affected one way or another. I have a list of counsellors, financial and psychological, should you wish to see someone about your changed circumstances.'

'And how am I going to pay for counselling? I won't be able to pay my mortgage. Thanks, but you can keep your list, Gemma,' he said sarcastically as he turned and walked out of her office.

'You won't be able to pay for your coke either, dickhead,' Gemma muttered, putting his file on top of the pile on her left and picking up the next one from that on her right.

Bryan was so angry he wanted to put his fist through the grinning gargoyle, painted by an up-and-coming artist, that decorated the wall outside Gemma's office. It was now official: he and Debbie were up the creek without a paddle.

He took the lift to the ground floor and walked over to the decorative fountain in the middle of the foyer and sat on the low grey brick wall that surrounded it. The sound of the water tinkling and streaming behind him made him wish he was up in the mountains beside a river, far, far away from this hell hole. He slid his BlackBerry out of his pocket and dialled Debbie's number.

'Hello.' Her voice was low, but at least she answered. And if the manager who'd been injured in the car crash had been back in the office, she wouldn't even have had the phone turned on.

'It's a three-day week for me. Jerry and a whole load of others are gone. We'd better decide what we're going to do,' Bryan said flatly.

'Well, we can't afford to go to that wedding we're invited to, for starters. I'm going to ring up and cancel and—'

'Debbie, the wedding's in the halfpenny place. We need to really talk about our future. I want us to get the hell out of Ireland,' he said grimly. 'There's nothing for us here.'

'Look, I can't talk now. Do you want to meet after work and go for an early bird somewhere?' He could hear the stress in her voice.

'No point in wasting money eating out. I've no appetite. I'll see you at home,' he said.

'OK. Bye.' His wife sounded as fed up as he was. Bryan stood up and stretched, and picked up the file with his new assignments. They could rent the house, which would pay the mortgage, and just get out of this damn country for a few years. They could get work somewhere, pay off the interest on the credit cards and keep that at bay, and go and have some fun for themselves, like they used to before they bought that friggin' house. And if she didn't want to – well, that would be her choice. He was going whether Debbie liked it or not. What did that say about the state of their marriage? It wasn't too strong at the moment. He and Debbie had been a carefree, fun-loving couple once. She had been so loving and mindful of him and he'd always been able to get around her. That had all changed in the past two years. She'd gone to all their friends' weddings and seen them buy houses and settle down, and she wanted to do the same. She wanted a home of their own, whereas he didn't give a fiddler's about owning a property. Maybe being reared in a one-parent family had made her long for roots and security, even though, in fairness, Connie had given her a very stable upbringing. But there was always a want and a need in Debbie, and he didn't have to be a psychologist to know that it was because Barry had been absent from her life for so long. He loved Debbie, but he wasn't going to suppress who or what he was any more. He'd given it his best shot. He wasn't cut out for mind-numbing mediocrity. He needed his spirit to soar, he needed vibrancy and diversity in his life, and if Debbie couldn't cope with the way he wanted to live his life, they weren't going to make it as a couple. He felt dread and sadness as he acknowledged a truth he'd been trying to ignore for the past few weeks. Debbie was going to have to make a choice: give him his freedom to live as he wanted and share it with him, or live this tedious, suburban life without him. He took a deep breath. He felt strangely exhilarated now that he had finally stopped running and made a decision.

The worst had happened but maybe it was a blessing in disguise – it might give him an escape route from the stranglehold of marriage and debt that was slowly but surely smothering him.

*

What did Bryan mean, he wanted to get out of Ireland? Where did he want to go? She had a good job that was well paid; did he want her to give that up in the middle of a recession? What about their home? What about the money they owed? They couldn't simply up sticks and leave, no matter how much he wanted to. Typical Bryan, with his head in the sand. When was he ever going to grow up? Debbie thought irritably as she picked over the bones of their earlier conversation. She felt a shiver of apprehension. Why did it always end up being about him? Had he factored in *her* feelings at all when he pronounced that he wanted them to get out of Ireland? Bryan was the master of the unilateral decision. She had often let him get away with things for the quiet life, choosing her battles wisely, but this was different. This was a totally life-changing proposal, and she had more to lose than he did right now. Besides, she didn't want to live abroad and, anyway, didn't Bryan realize that leaving the country wouldn't have any effect on the amount of money they owed. Was he that obtuse? Until today, it had only been a possibility that his job would be affected by the cutbacks. Now it was confirmed, and she knew they were going to have to face up to their precarious financial situation and, as usual, it was going to have to be her who took on the responsibility for doing something about it.

She got up from her desk and walked through the big swing doors that led to the lifts and the stairwell. There was a window with a ledge opposite the lifts, and she leaned her elbows on it and stared out at the clear blue sky, oblivious to the view of city rooftops and church spires that spread out below her. She took her phone out of her jacket pocket and keyed in a number, and heaved a sigh of relief when Barry answered.

'Debbie?' He sounded surprised. She didn't normally ring him. She was being a bit of a user, she thought guiltily, but needs must.

'Dad, I need to talk to you about something. Can we meet for lunch somewhere? I know it's short notice. I'll explain when I see you,' she said tersely.

'Ummm. Let's see. It will have to be an early one, I'm afraid, Aimee and I are bringing Melissa to see our GP today—'

'Oh sorry, Dad, I didn't meant to impose. Like I say, it's short notice. We'll leave it,' Debbie said hastily, cursing herself for being so impulsive.

'It's not a problem, Debbie,' her father said firmly. 'I'd love to meet for lunch. What's up? Nothing too serious, I hope.'

'I'll tell you when I see you, Dad. I have to get back to work. Where suits you?'

'How about the Morrison – that's not too far from you, sure it isn't? I've a meeting with some clients there at eleven. I could meet you at twelve, twelve fifteen? I'll have to leave around half one, but that would give us a good hour and a bit,' he suggested.

'Perfect. That would be great. Thanks a million, Dad. I'll see you then.'

'Take care, Debbie,' her father said kindly, and she felt a lump come to her throat. For the first time in her life, Barry was there for her in her hour of need. Memories of years of childhood hurts and sadness when he hadn't been around for birthdays, sports days and other special events in her young life smote her, and she had to duck into the loos and have a silent weep in one of the cubicles before she was able to compose herself enough to go back to her desk.

Barry frowned as he put his mobile back on his desk. What was up with Debbie? There was clearly something wrong. She sounded terribly stressed. She had never asked him to meet her for lunch before. She'd met him for coffee prior to the wedding to talk things over, but this was a first. It was unfortunate that it was the day he was bringing Melissa to the doctor. He didn't want his first-born daughter to think he was giving her the bum's rush. God knows she'd felt like she was playing second fiddle all her life, and now that she was finally building up a relationship with him again, he wanted to be there for her one hundred per cent.

How strange fate was. His two daughters were in trouble, needing him as never before in their lives. He was so pleased Debbie had felt they were close enough now that she could phone him and ask for his advice. Hopefully he'd be able to help her with whatever was troubling her and cement their relationship even further. Connie would be very pleased at this turn of events, Barry thought with satisfaction. At last he was being given the chance to make amends for walking out on them so long ago.

Mrs O'Doherty droned on and on about the square on the hypotenuse, and Melissa felt like screaming. She hated maths with a vengeance. The morning was really dragging, and she felt sick and dizzy. But she knew the sickness was not just because she hadn't eaten. It was because her parents were bringing her to the family doctor in the afternoon. Dr Burke would probably quiz her about her eating habits and try and tell her she had a problem. She was dreading it.

What was wrong with all of them? she fumed silently. Couldn't they see that she was happier than she had ever been? She wasn't huge and fat like a big whale any more. She still had a good way to go, but people were telling her that she looked great. Melissa felt for the first time ever that she was in control of some part of her life; surely that was a good thing? Why wouldn't they all leave her alone? Even Sarah was giving her funny looks and being a bit strange, and why was she digging her in the ribs? she thought irritably.

'. . . Do you think you could come out of your daydream there, Miss Adams? Melissa Adams, would you *concentrate*, please,' her teacher exhorted in exasperation.

'Oh . . . oh . . . sorry, Mrs O'Doherty.' She sat up straight and pretended alertness.

The teacher turned her back to the class and wrote some figures up on the board. 'Solve that theorem please, girls,' she instructed.

'You didn't have to dig me so hard in the ribs,' Melissa whispered petulantly to Sarah. 'It hurt.'

'That's 'cos you've got too skinny,' Sarah retorted tetchily.

'No conferring, you pair.' Mrs O'Doherty cast a gimlet eye in their direction.

They bent their heads to their work, each simmering with resentment as, for the first time in their long and loving friendship, the beginnings of a rift cast a long dark shadow.

Debbie's heart raced as the elegant façade of the Morrison loomed and she stepped in from the quays to the calm serenity of the hotel. It wasn't only the fact that she had practically jogged from the office down through Temple Bar and across the Halfpenny Bridge to the quays on the north side of the Liffey that was causing her heart to pound, it was because she was going to ask her father for financial help, and if he turned her down, she didn't know what she was going to do or who she was going to turn to.

Barry stood up when she walked into the lounge, a smile breaking across his tanned features when he saw her. He looked very handsome and successful in his grey bespoke suit and pale lilac shirt. 'Hello, love,' he said warmly, leaning down to kiss her and give her a hug, and she stayed motionless in the shelter of his arms for a moment as his embrace evoked memories of when she was very young. She remembered that she had always felt completely safe when she was in her father's arms.

'You look a bit wrecked – what's up?' he commented, concern mirrored in his eyes as he drew away from her and looked at her. 'You look a bit weary yourself,' she remarked, noting the bags under his eyes. 'Is it Melissa – are you very worried about her?' she asked shakily.

'Yeah, I'm worried. There's no talking to her, we just have to step in and see if we can get help for her. She's taking this slimming racket way too far. I don't suppose you have any idea what it's all about? I think she overheard someone calling her fat.' Barry had no intention of telling his daughter that the incident had occurred at her wedding.

'That's terrible. She hasn't said anything to me. I'm trying to get her to be as comfortable with me as she can so she feels she can confide in me. If I hear anything I think could be of help, I will tell you, Dad, but I think it's important that she feels she can trust me,' Debbie said as they sat side by side on a brown leather sofa and he handed her a menu.

'I appreciate that, Debbie, I really do. Aimee and I are at our wits' end.'

'I can imagine. It's very worrying.'

'Perhaps you'd prefer to go to the restaurant and have a proper lunch? It's not often I get a chance to treat my oldest daughter to a meal,' he suggested casually, hoping that she would accept his invitation. It would be good to make a fuss of Debbie and make her feel special. She'd kept him at arm's length for such a long time.

'I'm not really that hungry,' she murmured, scanning the bar-food menu in front of her. 'I think I'll just have a sandwich.'

'What's up? Don't tell me you're slimming too,' he said with an attempt at humour.

'No, Dad, nothing like that. It's just . . . well . . . to be honest, things aren't going too well for me and Bryan, and he's been put on a three-day week at work, and we can't afford our mortgage because we're paying off a massive credit-card debt, and Bryan wants to leave Ireland and I don't, and he doesn't even know I'm here talking to you about it. And I don't know what to do or who to turn to.' It all came tumbling out; the reasoned, calm speech she had prepared in her head on her way to meet him evaporated into the ether. Just this jumble of words pouring out willy-nilly, like an unstoppable flow of lava.

'Wait, wait, slow down. Start again.' Barry put the menu down and turned to face her.

'Oh Dad, I'm in real trouble, and I need to borrow about

twenty-five thousand, if you have it, and as soon as the property prices rise we'll sell the house and I'll pay you back. If we sell now we'll be in negative equity, and even if we tried getting another loan to pay off the cards it would still leave us short for the mortgage,' she floundered. 'If I could just get the cards paid off and only had to pay the mortgage, I think we could weather this, even with Bryan on a three-day week. I know you were very, very generous to us with the wedding, but this would be a loan, and I'd pay it back with interest,' she said earnestly. 'I'm only asking because you seem to be so wealthy, with the big car and the holidays abroad, and Aimee having that high-powered career, so I guess you've got two top salaries and would have . . . er . . . access to cash, if you know what I mean. I don't mean that in a smart or . . . em . . . intrusive way,' she rattled on. 'I'm just explaining how I felt that I could come to you for help. If Mum had spare cash, I would have asked her, but she's working part-time now and I know the wedding and the money she gave us ate into her savings.' She gave a little shrug and looked down at her hands, unable to look him in the eye.

'I'm glad you approached me,' he cut in quickly. 'I know you're not being smart or intrusive in the slightest. How did you get into such debt, Debbie?' he asked, mystified. 'How did you get a mortgage with such debt?'

'Oh, we didn't have a huge debt when we went looking for the mortgage.' She twirled a twist of hair nervously. 'It was what we spent on the wedding, ourselves, and the honeymoon, and buying stuff for the house after we'd got the mortgage where we went a bit mad. We used the cards until we maxed out. We'd no problem at all getting a mortgage, we got a hundred per cent variable one when they took into account both our salaries . . .' She tailed off helplessly. 'We're changing the car to a much smaller one, and I was thinking we could take in a lodger.'

'That's a bit of a pain. Who wants a lodger when you're just married?' Barry made a face.

'I don't think it would make much difference,' she said

glumly. 'We're not in a very good place at the moment. Things are really rocky.'

'Why, what's wrong?' Barry looked shocked at her disclosures.

'Bryan feels we shouldn't have got married and that we should have stayed living together and renting. He never wanted to buy a house. He didn't really want the responsibility of a mortgage and all that entails, and now he's pissed off about everything and feeling trapped and he's blaming me for it.'

Barry felt a jolt of reluctant empathy for his son-in-law. That had been him thirty years ago. Constrained by marriage and responsibilities, stifled, smothered, resentful, bored – he could understand *exactly* where Bryan was coming from and he pitied Debbie from the bottom of his heart. Not even settling their credit-card debt was going to sort out the way that young man was feeling, he thought grimly. Bryan wanted out, just as he had years ago. It pained him to recognize this. It brought back uncomfortable memories of his younger, unhappy self, and the knowledge that he had turned his back on his wife and child and walked away from his marriage. At least Debbie didn't have a child to tie her down. That was a small mercy.

'Do you want to emigrate with Bryan and try and make it somewhere else?' he probed, knowing Connie would be gutted if they went abroad to live.

'No, Dad. I've a good job here and I like living at home. I like going abroad for holidays, but not to live. We've done a lot of travelling, but home is home for me,' she said miserably.

'I can see why Bryan might want to try and make a fresh start elsewhere,' he said slowly.

'But Dad, we'll still owe money on the mortgage because we'll never get the price for the house that we paid for it.'

'Could you rent it if you *did* go abroad for a couple of years or so?'

'I suppose we could, but rents have dropped drastically and it wouldn't give us enough to cover the whole amount every month. There'd still be a shortfall. And where would we go? The recession is worldwide. I've friends in Australia and they say there's no work out there. Look at the unemployment in the US. The one place where Bryan might have got work was Dubai. He often talked about it. It's a financial hub, and there were a lot of offices being built in the boom times. But it's practically bank-rupt now; they had to be bailed out by Abu Dhabi and the property market has collapsed completely. Bryan hangs out with a guy who's pretty loaded, and he bought two properties out there and he can't sell them or rent them now, so that's not an option any more. I don't know where he thinks we're going to get work. And the thing is, would I get as good a job as the one I have here? It's OK to say we're leaving, but leaving for what?' She gave a sigh that came from the depths of her.

'It would definitely be foolish for you to give up a good job that's reasonably secure unless you had something else equally as good to go to,' Barry agreed. 'Look, I need to talk to my invest-ment advisor; it might take me a while to get my hands on that amount. Would that be OK?'

'Oh Dad, I don't want to be a burden. It was just if you had money that was easily accessible was what I was thinking, and I'm sure you'd need to talk to Aimee. I shouldn't have asked. I was just in a bit of a panic when I rang because Bryan had phoned to say he was going on a three-day week. Look, forget it, I can try MABS for advice, or maybe try and renegotiate our mortgage.' Part of Debbie wished that she'd kept her woes to herself.

Barry held up his hand. 'Don't do anything for the moment. And don't worry about Aimee, I'll deal with that side of things. We'll keep this between us for a while until I work out my strategy,' he said firmly.

'OK. But will I say it to Bryan? We're going to talk about it all tonight.'

'Tell him it might be an option and see what he says. Maybe he might not be so determined to emigrate if the credit-card issue was sorted. Maybe he's just panicking,' Barry observed, privately thinking that, unless he was very much mistaken, and he hoped he was, Bryan and Debbie might not last the course. He vaguely remembered Connie saying something similar before the wedding. He knew she wasn't that keen on their son-in-law. She'd actually called him a 'pretty boy with no substance' once. Maybe she was right, he thought gloomily. He, at least, had stayed married for a few years before he'd had his existential crisis. The way Debbie was talking, it didn't look as though her marriage would make it to the first anniversary.

'Enough of this, let's have something to eat and try and stop worrying,' he said calmly, and she felt herself relax a little. Even just being able to talk to him was a help. She would have hated to have to go running to Connie and spoil her happiness. Confiding in Barry was the perfect solution. Let him prove to her just how good a father he could be. Melissa had had a very affluent lifestyle and upbringing, far different from what she'd had; now it was his time to make up for what she'd missed out on. Debbie didn't feel as guilty about landing her burdens on Barry as she would have if she'd had to go to Connie. Barry had told her at her wedding that he wanted to be a real father to her, that he wanted her to know that he would always be there for her. Now was his chance to put his words to the test and come up trumps.

'Mother of God,' Barry muttered to himself, returning Debbie's wave as she stepped on to the Halfpenny Bridge to cross the Liffey. What crap timing for his daughter to come to him with financial problems! If it weren't for his ill-considered investment in the SCIP fiasco he would have been able to write a cheque for the damn money there and then, but now he was paying back a loan plus interest on 100,000 smackers and there was nothing for him at the end of it.

Kids nowadays were in desperate trouble, he thought angrily as he made his way past one of his favourite city sculptures, the two women sitting on a bench chatting, in front of the Woollen Mills. His car was parked in Arnott's car park. He'd want to get a move on. He was picking Aimee up from Meadows & Byrne on North Wall Quay in twenty minutes. She had taken the Dart and Luas to check out the length of time it would take to get to her new office.

What kind of madness had allowed bankers to give 100 per cent loans to the likes of Bryan and Debbie? He seethed as he drove down the ramp on to Abbey Street and swung right and then left to get on to the quays. When he and Connie had been saving for a house they'd had to have a down payment of 10 per cent of the price of the house and the loan was calculated on two and a half times the larger salary. They'd had to save bloody hard, and neither of them had had a credit card.

He'd seen a headline that Anglo was wiping off millions on directors' loans. He'd seen pictures of the massive houses they lived in. Why were they not forced to downsize to a semi-detached, in a half-finished estate, and then they'd see how the other half lived, the half that were paying the price for their greed. NAMA was bailing out the banks, but there was no help for the thousands of other mortgage holders who were in danger of having their homes repossessed because they were taking big cuts in their salaries. It was obscene, amoral, and the government was doing nothing to help them.

He was taking a hit because he'd been greedy and reckless, he admitted that, not that it made it any easier. But at least he had an asset to sell. His child had nothing. If it was the last thing he did he would get that money for her. He had shares he could sell or he could cash in an investment bond early. He would keep it to himself for the time being. He could see why Debbie would think he was rolling in it. The lifestyle he, Aimee and Melissa had was far removed from the way she'd lived with Connie, he reflected with a pang of shame.

Connie had only looked for child support and had gone back to work to support herself. She had never leeched off him, but there hadn't been foreign holidays, flash cars, designer labels and the like for his elder daughter, and if, in years to come, Aimee ever found out that he had helped Debbie financially he would be pointing out these things to her. If she hadn't so much on her plate he might have discussed it with her, but remembering his second wife's attitude to his contribution to Debbie's wedding he thought it might be prudent to keep it to himself. He tapped his fingers impatiently on the wheel as he sat at traffic lights at Butt Bridge.

Aimee wouldn't be at all sympathetic to Debbie's problems. It would only cause resentment on her part. He didn't need any more issues with his wife. They had more than enough to be going on with. It was lucky they had separate accounts as well as the joint one, and that had been Aimee's doing. She had been adamant that she wanted financial independence when they got married. Well, she had what she wanted, and right now he was very glad of their separate accounts. He could do what he wanted with his own money, and that was the tack he'd take when he eventually told her about his disastrous investment. Debbie's business he would keep to himself. There were some things his wife definitely did not need to know. She would have had a termination and not told him had Melissa not inadvertently discovered the pregnancy-test kit. They were good at keeping things from each other lately. It wasn't a good reflection on their marriage. He brushed the thought aside impatiently. Now he had to put all of this to one side and go and support his younger daughter as best he could in the ordeal that was to come in their GP's surgery. At least he and Aimee were at one about that.

CHAPTER SIX

'Honestly, Dr Burke, I'm fine. I needed to lose a few pounds and I've done that. And I'm eating really healthily, lots of salads and things,' Melissa said airily, putting on the act of her life. 'Mom and Dad are worrying over nothing.'

'Well, there's no harm in checking you out while you're here, Melissa,' Dr Burke said easily, tucking a strand of black hair behind her ear. She was in her early forties and easy to talk to, and Melissa usually had no problem going to her, but today was different. Today Melissa had to prove that there was absolutely nothing wrong with her, when everyone, Dr Burke included, seemed to think she had an eating problem.

'You know, eating salads is very good, and well done for being so health conscious, but you need a good balance of proteins and carbs. It's all about balance and moderation. You don't want to be at risk of having osteoporosis in later life. How are your periods? What's your cycle?' Dr Burke asked matter-of-factly, making a little note on the pad in front of her.

'What do you mean?' Melissa twisted her hands in her lap. She was so nervous she was perspiring profusely, doing a real Niagara.

'You know ... twenty-four days, twenty-eight days?' The doctor smiled at her.

'Oh, um ... well now I don't get them for ages, and sometimes they only last for a day. They're really light now, actually, compared to what they used to be. It's great,' Melissa enthused. 'They used to be really heav—' Too late, she suddenly remembered she'd read that eating disorders could have a very bad effect on your periods, and even stop them all together. 'Sometimes they're a bit painful,' she amended.

'Just hop up on the couch there behind the screen and I'll have a quick look at your tummy,' the doctor instructed.

'Honestly, there's nothing wrong with my tummy,' Melissa protested.

'What did you eat today?' Dr Burke probed, coming around from the desk and pointing to the couch that was hidden behind a wooden screen with some butterflies painted on it.

'Umm . . . cornflakes and a banana for breakfast, and a ham and salad roll for lunch,' Melissa lied. She hadn't actually had the roll, and she'd only eaten two bites of the banana.

'And what do you do for exercise?'

'I walk to school and back, and I walk on the pier sometimes,' Melissa said sullenly.

'How far is it to school?'

'About half a mile.'

'You go to the one at the other end of Sandycove?'

'Yeah.'

'That's a lot more than a mile, more like two at least.'

Melissa didn't answer.

The doctor lifted her top, ran her fingers lightly over her tummy and sides and then slid a weighing scale out from under the couch. 'Hop up on that like a good girl and then we're finished,' she said lightly.

'Do I have to? I hate weighing myself.' Melissa made a face. She thought that was a good move, to pretend to hate weighing herself, when she *lived* on the scales, morning, noon and night.

'Won't take a second,' the doctor said firmly.

Melissa stood on the scales and, with enormous willpower, refrained from looking at the display on the small square screen.

'Grand. Sit down there now, and we'll call in your mum and dad,' Dr Burke said non-committally. She picked up the phone and spoke into it. 'Orla, will you ask Mr and Mrs Adams to join us, please?'

Her parents looked so serious and concerned as they sat on the chairs Dr Burke had placed beside hers. Melissa swallowed hard and a big ball of anger lodged in the pit of her stomach. This was not the way it was meant to be. They were treating her like a child. She was almost fourteen, practically grown up. Why couldn't they see that? And she hated Dr Burke for interfering.

'Well, I've had a chat with Melissa and examined her and weighed her. I'm a bit concerned that she isn't eating properly. Her stomach is concave, her weight is too light for her height and body mass, her menstrual cycle has changed, and I think it would be wise to have a consultation with a specialist. I'm going to write a letter of ref—'

'There's no need,' Melissa burst out. 'If it makes you feel better, I'll eat my meals with you every day, Mom, and I'll take the Dart to school.'

'No, Melissa, we gave you a chance to act responsibly. You've lied to us too often,' Aimee said firmly.

'There's nothing wrong with me,' Melissa exploded. 'Why can't you get it into your thick skulls?'

'Melissa!' Aimee remonstrated.

'Apologize. Now!' Barry said in a tone she rarely heard.

'Sorry,' she muttered, close to tears.

'It's just a precaution, Melissa,' Dr Burke said kindly. 'It's easy to slip into bad eating habits at your age. You don't want to end up in hospital, now do you?'

'No.' She scowled.

'I'm going to give you a sheet with the food pyramid on it. It might be helpful to follow it to balance out your meals.' Dr Burke slid the coloured information sheet across the table to her and began typing the letter of referral. 'I'll fax this through and you should get a phone call from the secretary with an appointment. I have your number on the computer. Aimee, will I put yours down?' She looked out at Aimee over her glasses.

'That's fine, thank you, Audrey,' Aimee said with a stern glance at Melissa.

Melissa ignored her and stared stonily ahead. Let them write their bloody letters and give her information sheets and bring her to specialists. They couldn't stop her from living her life the way she wanted. She wouldn't let them undo all the progress she had made. The girls at school had been totally impressed. Their reaction had far exceeded her hopes and expectations. She would diet as much as she could between now and going to the specialist and hopefully lose another stone, and then she could start eating what they wanted her to eat for a while. And when they forgot about it, she would begin to eat the way *she* wanted to eat again, she decided, as her father took out his wallet to pay the doctor.

'That wasn't so bad, now was it?' Aimee said briskly as they walked to the car.

'It was horrible. I feel like a seven-year-old. I missed a whole afternoon of school for nothing. I'm going to meet Sarah to get my homework. You can drop me off at Costa,' Melissa retorted coldly, getting into the back of the car.

'We're just doing what any responsible parents would do, Melissa,' Barry said firmly, 'so drop the attitude.'

Can u meet me in Costa in ten?

Melissa texted Sarah, ignoring her parents. She hadn't told her friend she was going to the doctor; she'd fibbed and said she was going to the dentist. She wanted to make sure things between them were OK. Sarah had been a bit funny the last few days since they'd started back at school and she'd given her a really hard dig in the ribs in class today when she'd been daydreaming and hadn't heard Mrs O'Doherty speaking to her. She needed to find out what Sarah's problem was. She had enough going on in her life without having a moody best friend.

*

Sarah read Melissa's text and frowned. Her best friend had lied to her earlier and said she was taking the afternoon off to go to the dentist when Sarah knew full well that she was going to see her family doctor. Aimee had told her so, but instructed her not to let on that she knew. So Melissa had lied, just as she'd being lying the whole summer, thought Sarah bitterly.

Well, this was her last chance. If she were a real friend, Melissa would tell her the truth. They had always been very honest with each other, they were like sisters, and that was why all the deceit, as well as the fact that Melissa could be so stupid as to go down the road of dieting to extremes, hurt so much.

It felt almost like a betrayal, Sarah thought sadly. They used to think that people like Brenda Meyers were crazy to make themselves sick and turn themselves into lollipop heads. They had gazed at pictures of Posh Spice and Kate Moss in those celebrity magazines and jeered at their skinny little insect legs and balloon boobs. They'd read about their weird diets as they tucked into doughnuts and lattes. And now, just because of that horrible, big-mouth skanger at Debbie's wedding, Melissa was heading down that route, and Sarah was frightened for her.

OK on my way.

She sent the text and hurried to change out of her school uniform and put on some make-up. Some of the gang might be there. None of them ever went out without make-up. It was such a pain sometimes having to keep up with the cool girls.

Melissa was there before her, sipping a black coffee. No one from school was there, thankfully, Sarah noted as she cast a quick glance around. Just a group of teenagers from another school, and two mothers and their young kids, one of whom was squealing noisily.

'Hi, how did it go,' she said warily as she slid on to the seat opposite her friend.

'Fine.' Melissa didn't meet her eyes. She looked tired, and she had two big spots, which looked red and ugly against the pallor of her pasty skin.

'Did you have to get anything done?' Sarah pretended innocence.

'No. It's all fine.'

'Are you having something to eat?' Sarah asked flatly, feeling strangely apprehensive.

'No, I ate with my parents earlier.' Melissa shrugged. 'You have something if you want.'

'Why did you want to meet, then?' Sarah had an edge to her voice.

Tension crackled between them.

Melissa took a deep breath. 'Why are you being like, a bit weird with me since we came back to school?' She stared at Sarah in a hard, accusatory, unfriendly way.

"Maybe it's *you* that's being a bit weird, Mel,' Sarah said in a low voice, trying hard to restrain herself from causing a row.

'What do you mean by that?' Melissa demanded truculently.

'I know something's wrong with you. You stopped eating. You don't come out for lattes and doughnuts or a burger like you used to, and you've got way too thin and you're making yourself sick after eating, just like those lollipop heads do.' She couldn't hold back.

'I like totally am *not*, Sarah! Don't you dare say that to me.'

'Yes, I will dare. That's crazy what you're doing. I thought we were friends and all you're doing is lying to me.'

'I don't have to sit and listen to this. You know what's wrong with you, Sarah? You're just jealous 'cos I lost weight. You were always thinner than me, and now I'm thinner than you and you just can't deal with it. Just 'cos the girls were very compli-mentary to me the first day back and took no notice of you, you're jealous. Well, get over yourself, Sarah. Like I'm so not going to listen to this crap.' Melissa stood up, grabbed her bag and stalked down the wooden stairs out of the coffee shop, leav-ing Sarah pale with shock at the brutal sundering of their friendship.

*

'We can't afford to sell up and emigrate, Bryan,' Debbie protested, pushing her half-eaten plate of smoked salmon and pasta aside.

'I think we should offload this fucking house, take the hit and just go,' her husband retorted.

'Go where, Bryan? There aren't any jobs to be had—'

'We'll get something. Let me look into it, at least.' He took a slug of white wine.

'So if we sell we'll end up owing the shortfall for the house plus the credit cards, and I'll lose all my work pension and healthcare, which I've been paying since I started working in—'

'Christ Almighty, Debbie, you're talking like a middle-aged auld wan. Pensions, healthcare. We're in our friggin' late twenties, not our fifties. I'm telling you, I've had it. I can't hack it here any more. You stay if you want to. I'm outta here.'

'Look, I spoke to my dad today and I think he might help us pay off the cards. It would be a loan, of course. When property prices rise we can sell this place, pay off our mortgage and hopefully not lose a penny—'

'And when will that be – thirty years down the line? And why did you go talking to Barry about our business without talking to me first?' he demanded.

'Are you serious?' she flared. 'We're not talking. That's the problem, Bryan. We are not *talking*!' Her voice came out in a shriek.

'Calm down, Debbie,' he roared back.

She started to cry, great gulping, howling sobs that shook her body as the weeks of pent-up anxiety and hurt erupted out of her.

'Ah stop, Debbie. I'm sorry I shouted at you.' Bryan jumped up from his side of the table and hurried to put his arms around her. He hated to see Debbie cry.

'Bryan, we're in trouble, bad trouble,' she hiccupped. 'I thought if Dad paid off the cards we'd manage the mortgage even with the three-day week. We have to do something. We can't run away from it.'

'But Debs, this could go on for years,' he said frantically.

'Well, what's the point of being broke abroad? We'll still have to pay off the balance of the mortgage. At least if we manage the mortgage we have a roof over our heads. We have a home.' She raised her head from his shoulder.

'But at what price, Debbie?'

'Please, Bryan, let's see what Dad comes up with and give it a chance,' she pleaded. 'Let's get ourselves on an even keel first and then make decisions about our future.'

'We could go to one of those lending companies, remortgage the house, pay off the cards and just have one—'

'No, Bryan, they're *lethal*. I know someone at work whose brother remortgaged his house with one of them, even though he hasn't worked in years because he's addicted to prescription drugs, and now they're taking the house off him. He should never have been given a loan. The family are thinking of suing because he wasn't of sound mind when he signed the papers. Stay well away. I won't have anything to do with them. Let's see if Dad can help, please, Bryan, please.' She wound her arms around his neck and hugged him tight.

'All right, Debbie, all right. I'll give it until Christmas. But when the New Year comes, if things aren't any better, I'm outta here. OK?'

'OK,' she agreed, breathing a sigh of relief. It wasn't the ideal solution but it was better than nothing, and maybe Barry was right: once they had the cards paid off and only had the mortgage to pay, her husband might not feel so oppressed.

Bryan held his wife tightly. He only had to endure this misery for three more months and then she'd see the sense of what he was saying and they could hit the road and wipe the dust of this benighted country off their shoes. He could cope with that, and besides, Big Daddy Adams owed it to Debbie to help out. He was loaded. Twenty-five thou was nothing to the likes of him.

Debbie might talk about paying the money back, but he was sure Barry wouldn't hear of it. He wouldn't be that much of a heel. Maybe some good might come of this after all. It would give him some breathing space, and there was light at the end of the tunnel.

He kissed the side of her neck and slid his hands down to her curvy ass. 'Let's go to bed, babes,' he murmured huskily. 'It's been too long.'

'I love you, Bryan,' Debbie whispered, so glad to be back in his arms again.

'I love you too,' he whispered back as he bent his head and kissed her, then he took her hand and led her upstairs to their bedroom.

For the first time in weeks, Debbie forgot about their dire financial situation and gave herself up to a night of deeply satisfying lovemaking. Everything would be fine; the worst was behind them, she thought drowsily later on, as she lay in Bryan's arms. He was already asleep, breathing slowly and evenly, his breath creating a little breeze against her shoulder. This was what their marriage should be like: talking, sharing, making love, sleeping with their arms around each other. It was just like old times.

Approaching her father had been a good move. He'd been so kind and concerned, she thought with a little warm glow. He'd behaved just like a loving father should behave. She was sure Barry wouldn't let her down. More relaxed than she'd been in ages, Debbie fell into a sound sleep.

CHAPTER SEVEN

'It's lovely to see you, Connie, and you look wonderful.' Juliet
kissed her new friend on the cheek and was hugged warmly in
return. They were waiting for Karen to join them in Purple Ocean
for lunch. It was the first time they'd got together since they had
become friends on that eventful trip to Spain earlier in the summer.
'Will you have something to drink?' Juliet asked hopefully.

They'd had a boozy lunch or two on the Costa and it had been
great fun. When she'd been with Connie and Karen, she'd
been totally relaxed, much more so than with her social circle in
Dublin. At home she was conscious of her position as Ken's
wife. And there was always that element of bitchery and
snobbery and talking behind each other's backs, usually about
who had had work done and how good or bad it was, and Juliet
had never been comfortable with the backbiting. She tended
only to have one or two glasses of alcohol at social occasions in
Dublin, so it had been a real treat to go the whole hog and get
giddily tipsy in Spain with the girls.

'Why not?' Connie smiled. 'I've done my day's work. I'm a
lady of leisure. I'll have a spritzer. I've left the car at the station,'
she said regretfully. 'Otherwise I'd have a glass or two.'

'Pity about that. I'm lucky I can walk from Sydney Parade, or
take a taxi,' said Juliet lightly, hiding her disappointment, wishing she could get hammered so that she could forget the

afflictions of disillusionment and despair that had become her constant companions. 'Two spritzers, please,' she said to the waitress, who was hovering discreetly.

'So things haven't worked out as you planned,' Connie said sympathetically as she buttered a sesame bun then broke a piece off and ate it hungrily. She was famished.

'It was all too good to be true – a pipe dream,' Juliet said despondently. 'I was on such a high coming back from Spain. So determined to start a new life for myself. And when I found that apartment in Blackrock I thought I'd landed on my feet. I fell in love with it and the idea of living there on my own, doing as I pleased, coming and going as I pleased, was pure bliss,' she said regretfully. 'It would have been ideal if it weren't for this damn recession. In fairness to Ken, he told me the decision was mine whether we sell the house or not and split what we get for it, but he's right about the value of it falling. We'd never get what it's worth now, and he's worked too darn hard for him to end up living in some box of an apartment. I wouldn't do that to him. We've lost an awful lot of our nest egg as it is.'

'Well, Juliet, the fact that you can say that and that you worry about where he'd end up shows that you still have feelings for him,' Connie pointed out gently. 'So that's something to hold on to.'

'Oh!' said Juliet, thinking about it. 'I suppose that's true. We've been together for a long time, and he has his good points: he never questions what I spend; he buys me nice gifts too. I hadn't thought of it like that. It's just that I loved the idea of my freedom. Can you understand that?'

'Oh I do, I do. I'm having a taste of it myself, and it's wonderful,' Connie enthused.

'I've never had it,' Juliet said wistfully. 'I've always been the good little wife. Do you know what I was really looking forward to? I could see myself decorating that apartment and picking up bits of furniture and paintings and making it my own. I had it all planned out – colours, everything. Ken's taste in furniture and decor is much more old-fashioned than mine. He likes leather and mahogany, and dark greens and burgundy and so on. I would have gone for pastels and lots of light. But I'd feel terrible to sell the house at such a loss – not for myself, but for him,' she added hastily. 'But the way things have gone with our investments and savings, selling up is the only way I'd be able to buy the apartment – any apartment.'

'It's a shame, Juliet. A real shame. You couldn't divide up the house, could you?' Connie suggested.

'Well, I hadn't thought of that.' Juliet sat up straight and her eyes lit up. 'It's a fine big house with plenty of rooms. That might be an idea. I could have the morning room, and break down the wall between it and the family room – we hardly use it now that the children are all gone – and I could have all that space for myself. It faces out on to the back garden. I could have a deck, to have breakfast on in the mornings,' she said, her eyes beginning to sparkle. 'Connie, you darling. I was in such despair I couldn't see the wood for the trees and now you've shown me a way that would let us keep the house and give me my space – and it would be *my* space, to do with as I please. And what's more, I wouldn't be living in guilt because of Ken. What a wonderful solution. I would have missed the gardens terribly if I'd moved. They're rather lovely and I put a lot of work into them. This way I'd get to still have the joy of them. Will you come over some day soon and see what you think? I'd love your opinion,' she asked eagerly.

'Sure,' Connie said easily, hoping she wouldn't bump into Ken.

'Oh look, here's Karen.' Juliet waved as Connie's sister-in-law made her way to their table.

'Girls, are you on the ming already? I could do with a good stiff drink. I had the morning from hell at work! Thank God for flexi-time and time in lieu.' Karen kissed them both and sank into her chair.

'Will we go on the razz?' Juliet coaxed. 'I took the Dart over.'

'I took a taxi, in case of such an eventuality.' Karen grinned.

'I could ring Drew and get him to collect me from the station and leave the car there,' Connie said slowly.

'Hell, we deserve it.' Juliet waved gaily at the waitress. 'A bottle of Moët, please, to start off with,' she said happily, and the others laughed.

'We're right to go mad and enjoy ourselves,' Karen declared a few minutes later as they clinked champagne flutes and the bubbles of the golden liquid tickled their noses as they each took a sip.

'The perfect antidote to gloom and doom and that dreadful "R" word,' Connie agreed good-humouredly.

'And poor Ken, I'll be going home tipsy to tell him I'm taking over the ground floor at the back of the house and, if he doesn't like it, *he* can move out.' Juliet drained her glass and poured another one, topping up her companions as they all laughed heartily and clinked glasses again. 'Good times are coming,' Juliet smiled broadly, delighted to be in their company once more. They were true kindred spirits.

'What do you mean, you're taking over the ground floor at the back?' Ken blustered, loosening his tie and dropping wearily into his favourite armchair. Before Juliet had gone mad and had her brainstorm, as he privately called it, she would have brought him a glass of whiskey and the *Irish Times*, if they weren't going out, and he would have sipped the welcome drink and perused the paper while the smell of home cooking wafted from the kitchen. Since her rebellion, the fridge was full of bought-in meals that he had to heat up himself in the microwave. And now, to add insult to injury, his seriously deranged wife, who had obviously been drinking, was standing in front of him telling him she was taking over the ground floor at the back of the house, including the morning room, where he particularly liked to read the papers on a Sunday morning.

'If I can't buy the apartment I want to take the morning room and the family room to make into a living space for myself, to decorate as I please, Ken. It's perfectly simple. If you want to move back into the main bedroom, you can. I'm going to do up Aimee's old bedroom. It has an en suite. It overlooks the back garden. You can have the rest of the house and the front garden.'

'Are you mad? That's silly nonsense. And how much will that cost?' he demanded.

'A lot less than an apartment, I'd hazard a guess,' she said dryly. 'I'll get Freddy Walsh to draw up the pla—'

'No, Juliet!' Ken shot to his feet. 'I won't have it. I won't have our friends knowing about this . . . this charade.'

'Fine. I'll get someone who doesn't know us then, if that's more palatable to you, but if anyone says anything to me about the fact that we're not out and about together or entertaining any more, I'm not going to lie. I'm telling the truth and saying we're living separate lives. Believe me, Ken, this is no *charade*, and don't patronize me.' Juliet glared at him, her eyes unnaturally bright.

'Why are you doing this to me?' he said heavily.

'Ken, we've been through all this. It's not about *you* any more, it's about *me*. I'm going for a nap now. Drinking in the afternoon is rather delightful but it does make one a little tired. There're some Butler's Pantry meals in the fridge if you're hungry.' His wife picked up her handbag, gave a big yawn and went upstairs to bed. It was just gone six. The Angelus bell was ringing on the TV, and she was going for a *nap*! What sort of behaviour was that? If she wasn't careful she'd turn into a lush.

He trudged out to the kitchen, up-ended a carton of some sort of chicken and pasta dish on to a plate and shoved it into the microwave. Could there be any underlying pathological reason for this completely uncharacteristic behaviour? he wondered, baffled, pouring himself a glass of milk. She was going to ruin the house with this ridiculous plan of hers. Maybe Aimee would be able to talk her out of it.

Ken jabbed at the phone on the wall, dialling his daughter's home number. Melissa answered. 'Hello, Melissa, is your mother at home?' He didn't have time to indulge in any polite chitchat with his grandchild. He had a game of bridge scheduled in three-quarters of an hour.

'Hold on, Granddad.' Melissa didn't sound in the form for chat either. Her tone was rather churlish. What was wrong with these women anyway?

'Yes, Dad?' Aimee said crisply when she came on the line.

'Aimee, I want to see if you can talk sense into your mother. She was out to lunch and came home – a bit under the weather, I might add. She's had to go up and lie down,' he ratted self-righteously. 'Anyway, she has this notion that she wants to divide the house up and make some . . . some . . . "living space"' – he articulated the words with utter contempt – 'she called it, for herself. She wants to take over the morning room and the family room and make them into one big room, and then she's going to take over your bedroom and redecorate it and move into it.' His voice rose indignantly. 'And apart from ruining the house, it will devalue it, I'd say. It's just not feasible, Aimee. Could you please *try* and talk sense into her? Make her see reason?'

'I actually think that it's rather a good idea, Dad. This is no time to be selling the house, so this way you get to keep it until prices rise again, and yet both of you have freedom and independence to do your own thing. At least she won't be living in Blackrock, leaving you alone. Try and look at it like that,' his daughter advised calmly. He felt like shaking her.

'Well, you're not much help,' he said huffily. 'And aren't you concerned that she was out drinking this afternoon and is now in a drunken stupor?' That was a complete exaggeration, but Aimee wasn't to know that.

'I think it's great that she's meeting friends for lunch and enjoying herself. And she didn't sound at all intoxicated when I spoke to her earlier. She just sounded animated and excited about the refurbishment. Have to go, Dad, my mobile's ringing. Byeee.' And then Aimee hung up on him.

He should have known better than to go looking to *her* for support. She was firmly in her mother's camp. Juliet must have phoned her to sound her out about her great plan. There was no point in ringing the boys, they never got involved, they were much too cute, Ken thought angrily.

One sentence that Aimee had uttered did resonate though: 'At least she won't be living in Blackrock, leaving you alone.' She had a point. Lonely and all as it would be with Juliet living in this 'refurbishment' of hers, at least they'd still be under the one roof and she wouldn't be totally lost to him. Maybe he should go along with it. It was the lesser of two evils, to be sure, and maybe Juliet might come to her senses before too much damage had been done to their relationship, as well as to the house.

He finished his dinner, hardly tasting it he was so lost in thought, and when he went upstairs to change into casual wear he stood outside her bedroom and gave a sharp rap on the door. She didn't answer. He frowned and pushed open the door. Juliet was lying under the coverlet, one hand under her cheek in an almost childlike manner. His heart softened at the sight. An ash-blond strand of hair lay across her eyes and he pushed it back tenderly. Why did it have to be like this? He missed her. He missed her comforting presence by his side at functions, and the warm softness of her in bed at night.

He'd thought they'd had a good marriage. He worked hard to provide for her and the family. She had always been content to stay in the background, or so he'd thought.

'Arrogant and selfish,' she'd called him. That had stung. He wouldn't have got so far in his profession if he'd been a shrinking violet, if he'd been a walkover. And Juliet wouldn't have a house this size to 'refurbish' so that she could live apart from him. Ken turned and left his wife to her sleep. Perhaps in time she might miss him the way he missed her, this carry-on would be all forgotten and they would live out their old age in harmony. It wasn't too much to wish for, surely, after a lifetime of grinding hard work.

At least she seemed to have given up on the notion of selling up. That proposal, although it had come from him, had given him sleepless nights. Where would he have ended up? Rattling around in some strange house or apartment – he couldn't think of a worse nightmare. Maybe the recession was a blessing in disguise, he mused as he combed his hair. He wouldn't mind moving back to his old bedroom either. The bed was more comfortable than the one in the guest room. He felt like a stranger in his own house sleeping in it. So maybe, under the circumstances, he'd give his permission for her new proposal.

Relieved that at least he'd made a decision that might give them some breathing space, Ken set off for his card game in an easier frame of mind. His playing had slipped lately. He needed to smarten up and get back on form again. As he strode into his club, Juliet and the house were forgotten and Ken Davenport turned his thoughts to the game ahead.

Chapter Eight

'I do enjoy that programme, *Room to Improve*, and that young architect is quite handsome, with a lovely smile. I love watching house renovations,' Lily remarked, taking the cup of tea Judith had made for her.

'Me too,' her daughter agreed. 'Especially now that I'm on the hunt for a house of my own, those type of programmes have become much more interesting.' She held out the sugar bowl for Lily.

'I like the way they built the patio with the steps leading down to the lawn. I'd prefer a patio than a deck, myself, if I was ever to get anything like that done.' Lily stirred a spoonful of sugar into her fine-china cup, unwrapped a Club Milk and took a dainty bite.

'You know, you could have a very nice patio at the back door, Mam. It's a real suntrap there for the afternoon and evening sun, and it wouldn't take too much off the lawn, if you didn't want it to,' Judith suggested, settling down on the small sofa beside her mother's chair with the latest issue of *Hello!* It was raining, the cloudy evening hastening the dusk. It was getting dark much earlier now that September had arrived, and the evenings had grown chilly. They'd lit the fire in Lily's small front sitting room and settled in for a cosy evening.

'Do you know, I wouldn't mind losing some of the lawn

because, when you're gone, I won't have to cut as much grass,' Lily considered, a little frown furrowing her brow.

'Ma, just because I'm moving out doesn't mean I won't be coming back home to help out. I'll be cutting your grass, as normal,' Judith remarked.

''Tis not you should be cutting the grass, Judith, 'tis that Tom fella. And especially with you recovering from surgery,' Lily said crossly.

Her son rarely did anything around the house or garden. It had always been left up to Judith. Lily was still mad with him for his devious attempt to get a sneaky look at her bank statements and will when Judith had been in hospital. Her son was deeply concerned about what he would inherit when she passed on.

Lily's bright-blue eyes began to twinkle. 'I'm going to do something that will give me a lot of pleasure and will annoy Master Tom,' she announced mischievously, smiling over at Judith.

'What are you plotting, Ma?' Judith arched one of her perfectly shaped eyebrows. She'd been to the beauty salon and had a facial and an eyebrow and eyelash shape and tint, and looked much more like her old self.

'I'm going to treat myself to a patio, I've just decided. I'm going to get some big planters and fill them full of bedding and I'm going to buy a small round table and chairs. It will be nice to take tea out there in the afternoons. You're right, Judith. It *is* a suntrap. I should make more use of it. And do you know what I think I'll do? I think I'll get a big French door put in the kitchen. It would give much more light, and it would be nice to walk out on to the patio. It would be just like those houses they do up in those makeover programmes. I might as well spend my money on myself, and that's what will annoy Tom. He'll think I'm spending his inheritance, and he'll be right.' Lily gave a hearty chuckle and Judith joined in.

'Ma, you're *baaddd*!' she teased. 'He'll go ballistic!'

'I know, and we'll say nothing to him about getting it done. I know *exactly* who to go to for advice.' She put her teacup down and picked up her knitting, her needles clicking furiously as they flashed backwards and forwards.

'Who's that then?' Judith was intrigued.

'That lovely man Jimmy who painted the house for us. I remember him telling me that his brother was a builder,' Lily said triumphantly. 'He's the one we'll get. I'll ring Jimmy in the morning. It would be good to have it done before the winter sets in, and then I'll have it to look forward to next year. What do you think?'

'I think, if it's what you want, go for it. I think it's a great idea, and you could get a water feature, which might look good as well,' Judith suggested.

'And I could get nice outdoor lights around it. Wouldn't that be pretty?' Lily said excitedly, feeling a great sense of anticipation at what was to come.

'Perfect.'

'Yes, I think that's what I'll do, dear. After all, I have the money in the bank from my SSIA account that I never touched. What's the point of having it mouldering in the banks these days? They all might collapse, with the way the country is being governed. I'm going to start spending it. There are no pockets in a shroud, as they say. We might even have a launch party when it's done and invite Tom and Madame.' Lily tittered.

'It's worse you're getting, Ma.' Judith laughed.

'And better you're getting. You look very well after your trip to the beauty salon and the hairdresser's. I'm so pleased you're meeting your friend from work tomorrow for lunch.' Lily stopped knitting and smiled over at her daughter.

'I'm looking forward to it myself, Ma. We're having lunch in the Avoca Handweavers. I'm going to bring you home some of their beef stroganoff. It's to die for.'

'I don't know about those foreign foods, now,' Lily said doubtfully.

'It's just stew with cream in it – honestly, it's scrumptious. I'll bring you there for lunch someday. Even better, I'll bring you to Avoca Handweavers in Wicklow. We'll have a day out before I go back to work.'

'Well, that would be lovely, dear. I believe the food there is very tasty. I've seen several excellent reviews. We're becoming right ladies who lunch, aren't we?'

'Indeed we are, Ma, and not before time,' Judith said fondly.

The phone rang and Lily picked it up. 'Ah, Moira,' she said with pleasure. 'How are you? I'm just sitting here with Judith, we're having a grand chat.'

'I'm going to have a bath, Ma.' Judith got up and waved her *Hello!* at her mother, who waved gaily back at her.

Ten minutes later, Judith stepped into a steaming, scented bath and leaned back against a small air cushion, enjoying the feel of the hot, foamy water floating over her body, helping to ease the aches from her hip and shoulder. She had poured some perfumed oils and a few drops of lavender into the water, and the aromas wafted around her, helping her to relax. She flicked through the magazine until she found her horoscope. Jonathan Cainer always took a long time to get to the root of the forecast, so she usually just read the last line or two: 'New possibilities . . . new insights and understandings . . .' Umm, well, that was true, Judith reflected. She was looking for a new house and she was getting new insights into her mother's personality every day. She smiled, gazing up at the pretty seashell tiles that surrounded the bath. Lily *was* a revelation. She had a wicked sense of humour which was beginning to reveal itself a lot more. Tom would go bananas when he found out that their mother was going to spend a few thousand euros getting the back renovated. And she was dead right to spend it. It would be a very pleasant way for her to get fresh air and sunlight from late spring to autumn.

It was wonderful to see that Lily was becoming much more open and adventurous. All those wasted years she had spent in self-imposed imprisonment in the house, hardly daring to go out except to go to Mass or the bank. What a shame, when she could have lived such a vibrant life.

Judith had enjoyed watching TV with Lily earlier. It was pleasant, too, to be able to sit and enjoy an evening in her mother's company without feeling trapped and resentful, as she had for years before her accident. How her life had changed since she'd careered headlong into that tree, Judith reflected, blowing a bubble of sudsy water from under her chin. She was having follow-up sessions with the hospital psychiatrist since her meltdown, and his calm, reassuring and positive manner was helping her reach a turning point in her way of viewing herself. She no longer felt downtrodden, trapped, a victim of circumstances. Dr Fitzgerald had pointed out gently that, when you begin to accept the choices that you make and take responsibility for them, you become empowered. He had recommended that she read a book called *The Seven Spiritual Laws of Success*, by Deepak Chopra, and it was making her look at her life from a whole new perspective. It was all rather interesting, really, just taking a step away from the drama of all the emotional stuff and looking at her life with dispassion.

'Some people become addicted to drama and confrontation or victimhood. The choice is always there for you to step away,' Dr Fitzgerald counselled. She *had* felt like a victim for years, having to take care of her mother, but looking back, she realized that by making the choice to stay at home she had enabled her mother to be the victim *she* had become. When fate had stepped in, in the guise of her car accident, Lily had had to step outside her comfort zone and take responsibility for herself, and her mother was flourishing now, having taken those daunting first steps to independence.

Judith too felt a welcome sense of well-being, no doubt helped by the course of mild anti-depressants the doctor had prescribed for her. They had certainly made a difference, and he had told her he would wean her off them gradually, in the not too distant future.

Idle thoughts drifted in and out of Judith's head as she lay, relaxed, in the steamy, warm bath. She thought about what it would be like going back to work. She was meeting Janice Harris from HR for lunch tomorrow. It would be good to catch up on all the news. The company was managing perfectly fine without her, she thought wryly. No one was indispensable, no matter how much they liked to think they were. Young Ms Slater seemed to be taking it all in her stride as acting head of department.

She was definitely going to lighten up a bit at work when she went back. Work was not the be-all and end-all of life – another thing she had come to realize during the weeks of her hospitalization and recovery. She felt like one of those big Spanish onions being peeled, she decided, amused at the notion. Layers of burdens and self-imposed responsibilities were being shed, and that sweet white core, unblemished and untouched, was being revealed. She felt a lightness of spirit as never before, and an acceptance of herself with all her flaws and failings. It was new to her, but very, very welcome.

'Now, I wouldn't want you to be saying anything to Tom, if you don't mind, Jimmy. It's just he'll only be interfering, and Judith and myself have our own ideas for what we want,' Lily explained to the painter at the other end of the phone. 'Of course, if it was going to get you into trouble with him, now I wouldn't want that. I know you do a lot of work for him,' she added worriedly. 'Could we say we wanted to give him a surprise?' she suggested as inspiration struck.

'The perfect solution, Missus Baxter,' Jimmy agreed. 'Don't worry about Tom at all. Larry will build you a grand patio at a very reasonable price. You have the perfect aspect for it. You'll be able to sit there enjoying every ray until sunset. And the French doors will suit your kitchen very well. I'd go for triple glazing if I were you, though. It will cost a bit extra but will be well worth it in terms of heat conservation. And it's not a big job at all; a week or so will see it through. And I'll replaster and paint the wall when the doors are put in.'

'Well, it will be lovely to see you again, Jimmy. We had some very interesting chats.' Lily smiled, looking forward to seeing him. Jimmy was a real gentleman, something rare in today's world.

'You just keep that kettle on the boil and serve the tea in those lovely china cups of yours and we'll be away on a hack, Missus Baxter,' the painter responded genially, and Lily just knew that her beloved Ted was watching over her and Judith and had sent this kind man into their lives to assist them.

Although her husband was dead a long time now, he was only a thought away, and she often spoke to his photo and asked his advice on matters. And Lily knew without the shadow of a doubt that he was still very much with her in spirit, if not in body.

She put the phone down, delighted that she'd have good news for Judith when she came home from her lunch with her friend. It had been wonderful to see her daughter looking so smart, in her black trousers and jaunty red tailored jacket, with her hair done and her make-up on, going off to town earlier in the morning. Only the slight limp betrayed the fact that she'd been at death's door.

She peered out the window; a cluster of leaves took sudden flight down the garden path as the wind got up. She'd advised Judith to take a coat as well, and looking at the dark looming rainclouds moving up from the south, she knew it would rain before long.

Lily sat down in her chair and picked up her rosary beads. She'd say a decade for Judith, asking that she'd enjoy her lunch and that a suitable new house would come for her soon. She needed to say a prayer to St Anthony for that. The gentle saint was always *particularly* kind to her and most obliging when she called upon him.

'Dear St Anthony, I've a favour to ask of you. I want you to find the perfect house for Judith, please,' she asked crisply. 'And of course I'll put some extra in your collection box, needless to say,' she added, in case he would think she was taking him for granted. Petition to her favourite saint over, Lily closed her eyes and began to recite the rosary with fervour for her recovering daughter.

'Judith, you look terrific,' Janice Harris exclaimed, giving her a hug when Judith rose from the table to greet her. 'So much better than the last time I saw you.'

'Well, I was looking a bit of a wreck in hospital.' Judith laughed as they sat down. She had been feeling a little nervous about meeting up for lunch. She hadn't felt up to the rigours of city driving and parking so she'd taken the bus into town. She might even go mad and treat herself to a taxi home. This was her first social engagement, apart from the sorties out with her mother for coffees and lunches after viewings. But seeing her colleague smiling so warmly at her put her at her ease and she began to relax.

'So how have you been keeping, Judith? How is the recovery going?' Janice asked after they had ordered lunch.

'Slow but sure. My physio is very pleased, but she's a demon. I ache when she's giving me a going over, but it's working.' Judith speared an olive and ate it with relish.

'It must have been awful. Do you remember much of it?' Janice asked sympathetically.

'Not a lot, thankfully. I remember the wheel juddering and the tree looming up but that's about it. I do get flashbacks now and again and driving's a bit of an ordeal but I'm receiving . . . er . . . counselling.' She didn't want to say that she was seeing a psychiatrist. It was foolish, she knew, in this day and age, when there were ads on the TV encouraging people to be open and proactive about their mental health, but for Judith, it was just a step too far to share such information with a work colleague.

'I don't think I'd have the nerve to get behind a wheel again after such a bad smash.' Janice shuddered. 'I think you've very brave, Judith.'

'Thanks. I won't deny it's hard. My nerves are shot. But driving gives you such freedom. I'd hate to be dependent on taxis and buses.' She offered the olives to Janice.

'True. Taxis especially. I nearly freaked the other day when they were blocking the traffic with their protest. It took me two hours to get home. We've all been affected by the recession. Stop whinging and get over it,' Janice snorted, helping herself to a couple of the tasty appetizers. 'I was in a taxi recently and the driver drove like an absolute lunatic. I thought I was going to be killed, and his personal hygiene left a lot to be desired. The pong! I nearly puked.'

'I know, or then you get the ones that, whether you like it or not, are going to talk, talk, talk for the entire journey.' Judith made a face and the two of them laughed. 'Although, in fairness, you can get some very nice ones too; a few of them have been very kind to Ma.'

'I suppose it takes all sorts,' Janice agreed, buttering a bread roll. 'Did you hear that Peter Kennedy is taking early retirement and Coleen Flynn is expecting twins?'

'Really? She had to have IVF, didn't she? I'm delighted for her,' Judith replied. Coleen was a very quiet, hardworking girl, in reception, and she had sent a get-well Mass bouquet to Judith when she was in hospital.

'And Martin Anderson has left his wife—'

'*What?*'

They settled down to a good natter and a most enjoyable lunch.

'Do you know, I was just thinking, my sister goes to this woman in Dun Laoghaire for some sort of holistic healing – I think it's from India, I'm not too well up on these things – and she swears by her. Maybe you should give it a try. Una says it's very relaxing. She talks to you first for a while and finds out what your blocks – I think that's what Una calls them – are, and then she does the treatment. It might help you get your confidence back for driving. Una used to be afraid of flying and she's fine now. If you're interested I can text you the number,' Janice said as they stood outside the restaurant before going their separate ways.

'I think I'd like that. I've a very good friend, Jillian, who's really into that type of thing. I had a lovely few days with her recently and I had some very relaxing holistic treatments. The hot-stone massage was particularly nice,' Judith said, pulling up the collar of her coat against the chill breeze that whistled along the narrow street. Drops of rain spitter-spattered on to the pavement.

'Oh, I love them. I'll text it to you, so. I enjoyed our lunch, Judith. Don't come back until you're fit and well,' Janice instructed.

'I won't. There's no point. My days of being a martyr are over,' Judith declared light-heartedly.

'Good for you. Take care now.' Janice gave a wave, put up her umbrella and turned to walk briskly back towards the office. A taxi with its light on came around the corner and Judith waved it down, glad to avoid the rain. Fortunately, the driver was not inclined to talk and Judith sat back against the leather upholstery, observing the tapestry of city life that unfolded outside her window, glad she didn't have to go back to work after such an enjoyable lunch. She felt pleasantly weary and decided that when she got home she was going to indulge in a nap, a rare treat, and utterly decadent in the middle of the afternoon.

'I thoroughly enjoyed myself, Ma,' Judith told her mother as they had a cup of tea together later that evening. She felt rested after her nap. She'd fallen snugly asleep almost straight away after her head had hit the pillow, to the sound of sheets of rain hurling themselves in fury against her bedroom window, and hadn't woken up until after four.

'Janice texted me a phone number of some woman who does holistic treatments that might help me get my confidence back driving. Seemingly her sister was afraid of flying and she's fine now. I think I might give it a bash,' she confided.

'That would be terrific, Judith. It took a lot of nerve for you to get back behind the wheel of a car, and a strange car at that. You should be so proud of yourself. I'm *very* proud of you, and so would your father be if he were here,' Lily praised.

Tears came to Judith's eyes. Her mother had never been one for praise when Judith was growing up. That had been her dear dad's department. To hear her mother's laudatory words, even though Judith was now a middle-aged woman, was a moment of immense healing for her.

Lily was proud of her. There was no higher praise than that.

CHAPTER NINE

'So I'm afraid I won't be able to make it on Friday, due to unforeseen circumstances. I'm terribly sorry if I've caused any inconvenience,' Aimee said apologetically to the receptionist at the other end of the phone.

'Don't worry, it happens all the time, but we have a cancellation list so the slot won't be lost,' the woman replied calmly. 'Would you like me to give you another date?'

'Umm . . . let me see.' Aimee glanced at her diary, displayed on the laptop screen in front of her. There were several dates that were clear. One, the Thursday of the following week, seemed the most obvious. Her mobile phone rang and she saw Roger's name flashing up on the screen. 'I'm sorry, I have to take this call. May I ring you back?' she said politely.

'Of course, no problem. I'll take your name off the list for Friday and you can get back to me.'

'Thanks a million,' Aimee said quickly and hung up before Roger, who wasn't the most patient of men, hung up himself. 'Hello, Roger,' she said crisply.

'Aimee, good news, if a little on the short-notice side.' Roger got right to the point, as usual. 'Arthur O'Donnell is planning to invite a group of potential investors, yours truly included, to a presentation in Darnley Castle. He wants it to be as discreet as possible, that's why he's hosting it in his home. He usually uses

B&W to cater for him – that was until I got talking to him.' Roger laughed, as pleased as punch with himself. 'I've really talked you up, Aimee. Hibernian Dreams will be off to a superb start if we land O'Donnell. He's one of the few billionaires in the country who isn't in trouble. Between yourself and myself, Aimee, the half-dozen names he gave me who'll be at this are some of the few businessmen left who are completely solvent and have a secure financial base. None of these boyos are operating what I call The House of Cards business model, like a few well-known names I could mention. Do you get my drift, Aimee? You impress this lot and we're up and running. O'Donnell's PA will be in touch. So it's up to you to sell it. You can take it from here. I've done my bit. I'll see you on Friday.'

'Friday it is. Bye, Roger,' Aimee said, but he was gone and she was left talking to herself. She felt the old, familiar exhilaration rise. She'd been presented with a challenge. Roger had paved the way with his incomparable contacts. And the great thing about him was that he would let her organize the event as she saw fit if they secured it. He was the perfect boss in that regard. She glanced at the diary page still open on her laptop and closed it. She'd deal with that problem later.

She opened the file of suppliers she had and perused them. Nothing but the best for Arthur O'Donnell, one of the wealthiest but most self-effacing businessmen in the country. Darnley Castle, his home in Meath, never featured in the glossy society magazines, and neither did he. He rarely gave interviews; his wife would pass unnoticed in the street. But Arthur had one of the sharpest financial brains and he didn't take risks. Aimee knew instinctively that he wouldn't want glitz or anything too showy. Elegant sophistication and the highest quality organic food would be the order of the day. She hoped Arthur's PA would ring sooner rather than later so that she could lock down the contract and get planning. Humming to herself, Aimee opened a selection of menus on her computer and began to formulate a meal plan to impress her potential client.

*

'You have one Post Office cert. of twenty thousand and that Scope investment that's doing really poorly. You invested forty-five thou in it ten years ago and it's now worth, let me see . . .' Barry's investment advisor tapped a few keys on the computer. 'Thirty-five—'

'Huh, down ten and not a red cent in interest earned. That wasn't the best investment I ever made.'

'That was before I was advising you. I wouldn't have touched it myself,' Donal said dismissively.

'Cash it in,' Barry instructed decisively. 'Would you believe, I forgot about them. I know I have a biggie with 150k in it in a bond with An Post. I suppose it would be better to cash that one in than sell the bloody cottage now. That would cover that damn loan I borrowed for the SCIP shares.' Barry doodled on the blank page in front of him.

'Bloody shame about that,' Donal Reilly said. 'I would have sworn that was a safe bet. Anyway, you might as well pay off that loan and take the hit. It's crazy to be paying interest on it. Let me organize it for you. You'll have to sign some forms. I'll get them to post them to the office?' he queried. 'Or to your home address?'

'Yeah, I guess that's the best I can do. And yes, send them to the office. I haven't told Aimee about the debacle yet. I have to pick my moment.'

'A wise course of action,' Donal approved. 'I'll set that in motion. You should have the forms by the end of the week. Oh wait now' – he paused – 'were they joint investments? Because if they were we'll need Aimee's signature, so that might upset the apple cart.'

'No, we have joint ones all right, but the ones we're discussing were in my name only,' Barry clarified.

'Excellent. No hiccups so, talk soon,' Donal said in his usual businesslike manner and Barry put down the phone feeling a tad happier.

He'd completely forgotten about the smaller saving cert. and that damn Scope thing. They would get Debbie out of her situation without impacting too much on his, although they would have been handy to use to pay off the bank loan. Bad timing all round. Still, it couldn't be helped and he had a daughter who needed his assistance. He dialled her mobile number.

'Hello, Dad.' She sounded perkier, he noted.

'Morning, Debbie. Can you talk?'

'Just give me a minute. I'll take this outside to the landing,' she said hastily, and he could understand her not wanting to discuss her financial affairs in an open-plan office.

'I'm here, Dad,' she said moments later.

'Well, I can do that for you, Debbie. I should have the cheque for you very early next week so we can get you on the straight and narrow again,' Barry said with pleasure.

'Oh, Dad. Thanks a million. I'm *so* grateful. And I'll start saving to pay you back as soon as I can.'

'Get yourself sorted first, Debbie. We can come to some arrangement when things pick up. This can be a long-term loan and I won't be putting any pressure on you,' he assured her. 'Was Bryan OK with it?' he probed, wondering how their discussions had gone.

'He's very grateful too, Dad. He's going to give it to Christmas to see how things are going before making a decision about emigrating.'

'I see. Well, I hope it won't come to that,' Barry said. 'I would suggest cutting up the cards for a while and just dealing in ready cash,' he added casually.

'I think that's a good idea too. The cards are just too easy to use. We'll do that, Dad, don't worry.'

'Good.'

'How did Melissa get on? I didn't want to say anything to her, I'm sure she doesn't want her business discussed by all and sundry. I was going to text her and ask would she like to go to the pictures.'

'Would you, Debbie?' Barry said gratefully. 'She's not talking to her mother or myself. She's very annoyed with us, especially now that she's been referred to a psychiatrist who specializes in eating disorders. Melissa doesn't know she's a psychiatrist, so say nothing. Let her tell you whatever she wants to herself. And if you could get her to eat something it would be an extra blessing. Oh, and Debbie, this, ah . . . this loan is strictly between you and me. I won't be saying anything about it to Aimee, there's no need, and there's no need for you to say anything about it to Connie.'

'OK, Dad, and thank you. I hope you didn't think I was out of line asking you for help.'

'I'm glad you did, Debbie, very, very glad indeed,' Barry assured her. 'It's time I did something for you,' he added, hoping she would take it as a subtle apology for the times he hadn't been there for her.

'Thank you. I know I wasn't very nice to you a lot of the time. Mam told me you would have been more proactive in my life if I'd let you. I was—'

'Debbie, that's all water under the bridge, that's the past, let's build on what we have now,' he said gently.

'OK, Dad, thanks. Bye.'

Barry sat back in his chair and put his hands behind his head. One daughter almost sorted. If he could help Melissa to come to her senses he wouldn't be doing too bad at all, he reflected, indulging in a moment of self-congratulation he felt he deserved. He'd be the first to admit he'd been crap at parenting when Debbie was a child, but he'd been given a second chance and he'd taken it and risen to the challenge, and now he felt that it was one area in his life that he could truly say he was succeeding in. Despite her current blip, he and Melissa were very close and would be again. And now, that same sort of closeness, and a modicum of trust, was developing in his relationship with Debbie. Reasons to feel good, Barry acknowledged, picking up the phone to dial a client who wanted a better deal for his monthly trade magazine.

*

Debbie was on cloud nine when she sat back down at her desk and typed an email to Bryan to tell him the fantastic news. The knots in the back of her neck loosened as the burden of debt that had bowed her down seemed to melt away. She would never, ever, allow them to get into such a dire financial state again, she vowed. It would be hard cutting up their credit cards, but Barry was right, they had to go until things improved financially for herself and Bryan. They had to stop living beyond their means. It was going to be tough for a while, but the money they were currently using to pay off the interest on their credit cards would be back in their pockets again and would balance out the wages cut Bryan would be taking. And they'd be paying less tax, so that was another positive. This was the best day she'd had in ages. She actually felt quite cheerful as she winged off the email to her husband.

Great news. Dad's loaning us the money to pay off the cards. Things are looking up. Love ya, babes. D xxxxxxxxx

Well, that was a relief of sorts, Bryan thought, noting she'd written 'loaning' rather than 'giving'. At least the serious hassle was over, the noose around his neck looser. Debbie was happier as well, and that took the pressure off him. He could quietly suss out job opportunities, visa requirements and the like, so that when his deadline of Christmas came, he'd have all his ammunition ready. One thing he was sure of: in twelve months' time he was going to be living abroad, preferably somewhere in the sun, and not vegetating in dreary suburbia in a country that was bankrupt morally and financially.

The atmosphere in the office was toxic; the murky pall of fear, shock and apprehension permeated every corner. His colleagues who'd been made redundant were bitter and angry and, he could imagine, very resentful of the ones who'd been saved. The three-day weekers were pissed at the ones who'd been kept on full time, and everyone was pissed with management. At least he would be gone for the rest of the week, to supervise the fit-out of an office on the other side of the river. He had done the design for it and he was looking forward to seeing it take shape. It was the part of the job he liked the best, seeing his vision come together. He'd been given the brief when money was no object and he'd done a very classy design for the MD's office, all chrome and glass and sharp angles and minimalist furniture, with just one key abstract painting on the eggshell-blue wall opposite the bespoke desk.

It would be such a relief to be away from all this negativity and anger. He could feel it seeping into his pores. Well, not for too much longer, he comforted himself, gathering up his equipment and slipping the disk with the design plans into his jacket pocket before answering his wife's email.

Terrific! What a relief. Love U 2 babes, xx

He logged off and slid his laptop into the black Versace shoulderbag Debbie had bought him for his last birthday. He took the lift to the ground floor and headed out towards the Samuel Beckett Bridge. The sun was shining on the Liffey, prisms of silver shooting through the smooth green surface, glittering like diamonds. The gentle *slap slap* of the river against the quay walls, the gulls circling around and a small boat's outboard chugging sputter for some reason reminded him of the canals in Amsterdam. Would that be an option? he wondered. He and Debbie had had a great time there just before they got married. And the hash cafés would suit him down to the ground, he thought longingly, wishing he had a spliff to raise his drooping spirits and ease the stress that had become such a part of his day-to-day existence.

CHAPTER TEN

'Are you and Sarah, like, not talking?' Brenda Meyers murmured to Melissa as they stood in line at the vending machine to get coffee for their morning teabreak.

'Not really, at the moment,' Melissa muttered awkwardly. She had hated coming to school this morning. She and Sarah had never had a row before. It had been so strange sitting beside her in class and not talking. They hadn't sat beside each other in art, and they had gone their separate ways, Sarah back to their classroom, Melissa to get coffee, once the bell went. Brenda had obviously spotted something was up.

'She thinks you're losing too much weight. I heard her saying it to Kate Murphy yesterday when you were off for the afternoon.'

Melissa reddened. How dare Sarah talk about her behind her back? What an absolute betrayal.

'Of course, she's only jealous.' Brenda dropped her coins into the machine and selected the black-coffee option. 'I know what that's like; I've been there. Don't mind them, Melissa, you look fantastic. Keep going.' She took a little notebook out of her uniform pocket and wrote something down while she waited for the coffee to pour.

'It's my food diary,' she confided. 'It really helps me keep track and, if I put on any weight, I can see exactly where I've started to slip.'

'Oh! That's a good idea, I must start keeping one myself,' Melissa remarked casually.

'I can give you loads of tips if you want them. I'm an expert on calories,' Brenda offered.

'Thanks, that would be cool.' Melissa took a sip of the scalding coffee. She was starving and she felt quite dizzy. Her mother had sat beside her at the breakfast counter this morning and she'd had to eat toast and cereal, and it had nearly made her gag. As soon as she'd got to school she'd got rid of it, but she felt terribly faint today for some reason.

Her phone vibrated in her pocket and she moved away to a more secluded spot. They weren't allowed to use phones in school and were supposed to keep them in their lockers, but everyone kept them in their uniform pockets on silent. If the teachers caught you, your phone was confiscated and you had to get a note from a parent to get it back.

She had a quick look around. The teachers usually didn't come near the vending machines in the morning; they were all having their coffee in the staff room. It was a text from Debbie wondering would she like to go to the pictures. Melissa's heart lifted. It would be so nice to go to the cinema with her older sister and hang out with her, especially now that she and Sarah weren't talking. She sipped her coffee slowly as she dawdled her way back to the classroom. She didn't want to have to spend a minute more than necessary in Sarah's company.

'Hi, Melissa,' Nerdy Nolan chirruped chummily.

'Hi,' Melissa said coolly.

'Where's Sarah? Doesn't she usually come down for coffee?' her classmate said slyly. Word had got out that Melissa and Sarah weren't talking.

'We're not tied at the hip, Evanna,' Melissa snapped.

'Oh, it's just strange not to see the two of you together,' twittered the other girl.

'Yeah, well, you and Niamh Sampson don't have coffee so often now, sure you don't.' Melissa gave her little dig.

Evanna's cheeks reddened at this pointed reference to the rift of gigantic proportions that had split what had once been a solid friendship.

'Excuse me, Evanna. I'm just going to the shop to get a notebook.' Melissa wheeled away and headed to the school shop to get a little notebook so she could follow Brenda's example. She might be upset about the row with Sarah, but she'd never be upset enough to hang around with Nerdy Nolan. There were some levels you did not sink to, no matter how dire your circumstances.

Later that afternoon she stood in front of the mirror tying the belt around her khaki cargo pants. She was going to have to buy a whole new wardrobe, she thought gleefully; her clothes were swimming on her. She was calling to Debbie's first and they were going to go to the cinema from her house. Thankfully, her mother wasn't home, so she ate half a banana and half a Weetabix, mashing it up in a mush so that she only had to put the smallest drop of milk in to wet it. That would do her until the following morning.

Debbie had just got in from work when she arrived and was making herself a cup of tea. They hugged tightly.

'Hey, little sis, I'm just going to have a sandwich to keep me going. Would you like one?' she asked.

'I ate at home. I'll just have tea, black for me.' Melissa perched on a high stool trying not to look at the butter Debbie was slathering on her bread. She hadn't had bread and butter in yonks and she felt a sudden longing for a slice.

'How are things?' Debbie arranged ham and tomatoes and cheese on the bread. Melissa averted her eyes.

'OK,' she sighed.

'Bryan's on a three-day week,' Debbie confided. She hoped that perhaps Melissa would feel able to tell her about the trip to the doctor in return. Even though she'd only seen her sister ten days ago, she was shocked that she had lost even more weight.

'Gosh, that's rough.'

'I know. Life's a bit tough, to say the least. We're really having to cut back. We're changing the car at the weekend. We're getting a Fiesta. Bryan's really fed up.'

'Oh no, I loved your soft-top.'

'It's way too expensive,' Debbie said. 'We just can't afford it.'

'I had a row with Sarah.' Melissa made a face.

'Oh. Why? I thought you were the best of friends.' Debbie stopped munching her sandwich and gazed at her half-sister in dismay.

'Well, I thought we were too, but she says I'm being weird and she says that I've lost too much weight. She's even saying that to other girls behind my back.' Melissa couldn't hide her indignation. 'I think she's jealous, and I told her so, and the two of us got really mad with each other, so we're not talking,' she divulged miserably.

'Oh, that's terrible. It will sort itself out.' Debbie dropped a comforting arm around her shoulder.

'Well, I never thought Sarah would be jealous of me.'

'Maybe she's not jealous, maybe she's just a little bit concerned,' Debbie said delicately.

'Oh, for God's sake, Debbie. There's nothing to be concerned about. Honestly, Mom and Dad are driving me mad, they even brought me to the doctor yesterday 'cos they think I've got an eating disorder, and I've to go and see some specialist. I just wish people would, like, butt out of my life and leave me alone.'

'Oh . . . I didn't know that,' Debbie fibbed.

'Yeah, it's a bummer. I'm just watching what I eat, that's all.'

'I should watch what I eat,' Debbie sighed, deciding to say no more. She didn't want to say anything that would cause her half-sister to feel hostile towards her. She needed to try and keep Melissa on side so she could be of some support to her. She heard Bryan's key in the front door and was happy to see her husband walk into the kitchen. It was such a relief to be on good terms with him again.

'Hi, Debs.' He gave her a kiss and turned to Melissa.

'Hi,' he said politely, and then his jaw dropped. 'Jeepers, Melissa, I didn't recognize you. You've lost *tons* of weight.'

An iridescent beam illuminated Melissa's face. *Yessss!!!!* she shouted silently, the success of her diet affirmed beyond the shadow of a doubt. 'I've lost a few pounds,' she said modestly.

'A few pounds! A few stone more like it, I didn't recognize you,' he repeated, sitting on the stool next to her. 'So how's life?'

'OK. Back at school. Mom's got a new job, she's an MD now,' she declared proudly.

'MD no less, that's a good place to be. Did Debs tell you I'm on a three-day week?' Bryan ran his fingers through his jet-black hair and gave a rueful shrug.

'Yeah, that's awful. Will you try and get another job for the other two days?' Melissa asked matter-of-factly. 'My mom's getting a new office; you could do a nixer.'

Bryan looked startled: this option hadn't occurred to him. He'd been planning on trips to the IFC and a few galleries, and drinking lattes in Temple Bar.

'Umm, we'll see what turns up,' he answered non-committally.

'Thanks for thinking of us.' Debbie gave Melissa a hug. In a million years she wouldn't want Bryan to work for that stuck-up cow, Aimee, but of course she'd never let Melissa know that. 'We should go if we're going to be in time for the 6.20 showing.'

'Have fun,' Bryan said, hoping Debbie wouldn't start thinking about him doing nixers. He wasn't a nixer type person. He was a professional, he thought, a touch affronted that Melissa would see him in that light.

'Could you put a wash on? I didn't get time.' Debbie kissed him lightly on the cheek before following her half-sister out the door.

*

Melissa sat next to Debbie in the darkened cinema, chewing and spitting into a paper napkin from the stash she kept in her handbag for such eventualities. Debbie thought she was tucking into popcorn and M&Ms, as she was herself.

Melissa was buzzing. Her brother-in-law's reaction to her weight loss had brought her to a nirvana-like high. Nothing else in her life had given her such immense satisfaction, or such a sense of control. Even at night as she lay in bed starving, her stomach rumbling and growling, she felt powerful. How strong she was, what willpower she had not to go down to the fridge and savage everything in it. In a strange way she welcomed the by now familiar hunger pangs. She welcomed this nightly testing, because it only made her more determined to triumph over herself.

If she could lose another half a stone, she'd be really happy, she decided, as Jennifer Aniston emoted woodenly on screen. Jennifer was too curvy for Melissa's liking. She far preferred the way Keira Knightley looked, with her bony shoulders, flat chest and bird-like figure. Fabulous! She wanted to be that thin too, and she would be, she vowed, spitting the half-chewed popcorn into the napkin and taking a small sip of diet Coke.

'Jeez, I didn't recognize Melissa; she's changed completely in a few months. She's very pretty,' Bryan remarked as he and Debbie had a nightcap of Butler's hot chocolate.

'I meant to say to you not to remark on her weight loss. Mum and I think she's developed an eating disorder. Dad and Aimee brought her to the GP and she's been referred to a specialist.'

'How was I to know? Why didn't you tell me?' Bryan said defensively.

'We weren't really talking,' Debbie retorted, dipping a chocolate biscuit into the steaming drink.

'It suits her. She was a bit podgy.' Bryan ignored Debbie's last remark.

'I think she's too thin now. It did suit her a while back, but she's starving herself and upchucking after her meals, and now she's had a falling-out with one of her best friends because of it. That's awful for the poor kid.' Debbie couldn't help feeling worried about Melissa. She'd seen her chewing and spitting in the cinema and found it very upsetting.

'Did you hear her saying her mum's an MD? It was kind of endearing.' Bryan finished his hot drink.

'Did you hear her suggesting you could do Aimee's office fit-out?' Debbie grinned. 'As if.'

'I'd say Aimee has good taste. It's not beyond the bounds of possibility that we might get on, but I won't be looking to work for her, recession or no recession.'

'Did you put on the wash?' Debbie asked as she rinsed the cups.

Bryan smote his forehead. 'I knew there was something I meant to do. Sorry.' He gave his I'm-a-naughty-little-boy look, head tilted, looking at her through his long, silky lashes.

'I'll do it,' Debbie said resignedly.

'I'll have the bed warm for you when you come up.' He blew her a kiss and she tried to suppress a flash of irritation as she hurried upstairs in front of him, yawning, to get the dirty clothes out of the linen basket. What had he done all evening? Nothing, as far as she could see. She hoped that he'd make a start on doing something with the house and garden. In one way, it was the ideal opportunity to get the house the way they wanted it – as cheaply as possible for the time being, unfortunately. But paint and paper weren't hugely expensive and it would really freshen the place up.

Once she had the cheque from her dad, though, she was going to cut up her credit card, and insist Bryan do the same. He wouldn't like it, but tough. If her father was bailing them out and giving them breathing space to clear their debts, it was the least they could do. She hoped her husband wouldn't be too intransigent about it, but if he refused, the cheque was going back uncashed. This was one time Bryan couldn't have his cake and eat it.

*

Sarah checked her phone for the umpteenth time that evening as she lay in bed flicking through a glossy mag. No text from Melissa, no apology for being a bitch. Usually they would text for half an hour or so before going to sleep. It had been horrible at school, sitting next to her and not talking and avoiding her between classes. A tear slid down her cheek just as her younger sister, Jenny, came into the room they shared and flung herself down on her divan.

'Are you crying, Sarah?' She did a double take and sat up.

Sarah swallowed hard but couldn't answer.

'Hey, what's wrong?' Jenny got off her own bed and came and perched on Sarah's, looking at her in concern.

'Having a row with Melissa,' Sarah sniffled.

'Aw, poor baby.' Jenny slid back the duvet, got in beside her and put her arms around her. 'It will blow over,' she said kindly.

'I hope so. It's the first time ever. But she started it. She was, like, such a total bitch to me and I was only trying to help her,' Sarah said indignantly.

'Oh! Bad buzz!' Jenny kissed the top of Sarah's head and cuddled her.

She was such a sweet younger sister, Sarah thought gratefully. They got on fairly well too, in spite of sharing a bedroom. Melissa had no siblings at home, even if she had got a lot closer to Debbie since the wedding. Although she had often envied her friend her fabulous bedroom and not having to share, right now Sarah was extremely glad of her younger sister's comforting hug. When things were bad, family could actually be a comfort.

Melissa lay in the dark as raging pangs of hunger gathered strength for their nightly assault. She picked up her phone just to check there was no text of apology from Sarah.

Nothing. Nada! No welcome *You have 1 message* note.

She inhaled deeply then exhaled. Why was Sarah being such a bitch? How could she be so cold and unfriendly after all the years of being as close as sisters? Sarah knew more about her than anybody. It really hurt to see her laughing and chatting with Melody Johnston and Lizzie Gaynor. She'd wondered were they talking about her behind her back. Her heart had felt like it was being pricked by a thousand thumbtacks when she saw her best friend cast a glacial look in her direction and turn her back on her to giggle and gossip with her new best friends. She'd felt like bursting into tears. It had been one of the worst moments of her entire life.

In the soothing dark of her bedroom, broken only by a sliver of moonlight shining in through a gap in the curtains, Melissa felt the heartache anew. It was far, far worse than the hunger pains. It was even worse than the heartache she'd felt when Shane Kelly, whom she'd fancied like mad and who, she thought, fancied her as well, had asked Ellen Quinn to his family's end-of-summer barbecue. And *that* heartache had really hurt, she conceded.

Well, at school tomorrow, she would pretend Sarah's mean behaviour wasn't bothering her one bit. She would walk into class acting completely unconcerned. And if things got rocky she would simply escape to the memory of that wonderful moment when her brother-in-law had failed to recognize her, and when, as he did, his eyes had widened in shock and surprise and he'd told her she'd lost tons of weight.

'Tons of weight,' she whispered to herself as her stomach growled and gnawed. 'Tons of weight.'

CHAPTER ELEVEN

Debbie couldn't describe the relief she felt when she put down the phone after a call from her father after what had seemed like an age. It was like she could breathe again. He had the cheque for her. Would she like him to drop it in to her on his way home from work or would she prefer to meet him somewhere? he wanted to know. Whatever suited her was fine with him. It seemed churlish not to invite him to her home, especially when his generosity was going a long way towards ensuring that she and Bryan could keep the house.

It would be the first time her father would have been in their home, and she rang Bryan to tell him to tidy up and have the place looking presentable, but he had already left to go to the launch of some up-and-coming artist in a gallery in Temple Bar. He wouldn't be home until late. Typical, never there when he was needed, she thought irritably, turning her attention back to a set of complicated figures for a retiring employee's pension plan.

She rushed home from work, hoping that her husband had left the house spick and span before he went out, but it was a vain hope. Debbie scowled in frustration when she walked into the kitchen and saw the dirty dishes in the sink. Bryan had been too lazy to unload the dishwasher and had simply put his dirty lunch dishes into the sink until she came home to unload the dishwasher and fill it up again.

147

He'd really want to start pulling his weight a lot more. Being off for two days a week had so far not inclined him to up his game in the housekeeping stakes. Why should she have to act like his mother and nag him? They were supposed to be a partnership, a team. Why did he think so little of her that he felt it was OK to dump his dirty dishes in the sink for her to tidy up? She'd been working all day to earn a living; he'd obviously been on the doss. Debbie was hopping mad as she ran the hot water and squirted some washing-up liquid into the basin. She had to run around like a dervish, tidying the kitchen, giving the bathroom a quick clean, polishing the mirror in the hall and spraying polish and air freshener around so that at least the house would *smell* clean.

The grass needed to be cut, badly, but there was nothing she could do about that in the short space of time between her getting home from work and Barry's arrival. She wished she had some flowers to put in the Louise Kennedy vase they'd got as a wedding present that was on the hallstand. When they'd had money she'd often bought whatever flowers were in season and arranged them artistically, and they were a colourful focal point and the first thing you'd notice when you came in the front door. She barely had time to give her hair a quick brush, apply some lippy and a spray of DKNY Apple when she heard Barry's knock on the door. She ran downstairs, her heels clacking like castanets on the wooden floor as she hurried to open the door.

'Excellent directions.' Her father kissed her on the cheek. 'And a very nice little complex. Handy to the Dart and the village,' he approved as he followed her into the kitchen. 'I always liked Sandymount, a good mixture of old and new, and great restaurants too.'

'Yeah, we like it a lot, but in light of the financial meltdown, it's too expensive an area to have bought in. We'd have been better off in a less upmarket suburb, ' Debbie confessed.

'Well, you're here now and you can't do much about it at the moment. I have the cheque here for you; at least that will help you stay afloat.' He took a crisp white envelope out of his pocket and put it on the table.

'Oh, Dad, thanks so much. Are you sure? I'm a bit mortified,' she confessed, her cheeks pink with embarrassment.

'Don't be silly.' Barry put an arm around her shoulder and smiled down at her.

'I'm sorry Bryan's not here to thank you. He's at some exhibition in town. He was gone before I knew you were coming,' she apologized, giving him a quick hug back. It was strange but nicely strange to be able to hug her father without being submerged in a mire of resentment and anger.

'No problem at all,' Barry said easily. 'How's he finding the three-day week?'

'Well, it's very new still. I think he thinks he's on holiday. It hasn't sunk in yet.'

'Melissa mentioned it to me. I know that Aimee's going to be moving into a new office soon – I wonder does it need a fit-out? Or is it best not to involve family? Sometimes things can get complicated,' he queried delicately. 'It's just a suggestion.'

'You might be right about the family thing, in case anything went wrong, or Aimee might not want to use him and might feel bad if she had to say no,' Debbie murmured, not wanting Bryan to be involved with Aimee for any reason. 'Dad, where are my manners?' She changed the subject. 'Would you like a cup of tea, or something to eat? I have some fresh plaice, and I could do a baked potato and some veggies or I've a dish of macaroni cheese, and I could toss up a salad.'

'Macaroni cheese . . . I haven't tasted that in years.' Barry's eyes lit up. 'Is it your mother's recipe? She used to add crispy bacon and baby tomatoes, if I remember rightly.'

'Spot on! That's the one.' Debbie grinned. 'Would you like some?'

'I shouldn't really; I like to have dinner at home with Melissa. I'm always hoping that if she eats something she'll get some small bit of good out of it, even if she gets rid of it later,' he confided.

'Oh, right, that's understandable.' She was disappointed. It would have been a first, having a meal at home with her dad.

'I suppose I could have a very small portion,' he ventured.

'Think of it as a starter,' Debbie pressed. 'I just have to heat it in the microwave. I'll have the salad tossed in a second.' She bustled around getting herself organized, thinking she hadn't been as nervous when she was going on her first date with Bryan. But gradually, as they chatted, he sitting on one of the high stools, she relaxed, slicing mixed peppers to go with a dip on the side.

It was most agreeable to sit with him at the kitchen counter, elbows touching companionably as they ate the tasty meal. She was actually enjoying his company, she thought with a mild sense of shock, remembering how vehemently she had argued with Connie about not having him at her wedding. How true that line in the book by Neale Donald Walsch was; her mother had given it to her before her wedding: 'That was then. This is now.' Looking at it like that, any hurt could be forgiven over time. Letting go of her anger and bitterness was one of the best things that had happened to her in the past year. It had eaten her up for so long, she had been in danger of being consumed by it, defined by it even.

Debbie Adams who hates her father.

It was such a relief to let the burden of it go. And now here she was, eating a meal with him in her own house, laughing at things he said as if they had been close all her life.

It was he who had suggested they eat in the kitchen when she'd got out a tablecloth to set their small dining table. 'Kitchens are cosy,' he said, taking the tablemats and cutlery from her and setting two places for them at the counter. She was glad then that Bryan wasn't home, that it was just the two of them, father and daughter, spending time together. How she'd longed for that as a child. She'd have given anything to be the same as her peers who were lucky enough to have two parents living at home. Still, it was better late than never, and it was one of the most enjoyable meals she had ever had, she thought as she stood at the door waving him off. And at least he'd stood by her and supported her in her hour of need. That was what fathers were for. She was smiling broadly as she closed the door to go back into the kitchen to tidy up the detritus of their meal. Or maybe she should leave that for Bryan to do the following day? That was a better plan, Debbie thought, in great humour.

She needed to let Connie know that Barry had had a meal with her in her house. Her mother would be so pleased. She had always wanted Debbie to reconcile with her father. This breaking of bread had to be the final step: from now on, she would never look back in sorrow at her and Barry's fractured past. From now on, there was no separation. They would only move forward.

'Mam, he devoured the macaroni cheese. He said he hadn't had it in years. He asked me was it from the recipe that you used to make,' she burbled happily, remembering how Barry had stood absent-mindedly scraping the sides of the macaroni dish after she had dished out their food.

'That's wonderful, Debbie. It makes me so happy. I've wanted this for a long, long time,' Connie exclaimed joyfully. 'What made him call?'

Debbie took a deep breath. She'd never had secrets from Connie until now, and she didn't like it. Now that Barry had stepped in and rescued the day she felt she could tell her mother of the lead-up to his visit without her being too worried. 'Well, I haven't told you any of this, but things have been a bit rocky for Bryan and myself. We got into debt on our credit cards, and were finding it difficult to pay them off without letting our mortgage slip into arrears. I asked Dad could he help us out financially. Bryan's just been put on a three-day week as well,' she explained.

'For God's sake, Debbie, why didn't you come to me? Why

didn't you tell me this? How long has it been going on?' Connie was horrified.

'A while,' Debbie admitted. 'But look, I didn't want to worry you, you seem so happy with your new man, and besides, I felt Dad could afford to help. They're pretty well off.' Debbie walked into the lounge and flopped down on to the sofa.

'But you should have come to me. I'm your mother—'

'And he's my father and he was delighted I came to him. He was *so* pleased, honestly, Mum. He told me how happy he was to help me,' she said earnestly.

'Well, that's fine, love, but please tell me when you're in trouble. Me being happy with Drew is no reason for you not to tell me things, Debbie. You and I are a unit, and no one will ever change that,' her mother replied firmly. 'Is Bryan very upset?'

'Ah, you know Bryan,' she said off-handedly. 'He's adaptable. He's at an art-gallery opening tonight.' She certainly wasn't going to say anything to Connie about his talk of emigrating.

'And are you OK?' Connie still sounded concerned.

'I'm fine, Mam. Paying off the credit cards gives us a lot of breathing space, so that's a huge relief. I'm cutting up my card tonight, and Bryan will be too. I'm never getting into debt like that again. Once bitten, twice shy.'

'Well, that's very positive, love. How about you and Bryan come to lunch on Sunday and I'll introduce you to Drew?'

'Sounds lovely, Mam. We'll be over around one,' Debbie agreed.

'Great, see you then. Go and cut those cards up now.'

'Will do, Mam. See you, and thanks for showing me how to make macaroni cheese. I don't think that Aimee one can cook at all, she certainly has the look of it.' Debbie giggled.

'Stop it,' Connie remonstrated, but Debbie knew she was smiling.

It was after eleven when Bryan got home, and he'd had a few drinks. 'Hi, Gorgeous, you would have enjoyed the evening. Briony and Philip were in top form; they send their love.' He grabbed her and nuzzled into her.

'Hey, wait, I've something to show you.' She twisted out of his embrace and picked up the envelope from the top of the kitchen counter where she'd stuck it behind the biscuit jar, and waved it at him.

'What's that?' He'd obviously completely forgotten about Barry's promised cheque.

'The money from Dad.'

'Fan-bleedin'-tastic.' He grabbed it off her, opened it, took out the cheque and studied it. 'Imagine being able to get your hands on that amount of lolly.' He whistled.

'I'll be paying the cards off first thing tomorrow. Now, there's one thing we have to do, and I told Dad we'd do it tonight.' Debbie took the cheque back from Bryan and replaced it in the envelope.

'What's that, Dollface?' He was in high good humour.

'This,' she said, taking her wallet out of her bag. She slid her credit card out of the pocket and held it up. 'Get yours out.'

'For what?' He was suddenly wary.

'I told Dad we'd cut them up.'

'That's a bit extreme!' he protested.

'What's the difference? We haven't been able to use them anyway,' she said patiently. She understood his angst. A credit card was a real lifeline. It had been hard getting used to not using them; being told her card had been declined at a shop counter had been one of the most mortifying and scary moments of her life.

'We could be really, really careful about using them,' he wheedled.

'No, Bryan. We need to cut them up. It's too easy to get into debt. This is going to make a huge difference.' She waved the envelope at him. 'But if you don't agree to cut up the cards, I'm giving it back to Dad. It's up to you.' She eyeballed him and he lowered his eyes.

'OK, Bossyboots,' he acquiesced petulantly and watched with a pained expression as she got the kitchen scissors and, with two sharp cuts, cleaved the shiny plastic cards in half.

'This is our fresh start,' she said, opening the pedal bin and dropping the four halves into the kitchen rubbish.

'If that's what you'd call it,' he growled, all traces of good humour dispelled by her actions.

'Don't be like that, Bryan, we've been given a second chance. And please ring Dad in the morning to thank him,' she said resignedly, walking out of the kitchen to go up to bed and wondering why she always seemed to be the baddie.

'How high will I jump?' Bryan muttered grumpily, thanking all the gods in the universe that his wife knew nothing about his secret credit card. And that was exactly how it would remain: a secret. He wasn't a schoolboy to be bossed around, for crying out loud. He was a man, heading for thirty, and Debbie could frig off if she thought she was going to tell him what to do for the rest of his life. She was just like her mother, a bossy cow, he fumed, rooting in the fridge to see what was there to eat. He pushed aside a bag of Caesar salad looking for the remains of the macaroni cheese and saw that it was gone. In an even worse humour, he slammed the fridge door shut and went in and sat down on the sofa to watch TV. He could stay up as long as he liked, he didn't have to get up for work in the morning, and if the noise of the television kept Debbie awake, tough, he thought nastily, surfing until he found a documentary on the arts channel that grabbed his interest.

'Are you coming to bed?' Barry asked Aimee, standing at the door of their elegant red and gold dining room watching as her fingers flew over the keyboard of her computer.

'Soon, I just have to get this finished,' she murmured absently. He left her to it. Since Roger O'Leary had given her this new project to sink her teeth into she'd been going hell for leather – on the phone, on the computer. It was just like old times. Aimee had the bit between her teeth, and he and Melissa were utter distractions.

He wondered could he get away with giving Connie a ring, in

the bedroom? He was sure she'd be delighted to know that he'd shared a meal with Debbie in her house. He glanced at his watch. It was after eleven, a bit late to be ringing, he thought regretfully. She might be on the early shift in the morning and have to get up at the crack of dawn.

He locked up, looked in on Melissa, who was fast asleep, and went into his en suite and got ready for bed. He and Debbie had really bonded over the meal in her kitchen. It was worth the financial loss he'd made cashing in his savings early, just for the look of relief on her face when he'd given her the cheque. Hopefully she'd be able to keep up her mortgage repayments and ride out the recession and Bryan's cut in salary.

Their house was small enough for the price they'd paid for it, and in need of redecorating. Connie had claimed that Bryan wasn't great around the house. Barry had thought she was being a bit mother-in-lawish, but now he could see where she was coming from. That lad needed a good kick in the butt. A lick of paint in the hall and kitchen would spruce up the house. And the state of the gardens! Barry shook his head as he climbed under the duvet. Even he, and he was no green fingers and he hated gardening, had kept the front and back garden neat and tidy in the house he'd lived in with Connie in those first turbulent years of marriage. He'd had some pride; obviously Bryan had none. His oldest daughter had her hands full there, he thought, hoping that Bryan would pull up his socks and get his act together. It would be interesting to see if his son-in-law rang to thank him for the cheque. It wasn't something he'd bet money on, Barry thought grimly as he switched out the lamp on his side of the bed.

Connie lay in bed planning her menu for Sunday lunch, but she was distracted and her thoughts kept returning to the conversation she'd had with Debbie earlier. She wasn't surprised her daughter and son-in-law were up to their ears in debt. Bryan got through money like there was no tomorrow and he had very expensive tastes. Debbie had spent a fortune bringing him to Amsterdam before the wedding, for whatever reason she'd felt the need to. And with the millstone of a 100 per cent mortgage around their necks, it was no wonder they were in danger of sinking. The one positive thing to come out of all of this was Debbie and Barry's increasing closeness. That had to be the blessing in disguise.

At least Debbie had told her about their problems. It would be awful to think that her daughter felt she couldn't confide in her any more. She really had a lot on her plate right now; with Bryan on a three-day week things were bound to be tight. Connie's brow furrowed. Now that she was working part time herself, she had to be careful with her money, otherwise she could have helped out a bit; but she'd given them a hefty lump sum for their wedding present and she wasn't exactly rolling in cash. And it was such an irony, although Debbie didn't realize it, that Barry wasn't either. She couldn't have gone to him at a worse time for financial help, but he'd obviously given her a helping hand. She wondered if he'd told Aimee and what her response was. It was slightly galling that Debbie was beholden. No doubt Aimee would look down her shapely nose at the first family for looking for hand-outs. Debbie hadn't told her how much Barry had lent her and she hadn't asked. That was between Debbie and her father.

Connie sighed in the dark and turned over on her side. It would have been nice to have Drew beside her, to discuss it all and get his point of view, but she hadn't seen him today. He'd had to go to an equestrian event in Galway and wouldn't be back until the following day.

It was a pity she had to invite Bryan to lunch, she thought gloomily. She just did not like her son-in-law, and hiding her antipathy was very wearing. She wouldn't hurt Debbie for anything, so she always put up a friendly façade when she was with him, but sometimes she felt like giving him a good hard slap. He was a lazy lump. She could bet her last euro that he would not be spending his enforced days off doing up the house and garden or looking for alternative work. 'Stop thinking about him, you're only putting yourself in bad humour,' she muttered, pummelling her pillow into a more comfortable shape. Miss Hope, her little black cat, stretched out a silky paw and placed it proprietorially on her wrist.

'And I love you too.' Connie smiled as she reached out her other hand to stroke the cat's soft furry head. I wonder what Drew will make of Bryan, she thought before her eyes closed and she fell into a dreamless sleep.

CHAPTER TWELVE

Connie shook the par-boiled potatoes in a sieve and then placed them into the bubbling goose fat and slid them into the top oven. She blew the hair off her forehead at the gust of heat that rushed out, adding to the heat she was feeling from a most awkwardly timed hot flush. Those bloody things were such a nuisance. It was just her luck to find an attractive man and have a lifestyle that was a lot more relaxed than it had been and then to be smitten with the dreaded 'change', she thought wiping her forehead with some kitchen paper.

She opened the bottom oven to check on the roast beef. She had two roasts in the oven, one for herself, Drew and Debbie that had been in for almost an hour and fifteen minutes, and one a separate, smaller joint she was cooking for Bryan, who liked his meat rare. Fussy little brat, she fretted, hoping it would be pink enough for him. She wasn't having her son-in-law sitting there looking down his nose at her cooking. He'd once told her that he didn't like 'cremated' meat as he'd sat pushing his fork around a slice of roast pork. She'd wished heartily that she *had* cooked the pork pink for him and given him a dose of the squits. She'd never served him pork again.

Everything else was under control, she decided as she surveyed the cooker top: the vegetables were ready to be steamed and the gravy was cooked. Just time to slap on some make-up to tone down her red face before her guests arrived.

She scowled when she saw her bright-red face in the mirror, the beads of sweat dripping down her temples and down her cleavage. She was baked. It wouldn't take five minutes to have a quick shower. She hurried into the bathroom, turned on the spray to lukewarm and undressed rapidly. That was so refreshing, she thought gratefully a few minutes later as she wrapped a soft terry towel around her. The zzzzz of the doorbell made her jump and she looked out the window and saw Drew's jeep in the drive.

'Come around the back, the door's open.' She stuck her head out the window and called down to him.

'OK,' he squinted up to her, grinning.

'Are you decent?' he called at the bottom of the stairs a minute later.

'No, I just had a shower, I have to get dressed.' She stood at the top of the stairs, thinking how handsome he looked in his black trousers and light-blue shirt, open at the neck. He'd had his grey hair cut, tight, and she had the urge to run her fingers over the top of his head.

'Nice view,' he teased, and their eyes locked.

'Don't come up here,' she warned, grinning like a schoolgirl. 'No, Drew, I mean it,' she laughed as he bounded up the stairs two at a time and grabbed her.

'I'm only saying hello,' he said innocently, bending his head to hers and giving her a long, slow, sensuous kiss.

'Stop it.' She pushed him away. 'Debbie and Bryan will be here soon.'

'Traffic's very heavy,' he said, lowering his head again. 'Your turn to say hello to me.'

A minute later they were rolling on the bed and she was unbuttoning his shirt with one hand and tugging at his trousers with the other as he opened his belt and kicked off his shoes.

It was hot and fast and deeply satisfying, and they lay together afterwards, panting and laughing, enveloped in a bubble of happiness, touching each other's faces tenderly.

'What are we like?' She raised her head and rested it on her hand, looking down at him.

'You only live once, you have to make the most of it.' Drew smiled up at her, his eyes crinkling in his tanned face as she traced her forefinger along the jut of his jawline.

'This is the best fun I've had in years.' Connie kissed him lightly on the mouth. 'I've never felt so light-hearted.'

'Me too. Strange, isn't it? I don't ever remember feeling like this.'

'No, me neither, not even when I was first married,' Connie reflected.

'I'm looking forward to meeting your daughter.' He twirled a curl around his finger.

'She's dying to meet you too, especially when I told her who'd play you in a film,' she teased.

Drew snorted, laughing. That would be something to see all right. 'Dinner smells nice.' He sniffed appreciatively at the aromas that were wafting up the stairs.

'Oh drat! That bloody joint for Bryan! Quick, let me up, I have to get out of here. And now I smell of sex.' Connie shot up off the bed.

'You smell gorgeous and you look gorgeous,' Drew said lazily, his eyes running up and down her.

'Stop looking at me,' she blushed, grabbing the sheet and covering herself. 'Get up, you. I was supposed to be all calm and unflustered, and look at the state of me. Look at my hair,' she wailed as she saw her reflection in the mirror and the wild, coppery muss sticking up all over the place.

'I don't have a hair out of place,' Drew said smugly as he got off the bed and started to get dressed again. 'Bedhead suits you,' he added as he went into the en suite to wash his hands.

'Go down and take that small joint on the lower shelf out of the oven, quick,' she urged, panicking when she heard a car drive along the road.

'Yes, ma'am. Whatever you say.' He picked up the towel from the floor and handed it to her. 'It was good, wasn't it?' His blue eyes shone, warm and loving.

'It was fantastic, Drew. You make me so happy.' She leaned her head on his shoulder and he held her close.

'Not half as happy as you make me, Connie,' he said huskily. 'How lucky are we?' They kissed tenderly, and reluctantly he drew away and said, 'I better take that meat out that you're so worried about.'

'It's for Bryan, he likes it rare,' she said dryly.

'Better be rare so. Get dressed, woman.' He patted her ass and went striding out the door to rescue the beef.

She had just joined Drew in the kitchen when she heard Debbie's key in the front door. Her heart lifted at the sight of her daughter as she poked her head around the kitchen door. 'Hello, Mum. You can smell the dinner down the road. I'm starving.' Debbie looked beautiful in a pair of white jeans and a pink floaty top that highlighted her blue eyes and creamy complexion.

'Hello, love.' Connie hugged her daughter tightly and was tightly hugged in return. 'Bryan, hello.' She lightly kissed her son-in-law's cheek but didn't hug him. His own kiss was perfunctory, but that didn't bother her.

'Hi, Connie, thanks for the invite,' he said politely. He wasn't in good form, she could tell. His brown eyes were cold and unfriendly, his body language stiff and tense. He was clearly at lunch under sufferance. Or maybe she was imagining it, Connie decided, chiding herself for getting on his case the minute she'd seen him.

'Debbie, this is Drew. Drew, my daughter, Debbie.' She turned her attention to the most important matter to hand and introduced the two most precious people in her life to each other.

'Very nice to meet you, Debbie.' Drew held out his hand and shook Debbie's firmly, meeting her intense gaze with a smile.

'Really nice to meet you too, Drew. Thanks for making Mum so happy,' Debbie said with heartfelt sentiment, smiling broadly, and Connie knew instantly that Debbie liked him and that they would get on.

'Thanks, Debbie. It's a two-way thing.' Drew slipped an arm around Connie's waist.

'And Drew, this is Bryan, my son-in-law,' Connie said, conscious of the younger man studying them with undisguised superiority.

'Nice to meet you.' Bryan held out a limp hand and almost gasped when it was gripped in an iron handshake.

'Likewise,' Drew returned, eyeballing the younger man.

'So who'd like a drink?' Connie asked lightly. 'Which one of you is driving today?'

'I am,' Debbie said. 'Bryan can indulge.'

'Wine, beer, spirits?' Connie asked, thinking it wouldn't have killed him to drive and let Debbie have a drink. She was sure if they were going to his mother's he wouldn't have to drive.

'White wine would be super,' Bryan said languidly.

'Debbie?'

'I'll have a spritzer, please,' she said, and Drew poured the drinks for them, perfectly at ease in Connie's kitchen. 'Dinner smells gorgeous, Mum. I've been so looking forward to it.' Debbie stood against the cooker and stirred the gravy like she used to when she was young.

'I made an apple and cinnamon crumble for you, I know it's your favourite.' Connie smiled as she took the glass of chilled white wine Drew had poured for her.

'Mum, you're the best,' Debbie declared, snaffling a fat, juicy prawn from a platter on the countertop before taking the spritzer Drew offered her.

'Leave those alone, they're for the starter.'

'You should be on *Come Dine With Me*,' Debbie teased.

'Oh, I love that programme.' Connie laughed and saw the brief flash of disdain in Bryan's eyes.

'So Bryan, have you any advice for me about dealing with these Adams women?' Drew said jocularly as he handed him a glass of wine.

'Don't let them boss you around,' Bryan riposted smartly, with an edge of sarcasm, sniffing the bouquet before taking a sip of the wine.

'Oh!' Drew's eyes narrowed. 'Bossy! Hmmm, not an adjective I'd use to describe Connie.'

'I wouldn't imagine you're someone who'd be easily bossed, anyway,' Debbie retorted, glaring at her husband.

'I've been henpecked a few times in my life.' Drew smiled at her.

'A few times? You're lucky! I'm henpecked *all* the time.' Bryan pretended to joke.

'Why don't you all go in and sit down and I'll serve the starters,' Connie suggested smoothly, preceding them with the big seafood platter, which she placed in the middle of the table. 'Help yourselves,' she invited, wishing she could stick the crab claws into a delicate part of Bryan's lower anatomy.

'That was delicious, Connie, thank you. I'd give you a 10,' Drew said after they'd finished the tasty starter. 'I look at *Come Dine With Me* too when I'm with your mother.' He winked at Debbie.

'I think you and I will have a lot in common, Drew,' Debbie assured him. 'I love the countryside, walking along the beach, Elvis and Leonard Cohen, too.' She giggled.

'Elvis was overrated,' Bryan drawled dismissively.

'That's your opinion,' Debbie sniffed. 'I think Van Morrison is overrated and can't sing for peanuts.'

'To each his own,' Drew said, standing up to help Connie gather the plates.

'Debbie's a lovely girl,' he said to her in the privacy of the kitchen after he'd closed the door behind them. 'She has your sense of humour.'

'And what do you think of Bryan?' Connie arched an eyebrow at him as she carved the meat.

'Not what I expected. He has a bit of an attitude problem.' Drew loaded the dishwasher with the starter plates.

'I hope this is pink enough for him,' Connie muttered, slicing Bryan's joint and slapping the meat on his plate.

'Rare for you, isn't it?' she said coolly as she placed the plate of pink beef in front of him.

'Oh, you remembered. Thanks.' He took a swig of wine, and she could see that his eyes were a little glazed. He'd polished off half a bottle of white wine and was now slugging the red. Drew and Debbie resumed chatting away nineteen to the dozen as she sat down at the table. It was comforting to see them getting on so well. Debbie clearly liked him, and it appeared that the feeling was mutual, and that was all Connie cared about. Bryan could go and take a running jump for himself.

'Lovely dinner, Connie, thank you,' Drew said appreciatively as he cut into his last crispy golden roast potatoes.

'You're welcome. Glad you enjoyed it.' Connie beamed at him. She'd given him an extra roastie, knowing how much he loved them. Because Drew was pulling out all the stops with Debbie, she felt she should make more of an effort with Bryan. Maybe he was down because of his bad luck at work, she decided, trying to make allowances, sitting back down next to him after serving the dessert.

'So how are you finding the three-day week, Bryan?' she asked, offering him more ice cream for his crumble.

'Difficult,' he mumbled. 'It's the pits having no money. If we hadn't been railroaded into buying a house, we'd be fine.'

'We weren't railroaded, Bryan.' Debbie looked at him in irritation. 'And who was to know all this was going to happen?'

'I remember saying that house prices were far too high, *artificially* high, and that there was going to be a crash, but as I remember, you felt we should buy to get on the property ladder, didn't you, Connie?' he said smarmily.

Connie couldn't believe her ears. Was he, in a roundabout way, blaming her for their financial problems? 'I always felt renting was dead money for you,' she said slowly. 'And I'm sure you could have bought a house where the mortgage would have cost you the same amount as what you were paying in rent, if you'd bought in another area. Sandymount *is* expensive, there's no denying that.'

'It's a renters' market now. Rents have dropped drastically while mortgages are going up. Anyone who was renting is on the pig's back and *now* is the time to buy a house, when prices have halved. Not when we bought – but no one would listen to me.' He took another slug of wine and stared at her. 'We'll be lucky not to lose the house, I'd say,' he added with almost undisguised hostility, as tension crackled around the table.

'Stop, Bryan. Don't be like that. We're not going to lose the house,' Debbie snapped. 'And Mum's right, if we hadn't gone for the house in Sandymount, we wouldn't be paying such a high mortgage. We can't have it every way.'

Bryan shrugged. 'Whatever you say, babes.' Debbie flushed puce. Her husband was being obnoxious. He hadn't wanted to come to lunch and had made a face when she'd told him Connie had issued the invite. Now he was drinking too much and being rude and insufferable, and in front of her mother's new partner. It was absolutely mortifying.

'Let me take out these dishes and bring in the coffee,' Connie interjected. Drew and Debbie were finished; she couldn't care less if Bryan wasn't. He was an ignorant little toad and she'd had enough of his bad behaviour.

'I'll help.' Debbie stood up, subdued.

'Thanks, darling,' Connie said gratefully.

They collected the dishes and cutlery and carried them out to the kitchen. When they were gone, Drew stretched like a panther and fixed a stern eye on Bryan. 'Sonny, seeing as we're here on our own, a word in your ear. You treat Connie and your wife with respect when you're in my company, and don't embarrass them. Just so we understand each other.' His tone was glacial, and Bryan looked taken aback at the unexpected full-on onslaught. 'And I think you've had enough to drink while we're at it,' Drew continued tersely. He gave Bryan a flinty-eyed stare, and the younger man dropped his eyes under Drew's disgusted gaze. A frosty silence descended and they sat there, Bryan fiddling with his napkin, until Connie reappeared with the coffee pot and Debbie placed the cups on the table. The tension abated a little, and after the coffee was finished Connie suggested a walk on the beach.

'Mum, we have to go,' Debbie said hastily, seeing the look of dismay on her husband's face. 'We're meeting some friends who are emigrating for a drink later. But lunch was delicious, and thanks so much for going to all the trouble.'

'Very nice, Connie, as always,' Bryan said silkily, slanting Drew a look as if to say, *Was that all right for you?* as the older man stood up to say goodbye to Debbie.

'He's something else, isn't he, the little scut?' Connie murmured as she and Drew stood waving at the door. 'I don't know what she ever saw in him, she could have had anybody.'

'That's the way it goes, Connie. People could say that about us and our first marriages,' he said calmly. 'They'll have to sort it out for themselves.'

'I suppose you're right, but I find it very difficult to be in his company, and he's so lazy, Drew, Debbie has to do everything.'

'What do they say about people coming into our lives to be our teachers? Maybe she has to learn balance and to put herself first sometimes. We all had to learn that lesson, didn't we?' he said kindly, closing the door and taking her in his arms. 'Debbie has her own path to walk and her own lessons to learn, but we can support her on that path, Connie. You can't live her life for her. It's time to live your own life now.'

'I know, and at least she and Barry are becoming much closer. I always wanted that.'

'Well, it's happening, and take comfort in the fact that you've reared a lovely girl. I see so much of you in her. She'll be fine, Connie. Now let's clear the dishes away and go for a walk. It looks like it might rain later, so we can light the fire and read the papers together, just like Darby and Joan.'

'Who are Darby and Joan, anyway?' Connie chuckled.

'I have no idea.' Drew laughed. 'But I bet they don't do this.' He turned her around to face him and kissed her soundly, and was soundly kissed in return.

'You were *so* rude, Bryan. I'd never treat your mother like that. I'm disgusted with you.' Debbie swerved to avoid a pothole.

'Yeah, well, my mother didn't bang on and on about us getting a house—'

'Mum was only concerned that we were losing money by paying rent and she was right, and it was you that wanted to live in Sandymount because it was D4, so get over yourself, Bryan, and take some responsibility for the decisions we made. I'm sick of you blaming Mum and me for everything. I gave you an opportunity to back out of getting married. You had the chance, you could have taken it.'

'Yeah, well, right now I'm sorry I didn't,' he growled.

'Right back at ya, Bryan, right back at ya, because, trust me, this is not what I thought it would be.'

They drove the rest of the way home in resentful silence and when they got in he stalked upstairs and flung himself on the bed for a nap.

Debbie changed into a tracksuit and fleece and slammed the door behind her. She could see dark clouds rolling in from the south; she would go for a brisk walk and then go and have coffee and a read of the papers in Itsa 4. She needed a break from her sullen, childish husband, who was taking everything out on her. He had been in a bad humour since she'd made him cut up his credit card, but he could get over himself. It was no picnic for her either, she thought furiously, walking swiftly towards the seafront.

Connie was so happy with Drew, she thought, feeling envious in the nicest way. They were so into each other, so careful and mindful of each other. They were like newly-weds. They were like what she and Bryan should be. They *had* been like that once, but marriage had changed their relationship. Was it like that for every couple? she wondered.

Drew was a fine man, and she could see why Connie had compared him to Gary Cooper and McSteamy. He was undeniably handsome in that manly, rugged sort of way. And he had a quiet strength. He wouldn't run away from his responsibilities. She was so glad for Connie and so relieved for herself that she liked Drew. It would have been awful if they hadn't clicked.

Would she and Bryan last the course? She bit her lip as she headed for the Martello Tower. So far, marriage was not all it was cracked up to be. Not what she'd fantasized about. Maybe it would be different once their finances were back on track and this rocky stage was over. She had to keep positive, it was the only way, Debbie told herself as, head down, she faced into the rising wind.

Bryan lay in bed staring lethargically at the ceiling. He was delighted he'd made his point to Connie. That had been a long time coming. She'd been discomfited. He could see it in her eyes. Good enough for her. It would give her something to think about. And what about that bloke of hers having a go at him? That was bang out of order. He wouldn't get the chance to do that again, Bryan vowed. He wasn't even going to wait until Christmas. If an opportunity came for him to get out, he was going, and right now, he wasn't particularly fussy whether Debbie came with him. A solo run seemed like a most enticing option. He turned over on his side and pulled the throw over him. His mother-in-law's choice of wine had been rather good, and he was glad he'd quaffed a good portion of it. It had been the only good thing about the lunch, he thought, as he fell asleep and dreamed of surfing on Bondi Beach with a redhead and a blonde in tow.

CHAPTER THIRTEEN

She felt most peculiar, Melissa thought weakly as the girls in front of her seemed to swim away, the racket of chat and laughter faded, the light in the corridor dimmed – and then utter blackness eddied around her and she fainted.

'Give her room, girls, step back. Step back, please,' she could hear someone say from very far away. A face, distorted, whirling, spinning, made her close her eyes again as nausea overtook her.

'Breathe deeply, Melissa,' the authoritative voice instructed, penetrating the stupor she was in. 'Get me a glass of water, one of you.' Melissa kept her eyes closed until she heard the voice say kindly, 'Try and drink some water, Melissa.' She opened her eyes again and Miss O'Byrne's face swam into focus. 'Try and sit up, there's a good girl.'

'I . . . I . . .'

'Don't talk, just take a sip.' Melissa felt the cool liquid trickle down her throat. It felt good, but she still felt very weird.

'Bring a chair, girls,' Miss O'Byrne ordered, and Melissa could hear the sound of feet on the marble floor and the hushed tones of her classmates.

Willing hands helped her to her feet, but it was too much effort for her. The darkness came for her again and she crumpled up in a heap.

She came to in an ambulance, with the paramedic calling her name. Dazed, she gazed around her and saw Miss O'Byrne sitting opposite her, looking very concerned. She closed her eyes again. Keeping them open was such a strain. It was much easier to drift away and just listen to the roaring sound her thumping heart was making. She was having terrible muscle cramps. She felt as though she'd run a marathon.

Then the doors were opening and she felt fresh air on her face as she was lifted down on her trolley and wheeled along, with Miss O'Byrne walking beside her. The sun was too bright and it hurt her eyes, so she closed them and floated away again.

She was vaguely aware of nurses, a doctor in a white coat. People talking to her. She was wired up to some sort of a machine. Someone stuck a needle in her arm, and that hurt.

Her parents arrived, some time later, Aimee white-faced with worry; Barry grey, anxious. She could hear them thanking Miss O'Byrne, could hear them speak in low, worried tones. She wanted to hide away from them. Causing them hassle was the last thing she wanted. They didn't need hassle, especially her mom, with the stress of her new job and being pregnant.

She could hear a doctor saying something about her electrolytes being out of balance, whatever they were. Loss of potassium . . . The blood test would be back in an hour or so . . . they could start treatment . . . a drip . . . The words lodged in her brain for a moment or two and then they were gone just out of reach and she faded into oblivion once more.

'Did you see her? She was as white as a ghost.'

'Maybe she's preggers.'

'Great way of getting out of a maths exam.'

'Bet she's not eating – look at all the weight she's lost.'

Sarah bit her lip as she heard the conjecture doing the rounds. It was lunchtime and Melissa being carted off to hospital in an ambulance was the main topic of conversation, apart from scathing comments about Mrs O'Doherty's horrendous maths test which few, if any of them, expected to pass. At least Melissa had missed that ordeal, she thought, nibbling on a Danish.

She wasn't really that hungry. She was desperately worried about her friend. She finished the last drop of coffee, dropped the cup into the bin and headed out to the yard. There was a small, secluded garden around the side of the school, and she bypassed the basketball and tennis courts and made her way to the garden. Once there, she sat on one of the wooden seats and raised her face to the sun. The sound of basketballs being dribbled along the courts and the thwack of tennis balls hitting tightly strung racquets mixed with the sound of skylarks and a bee buzzing in the rose bushes under the library windows.

What was happening to Melissa? Maybe it was a good thing that she had fainted. If she was in hospital, she'd have to eat. Maybe she might get sorted then and get back to normal. She glanced around: no teachers near, just a couple of other girls lounging on the grass. She did a quick text.

Hope ur feeling ok. Let me know. Love Sarah xxx Ps Maths was crap. Am sure have failed.

She deliberately put 'love' and not the just the 'Sxx' that she usually ended a text with. She pressed send and hoped against hope that her friend would respond.

'Melissa, I just want to change your drip. This is to replenish your potassium. You do understand, don't you, that your electrolytes are completely out of balance? Your potassium is only 2.2. You could potentially do damage to your heart or even be at risk of a heart attack. These are consequences of starving your body,' the nurse said sternly as she put a full bag of colourless liquid on to the drip that was feeding into the needle in Melissa's hand, a drop at a time.

Melissa said nothing. She felt really scared. Her parents were grim-faced on either side of her bed. What would happen if she had a heart attack? She could die. She wasn't in control of this any more. Her body had let her down. She lay back against the pillows, furious. Just when she had been doing so well. At least she didn't feel so weak any more. She could hear someone in the next cubicle puking and, further along, a child was crying, 'I want to go home. I want to go home.'

Melissa knew exactly how she felt. She wanted to get out of here as quickly as she could, but she'd been told she wouldn't be allowed home until they were satisfied that her potassium levels were sufficiently up. She could be in A&E for hours.

'Melissa, this has to stop,' Aimee said sternly when the nurse had gone, swishing the curtains closed behind her. 'I want you to eat that tea and toast they want you to have.'

'Mom, I don't feel hungry,' she said desperately.

'Melissa, you are well on the way to ruining your life – you heard what the nurse and doctors have been saying to you.' Barry tried to reason with her.

'I just don't feel hungry,' she repeated. She wasn't lying either. She felt she'd choke if she had to eat anything.

'Melissa, you're going to end up staying in hospital. Is that what you want?' Aimee demanded.

Melissa burst into tears. This wasn't the way it was supposed to be. Barry took her hand. 'Stop crying, Muffin,' he said, using his pet name for her. 'We'll get you sorted.'

'We're only worried about you, darling.' Aimee took her other hand in hers and stroked it tenderly. We're all worried about you. Poor Sarah was in tears on the phone, and she says to tell you she sends her love.'

This, and their kindness, only made her cry harder.

On way home, everythin ok. Talk 2 moro. Tks 4 text. Sorry I was a bitch. Mxxxxxxxx

Sarah felt a wave of relief wash over her as she read Melissa's text. It was brilliant that she was on the way home from hospital. She'd spent the day imagining one dreadful scenario after another. She'd Googled anorexia when she'd come home and what she'd read had terrified her even more.

The relief when her phone had tinkled to let her know she had a message, and then seeing Melissa's name and not Aimee's, had been indescribable. Their friendship was back on track again. Melissa had even apologized.

She replied, utterly relieved that a long and very worrying day was almost over:

Really glad ur home. Have a good rest. Love u. Sxxx

'Oh Lord, what a day.' Aimee sat, shattered, at the kitchen counter and picked at the chicken salad Barry had prepared for them. It was nine thirty, and Melissa was tucked up in bed, having fallen asleep almost straight away, she was so exhausted. It was after eight when she'd been discharged from the A&E. They had been told that Melissa needed specialist care, urgently. Aimee had phoned the consultant that Dr Burke had referred her to and they had an appointment for the following Friday.

'Well, at least she's going to be in the hands of the professionals. We won't be struggling on our own with her.' Barry poured a glass of white wine and looked at Aimee questioningly, bottle raised.

'No, I don't think so.' She shook her head.

'Did you reschedule your . . . your trip to London yet?' Barry took a mouthful of the welcome chilled wine and hungrily ate some chicken.

'That's another thing.' Aimee rubbed her eyes tiredly. 'When we were at lunch the other day, Melissa told me she was looking forward to being "the older sister" to the new baby. You can imagine how I felt when I heard that.'

'It might give her something to get well for,' Barry mused, and then remembered that Aimee had other plans for their unborn child.

'I know. How am I going to be able to go to London and have a termination having heard that, especially with the day we've put in?'

'Don't let it sway you if it's not what you want,' he said steadily, although it broke his heart to say it.

'Thanks,' she said quietly. 'I did actually go as far as dialling the number to reschedule, but I couldn't. Roger was adamant I take maternity leave. He has no issues with me being pregnant, even though it's the worst possible time in terms of a business start-up. Melissa's looking forward to me having it, you want it, and I suppose, now that the initial shock has worn off, I've got used to being pregnant. I knew I could have drunk coffee and wine any time these past few days since I'd got a date for the termination, but somehow I couldn't indulge. What does that say?' she asked wryly. 'Since our chat over lunch, I just keep seeing Melissa holding it. Maybe it will give her something to focus on in her battle to get well. And even though I've been a bit annoyed with Debbie these past months, it is nice to see the pleasure Melissa gets from their relationship. She really enjoyed going to the pictures with her the other evening.'

'I know – that gives me great happiness too,' Barry admitted. 'And honestly, Debbie's a good kid when you get to know her, she just had a much harder time growing up than Melissa has had. I wish you'd mend fences, Aimee. At the end of the day, family is more important than anything and, right now, we need everyone on board to help Melissa get through this. Are you *absolutely* sure you want to keep the baby? It really is your choice, and I mean that.'

'Maybe it's meant to be. Maybe this child has to be born to help Melissa, so yes, I'm not going to go to London. I just couldn't.' Aimee started to cry, and as he put his arms around her, Barry felt his own cheeks wet with tears as he realized that the child he wanted so badly was the one bright shining light in all their lives, and that bright light was not going to be extinguished in some cold, sterile clinic far from home.

CHAPTER FOURTEEN

Tom Baxter was not in good form. A letter in the post had informed him that his son's private-school fees were going up the following January. And he'd got an update he'd requested on his investment portfolio which did not make for good reading. To crown it all, his sister Cecily had mentioned to his wife in one of their interminable phone conversations that she had been to visit their mother and Judith, and that Lily was getting some sort of building work done. He hadn't been informed about that.

This was Judith's doing, he seethed. She probably had Lily spending a fortune on the house. She'd have their inheritance spent. He cursed explosively as a woman driver cut across him just shading the red light at Botanic Avenue and causing him to hit the brakes. 'Lane jumper,' he roared, shaking his fist, but she had taken the right turn down Richmond Road without a backward glance. 'Bloody women drivers,' he muttered as he took the left turn to get to Lily's. From out of nowhere, childhood memories that he thought he'd outgrown or at least buried deeply in the recesses of his mind smacked him hard in his gut. Maybe it was the time of year, settling back at school, leaves in free fall, a chill in the breeze, the long days of summer a diminishing memory. Tom sighed, remembering how he'd felt when he was ten years old going home after school, his satchel a lead weight on his back, wondering would his mother be in bed, huddled up in a ball under her quilts, her eyes big and agitated as she told him not to make too much noise. If she was having a good day there would be a dinner cooked. On very bad days, he'd rummage for food for himself and Cecily, waiting until Judith came home from secondary school to cook their dinner.

He'd always envied his pals racing home to feast on dinners and cakes and scones their mothers had made to have ready for them. He envied them that they could bring friends home to play in their homes and gardens. Lily's 'nerves' had been too bad for her to have to listen to the noise of rowdy boys playing boisterously and so his house was off limits. All he'd wanted was to be like the other boys, and to have a mother who was fun to be with, and who didn't mind if you played with your friends in the house – a mother who didn't behave oddly and spend a lot of her life in bed.

When their dad had died, Lily had taken to the bed almost permanently and he'd hated coming to visit, because he'd left home by then. He remembered the sun trying to stream through closed curtains on a hot, airless, sunny Sunday afternoon and Judith, bad-tempered, clattering pots around downstairs in the kitchen, washing up after the Sunday lunch that Lily might barely have picked at. He remembered the relief of saying good-bye and giving Lily a brief peck on the cheek before leaving, getting back out into the fresh air after the visit, knowing he'd have a week's respite before he had to call again. Tom gave a little shiver, dampening down those lonesome memories that made him feel strangely vulnerable. That was a long time ago. What in the name of God was he doing revisiting those miserable times?

He drove slowly down the tree-lined street, noting the skip outside his mother's gate. His lips narrowed into a thin line as the familiar irritation where his mother and sister were concerned returned. Lily was as cute as a fox and Judith was no better. He had visited them less than a month ago and neither had said a word about any renovations. Sly, that was what they were. As sly as bedamned. The house looked well kept, he thought absently, pulling up outside the gate. Pink and yellow roses still bloomed in the mulched bed under the window. To give Judith her due, she kept the place very ship-shape. He gave a sharp bang on the gleaming door knocker. He could hear the sound of a Kango hammer coming from the rear of the house.

Lily opened the door to him. 'Hello, Tom. I wasn't expecting you,' she said matter-of-factly, stepping back to allow him to enter. She was wearing a lilac blouse, decorated by a brooch his father had given her, and a green tweed skirt. She looked very smart. She had always been particular about her appearance, except for the times she had taken to the bed, when she'd been dishevelled and unkempt. There'd been a lot of that when he was growing up, he remembered. He followed her into the hall and felt the welcome warmth of the house. It was a chilly day; the breeze would slice through you despite the sunshine and clear blue skies.

'What's going on here?' He toned down his bad humour with difficulty. Lily was prickly; she didn't take kindly to what she had once called his 'interference'.

'I'm getting a job done,' she informed him briskly, and he could see by the look in her beady blue eyes she was daring him to make an issue of it.

'And what's that, Mother, or dare I ask?' He couldn't keep the irritation out of his voice. He shoved his hands in his trouser pockets and followed her into the kitchen. His jaw dropped when he saw the floor-to-ceiling French door where the old wooden and glass back door had been. It changed the room totally and gave it a completely different air, even though nothing else had been done to the small, compact kitchen. Light flooded in, enhancing the honey tones of the wooden floor and spreading brightness into every corner of the room. 'Very nice.' He gave his reluctant approval. 'Thick glass.'

'Triple glaze. I was advised it was the best,' Lily said knowledgeably. 'I'm thinking I might even do the same kind of thing in the back room and have it all glass, like they do on those TV programmes. And some cane furniture would look good in it. It's about time I did something with the house. I might as well enjoy it for the years I have left. Your father would be pleased,' she said, almost to herself. 'He liked bright rooms.'

'Good God, that will cost a fortune, Ma. Triple glazing on floor-to-ceiling windows! And how much is all this costing?' He couldn't contain himself. Was she gone barmy, spending all around her when for all she knew she might end up in a nursing home and need her savings to keep her?

'Sure, what matter what the cost is, Tom?' Lily smiled sweetly and patted him on the arm. 'I have the money and, as the old saying goes, you can't take it with you. There are no pockets in a shroud.' Was Lily smirking at him? he thought, disconcerted.

'I suppose this was Judith's idea,' he said sourly, shocked at what he was hearing. Had his mother lost some of her marbles? Was it the onset of dementia or something like that? There were illnesses that made people do irrational things and spend money like it was going out of fashion. There had to be something behind all this most uncharacteristic behaviour.

'No, it was actually Cecily's idea to do the back room, but Judith gave me great encouragement to "Go for it," as she said herself,' Lily said firmly.

She would, she'll reap the benefit of all this, living here like a lady, with no expenses, Tom fumed. 'Where is she, anyway? I didn't think she was going back to work for another couple of weeks.'

'She has an appointment in Dun Laoghaire and won't be back until this evening.' Lily picked up a cloth and began to wipe the fine dust off the countertop.

'What's going on outside?' He peered out into the garden, where a lanky, thin man wearing earmuffs was drilling into the concrete yard.

'I'm treating myself to a patio, Tom. It will be very pleasant to have somewhere nice and peaceful to sit in the summer afternoons and evenings. I'm hoping to have a water feature and a pergola to enhance it. Would you like a cup of tea?' Still the matter-of-fact tone. Was he dreaming? Tom wondered. This was surreal.

'Eh . . . I suppose I could, seeing as I'm here,' he said. 'I'll go out and have a look and make sure he's doing a proper job out there. I hope you got a few quotes and that this fella isn't ripping you off.' Tom put his hand on the handle of the new door to slide it open.

'Indeed you won't,' his mother declared authoritatively. 'He's doing a grand job, there's no need for any inspection, and I was more than satisfied with the quote I was given.'

'And what do you know about building work and quotes?' he sneered.

'I know enough to know that the person I picked to do the job knows what he's doing and is very, very dependable, and that's enough for me, mister,' Lily said snippily. 'Now I want you to do something else for me while you're here. And I'll have the tea for you when you're finished.' Tom stared at his mother. It was as though he hardly knew her any more. She'd always been bossy, but never confident. She'd always seemed bowed down by her cares and worries, shoulders slumped, working her hands together agitatedly. Now she was bright-eyed, upright, still wiry, but full of energy. Her transformation since Judith's accident was unbelievable. She would never in a million years have dealt with a builder by herself previous to this.

'What do you want me to do?' he said warily, rattled.

'Would you ever bring the car down to the supermarket and get these few things for me. They're heavy, you see – washing powders, bottled water, cleaning liquids: I have a list here. Judith would get them, but I don't like to see her pushing big trolleys and lifting heavy bags. She still has pain, especially if she over-does things.' Lily took a sheet of paper off the kitchen table and pressed it into his hand. 'And I'll have a slice of that lemon cake that you're partial to for you when you get back.'

For crying out loud, he yelled silently. He didn't have time to be doing supermarket shopping. He had a business to run. What did his mother think, that he did nothing all day? He took the list, written in her elegant script, and stomped out the door.

Why couldn't Judith buy one heavy item at a time when she was doing the shopping? She was a bloody lady of leisure still. She was having a grand old time of it, off work on full pay, no mortgage repayments. And letting their mother spend a fortune on the house while she'd enjoy the benefits. Triple-glazed floor-to-ceiling windows indeed! There'd probably be new wooden floors to replace the old carpet, and new curtains to go with the new cane furniture. Oh, she was a cute one, all right, Tom raged as he got into the car and did a three-point turn on the narrow street of neat redbrick houses where he'd grown up.

Miss Judith was playing a very, very clever game indeed. He'd never known his mother to sit out in the garden at any stage of her life. It was Judith who would be sunning herself on this damned new patio with pergolas and water features. It was far from pergolas and water features she was reared, he thought wrathfully as he drove past the library to emerge on to the Drumcondra road.

This day was going from bad to worse. There was no doubt about it.

Lily chuckled to herself as she watched Tom wrestling with the steering wheel, twisting this way and that turning the BMW on the narrow street. That would cool his porridge for him, she thought, highly entertained at the fast one she'd pulled on him. She'd known as sure as eggs were eggs that she'd have a visit from her son at some stage once his sister Cecily had told him about the renovations.

Cecily had come to visit at the weekend and been as surprised as her sibling at what was going on in her old home. She'd been surprisingly positive about the makeover, though, and it was *she* who had put the thought into Lily's head about getting the back room done. In fairness to her younger daughter, she didn't go on as much about Lily spending money as Tom did. And she had offered to drive Lily and Judith to the big furniture stores out in Navan if they were refurbishing the rooms. She'd even told Judith of a place that, although a pit pricey, did lovely garden furniture.

The two sisters were actually getting on much better since Judith's accident, Lily was glad to see. Cecily had been very shocked by the accident and Judith's subsequent coma, and she was now making much more of an effort. They should invite Cecily to lunch on their next day out, Lily thought. It would be good to strengthen family ties. They would be three ladies who lunched on the jaunt to Navan.

She had been right on the button about Tom's visit though. And that was why she'd had her list of shopping prepared. He got off lightly and had done for years; it wouldn't kill him in the slightest to run around the supermarket down the road. She filled the kettle. She'd make him put everything away too, before Judith got back. She hoped her daughter was having a relaxing time at the healing woman she was going to. Judith had been waiting a good while for the appointment and had been looking forward to the session. Lily would be most interested to hear how she got on. She'd almost be tempted to go herself. Judith had decided to drive to Dun Laoghaire, and Lily knew driving was still an ordeal for her daughter. She paused from her tea making and looked heavenwards. She wanted someone *special* to take care of Judith today.

'St Joseph,' she prayed, to another of her favourite saints, 'sit beside our precious Judith in the car and give her confidence and, while you're at it, I know she's lonely. If you could find her a good man, someone like my Ted, I'd be very obliged to you. Thank you for your kindness.' She bowed her head. Lily was very impressed with St Joseph. He'd done her many favours and she thought he was a good manly sort of saint who had no nonsense about him. And he was like her Ted, a carer. Had he not taken wonderful care of Mary and Jesus? Lily sighed. The saints had been her sustenance all her life. She would never stop asking them for help.

She took the lemon cake out of the cake tin and cut a slightly bigger wedge than normal for her put-upon son. She did give him a hard time, she supposed. He was possibly the most like her, she thought with a little shock of awareness. Both of them had that streak of self-centredness that she was doing her best to eradicate in herself. There were times too, when she was quite certain that when her time came to depart the mortal life, not one tear would be shed by him at her grave. And that had to be the fault of her parenting, she thought regretfully. Lily gave a another sigh. That was the way of it with families sometimes. The Baxters had never been the Waltons, and they never would be. A bigger slice of lemon cake than normal was the best she could do for Tom at the moment. It was better than a kick in the rear, Lily decided, replacing the cake in the tin.

CHAPTER FIFTEEN

Judith sat in a small, windowless waiting room, decorated in blue and gold, incense wafting around her. It was a peaceful room, with a statue of a laughing Buddha, one of Jesus, and a picture of an Indian woman with a red dot on her forehead on a small round table with a white cloth draping in folds around it. Small night-lights burned brightly to the front and the table-top was covered in rose petals. Soft piano music played in the background. A selection of magazines was placed neatly on the low coffee table in front of her. *Kindred, Paradigm Shift, Spirit* – they all seemed of an esoteric and spiritual nature.

Judith flicked through one of them. People were increasingly interested in this type of stuff now, she mused. Jillian, her best friend, was a real convert. She read this type of material and very much enjoyed it. Jillian believed that souls came to earth to learn lessons, that life on earth was like being at school and that the real home was in the spirit world, or heaven, as they had been taught as children. The harder the life, the greater the lesson and reward, seemingly. It was an interesting concept, to be sure, and if she applied it to her own situation Judith could see that it had taken her car crash to bring her to the realization that life was about choices and how you reacted to situations rather than the situations themselves. She was deeply engrossed in an article about past lives when a small, dark-haired woman opened the door and held out her hand in greeting.

'Judith. I'm Sheeva de Burca, welcome. Could I offer you a cup of herbal tea? I don't give my clients caffeine before a treatment.'

'That would be very nice, thank you,' Judith agreed politely, although she didn't particularly like herbal teas.

'I won't be a jiffy.' Sheeva smiled. She could have been any age between fifty and seventy, Judith decided. Her skin was clear and translucent, her hazel eyes bright and friendly. She wore a flowing red kaftan over white trousers, and her hair was piled high on her head in a top knot that looked as though it would fall apart and come tumbling down any minute. It had to be dyed. It had that orange, hennaed look about it. She spoke with a foreign accent.

'Now, let's settle ourselves down for a chat.' Sheeva came back a few minutes later with two cups of herbal tea in fine bone china and a plate of rice cakes on a gold tray. She busied herself placing the cups and rice cakes in front of them and then, to Judith's surprise, sat on the floor with her legs folded up under her as if she were about to go into a meditation. She was lithe and agile and Judith envied her her physicality.

'Is Sheeva an Irish name? I never came across it before,' asked Judith, curious about the other woman's background.

'Oh no, my birth name is Monique, but I was told by Spirit in deep meditation one day that I was the reincarnation of the Celtic goddess Sheeva and that I was to use that name henceforth. I'm French by birth but I'm married to an Irishman.' Sheeva handed her a cup of green, sweet-smelling tea.

'Oh, I see,' Judith murmured nonplussed. She'd never encountered anyone like Sheeva before and wasn't at all sure what she was letting herself in for.

'Now what I like to do is have a chat with you, get to know a little of your background,' Sheeva said briskly, getting down to the business at hand. 'I like to see what might be holding you back, blocking you, or what issues might be causing you concern. Then, when I have an overall picture, I'll bring you into my healing room and I'll explain the treatment to you before I begin.'

'That's sounds—'

'A moment!' Sheeva interrupted her and held up her hand, imperiously studying Judith intently. 'Your aura is a little shaky, we may need to do some grounding exercises.' She waved her hands expressively in the air and then let them flutter down into her lap.

'Fine.' Judith was willing to give it a bash. This woman had a two-month waiting list: she must be good – if a little intense.

'So tell me about yourself,' Sheeva invited. 'Start with family, husband, children, parents, siblings, and tell me about your work if you have a career, and so on.'

'Well, I'm not married, and I don't have children. My father is dead, and I live with my mother,' Judith began, thinking how sad and lame it sounded at fifty years of age still to be tied to her mother's apron strings, manless and childless.

'And is this by choice?' Sheeva probed perceptively.

'For a long time, not really.' Judith sighed and haltingly gave the woman on the floor a brief synopsis of her life thus far.

'Hmmm. Family issues, feelings of unworthiness, lack of confidence, loneliness, anger, resentment, deep, deep hurt. A lot to work on,' Sheeva remarked kindly. 'You have chosen your pain, emotional and physical, to help you grow—'

'I chose this!' Judith interjected, shocked.

'Indeed. We choose all our growth opportunities. It is bringing you to awareness. It was the only way the "I", your true self, could connect with you to get your attention,' Sheeva said airily. 'Tell me, did you ever consider that perhaps you chose the family you were born into? That you chose your parents, and siblings?'

'Er ... no ... no, I hadn't actually thought of it like that,' Judith admitted, somewhat at a loss.

'You see, we've been here many, many times and we usually choose the soul group we come back to. Have you ever felt you knew someone even though you'd just met them?' Sheeva waved her hands again before dropping them back down to her lap.

'Er . . . yes, sometimes.'

'Past lives, my dear, past lives. You never lose the connection. You and your mother have been together many times. She will have been your daughter in another life and you will have been the mother. She will have been your father, husband, sister, lover. All the roles have been played out in the wonderful karmic dance we choose.'

That sounded a bit far-fetched, Judith thought sceptically.

'You and she are playing out a karmic dance. You are teaching each other unconditional love – the whole *raison d'être* for our being here. You see, my dear, you may have spent all those years looking after your mother, but it was time wasted. Filled with anger and resentment. If it is not done with love' – Sheeva pronounced it *loff* – 'if it is not done with *loff*,' she repeated, her hands thrown palm-up to the heavens, 'it is no use. None whatsoever.'

'But what was I supposed to do? Leave her? She was in such a state when my father died she couldn't look after herself,' Judith protested.

'You gained no benefit from it. Neither did she.'

'But she was looked after. Who else would have done it?' Judith's voice rose an octave.

'Someone would have come.' Sheeva was unperturbed by Judith's indignation. 'We are responsible for no one but ourselves.'

'Who? A stranger? My brother and sister certainly weren't volunteering,' Judith snapped irritably. Was this one for the birds? she wondered, angry that her sacrifice on Lily's behalf had been so summarily dismissed. And how could she sit there and make pronouncements like 'We are responsible for no one but ourselves.' What planet was she on? Mars?

'The Universe always provides,' Sheeva said equably.

'Well, I don't agree with you at all,' Judith said, incensed.

'What about all the people who are neglected? What about people who live alone and have no one? What about the homeless? What about all the carers who have elderly parents to look after and need respite and don't get it? When does the "Universe", as you call it, provide for them? What about the sick and disabled? Someone has to be responsible for them. That's a *ridiculous* thing to say!' She couldn't hide the note of angry sarcasm that crept into her tone. Just like the Judith of old, she thought crossly.

'Interesting response, Judith. I have touched a nerve. This is good. Very, very good.' Sheeva was completely unruffled by her hostility. 'Express your anger, your hostility. Verbalize it. Let it out and let it go. Release. Release. Release it to the Universe.' She waved her hands skyward in a circular motion. 'Your relationship with your mother will be so much better. It will be one of *loff*!' Sheeva gazed heavenward in ecstasy.

'You didn't answer my question,' Judith pointed out.

'Still the anger. Let go, let go,' Sheeva urged.

'You're avoiding the question,' Judith repeated, determined to get an answer and not to be fobbed off with airy-fairy balderdash.

'You know, it is so necessary to trust. Trust the Universe, my dear, and in the twinkling of an eye all will be healed. Release control, take your hands off, don't block and you will see outcomes you never dreamed of. People cannot blame the Universe if they don't stand back and allow the great plan to unfold. People must take responsibility for blocking the gifts that Spirit wants us to have. People must take responsibility for manifesting lack and—'

'You know, I'm not sure if this is what I'm looking for,' Judith retorted, standing up. 'I didn't come here to be told everything is all my fault, when I was only trying to do my best. I don't want to be in pain and, as you say, "grow". How can you "grow" through pain? And I don't think it's a good thing to be ladling guilt on to people's shoulders. I think your premise is unreasonable.' She felt like saying it was barking mad but restrained herself.

'Aahh, not quite ready yet. Not *quite* evolved enough. But you're getting there, Judith. You have taken the first tentative steps. The fact that you came to me proves that. You'll be back.' Sheeva jumped up from the floor, and Judith, again, had to marvel at her agility.

'How much do I owe you?' she asked stiffly.

'Well, I have to charge you for my time, I'm sure you understand. It's all about energy, giving and receiving. I won't charge you for the treatment, although, you'll appreciate, this session is now of no use to anyone else. Seventy-five euros will cover it.' Sheeva joined her hands together and bowed her head.

Let me out of here, thought Judith, extracting the notes from her purse.

'*Namaste*.' Sheeva palmed them and put them in her pocket under the flowing kaftan in a swift, fluid movement that would have impressed Fagin.

'*Loff* and Light, Judith,' she warbled as she closed the door behind her.

'*Loff* and Light yourself,' Judith muttered. That woman had some nerve telling her that all she had sacrificed for her mother had been in vain because, according to her, she hadn't done it with *loff*. If she hadn't loved Lily at some level, she would have abandoned her. All right, she hadn't been all sweetness and light and things had been difficult between them, she'd concede that point, she argued furiously with herself as she walked down the garden path where dancing leaves whirled like dervishes around her ankles. But the nonsense of leaving it to the Universe and some stranger coming to look after her mother was just one step too far to accept. And Sheeva had neatly sidestepped the question about the homeless and carers and the sick and disabled by throwing it back at Judith and telling her to let go of her anger. The daft woman couldn't see that it was Sheeva and her nonsense that had made Judith angry.

Well, that was an afternoon wasted, she thought crossly as she made her way down Marine Road and took the short cut through the Royal Marine Hotel to get to the car park.

Her stomach growled. She had only had a Ryvita and banana for her lunch and she was peckish. She didn't want a full meal, but a cup of coffee and a Danish would be nice, she decided. It would keep her going for the journey home. Instead of turning right for the car park, she carried on the few yards to the coffee shop. As she walked up the stairs of Costa, still highly annoyed at her encounter with the ethereal Sheeva, she almost bumped into a young girl who was about to descend.

'Sorry, I beg your pardon,' she apologized, and saw with a sudden, lurching shock that Debbie Kinsella was standing behind the teenager.

'Oh, oh! Hello, Debbie,' she managed. Judith was painfully aware that the last time she had seen the younger woman was when she was in hospital and looking her very worst, in her bed-clothes and with no make-up. It had been a bruising encounter. Debbie had accused Judith of bullying her at work, and she had been right. Judith could not deny she was guilty as charged. Of all the people to have to walk into, why did it have to be her? Judith groaned inwardly.

Debbie looked equally disconcerted to see her.

'Hello, Judith. How are you keeping?' she asked politely.

She looked pale, tired and stressed, Judith noted in surprise. Not how she would have expected a happy newly-wed to look.

'I'm doing OK,' Judith said awkwardly. 'Getting there.'

'I took time in lieu, that's how—'

'Oh Debbie, it's fine. I'm not your boss today,' Judith said hastily, taken aback that the younger woman felt she had to explain why she wasn't working on a weekday.

'This is my sister, Melissa.' Debbie introduced the teenager, a thin young girl with an unhealthy pallor and very dark circles under her eyes. 'Judith is my boss. She had a very bad accident around the time of our wedding – in fact, she was in a coma,' she explained to Melissa, who held out her hand courteously.

'Nice to meet you,' she said shyly. 'I never met anyone who was in a coma before. Was it scary? Could you hear people and not speak to them? Were you, like, trapped in your body?' She couldn't hide her fascination.

'Melissa!' chided Debbie.

Judith shook Melissa's hand lightly and smiled at the question. 'It's fine, Debbie, people always ask me that when they hear that I was in a coma.' She turned back to Melissa. 'Thank God, nothing like that. I don't remember anything about it, to be honest.'

'Oh. That was good, I guess.'

'Yes, I don't think I'd have liked to have been, as you put it, "trapped in my body".' She made a face. 'So Debbie, everything seems to be going smoothly in Wages and Salaries. I had lunch with Janice a couple of times and all reports are positive.' She had to make some sort of an effort, for politeness' sake.

'Everything's fine. Er . . . Judith. I'd just like to thank you again for . . . for sorting my increment. I sent you a thank-you card. I hope you got it,' Debbie murmured.

'I did indeed, and thank you for the good wishes you expressed in it.' Judith's heart softened at the memory. She had given her young colleague a hard time at work and, in fairness, Debbie had not held it against her. There'd certainly been a lack of *loff* between herself and Debbie, she admitted.

'It's good to see you, Debbie. Your increment was well deserved. And very nice to meet you, Melissa. I won't delay you any longer.' She stepped aside to let them pass down the stairs. 'You can tell the girls to roll out the red carpet in a couple of weeks' time when I'm coming back,' she said with a rare flash of humour, and was pleased when Debbie laughed.

'I'll pass on the message,' she said good-humouredly.

'Bye, Judith.' Melissa turned to smile at her. 'Get well soon.' And then they were gone, clattering down the stairs and out the door.

What an unexpected meeting. And, after the initial awkwardness, rather pleasant, Judith reflected, standing in the queue for coffee.

Melissa was a nice, mannerly young girl. She hadn't realized Debbie had a sister. Certainly, bumping into them had taken the sting out of her episode with Sheeva. She wondered what Sheeva would have had to say about that *particular* occurrence. Just as well she hadn't mentioned anything to her about the bullying accusations. God knows what 'Ms Do-it-with-*loff*' would have made of it, she shuddered, wondering whether to have a doughnut or a Danish. She'd buy a Danish for Lily, who was very fond of the ones with custard in them, and if that wasn't *loff* she didn't know what was, Judith thought with wry humour as she gave her order.

Chapter Sixteen

'I wouldn't like to be in a coma – like how scary would that be? Your boss was lucky she didn't know anything about it,' Melissa remarked to Debbie as they made their way down to the seafront. They were heading for Teddy's, the famous ice-cream parlour. Debbie always treated herself to a 99 if she was in the vicinity of, as she termed it, 'The Occasion of Sin'.

She wasn't expecting Melissa to join her in indulging. Her half-sister had flatly refused to have anything to eat with her black coffee, no matter how hard Debbie had tried to persuade her. She'd been shocked when she'd seen Melissa. She was still clearly losing weight, even after the hospital episode. It didn't seem to have had any impact on her at all. Barry had told Debbie that they were waiting to see a consultant who specialized in eating disorders the following week, and seeing her half-sister's scrawny appearance, the visit couldn't come soon enough.

'You know, Mellie, people who aren't eating properly and develop anorexia can end up in comas—'

'Oh, for God's sake, Debbie, *please* don't lecture me. I get enough of that at home. I *don't* have anorexia. I wish you and Sarah would stop saying things like that,' her half-sister said grumpily. 'I'm just watching what I eat. How would you like it if I said you shouldn't be eating ice cream? I don't tell you what to eat, so you don't tell me, OK!'

'I'm just worried about you,' Debbie snapped irritably.

'There's nothing to worry about. Honest! What's your boss like?' She changed the subject.

'She was a bit of a wagon actually, and she gave me a hard time at work coming up to the wedding, but she seems to have calmed down a lot. She was quite nice today. She nearly died in that car crash.'

'Maybe she had a near-death experience and was told to start being nice to people,' Melissa speculated. 'I saw a programme on TV about them, it was cool.'

Yeah, well, you'll be having a near-death experience yourself if you don't cop on to yourself soon, Debbie was tempted to say, but she refrained. She was like a demon today, for several reasons, Bryan's laziness being one, closely followed by a severe dose of PMT.

Her husband was driving her mad. He had done nothing to try and find part-time work on the two days he wasn't working, and neither had he improved his housekeeping skills. The gardens were in dire need of attention, the weeds were growing as dense as the forest of Arden around the small shed in the back garden, and there was no sign of his great plan to paint all the interior walls off-white so he could hang the various paintings they'd acquired. Of course he was insisting on Farrow & Ball, like they could afford it, in their current economic crisis, thought Debbie bitterly, wrapping her coat tighter around her. A chill breeze blew in off the sea, whipping her hair around her face. She was so fed up nagging him, it was driving a wedge between them, but why could he not see that his enforced two days off work were not an excuse to spend all day in IMMA and other art galleries, or going to avant-garde films in the IFC and discussing their merits and demerits with other film-goers who shared his interest and who weren't working either?

He was having a wonderful time, and she was slaving away at

work and trying to keep the house in some sort of presentable shape.

The trouble was, he'd given up on their home, she thought sadly. He wanted to be rid of it. It was a millstone around their necks, as far as he was concerned, and whatever appreciation he'd had for it when they'd bought it first had diminished so much that it was practically non-existent. But there was no way they were going to be able to sell it and get what they'd paid for it, and she felt they should try and stick it out until the markets rose again in a few years' time. The recession wouldn't last for ever, but trying to explain that to him was like banging her head off a brick wall. Bryan just didn't want to know.

'Are you having a 99?' she asked Melissa when they got to Teddy's, although she figured it was a pointless exercise. She'd been longing for one of their orgasmic creamy ice creams all day.

'Um . . . no thanks,' her half-sister muttered.

She couldn't even enjoy her ice cream in peace, Debbie thought crossly when the girl behind the counter handed her the cone. It had been the same in Costa when she'd been eating her Danish. She'd almost felt guilty eating it in front of Melissa, sitting opposite her taking small sips of coffee, warming her hands around the cup and casting longing glances at the pastry. 'You don't know what you're missing,' she said, and shrugged, licking around the chocolate flake.

'A minute on the lips, a lifetime on the hips,' countered Melissa brightly.

'Melissa, if you're not careful I'll dunk you in the sea,' Debbie retorted. 'I've got a serious case of PMT.'

'Yeah, you're very crabby all right, but I forgive you.' Melissa gave her a dig in the ribs. They smiled at each other.

'Have a lick, just one,' Debbie urged, holding out the cone.

'Just for you, I will,' said Melissa, taking the tiniest lick and savouring it.

That sight, more than any other thing that was going on in her life, made her want to cry, Debbie felt, struggling not to burst into tears and cursing the PMT that had her hormones all awry.

'She's doing my head in, Ma, I just can't take much more of it. Debbie just won't listen to reason about selling the house. We can't afford it and that's all. That's about it, and I think we should cut our losses and run, but she won't hear of it. She wants to decorate the place. She's always going on about it, but what's the point if we're going to sell up? It's throwing good money after bad, money we don't have,' Bryan whinged, tucking into a plate of scallops cooked just the way he liked them.

'That's *terrible*, son,' Brona declared, handing him a basket of buttered homemade brown bread. 'After all, you've been put on short time. Debbie should be more reasonable.'

'*Exactly*, Ma. It's not easy, and it's not finished yet,' he said gloomily, dipping his bread into the white wine and butter sauce that Brona had made to accompany the scallops. 'There's talk of more redundancies.'

'Don't worry, love, your father and I won't let you starve. I told you before, there's plenty of room for you both here if you want to come home.' Brona patted his arm sympathetically.

'I don't know if Debbie would agree to that,' Bryan murmured. He didn't want to come back home to live under his parents' roof under any circumstances, he'd gone far beyond living at home, but of course he couldn't say that to his mother.

'Well now, Bryan, you might just have to put your foot down with her. I know she's your wife and everything and, far be it from me to interfere' – Brona pursed her lips – 'but she can't have it *all* her own way.'

'We'll see.' Bryan sighed heavily, mopping up the rest of the sauce.

'Have another few,' Brona urged, passing some of the scallops on her plate over to his.

'No, no, Ma, eat your scallops,' Bryan protested.

'I've plenty,' his mother assured him. 'And I've your favourite,

homemade Pavlova, in the fridge. When you said you were calling in I made one up for you.'

'Ah, you're the best, Ma,' Bryan exclaimed. 'When all's said
and done, there's no place like home.'

'My sentiments entirely.' Brona beamed at her youngest son,
overwhelmed with love for him.

'Oh, Mum, I'm so worried about Melissa. She looks awful,'
Debbie said to Connie, pausing from slicing mushrooms to go
with the chicken and pasta dish she was making for dinner to
talk to her mother on the house phone. She'd tried to persuade
Melissa to come back home and eat with her and Bryan, but
she'd said that she was meeting up with Sarah to do maths
homework.

'I haven't seen her in a while, I've had to do double shifts
because Fiona broke her wrist, so I haven't brought her to see the
horses. I must give her a ring. I know they're bringing her to
the specialist next week,' Connie said.

'Let's hope she can help, because it's getting serious,' Debbie
said. 'Oh Mum, my mobile is ringing, can I call you back?'

'No, I'm going on a date with my young man. I'll talk to you
tomorrow,' Connie said chirpily.

'Bye, Mum, have fun.' Debbie laughed, hung up and rooted
for her mobile in her bag as the ring tone got louder. She saw
with surprise that her mother-in-law's name was flashing up on
the screen.

'Brona, hi, is anything wrong?' she asked anxiously. She rarely,
if ever, got calls from her mother-in-law.

'Well, yes, actually, Debbie, there is. Now, as you know, I'm
not one to interfere,' Brona said quickly, with a slight tremor to
her voice, and Debbie realized that her mother-in-law was
annoyed about something, to say the least. 'I've had Bryan over
here; actually, he's just left, and he's quite upset about things. In
fact, I don't think you quite appreciate just how upset my son is,'
she carried on. Debbie's jaw dropped in astonishment.

'What's he upset about?' she asked, perplexed. Bryan had been whistling in the bathroom this morning when she was leaving for work.

'Well, Debbie – and I can see his point – he thinks you can't afford to keep your house. He thinks there's no point in decorating if you're going to get rid of it, despite you going on and on about it. You know, he's quite shattered about being put on a three-day week and he's worried that there are more redundancies coming down the line. Now I've told him that the two of you are more than welcome to come and live with us. I think it's something you should give plenty of consideration to,' Brona declared. 'And you should give him some leeway, considering his difficult circumstances. I don't think you quite understand the *pressure* he's under these days.'

Debbie took a deep breath. How *dare* Bryan run blabbing to his precious ma about her, and about their business?

'If you don't mind my saying so, Brona,' she said tightly, 'the fact is we *can* afford the mortgage now, thanks to a very generous loan my dad gave us to pay off our credit cards. Things are going to be tough for a few years, sure, but there's a recession and *everyone* has to tighten their belts. Selling up now would be a crazy move. We'd lose all the money we put into the house and we'd be in negative equity, we'd be ruined financially and we wouldn't have a roof over our heads. We have to ride out the storm, and Bryan's just going to have to deal with it, Brona. He can't run away from everything. Thank you for your offer of accommodation, but it's not necessary.' Her voice was shaking she was so mad.

'Well, I was only trying to help, Debbie, there's no need to take that tone with me,' Brona said snippily.

'Just as a matter of interest, has Bryan eaten with you?' Debbie asked curtly.

'Yes, I fed him,' Brona snapped back.

'Well, it's a pity he wouldn't have the manners to let me know. I'm here making dinner for him,' Debbie retaliated. 'He's off all day visiting art galleries and the like, and I had to come home and make dinner. A bit lopsided, if you ask me, Brona. He's not the only one under pressure. Excuse me, I have to go, the pasta will be overcooked.' She hung up and threw her phone back in her bag. The nerve of her mother-in-law interfering, and how childish of Bryan to go moaning to his mammy! It was time he grew up, she thought in disgust, straining the pasta before pouring it into a serving dish. This was a new low in their marriage.

He arrived home half an hour later and strolled into the lounge, where she was watching a rerun of *Glee*. 'Hi, hon.' He bent down to give her a kiss. 'Something smells nice in the kitchen.'

'I believe you've already eaten,' she said shortly.

'Oh! Yeah, I had a bite to eat at Ma's. How did you know?' He flung himself down on the sofa and stretched out.

'Your mother rang me, Bryan, to tell me you were under pressure and to invite us to go live with them because you think we should sell the house. I don't appreciate you going over there and blabbing all our business to her.' Debbie glowered at him.

'Oh for chrissakes, Debbie, she's my mother – we talk. I bet you talk to Connie about stuff,' he growled.

'Stuff, yeah; our private business, no. I do *not* go to my mother whinging! It's time you copped on to yourself, Bryan, and grew up. Life's tough at the moment and we can't run away from it. Deal with it!' She stalked out to the kitchen leaving him scowling on the sofa.

'I will be dealing with it, babes, and sooner than you think, and we'll see how smart you are then,' he muttered, flicking over to a soccer match on the sports channel.

CHAPTER SEVENTEEN

'So have you any plans for this evening, Connie?' Mrs Mansfield asked after Connie had given her her meds one windy evening as the nights were drawing in.

'I'm having a girls' night with my sister-in-law, Karen, and another friend, Juliet.' Connie locked the medication cabinet and filled in the chart for Jessie, who was doing the nightshift.

'Ah yes, the woman you were telling me about who's getting the renovation so she can have her own space. I do like the sound of her, Connie. A woman of spirit.'

'You're fairly spirited yourself, Mrs M.' Connie grinned, propping a cushion behind her employer's back and placing her thin legs on a cushioned footstool.

'Well, do you know, you have to be, don't you? And in my day, if you weren't, men would walk all over you. I'm reading a fascinating book about Margaret Anna Cusack, or the Nun of Kenmare as she was known; now *she* was a spirited woman. The love of her life died before they could marry and she became a nun and, my goodness, what battles she had to fight with the Church hierarchy. She was a prolific writer, you know. Of course, it was such a patriarchal society then, but she battled those men and didn't give them an inch,' Mrs Mansfield said with relish. 'A woman after my own heart. Your friend Juliet's husband sounds as though he would have enjoyed living in Margaret Anna's time, a touch of the old patriarchy there, I think, from what you've told me.'

'I think you're right.' Connie laughed, picturing Ken Davenport in bishop's robes holding out his hand for his episcopal ring to be kissed. Mrs Mansfield took a keen interest in all her nurses' lives and enjoyed hearing what was going on with them.

'And how is the lovely Drew?' Her periwinkle-blue eyes twinkled. 'He's been neglecting me. He didn't come to visit me this week.'

Connie shrugged. 'I haven't seen much of him either. His ex-wife Marianna's mother crashed the car, and Marianna rang Drew from the States and asked him would he sort it, and he's had to bring Mrs Lynley up to Dublin to see her husband in the Blackrock Clinic a few times, so I'm as deprived as you are, but Marianna's coming back to Ireland at the weekend, so that should free him up,' she said lightly.

'Tsk.' Mrs Mansfield tutted. 'Don't let that one get her claws back into him. She sounds like a demanding little baggage to me, from what I've heard over the years.'

'A perfect description, Mrs M. I'm afraid Marianna takes a lot for granted.' Connie sighed.

'Fight your corner, Connie. Don't let that one take advantage of Drew's kind heart,' her boss counselled.

'I don't feel it's my place to say anything, really. I don't want to start dictating. Drew's his own man, as you well know. And besides, we're still relatively new to our relationship.'

'Mmm . . . I take your point. Nevertheless, she's the type that would walk all over you. Stamp it out early, I say.'

'I'll keep your advice in mind. Sleep well tonight, and enjoy your book.' She leaned down and kissed Mrs Mansfield's creamy, unlined cheek. Her employer had the most perfect peaches-and-cream skin, even in her seventies.

'And you have a good girls' night. I'll be looking forward to hearing all about it.'

'I will.' Connie smiled, closing the door behind her. She could imagine Mrs M. enjoying putting her foot down with Marianna. For all her quiet dignity and her debilitating illness, she was a fairly formidable woman, and Marianna would be hard put to get the better of her. 'Heading off, hon. The boss is fine, reading a book about a spirited woman, so she'll be engrossed in that for a while. Meds done, see you tomorrow. Have to rush, I'm picking Karen up from the station and I'm running late,' she said to the other nurse, who was sitting in the kitchen with her feet up on a chair, drinking coffee and flicking through the latest *Hello!*

Jessie waved the magazine at her. 'I'll keep this for you.'

'Good woman,' said Connie, grabbing a gingernut to keep her going and shivering as the biting northerly wind enveloped her when she left the warmth of the house. She switched her phone from silent walking to the car, disappointed not to have got a text from Drew. She had a day off later in the week and he was going to take her to dinner and stay over and not go into work until late the following morning, and she was *so* looking forward to it.

He was pissed off having to run around after his ex-mother-in-law. There was no point putting him under pressure by complaining about it, but he'd want to be careful for his own sake that it didn't become a habit. It was very convenient for Marianna to have him in Wicklow to turn to now that her parents were ageing. She had some nerve, Connie thought indignantly, especially after the way she had treated him in the past. Drew was a fool to let her get away with it. Anyway, she wasn't going to let it rile her tonight, Connie decided, switching on her full headlights as she emerged on to the pitch-black country road. It was freezing, so she turned on her heater and tapped the CD button on the dash. The strains of Leonard Cohen singing 'I'm Your Man' filled the air, and she sang along, thinking that, less than five months ago, she'd been lonely and single. Not even Marianna Delahunt was going to spoil one second of her time with Drew.

*

'We'll be eating in the dining room and, afterwards, we'll be in the sitting room, so if you don't mind watching TV in your study I'd be obliged.' Juliet moved around the kitchen, preparing her signature Moroccan lamb dish – one of Ken's favourite meals – for her girls' night. The three friends had decided they should each cook a meal at home every couple of weeks and have a catch-up. Eating out in restaurants had become too expensive to be doing it every time they met, they decided pragmatically. It was Juliet's turn to cook tonight, and she thought how relaxing it was cooking for Connie and Karen rather than having the whole dinner-party palaver when she'd cooked for her and Ken's social set. Everything had always had to be just so: the perfect meal, the perfectly dressed table, the wines and champagnes, the brandy and spirits, the cheese boards and petit fours. It had all been quite competitive, worse than *Come Dine With Me*, Juliet reflected as she scattered some flaked almonds and chopped dates into the saffron-flavoured sauce.

'Fine,' clipped her husband. 'I'll just get myself something to eat now. What time are your . . . er . . . guests coming at?'

'Around seven,' Juliet said airily.

'I'll be out of your way by then,' he said heavily, opening the fridge door to take out a Butler's Pantry beef dish and some duchess potatoes.

'If you can wait twenty minutes or so, I can give you a plate of this,' Juliet offered, feeling a tad sorry for him, observing the slump of his shoulders and listening to his gale-force sighs. Ken hesitated, and she could see him mentally deciding whether to carry on with his martyr act or enjoy his favourite meal. 'Sure, you might as well, I know it's your favourite,' she said matter-of-factly, making it easy for him.

'Well, if you insist then, thank you,' he said, replacing the food carton in the fridge. 'I'll get out of your way.' He plodded down the hall to his study and a comforting glass of whiskey.

Juliet hid a smile. 'Insist' indeed! Ken had caved in, just as she knew he would. But it would have been churlish not to offer him some of the food she was cooking, especially when he was very partial to her Moroccan lamb. She wasn't that much of a bitch. There were times lately, especially as her renovation progressed, that she felt the teeniest little bit sorry for him. It wasn't easy having the builders in, although thankfully he wasn't there during the day when the hammering and banging was going on. But still, having walls knocked down and rooms renovated in a way that would change his home completely could not be easy for her husband, no matter what had happened between them. He was quite deflated these days, finally accepting the inevitable, but completely mystified and unable to fully comprehend the reason she had instigated such a dramatic shift in their lives.

She wasn't sorry that she had, Juliet reflected as she grated some Parmesan shavings for the salad that would accompany the main course. Having the prospect of a lovely living space for herself had given her a new lease of life. Released from the tyranny of being the 'consultant's wife' and leaving Ken's grocery shopping and meal planning to their part-time house-keeper, Gina, who was doing an extra couple of hours' work a week, Juliet felt a great sense of relief. For the first time in almost forty-five years, she was living life to suit herself, and loving it. And Ken wasn't doing too badly out of it either, she assured her-self. He wasn't being left completely to his own devices; he didn't have to go out and buy his own loo rolls or anything like that. Juliet smiled at the notion, imagining the lordly Ken Davenport going around a supermarket chucking Kitten Soft loo rolls into a trolley.

The doorbell rang and she hurried out to greet Connie and Karen. 'Hello, girls,' she greeted them cheerfully. 'Come in and welcome.'

'Something smells scrumptious.' Connie sniffed appreci-atively, handing Juliet a bottle of Freixenet and a box of Butler's Irish, while Karen waved a bottle of Bailey's and a box of After Eights as they followed her into the kitchen.

'You shouldn't have, girls. Let the feasting and drinking begin. I have a bottle of Veuve Clicquot chilling – I wanted to celebrate the first viewing of my new pad.' Juliet led them through a door in the elegant cream and green fitted kitchen to what had once been her breakfast room.

'Oohhh!' Connie exclaimed, looking at the big rectangular room, which had two sets of large French doors.

'I decided not to go for the floor-to-ceiling glass in the end. It would have ruined the look of the house from the outside. It *is* an old house, that's part of its charm, so I stuck with the French doors I have here in the middle of the room and removed a window and put in another set here where the dining area is,' Juliet explained.

'I think you're right, sometimes those big plates of glass from floor to ceiling look very incongruous in period houses,' Connie approved.

'And probably not as expensive to heat the way you've done it now,' Karen added. 'Quite a consideration after the last two winters we've had. My gas bills were double what I usually pay last winter.'

'Absolutely, same here,' Juliet agreed. 'And this will be my little galley kitchen.' She led them into a small, tiled Shaker-style fitted kitchen, complete with hob, microwave, small fridge and mini-dishwasher. 'And this will be my dining area' – she indicated the area beside the kitchen – 'and then, along here' – she moved down the room to where the second set of French doors were – 'I'll have my living and lounging area. And I'm going to have a wood-burning stove, a bit like the one you have in your kitchen, Connie. Even though the house is centrally heated, it will be a cosy focal point in the winter.'

'Oh, I love mine, just chuck in a fire log and you have heat and flames instantly.' Connie peered out the window, where a new patio was being laid.

'The garden is truly lovely. I would have missed it so much if I'd moved. I do think, in a way, this is the best of both worlds and "himself"' – she pointed in the direction of the hall – 'is slowly adapting to the new regime, and I don't have to be worrying about him living here on his own.'

'Well, the best of luck with it,' Connie said warmly.

'And what happens if you're entertaining a toy boy?' Karen teased.

'I'll stick a "Do Not Disturb" sign on the door.' Juliet laughed. 'And chance would be a fine thing. Come on, let's open the bubbly.'

'You'll get no argument from us.' Connie grinned. She and Karen perched on the kitchen stools sipping the champagne while Juliet put the finishing touches to their meal.

How lovely and relaxing it was with her new friends, Juliet thought contentedly, sprinkling a few pine nuts over the salad. Chatting and laughing and tasting and sipping companionably, no topic was off limits: her marriage, Melissa's eating problems, Marianna's utter cheek, Karen's frustration with her job – all were tossed into the melting pot of their conversation over a most enjoyable dinner.

Juliet had one or two other close friends but none that she would have spoken to about her marriage and Ken the way she did with Connie and Karen. They had come into her life at a time when she most needed them and, for that, Juliet counted herself lucky indeed.

Ken listened to the gales of laughter emanating from the dining room, which adjoined his study, and shook his head. That pair that Juliet was hanging around with were the cause of all his trouble, he reckoned. It was since she'd met them that all this upheaval had occurred. That Connie woman had no sense of deference whenever she met him, and he was due *some* regard for his position – but that was nurses for you these days, wanting to be 'on the team', as he'd heard one staff nurse say recently. And the younger consultants were all for it. It was all about 'team work'. They were all watching too much of that *ER* and

Grey's Anatomy type nonsense. Ken scowled, listening to more giddy cackling coming from next door.

Still, at least he'd got his dinner tonight, and very tasty it was too. There was a hint of thaw these past few days, now that Juliet's bloody renovation was happening. His lovely morning room appropriated just like that. It rankled. Still, he supposed Aimee was right: at least his wife was still living under the same roof as him, and he wasn't rattling around the house on his own. And maybe once this bloody revamp was finished and Juliet had her own 'space' downstairs she might change her mind about moving into Aimee's old bedroom and he might be allowed back into the marital bed.

Ken gave a wide yawn and glanced at his watch. Ten forty-five, and they were still yakking away. He was going to bed. His first surgery was at seven thirty the following morning. He had to be needle-sharp. Juliet seemed to have forgotten that patients' lives were in his hands and that the stress she was putting him under had wider implications. He held a beating heart in his hand when he operated; did she not understand the *responsibility* of it? It was a heavy burden to carry at the best of times, Ken thought mournfully, switching off the light, and under no circumstances could these be called the best of times.

CHAPTER EIGHTEEN

'Morning, Caitriona. Morning, Rachel.' Drew greeted his two favourite instructors with a cheery grin. 'Everything OK in the yard?'

'Everything's fine, Drew.' Caitriona smiled back at her boss. 'I took Swift out for a ride, and Frisky's in tip-top form. Mandy Jennings has someone coming to look at White Socks. She's devastated she has to sell him, poor kid.'

'Lots of people are having to sell their children's horses. They can't afford to keep them any more. Tell her she can come and ride Black Magic and do some mucking out on Sundays to keep her hand in,' Drew said briskly. The Jenningses lived in a big pile near Druids Glen, but Dean Jennings's construction business had gone pear-shaped and he owed the banks a fortune. They were hounding him for loan and interest repayments and he was selling off his assets, his daughter's mare included.

'I'll tell her,' Caitriona said. 'You're such a softie,' she added approvingly.

'A softie, me?' He raised an eyebrow at her. 'Naw, I'm as tough as nails. I'm going to tack up Marino and take him for a gallop in Big Tree Meadow, and then we'll get to work on the tack room.'

'Sure, enjoy the ride, it's a perfect day for it. Swift was really giving it a hundred-and-ten per cent.'

'Yep, I'm looking forward to giving Marino his head. You know him, no holding him back.' Drew smiled as he headed into his horse's stall. Twenty minutes later he was galloping across the verdant countryside, the powerful horse beneath him relishing the freedom to run like the wind. They knew each other well and trusted each other implicitly, and as they settled into their rhythm, Drew reflected that his life was the best it had been in years. It really didn't get much better than this, he mused, as the breeze cooled his face and Marino whinnied with joy.

He'd have to get Connie into horseriding; she'd love it, he was sure of it. And how perfect it would be to ride out together early in the morning or late in the evening. It was so nice to have someone to share his life with again. He loved talking to her, loved her sense of humour, which was so in tune with his own, and he loved lying with his arms around her as she snuggled into him after lovemaking, drowsy and contented. All the grief, pain and despair he'd suffered when his ex-wife Marianna had taken their little girls to America all those years ago seemed like a bad dream. The years of loneliness seemed to have happened to someone else. Now he was more alive, more vibrant and happier than at any other time than he could remember, and he sent up a prayer of silent thanks for the miracle that had taken place in his life.

Two hours later, he was at his desk working on his VAT receipts when his mobile phone rang. 'Yes?' he said crisply, rooting under a sheaf of papers for a notepad.

'Drew, Drew,' a woman sobbed into the phone, and he recognized his ex-wife's slightly Americanized tones.

'What's wrong *now*?' He sat up straight, unable to conceal the edge of irritation he felt at hearing her voice on the line. She had been plaguing him for the past month since her mother had crashed the Merc into the side of a bollard in a car park when she'd been doing some shopping. Dorothy Lynley wouldn't drive the replacement Toyota the insurance company had offered, petrified she'd damage it too. Marianna had phoned him from America and begged him to help her out.

'What about your own family, Marianna?' he'd retorted. 'She's managed fine all these years without *my* help,' he added coldly.

'Oh Drew, don't be like that,' his ex-wife had remonstrated. 'Uncle Bert's practically blind, even though he won't stop driving. I couldn't expect him to drive Mama up and down to Dublin. And Phil drinks and drives. I wouldn't trust him behind the wheel. And the nephews and nieces, well, they're not very helpful.' She tailed off.

'Well then, you better get back here, Marianna,' Drew snapped. 'I'm a busy man. I can't be traipsing up and down to Blackrock Clinic. I'll give her a hand out this time, but that's it, Marianna. Sort someone else to step in the next time there's an emergency,' Drew said firmly. 'And I won't be going in to visit your father either, in case you think I will be. That's not on the cards.'

'You're very unforgiving, Drew,' Marianna scolded.

'Yes I am, and I intend to stay that way. You never thought of my poor mother when you took the girls to America, and your father fleeced me in the divorce settlement. So I'm not going to be a hypocrite about it all, that's not who I am,' Drew had barked before hanging up and phoning his ex-mother-in-law to help her sort out her dilemma until Marianna could book a return flight to Ireland. Now his ex-wife was back in the country, and he'd been hoping not to be troubled by her again.

'Drew!' Marianna's increasing sobs brought him back to reality.

'Is something wrong with one of the girls? What *is* it, Marianna?' He felt a sudden fear.

'It's Daddy, he's had another heart attack and they've called us in. We need to get there as soon as we can. Please could you drive us? I just couldn't . . . couldn't concentrate on driving, and Mama's in hysterics. Daddy may be dying,' Marianna wept.

Ah crap! Drew cursed silently. He *loathed* his ex-father-in-law. He couldn't give a toss if Charles Lynley kicked the bucket. Why couldn't Marianna get one of her friends to drive her? He was damned if he was going to do a bedside vigil beside that old coot.

'Are you there, Drew?' Marianna demanded.

'Yes, I'm here,' he said heavily, knowing he couldn't refuse to take his ex and her mother to Dublin. 'I'll be over to you right away.'

'Oh, thank you, Drew, I knew I could depend on you.' Marianna hiccupped.

'See you shortly,' he said and hung up. Typical, he thought angrily, that was what he got for thinking his life was almost perfect earlier. Trust Marianna to come and stick a pin in his balloon. He dialled Connie's mobile but got her voicemail.

'Connie, it's me. Marianna's dad's had another bad heart attack and they've been called in, it looks like the old buzzard isn't going to make it. She's asked me to drive them to Dublin. I couldn't really say no. I might not get to take you to dinner tonight. I'll try you again later. Sorry about this. See ya.'

He grabbed his keys and headed out to the yard grim-faced. If it wasn't for their daughters, he would have had nothing to do with his former wife, and it was because of them and only them he was doing this, but if Marianna felt she could continue to ring him at the drop of a hat when things were going wrong in her life, she could think again. She had a husband, even if he was in America. Let him come over and hold her hand at her father's bedside. Marianna had walked all over him once; he wouldn't be giving her the opportunity to do it again, Drew vowed wrathfully, Old Man Lynley on the way out or no.

Marianna felt a wave of relief watching Drew's dusty Range Rover scorch up the drive; it was more comfortable than the jeep. Her ex-husband was so solid and reliable, especially in a crisis. The traits she'd seen as negatives and dismissed so easily when she'd been unhappy in her marriage were now so comforting and reassuring and just what she craved.

'Mama, Drew's here. Are you ready?' she called up the stairs, where her mother was silently weeping in her bedroom.

'Coming,' Dorothy Lynley quavered as Drew gave a sharp ring on the doorbell.

'Thank you, Drew,' Marianna said quietly when she opened the door to him.

'Are you ready?' he asked coldly.

'Drew, my father may be dying, can't you drop the hostility?' she sighed, her lower lip wobbling.

'I'm very sorry for your troubles, Marianna, I know what it's like to lose parents, that's why I think you should have your husband here to comfort you. That's not my forte, as you well know,' he said dryly. 'We should get going if time is of the essence. Hello, Mrs Lynley,' he said politely as the elderly lady made her way down the stairs.

'Hello, Drew, it's very kind of you to come to our assistance yet again,' Dorothy gulped, trying with difficulty to compose herself. Marianna watched her ex-husband's face soften, the hardness that was so evident when he was interacting with her not so intense when he engaged with her mother. There was an innate kindness in Drew, especially around old people, that came from a lineage of good, kind country stock. Years ago, Marianna had looked down her nose at countryfolk, thinking that she, as a townie, was far more sophisticated and superior to them. Of course, being a solicitor's daughter in a small rural town in those days had meant that she was 'someone' and her parents encouraged the notion that they were, like the doctor, the banker and other 'professionals', the elite of the county. They had been utterly disappointed when she had fallen in love with Drew, who came from 'farming stock' as opposed to the landed gentry they mixed with who had money and land and managers to run their farms. And she had always felt superior to Drew's family, loathing their interminable family gatherings which they seemed to enjoy so much. His mother had welcomed her warmly into the Sullivan clan and put no pass on her airs and graces, much to Marianna's disgust. After all, Marianna felt she was 'someone' and that she should be treated like 'someone', not like the other daughters-in-law, who were quite ordinary and not of the social elite.

Marianna followed Drew and her mother out to the car. She had been a bit of a madam in those years, she admitted silently. And Drew was right. She'd never given his mother or the rest of his family a thought when she'd taken the girls to live in America. Her all-consuming desire to hurt and punish him had affected a lot more people than Drew, she supposed. Marianna frowned. Why was she thinking like this, now of all days? She didn't need to add guilt to grief, she told herself as she watched Drew assist Dorothy with her seatbelt in the front seat.

The journey to Dublin was mostly silent, apart from her ex-husband asking if the heating was sufficiently warm for them and pointing out tissues and a bottle of water in the door pocket should Dorothy require them. As they approached the entrance to the clinic, her mother broke down in tears. Marianna saw Drew silently reach across and squeeze Dorothy's hand and felt a stab of grief that he would never, ever, look upon her with the desire to comfort and console her in her hour of need again. 'I'll let you out here and I'll go and park,' he said, drawing to a halt near the entrance.

'Please come up, Drew,' Marianna entreated, her lower lip wobbling again. She was trying to keep strong for her mother but she was frightened out of her wits; she'd never seen anyone dying before, let alone someone she loved as much as her dear Pops.

'Oh, yes, please, would you, Drew? You've been so kind. I know we don't deserve it and you were angry with Charles, but it's so comforting to have you here.' Dorothy grasped Drew's hand in her thin, bony one. Marianna almost held her breath as she saw the tautness of his jaw and knew he was battling with himself. He had been so adamant to her that he wouldn't come next or near her father.

'I'll be up, Mrs Lynley, just as soon as I park,' he said steadily. 'Go on up, I'll see you there.' He glanced at Marianna in the rear-view mirror.

'Thanks,' she managed, and hurriedly got out of the car, afraid of disgracing herself. She felt absolute terror as she clasped her mother's hand and they hurried up the steps. A white-haired, imposing, handsome man was striding briskly through the doors, and he slowed down when he saw them.

'Mrs Lynley.' He stopped.

'Oh! Professor Davenport. How . . . what . . .' Dorothy stammered. He ushered them inside and stood in front of them to shield them from the gaze of other hospital staff and passers-by.

'Mrs Lynley, Mrs, er . . .' He looked questioningly at Marianna, having forgotten her name.

'Delahunt,' Marianna supplied faintly, noting his sombre expression.

'Ah yes . . . I'm so sorry. There's nothing more I can do. We've given it our best, but his heart is too badly damaged to recover from the last coronary. I'm sorry. It's just a matter of time, but he's in no pain. Actually, my dear, it won't be too long now.' He took Dorothy's small hand in his. 'I've just been with him, and he's as comfortable as we can possibly make him,' the consultant said gently, and it was his quiet timbre rather than his usual booming, stentorian tone that Marianna would always remember in years to come, when she would look back on that dark day and know that that was the moment she realized there truly was no hope.

'Thank you, Professor, I know you did your best,' Dorothy said brokenly, and then burst into fresh tears, burying her face into her laced-edged handkerchief.

'You should go up to him,' Professor Davenport said, giving her a sympathetic pat on the back before taking a deep breath and marching out the door. Marianna took her mother's arm and propelled her along to the lifts. Her heart was thudding against her ribcage. She thought she might be sick. Would it be horrible? Would her father struggle for breath and be in pain as he gasped for air? Would there be the awful death rattle that she had heard about? Would blood come out of his mouth? Would he have a seizure? Would she be able to cope without fainting or being paralysed with fear? All these thoughts raced through her mind as she slowed their pace, reluctant to face what lay ahead.

Drew, Drew, please hurry, she urged silently as they neared her father's room. 'Come on, Mama,' she whispered.

Her mother's shoulders sagged and she came to an abrupt halt. 'I can't go in there. I just can't do it,' Dorothy wailed. 'I'm too frightened.'

'Oh Mama, you can't let Daddy go without at least saying goodbye,' Marianna reproached, and then saw with huge relief Drew striding down the corridor towards them. 'Mama's afraid to go in,' she said in desperation.

'I just can't, Drew. I've loved him all my life, I just can't say goodbye. Professor Davenport said it won't be long, there's no hope,' Dorothy said with mounting hysteria, her eyes beseeching him to give her permission to stay away.

'Yes you can, Mrs Lynley. It's very important that you say goodbye and let him go, so that he can pass easy and that afterwards you won't have regrets, and when you're finished, Marianna and I will sit with him,' Drew said quietly.

'Will you come with me?' She was almost childlike in her pleading.

'Yes I will.' He took her arm and opened the door. Charles Lynley lay underneath pristine sheets, small and shrunken, his eyes closed, face waxy. He hardly seemed to be breathing. A nurse stood up when they entered and gave them a sympathetic smile.

'Mrs Lynley, Mr Lynley is very comfortable. Please don't worry that he's in pain of any sort. We've taken care of that.'

'Can he hear me?' Dorothy trembled, clasping Drew's hand tightly.

'Hearing is the last sense to go,' the nurse said as she moved out of the way to let Dorothy take her place.

'Would you like us to give you some privacy, Mrs Lynley?' Drew asked.

'Just for a minute or two,' she murmured, taking her husband's limp hand in hers and sitting down in the chair the nurse had vacated.

'We'll just be outside the door,' Drew said reassuringly as he shepherded Marianna out, followed by the nurse.

'I can't thank you enough, Drew. I didn't think she'd go in,' Marianna whispered as the nurse moved away.

'I've been by enough deathbeds in my time to know it's important to say goodbye if the opportunity is given to you,' Drew said grimly. 'If she didn't she'd regret it for the rest of her life.'

'But sometimes people don't get the opportunity. Mama didn't get to be with Gran when she died.' Marianna sighed.

'Sometimes people can't go if loved ones are near. It's too hard for them to leave, so they go when they are on their own.'

'How do you know all these things?' She was intrigued.

'My mother was a very wise woman, Marianna. People in the village always called on her when someone was dying. She knew what to do; her mother and grandmother were the same. It was knowledge that passed down through the generations.' Drew folded his arms and leaned against the wall.

'I'm scared of it,' she said, wishing he would put his arm around her or hold her hand like he'd held her mother's.

'Why wouldn't you be? That's natural. Have you told the girls?' He kept his arms resolutely folded.

'Yeah, but I don't know if they can get over in the next few days. Erin is in Los Angeles for some relocation project; I'm sure she told you about it. And you know what they're like in Katy's work. In America work is the Holy Grail and getting time off is next to impossible, and it's expensive. But it would be nice to have them here all the same. Just for the support. I'm finding it very difficult doing it all on my own.'

'I'll pay for their fares if it's a question of money,' he offered diffidently. 'I'll ring them later—'

'I think something's happening, he sounds peculiar.' Dorothy's stricken face appeared at the door, lily-white.

'Oh Jesus!' Marianna grabbed Drew's hand.

'I've said my goodbyes, Drew.' Dorothy stared at him wildly, her brown eyes glazed with grief and fear as she edged past him. Her mascara had run and her slash of red lipstick was vivid in her white face. She reminded him of an ageing film star, in a Piaf, Garland sort of way, he thought, distractedly, as she batted her thin eyelashes in distress.

'Marianna and I will stay with him. Don't worry. You did very well, Mrs Lynley. We'll take over now.' He knew it was what she wanted to hear. He knew she didn't want to be there for the end but she needed permission to leave.

'Why don't you come and have some tea, Mrs Lynley?' A nurse came over from the nurses' station as another two nurses slipped into the room to attend to their dying patient. Drew took Marianna's hand and led her to the bedside.

'Daddy, Daddy, don't go,' Marianna sobbed as her father took a deep, gasping breath.

'Don't say that to him, Marianna,' Drew murmured. 'Don't make it hard for him. This is about him now, give him per-mission to go and don't cry if you can help it,' he urged, tightening his grip on her hand.

'I can't,' she whispered back, tears streaming down her face.

'You *can*. Tell him you love him and let him go in peace.' The authority in Drew's voice made her pause. Marianna took a deep breath.

'Daddy, Daddy, I love you very much. You were a wonderful father. Go if you want to, don't struggle any more,' she managed, taking his wasted hand in hers and kissing his fore-head. Her father gave a gasp, took another long breath and exhaled, and she held Drew's hand so tightly she almost got a cramp. Every other external sound – the clatter of a trolley, a call bell ringing further along the corridor, an ambulance siren in the distance and the drone of a plane's engine overhead – faded, as time seemed to stop, and all she could focus on was her father and the sound of that long-drawn-in breath and the deep exhale. He gave another long, sighing breath. 'Go if you want to, Daddy,' she said, more clearly this time.

'Well done,' Drew praised, rubbing his thumb along the side of her hand, just as her father gave another lingering sigh. She waited for him to inhale again, holding her own breath in anticipation, but a moment later the nurse was by her side. 'He's gone,' she said softly. 'I'm very sorry for your loss. It's two minutes past twelve,' she murmured, glancing at her watch as she stroked Marianna's arm.

'Oh my God, is that it? He's *dead*?' Marianna stared at her father in shock. He looked so peaceful, just as if he were asleep.

'Oh Drew, Daddy's dead!' she cried in disbelief, and buried her face in his chest as his arms tightened around her.

CHAPTER NINETEEN

'Ah, shag it,' Connie cursed when she listened to Drew's message at lunchtime. She'd driven Mrs M. to a dental appointment and had put her phone on silent. Her employer was resting in her room after the ordeal of having had a wisdom tooth removed, her mouth very sore. Connie knew from experience with other patients that it could be two to three weeks before the pain settled down in Mrs Mansfield's jaw. The dentist had put her on a course of antibiotics to prevent infection and Connie took a jar of natural probiotic yogurt out of the fridge to take the chill off it before she gave it to the elderly lady.

She made herself a cup of coffee and stared out at the waterfall of leaves tumbling in graceful flight from the great oak and horse-chestnut trees along the drive, whooshing down in great piles as the wind puffed playfully through the branches. Normally this spectacular autumnal vista evoked pleasure but today her disappointment was so strong Connie hardly noticed.

She'd been so looking forward to her night out with Drew. She had the next day off, and he was taking the morning off. They had planned to go for a walk on the beach later, when she was finished work, before it got dark. Afterwards they were going out to dinner, and then they were coming home to sit in front of the fire for a while to kiss and cuddle and make love, either in the firelight or in bed. They were so eager for each other still and took such delight in each other it was glorious, Connie reflected, smiling. They were still at that sweet juncture in their relationship where they found it hard to believe they had met each other. Connie was old enough and wise enough to know that it wouldn't always be like this – no relationship could ever sustain the intensity of the early months – but she was enjoying it so much she wanted to make the most of every second. And she *was* enjoying every second – or would be, if it wasn't for Drew's ex-wife.

She was getting heartily sick of Marianna Delahunt and her friggin' mother and ailing father, even if he was at death's door, Connie decided crossly, opening the cookie jar and taking out a mini-Crunchie, her absolute favourite.

Over the course of the last month Drew had had to sort out his ex-mother-in-law's damaged car and drive her up and down to Dublin to Blackrock Clinic. Marianna really had some nerve expecting so much of him after the way she had treated Drew during their divorce.

Connie sighed, finished off the Crunchie and took a gingernut out of an open packet and dunked it in her coffee. Irritated as she was by the other woman's behaviour she felt she couldn't really say too much to Drew about it. It was none of her business if he felt he had to help out his ex-wife in a crisis. She was his children's mother, after all. But Connie and Drew's time together was precious and special and it was frustrating and disappointing lately that he'd had to cancel arrangements to do his ex-wife's bidding. That was the way of it with second relationships, she thought gloomily. The ties to the past were never cut completely. There was *always* baggage.

She ate the last of her biscuit, annoyed with herself for reverting to food for comfort, and tried Drew's phone, but it went into voicemail, as she had guessed it would. If Marianna's father was on his last legs and Drew was with them in the hospital, he'd no doubt turned it off. He could be there for hours, days even, she thought grumpily. She was beginning to get pre-period cramps, which, for her, sometimes lasted three or four days. It would be just her luck not to see Drew for a few days and then, when he was free again, Flo would come to town at just the wrong moment. 'You are turning into a nymphomaniac, Connie Adams,' she muttered, grinning in spite of herself. Just when lots of her contemporaries were going *off* sex, she was having a whole new lease of life and couldn't get enough of it.

She wouldn't tell Mrs M. of the latest developments, in case she got another lecture about 'fighting her corner', she decided, rinsing her cup under the tap, straightening her white cap and pouring the yogurt into a small dish to bring to her stricken employer. Just as she was leaving the kitchen her mobile vibrated in her pocket, and her heart leapt when she saw Drew's name flash up on the screen.

'Hello, darling. How are things?' she asked sympathetically.

'Daddy's croaked it. At least he didn't hang around too long. He did the decent thing for once in his life, the slithery old buzzard,' Drew murmured down the line.

Connie giggled. 'You're awful. I can see you're devastated.'

'I *am* devastated. Devastated that I'll have to go and bring the other pair to an undertaker's to pick out Pop's coffin – that will be interesting – and then help sort out funeral arrangements, when I'm supposed to be taking my gal for a walk on the beach and to dinner afterwards,' he said glumly.

'It can't be helped,' she soothed.

'Can I call over and see you, even if it's late?'

'Of course you can. I'll wait up.'

'Well, I'm hoping I won't have to hang around for *too* long once I bring them home. They can get their relations to come and give them comfort; I've done my duty big-time,' Drew grumbled. 'I'd better get back; the nurses are giving them tea and sympathy. I told them I had to ring work. I'll see you as soon as I can. Sorry about this, Connie. I couldn't just turn my back on them when it came down to the wire.'

'I know you couldn't, that's why I love you,' she said gently, wishing she could wrap her arms around him and give him a hug.

'See you later,' Drew said, and she knew he was smiling. Connie was smiling too as she made her way along the hall. The day wasn't a total disaster: she'd get to see her dearest and she didn't care how long she had to wait up. She would make a fuss of him after his long and exhausting day, just as he would do the same for her if it were the other way around.

'But you can't leave now,' Marianna protested, several hours later, as the house filled up with relatives and neighbours offering their condolences.

'Marianna, I need to see if everything's OK at work—'

'Some things never change. Still the workaholic,' she riposted tartly.

'And I want to see Connie. We had dinner reservations, which we had to cancel,' he said evenly, ignoring the barb.

'*Oh!*' she said stiffly. 'You should have told me. I wouldn't have dreamed of putting you out.'

'Don't be like that, Marianna,' he reproved. 'You didn't put me out in the slightest. I was glad to be able to help out. And you did great, you were very brave, and that helped your mum and your dad much more than you realize now,' he said kindly, seeing her crestfallen expression and the pallor of stress and grief etched in her face.

'Thanks. I don't think I could have done it if you hadn't been there. I *am* grateful for that, Drew. I always will be. And thanks for helping with the funeral arrangements and all of that.' Marianna managed a weak smile.

'Don't stay up too late. Get your mother to bed. She's done for,' he advised, walking out to the hall.

'Are you sure you couldn't stay? I don't want to talk to all this lot.'

'Don't, then. Go to bed. No one will think any the less of you. You've just been through one of the most traumatic events you'll ever have to endure, and you have the funeral to get through. Go to bed, Marianna. Your husband will be here tomorrow, won't he?'

'Yes, he's taken a Red-eye,' she said tiredly.

'Well, you won't need me then. I'll see you at the church tomorrow evening.'

'At the church!' she exclaimed. 'Are you not going to come up to Dublin to the funeral parlour?'

'That's for family only. I'm not family any more, Marianna. You'll have your husband with you, and all your relatives. I'll see you at the church,' Drew said firmly. 'Goodnight.'

'Goodnight,' she said sulkily, and turned her back on him and walked into the kitchen, leaving him to let himself out.

An hour later, as he sat at Connie's kitchen table and tucked into a plate of steak and homemade chips, Drew couldn't contain his anger. 'Do you think I should have to go up to that bloody funeral parlour? Heck, Old Man Lynley's lucky I'm even going to his removal, and I'm only doing that for the girls' sake. That man caused me huge grief in my life, I'm not going to pretend to mourn him and stand like a hypocrite at his coffin spouting prayers.'

'I think he did very well to have you at his bedside when he died. I don't know if I could be so forgiving. Marianna should be on her knees with gratitude,' Connie said crossly. His face softened into a smile.

'Ah you're biased,' he teased, amused and touched at her indignation.

'No, I mean it, Drew. You got her and her mother through a most difficult time, you really supported them, and you went and picked the coffin with them and sorted out the undertaker's for them. I think you've done more than your share. And you're right, her husband will be with her tomorrow.'

'I think she was hoping I'd offer to collect him from the airport, but she's got plenty of extended family; let one of them do it. Do you know, not one of them came to my mother's funeral,' he said, putting his knife and fork down and taking her hand. 'Imagine, none of them had the decency even to come to the removal.'

'That's despicable.' Connie was shocked. 'You've given them far more than they deserve. Put it out of your head, Drew, and let them get on with it now. And if you even think of going up to Dublin, I'll throw thumbtacks in front of the car.'

'It might take more than a thumbtack to puncture that old banger.' Drew grinned.

'It would be different if the girls were coming home for it,' Connie said as she topped up their wine glasses.

'I spoke to both of them today. They would have tried, but Marianna told them not to. She doesn't want to delay the funeral. Mama Lynley's at the end of her rope – it's been a long ordeal for her these past months – and I think Marianna's right to get it all over and done with as soon as possible. They weren't that close to old Pa Lynley, he didn't have a natural affinity with any of his grandchildren, from what I could see. He was of the 'children should be seen and not heard' school of thought, although he adored Marianna. His greatest affinity was with the whiskey bottle, to tell the truth.' Drew raised an eyebrow at Connie.

'My greatest affinity is with chips, tragically,' Connie sighed, enjoying a particularly crispy one. 'Will it be a big funeral?'

'Huge. He had a big social circle, and of course a lot of clients – they hobnobbed with all the hobnobs in Wicklow and beyond. Connie, you should see the coffin they picked. I said nothing. I just left them at it and said, "Very nice. I'm sure he'd love it," when they asked me what I thought of the one they chose. It's got a carving of the Last Supper down the two side panels.'

'Oh dear,' she murmured.

'Nothing but the best for Daddy dearest. It cost an arm and a leg. He'll be going out in style – if you call that style. I think, from listening to the conversations back at the house, there's going to be about five priests on the altar concelebrating Mass.

That would suit old Chas down to the ground. Pity he had no Christian decency when he was dealing with me.'

'Are you still very angry about it?' Connie pushed her plate away and took a sip of wine.

'I'd kind of let it go, to be honest, but it all seemed to come roaring back when I saw him lying there having a more peaceful death than he damn well deserved. It was the grief and upset he caused my mother and the family that bugged me more than anything. I never forgave him for that.' He saw the worried look on her face.

'Don't worry, I'm not going to get all bitter and twisted again. As I say, it was just seeing him lying there and having Marianna and her mother expect so much of me that brought it all back. Once this lot is over I won't have to have anything to do with them and it will all recede again and I won't give it another thought.'

Drew drank some more wine and felt the tension begin to ease out of his body. It *had* been a day of very mixed emotion watching his detested father-in-law expire. He had put his personal feelings aside and helped Marianna and her mother get through the ordeal as much as he could – common decency would demand that, he acknowledged – but he would go so far and no further, and by the time he'd left the big, imposing detached house up by Blainroe Golf Club, he felt he'd well and truly reached that limit. He could see Marianna slipping back into old ways. Expecting a lot more than he was prepared to give, or than she was entitled to.

Helping her through her father's demise was a one-off. It was not the start of a new rapprochement, no matter what she might think. He had no desire to get involved with *any* of the clan again. Been there, worn that particular T-shirt, and didn't like it, he reflected grimly, remembering how snooty, snobby and condescending his in-laws had been. It truly was an irony that Old Man Lynley had drawn his last breath in Drew's presence. Drew's late mother would have appreciated that, he thought with a little smile.

It was so relaxing to sit with Connie telling her all the events of the day. It would have been lonely having to go home alone after the day he'd put in. Watching someone take their last breath, even someone as detested as his ex-father-in-law, gave a man food for thought and brought up reflections of his own mortality.

'What would you think of us getting away together for a few days?' he asked impulsively.

'Oh Drew, I'd *love* it,' Connie enthused, eyes sparkling at the notion.

'Let's make plans, woman,' he grinned, leaning over and kissing her soundly.

Chapter Twenty

She'd hoped against hope that Drew would change his mind and come to the family gathering at the funeral parlour, but gazing around at those assembled, now saying a decade of the Rosary, Marianna felt a sharp jab of disappointment to see that Drew was not among them. Out of the corner of her eye, she saw the door open and her heart lifted in anticipation, only to drop again when she saw it was her cousin Hilary and her husband Rory.

She kept her eyes averted from the open coffin; she couldn't bear to think of darling Daddy being dead. She sniffled and swallowed the huge lump in her throat, desperately wishing it were Drew that was standing beside her and not Edward, stifling his yawns and belching discreetly behind his hand.

Her husband was not the source of comfort Drew seemed to imagine he'd be, Marianna reflected despondently. Back in America they were sleeping in separate rooms, since her discovery of his fling with a trashy, blond, divorced neighbour. Edward could sleep in the guest room tonight and tomorrow, she decided. She couldn't stop thinking how lovely it had been to rest within the shelter of Drew's arms and lay her head against his chest as he comforted her in those surreal moments following her father's passing. All the years of bitterness and anger seemed to dissolve, and for a fleeting moment before being overwhelmed by raw grief she'd remembered how wonderful her first marriage had been at the beginning, when she and Drew were happy. She should have stuck it out, she thought regretfully, as the priest began the 'Glory Be to the Father', signalling the end of the prayers. She had lost much more than she had gained. She'd lost a really good man because she'd been immature and selfish.

Was there any way she could get him back? Marianna wondered, thoughts drifting as the murmur of prayer ceased. What was this Connie woman to him anyway? She'd thought she was making some headway with him yesterday. He'd been so kind – holding her, comforting her – and then he'd refused point blank to come to the funeral parlour. That had been like a cold shower, just as she'd been lulling herself into a false sense of anticipation and expectation. That was Drew though. Straight as a die, you always knew where you stood with him, and right now her standing wasn't too high. Marianna bit her lip as everyone made the sign of the cross and the undertaker began to discreetly usher the extended family out so that only the immediate family remained for the last goodbye.

Watching the lid come down on the coffin, knowing that she was seeing her father's face for the last time, brought forth a wail of grief that she could not contain. Dorothy joined in, and they sobbed brokenly as Edward did his best to console them.

'There, there! There, there!' he muttered awkwardly, wishing he was a million miles away. He had told Marianna that he would be flying back to the States the day after the funeral; he couldn't stay away from work any longer. His investment businesses had been hit badly in the recession. Belt tightening was the order of the day. She wondered should she just get the divorce over and done with, take what she could and come back to Ireland to live? The girls were living their own lives now, and a lonely future beckoned in America.

Just before she took her place in the funeral limousine, Marianna excused herself, took her phone out of her bag and dialled Drew's number. 'Yes, Marianna?' he answered after the fourth ring.

'Drew, you will sit up in the front of the church with us for the removal and the funeral? Seeing as the girls aren't here, I think you should be their representative. And you will come to the meal tomorrow after the burial, I hope?' she said, hoping her mention of the girls would bring a positive response.

'Did Edward make it over?' Drew asked, and she could hear the annoyance in his voice.

'Yes, he's here, but that's not the point, Drew—'

'Marianna, you have enough to be worrying about. I'll see you at the church soon,' Drew said briskly.

'Please, Drew,' she whispered. 'I *need* you there.' There was a long silence. 'Please.'

'All right,' he said flatly. Marianna felt a surge of satisfaction. She could still get to him. He still found it hard to refuse her. There was hope for them yet, she was convinced of it.

'For crying out loud,' Drew muttered, flinging the phone on to the passenger seat. He sat in the jeep staring into space, mulling over his ex-wife's phone call. What the hell did she want him up in the front with the family for? That was a low shot, saying he was the girls' representative. How he longed to tell her to get lost and stop annoying him. If it wasn't her father's funeral, by God he would be telling her, he fumed. Marianna need not think that she could start her old shenanigans and have him dancing attendance on her. The past was the past and there was no going back to it. Their relationship was well and truly over. Once this damn funeral was over he didn't care if he ever set eyes on her, Mama, Bert or any of the other motley crew again. He glanced at his watch. He needed to change into his suit. He'd got his hair cut that morning, and thanks to bloody Charles Lynley, he'd hardly have time to take Marino out for a ride.

The only thing turning this day around was the thought of his forthcoming few days away with Connie. She was checking out when she could get the time off and then they were going to make plans and Marianna and all her carry-on would be a distant memory.

Marianna scanned the enormous crowd outside the church awaiting the arrival of the hearse and the family, and eventually located her ex-husband, standing tall and grim-faced and looking exceedingly handsome in his charcoal-grey suit. She was so used to seeing him in jeans she'd forgotten how well he spruced up. He was so fit-looking, she thought, trying not to notice Edward's paunch straining the buttons of his navy blazer and the roll of his jowls overhanging the collar of his shirt. 'I invited Drew to sit with the family, seeing as the girls aren't here,' she said to her mother.

'By all means. He's been very good to us, under the circumstances.' Dorothy agreed without hesitation. 'I wouldn't want him to feel left out. But he won't be in the front row . . . that might look a bit odd.'

'Oh no,' Marianna said hastily. 'He wouldn't want that.'

'It *is* a Catholic ceremony. Two husbands might be a bit much,' Dorothy murmured to Edward.

'Of course,' agreed her current son-in-law, wishing Drew *would* sit in the front row and let him off the hook. A respectful silence fell on the crowd of mourners as the family exited the car and the undertakers slid Charles's coffin out of the hearse. The priest came and uttered words of condolence and said some prayers before leading the procession into the church. Marianna tried to catch Drew's eye but could not as the crowd jostled forward to join in the procession.

It was a long, tiring ordeal. Although the prayers took only twenty minutes, the line of people who queued to offer their condolences afterwards snaked down the aisle of the church as far as the main door, and it took at least another hour before she was finally able to turn around and locate her ex-husband, sitting about three rows behind, staring into space.

'You should have sat right behind us,' she remonstrated when he came over to greet them as they left the church.

'I was fine where I was. Mrs Lynley, I hope you're bearing up all right,' he said politely.

'Thank you, Drew. I'll be glad when it's all over,' Dorothy said wearily. 'You will come back to the house for refreshments, won't you?'

'No, I won't, if you don't mind,' he said. 'I'm under a bit of pressure workwise. I'll see you tomorrow.' Marianna glared at him, but he ignored her and turned to Edward.

'Hello, Edward.' He held out his hand. 'Sorry to meet again under such circumstances.'

'Hello, buddy, yes indeed. Sad times, sad times,' Edward said jovially, sounding not in the least bit sad. 'Are you sure you couldn't come back?' he asked hopefully.

'Not tonight. I'll see you all tomorrow,' Drew said resolutely and turned to walk away.

'Drew, sit behind us tomorrow,' Marianna said, with a sharp tone to her voice. 'And you'll be at our table in the hotel.'

'Excellent,' Edward said cheerfully, oblivious to any undercurrents. 'We'll shoot the breeze.'

'Whatever you say, Marianna,' Drew said coolly, turning back to face her. 'Till tomorrow.' His eyes were chips of ice as their gaze locked.

She watched him leave, striding purposefully down the aisle, and could have slapped him. He wasn't giving her an ounce of leeway. He was as intent as ever on keeping his distance. It was downright *rude* of him not to come back to the house, and she'd let him know that one of these fine days. It was obvious when he'd put forward no argument about coming to the meal in the hotel or the seating plan that he was doing whatever she wanted and taking the line of least resistance. Which was exactly what she *didn't* want. Marianna wanted Drew to *want* to comfort her, to *want* to support her, not to be dragged unwilling to the church and the meal afterwards.

You gave him no comfort when his mother died. The thought came unbidden and she banished it swiftly. She couldn't deal with that now, she didn't want to deal with it. She had enough on her plate as it was. This was not the time to face up to the fact that Drew wanted nothing more to do with her. That realization was as much a grief to her as the loss of her father, and she sobbed her way out of the church and home.

'You did well not to go back to the house last night. I envied you,' Edward remarked as he and Drew followed Marianna and Dorothy out of the graveyard after the burial the following day.

'We all have our crosses in life,' Drew said with dry humour.

'And some are heavier than others.' Edward gave a wry smile, and Drew hid his amusement as Marianna gave them a dark look before they went their separate ways to the hotel.

'So, buddy, you did well for yourself in spite of Pops and the divorce settlement all those years ago. It must have been a sweet moment to watch him pass on,' Edward murmured out of the side of his mouth as he and Drew drank a glass of beer at the hotel bar before sitting down for lunch.

'You could say that,' Drew agreed.

'He was a damn contrary man, could never get on with him, couldn't cotton to him at all,' Edward remarked. 'Whiskey made him a nasty drunk. It won't cost me any tears not having him visiting us again.'

Drew laughed. 'You'd better not let Marianna hear you say that.' Edward was a cheery, hail-fellow-well-met, outgoing sort of guy – anathema to pompous, reserved Charles. What you saw was what you got with Marianna's second husband, and Drew liked him well enough. He'd been a good stepfather to Katy and Erin, and that was all that mattered as far as he was concerned.

'We're not doing too good, buddy, as it happens. Between you and me, I think we're gonna end up taking the divorce route one of these fine days,' Edward divulged. He'd had several beers to Drew's one.

'Sorry to hear that,' Drew said in dismay. This was not good news. If Marianna divorced Edward and came back to Ireland to live, he was damned if he was going to be in the firing line every time there was a crisis.

Marianna appeared beside them, taller than normal in her skyscraper slingbacks. She was wearing a tailored black suit that outlined her toned, well-preserved shape and a black pillbox, à la Jackie. She'd had a beautician come and professionally make up her face before the funeral as well as having her hair coiffed. She, no less than her mother, was the centre of attention today; it was important to look her best. And she'd hoped, with her sophisticated look, that Drew would be impressed. Her husband's appreciation hadn't been a consideration in her choice of outfit. 'They're ready to serve the meal. We should go in first.' She tilted her head and looked up at Drew.

'Whatever you say, honey.' Edward shrugged and Marianna flashed him a look of impatience. 'How many of those have you had?' She indicated his pint glass.

'Enough to make this bearable,' he drawled sarcastically.

'You would think,' she said to Drew, 'that a woman's husband would be more concerned about her than himself on the day she buries her father, would you not?'

'Leave me out of this, Marianna,' Drew snapped, walking off, disgusted that she would draw him into an argument between her and Edward. He wasn't interested in her affairs – how could he make it any more obvious to her? Why was she so determined to draw him back into her life when he was clearly so totally against it? He'd been blunt with her, he'd bordered on rudeness with her, and she still wasn't getting it, he thought in frustration as he made his way into the dining room, wishing the whole damn episode was over.

The meal was interminable, and Drew was itching with impatience to get away the longer it dragged out. Marianna had seated him opposite her at the round table, between her uncle Bert's wife, Nancy, and her cousin Phil, who was pissed as a newt before they even sat down.

'Great turn-out,' he'd slurred, and that was it, then he'd sat drinking silently without another word, which had suited Drew just fine.

Nancy had tried to engage him in conversation but after some pleasantries about Katy and Erin it had fizzled out and he had done nothing to try and revive it, so she had turned her attention to her husband. Drew presumed that Marianna had hoped to talk to him across the table, but she hadn't taken into account the high ceilings of the dining room, which made everything seem louder, amplifying the noisy babble from the several hundred mourners who had come back for the meal after the burial. She'd had to shout across the table at him, and it had given him some satisfaction that, even though she'd got her way about him attending the meal, she'd had to give up trying to converse with him.

The minute he'd finished his coffee he stood up, said his farewells to Dorothy and Edward and then come to stand beside his ex-wife. 'I'm sorry for your trouble, Marianna. I hope you can get some rest soon. I'm heading off now,' he said politely as she stood up.

'You can't get away quick enough, sure you can't,' she accused him bitterly.

'If you want the honest truth to that question, I think you know the answer is yes. I've done what you asked of me, for the girls' sake. I hope all goes well with you in the future. Goodbye, Marianna.'

'And that's it?' she said in disbelief, staring up at him, aghast at his lack of compassion.

'That's it, Marianna,' Drew said emphatically. He nodded to Edward, who raised his hand in farewell, and walked out of the dining room with an enormous sense of relief as his ex-wife stared after him with her mouth open.

That night, as they sat in front of the fire chatting, he said to Connie, 'I did my duty, she can't tell the girls I didn't stand by her in her hour of need – but if I never see the woman again it won't cost me a thought, and I think she knows that. I don't expect to be hearing from her for the foreseeable future.' Drew felt a huge sense of freedom. He'd behaved with decency, done what he could to help out, supported Marianna when she needed it but, after this, she should be under no illusions that she'd be hearing from him again unless something came up about the girls.

God bless your innocence, thought Connie, but she said nothing, not wanting to ruin his evening. Somehow or other she didn't think it was the last he'd heard of that bloody woman. In fact, from what she'd seen of Marianna's behaviour, she was damn sure of it.

CHAPTER TWENTY-ONE

'Thanks for coming tonight.' Barry glanced over at his wife as he reversed the car out of the parking space and headed out of the underground car park.

'Well, seeing as it's a charity bash and we'd bought the tickets months ago, *and* they cost a fortune, it behoves me to go. Besides, I wouldn't give Frances Reed the satisfaction of being a no-show. I've had to listen to her for the past six months telling me what a fabulous evening she's putting together. And the spot prizes are, as she said herself, "bang on trend". She's such a mega pain in the ass.' Aimee scowled as she pulled down the sun visor and studied her make-up in the mirror.

'She was lucky to get them when she did. I don't think it will be so easy to get sponsorship and luxury prizes these days. *We* won't be as generous as we've been tonight, for sure.'

'Tell me about it, Barry. Honestly, I can't believe I'm setting up a high-end company in a bloody recession – who would have thought it? It all happened so fast. That bloody Anglo fiasco. Unbelievable, what was going on and what they were getting away with.'

'Let's not depress ourselves. Let's try and enjoy this evening as much as we can. We haven't been out together in ages,' he said casually, not wanting to get into a discussion about anything to do with finances.

'Yeah, well, being pregnant is not exactly a barrel of laughs and, with Melissa's difficulties, it's so draining the only place I want to go to when I get home from work is bed,' his wife moaned.

'Look, again, all I can say is, I'm really sorry I was so heavy-handed about you being pregnant. I know I gave ultimatums, I know I didn't take your feelings into consideration, Aimee, but now that you're having it, I wish you could try and be happy about it. It's *our* child. Look how special Melissa is. This child could be as special. I'll be absolutely hands-on, you know that. We're in it together, Aimee,' he said earnestly, reaching over to take one of her hands in his.

'I know, and Melissa's looking forward to it, once it's born. It might help her to eat properly, having a baby to take her mind off herself. I didn't tell you, but I had the scan today, everything's fine,' she added flatly.

'I would have gone with you, Aimee,' he said, bitterly disappointed.

'I know. It was just something I wanted to do on my own. Please don't be annoyed.'

'Didn't you feel *anything*?' he ventured.

'Barry, if you want me to say I was thrilled, I can't. I was relieved that everything's OK. I was irritated because I had to wait longer than I thought, and I had a lunchtime meeting that I knew I was going to be late for. I'm sorry, but that's the best I can do, and that's why I went by myself. I'll show you the photo when we get home. It's in my briefcase.'

'OK,' he said, trying to hide his dismay. He'd hoped the excitement of the scan would bring them closer together and give Aimee some joy about the baby.

'I'm impressed with Dr Morton. Are you?' Aimee changed the subject and played with her diamond pendant, unwilling to meet his gaze. They had brought Melissa to the eating-disorders specialist and she had told them that she'd like to give Melissa the option of working on the programme, as an outpatient, initially. If Melissa made progress, that would be a step forward; if not, she would be hospitalized. Needless to say, Melissa was all for the outpatient suggestion. Her episode in A&E had scared the daylights out of her and she was desperate to avoid a hospital stay at all costs. She was making a great pretence of eating, particularly on the days before she was due a consultation with Dr Morton, which included a weigh-in. As the doctor had said to them, it gave Melissa some sense of control and responsibility to try and stay out of hospital but, she warned, more often than not, a spell as an inpatient was required.

'She's very no-nonsense, authoritative in a subtle way. Melissa can't fool her.' Barry slowed down when he caught sight of a squad car in his rear-view mirror. 'But to be honest, I think she'll have to go into hospital. She's struggling, in spite of our best efforts, isn't she?'

'Yeah,' Aimee agreed despondently. They drove in silence, lost in their own thoughts, until he swung into the grounds of the golf club. 'I guess we'd better sparkle,' Aimee said wryly, slanting a glance at him as she retouched her lipstick.

'On with the façade. Like half the other couples here,' Barry countered, parking the Merc beside a Series 7 BMW. 'Let's do what we have to do and go home at a reasonable hour.'

'Suits me fine,' she agreed, composing her features and pasting a smile on her face as she waved at the Grants, who had just drawn up alongside them.

'Aimee, we see so little of you – how nice to see you,' Doreen Grant trilled, air-kissing her as they stepped out of their respective cars. She was like a bandy little sparrow in her gold one-shoulder mini. Her fake tan against the gold gave her a faintly jaundiced appearance. Not a good look, Aimee thought privately, thinking if she had knees as bony as Doreen's, she would *never* display them in public.

'Looking particularly stunning tonight, Aimee,' Terry Grant leered, his gaze sliding over her strapless black evening gown, which enhanced her slightly fuller, rounded figure. Pregnancy had given her a décolletage that was decidedly sexier than her usual petite silhouette.

Doreen, eagle-eyed where her husband was concerned, frowned. 'I wonder whose table we'll be at?' She changed the subject speedily. Terry had strayed before, and she kept him on a tight rein. Not that Doreen had any fears from her, or indeed, Aimee suspected, any woman who would be at the do tonight, she thought in amusement, watching Doreen link a proprietorial arm through her husband's. Most women in their social circle steered well clear of him.

'Your table, I hope.' Terry winked lasciviously from behind his thick-framed black glasses, the sodium light overhead making his bald pate glow.

'I'm sure Frances will have put a lot of thought into the seating plan,' Aimee said smoothly as she led the way into the clubhouse, hoping to God he wasn't at their table. She couldn't stand Terry Grant; he was convinced that he was God's gift to women, rather than the sleazy, oily geezer that he was.

'Aimee, Barry, good to see you.' Simon Heston, the captain of the golf club, greeted them warmly. 'Have a glass of champagne.' He indicated a table laden with flutes of golden bubbly.

'You have one, Barry. I'll drive home,' Aimee said, taking a glass of sparkling water instead.

'Aimee, I haven't seen you in ages.' Rita Lawson, the lady captain, looking like Harry Potter's Dumbledore in a flowing purple glittery kaftan, her unruly grey hair tumbling to her shoulders, grabbed her hand and pumped it up and down. 'Heard you did a magnificent job for Roger O'Leary's daughter's wedding in the summer. I wanted to give you the gig but Frances muscled in and said it was only right that a member should organize it. She's such a bully. Honestly, you really should take up golf and then you could do all our functions.'

'Wouldn't have the time to play unfortunately, Rita,' Aimee laughed. 'I'm sure Frances has done an excellent job.'

'Oh, she just witters on so much about such trivial nonsense.

Honestly, she nearly had a coronary because the balloons weren't the right shade of silver,' Rita confided, *sotto voce*. 'Here she is now – a bird could nest in that hairdo.'

Balloons! How tacky, thought Aimee, noting a clump of silver balloons on either side of the doors leading to the marquee. She hid a grin at Rita's deliciously bitchy but spot-on remark as she watched Frances heading in their direction, baring her teeth in a smile that didn't quite reach her eyes.

'You made it, Aimee. No lavish function needing your magic touch?' Frances purred sweetly.

'Wouldn't have missed it for the world. *Love* the balloons.' Aimee was equally sweet. Frances's eyes narrowed, not sure if she'd been stung or not. Rita smirked behind the other woman's back.

'A little bird tells me you've left Chez Moi,' Frances probed, her hard, walnut eyes glinting from underneath their forest of false eyelashes. A mountainous bouffant of blond hair framed her narrow, sharp-angled face.

'Your little bird was absolutely right, Frances. Well sussed. I have indeed.' Aimee wondered why no one had told the other woman that the blond bouffant and thick false lashes look was so over. She looked like a badly made-up drag queen.

'And what are you up to now? Or have you left the business entirely? I heard mention Roger O'Leary and yourself are up to something.'

'All will be revealed in good time,' Aimee stonewalled, still smiling, enjoying the fact that all the other woman's angling was getting her nowhere. Her ex-boss Ian must have been blabbing. He was still spitting feathers that she'd left his company so abruptly. He'd be spitting more than feathers when she poached her old PA and his receptionist, once she was up and running. Roger was having the offices revamped, and she was hoping to be in situ in the next couple of weeks.

'Oh look, Barry, there's the O'Dwyers. We should say hello.' She slipped her arm into her husband's and gave Frances and Rita a nod.

'You can be such a bitch.' Barry grinned as they moved away.

'Well, she's a nosy cow,' Aimee retorted. 'Let's go find out where we're sitting and who's at our table. If it's Terry and Doreen I'm changing the place settings.'

'OK,' agreed her husband as they went and perused the seating plans. They were pleased enough with their seating arrangements. Terry and Doreen had been consigned to a table near the door. 'No crashing bores at least,' Aimee murmured as they headed for the marquee that adjoined the clubhouse. Blue and silver balloons floated along the tops of the columns that held the massive white tent in place. Second-rate tack, Aimee decided, running a professional eagle eye around the venue. She noted that the marquee was worn and shabby in places, and the silver and blue theme that Frances had chosen gave off a cold, sterile ambiance for an autumn event – for *any* event. It certainly wouldn't be a colour scheme *she'd* ever use, Aimee thought with a hint of smugness, knowing that Frances wasn't in her league at all.

'. . . He's absolutely and unequivocally responsible for the state of this country. He should never be allowed to hold public office again . . .'

'. . . I wonder who's paying for his make-up now? . . .'

'. . . I don't understand why Seanie and all that other shower seem to be getting away with it, and as for Fingers . . .'

'. . . If they were in America they'd be doing the perp walk. Look at Madoff, arrested in his office. Handcuffed . . . jailed . . .'

'. . . But how could the banks hand out loans of such magnitude without checking the creditworthiness of those developers? . . . Billions to Quinn . . . mind-boggling . . . Con House would be much more apt. I blame the regulator . . . or non-regulator, I should say. Thank God for the new chap . . .'

'. . . So much for the auditors. How have they any clients left? . . .'

'. . . They're all in cahoots. They think they're all above the law . . .'

'. . . Look at bloody SCIP, how fast that went down the tubes. A lot of people here got burnt in that, lost their entire life savings between Anglo, ISTC and SCIP . . .'

'. . . Don't mention *that* war . . . Greed. Greed. Greed. So what's happened to Jeremy Farrell? Not that I was expecting him here tonight . . .'

Barry let the animated, drink-fuelled waves of conversation wash over him as he sipped a brandy after the meal. Aimee was talking to Edmund Wallace, a retired architect, and Ella Burke, Barry's table companion, had gone for a smoke.

'Hey, Barry.' Nick Ross leaned across the round table. 'You invested in SCIP, didn't you? Have you heard anything from Jeremy?'

Barry came to with a start. He didn't want to get into discussing his losses in front of Aimee, now that things were on a much more even keel between them. He would choose his moment to tell her. She had enough to deal with as things were.

'Not a word. I'd say he's still in the villa in the Algarve, or in the holiday home in the west,' he said off-handedly.

'I bet he didn't lose a bloody cent; he's too cute for that. Only us suckers went down the river without a paddle.' Nick was slightly tipsy and his voice rose a decibel. 'Oh yes, that little toad, Farrell, his reputation as a smart boy is in tatters, but his reputation as a wide boy remains very much intact.'

'Ummm,' Barry murmured.

Walt Jenkins laughed. 'I like that, it describes Jeremy perfectly. A smarmy little wide boy if ever there was one.'

'Did you invest in SCIP, Edmund, or were you too cute? What about you, Aimee? Did Jeremy part you from your hard-earned money, like he did Barry?' Nick leaned across the table.

Barry felt a knot of tension dissipate his post-meal lethargy. Why the hell couldn't Nick keep his big mouth shut?

'What's SCIP?' Aimee looked puzzled. 'I've heard that name before.'

'SecureCo International Plus. Jeremy's great investment tip

that was going to make us all multimillionaires, Barry included.'

'I vaguely remember him boring the pants off me about some investment in hotels that Anglo were involved in—'

'I hope you didn't get involved in *that*,' Nick interjected in horror.

'No way. I wouldn't trust him as far as I'd throw him, patronizing little git. He told me I was far too cautious and that he met people like me every day of the week. He wanted me to invest a million and to borrow for it. I told him he was crazy, but that was ages ago. Is that what you're talking about?' Aimee asked.

'No, SCIP is much more recent. It was a grey market, due to be floated, the greatest thing since fried bread, allegedly. Shares went as high as €350, I bought mine for €340 – what did you buy yours at, Barry?'

'Not as much as that,' Barry mumbled.

'Three hundred and forty euros a share, good God!' exclaimed Aimee, who wasn't particularly into stocks and shares. 'What's happened? Have you lost much money?'

'Only half a million.' Nick laughed mirthlessly. 'But that's nothing, Barry and I are minnows compared to some of the high fliers. See the Bennets over there? Three million smackers gone, and they were friends of Doris and Jeremy. He sold his friends a pig in a poke—'

'Barry, you never said anything to me about investing in one of Jeremy's scams—' Aimee turned to her husband. 'Have you lost much?'

'Well, not half a million or anything like it – I'm not like Moneybags here,' Barry laughed, putting on the best act of his life. He certainly wasn't going to discuss the extent of his losses in a round-table discussion in the golf club in front of his wife, who knew nothing about it. 'The last scheme I invested in was only a couple of thou, and I made a good profit.' He threw in his red herring, hoping that it would distract from the topic at hand.

'I made a few bob out of that, but not half enough to cover this loss,' Nick said mournfully. 'No wonder the little shit hasn't been seen since the summer – half the people in this club have lost a fortune because of him. I bet he offloaded his stock and made a whacking great profit. He'll never be able to show his face here again.'

'I wonder how Doris feels about it all. She was always *so* superior, looking down her nose at us poor plebs. I wonder is she mortified?' Carla Ross mused as she held out her glass for her husband to pour her another glass of wine.

'She's a cold fish, she won't give a toss.' Ella Burke, reeking of smoke, had resumed her place beside Barry for the latter part of the conversation.

'I think you're wrong, I think she *will* be mortified, not that she'll ever let on to us, but let's face it: as Nick says, her precious Jeremy's reputation is in tatters. No one will ever take advice on investments from him again. His credibility is zilch. He's ruined a sizeable amount of their friends and acquaintances. Their mantelpieces won't be groaning with dinner-party invites, and they'll be hard pushed to find enough to fill a table at their monthly soirees, and that's what will upset Doris more than any-thing. Her place in society is lost, all the names she and Jeremy have brown-nosed gone,' Carla argued knowledgeably. She'd been to several of the Farrells' pretentious dinner parties.

Barry exhaled slowly as the conversation continued. The danger had passed for the moment. He'd had a near miss, but he was going to have to tell Aimee sooner rather than later about the magnitude of his losses now that she was peripherally aware of them. He just hoped she hadn't absorbed all Nick's drink-fuelled revelations. The last thing he needed was a row about their finances. If he could get his hands on Farrell he'd kick him from here to kingdom come, Barry thought irritably, on edge in case the conversation reverted to SCIP and the amount of his losses.

Chapter Twenty-two

'So how much did you, or should I say *we*, lose in that SCIP thing and when *exactly* were you going to tell me about it?' Aimee said grimly, reversing the car out of the golf club car park.

'Aw, Aimee, don't. Not tonight,' Barry groaned.

'Tonight's the perfect night. Melissa's on a sleepover at Sarah's, don't forget, so we have the place to ourselves,' she retorted coldly.

'Well, at least wait until we get home before you begin the interrogation then,' he growled, wishing heartily that Nick Ross had kept his big bloody trap shut.

Aimee's mouth was a thin line as she drove the Merc along the winding drive of the grounds towards the main road. 'Did we lose much?' she said tightly.

'Enough.'

'How much?'

'Just drive. I'll tell you when we get home.'

'Are we in trouble?'

'No.'

He saw her hands loosen their grip on the wheel a little and the tension eased out of her shoulders.

She stalked past him into the lift when they got out of the car, and his heart sank at the impending confrontation. In his dreams he had imagined that the evening would end with a much-needed session of lovemaking, especially when he'd seen Aimee looking so sexy in that long, black, strapless gown that moulded itself to her breasts, which were at least a size bigger than they used to be, and absolutely gorgeous to boot. He had two chances of sex tonight: slim and none, thought Barry glumly as they rode the lift in silence. He opened the door of the apartment and Aimee marched in, stony-faced. 'I'm just going to get a beer. Do you want anything?' he asked.

'Nothing, thank you,' she said icily, folding her cerise pashmina in a neat square before walking into the lounge.

'Aw hell,' he muttered, heading for the sanctuary of the kitchen. He grabbed a bottle of Miller from the fridge, opened it and took a slug. There was no point skulking; he might as well get it over with. He took another draught. He'd had quite a lot to drink at the dinner and should have been feeling pleasantly tipsy. No such bloody luck. Aimee's scowl when they'd got into the car was like an ice-cold shower.

'So how much have you lost us?' Aimee got straight to the point when he ambled back into the lounge.

'A hundred thou.' He took another slug of beer.

'Jesus, Mary and Joseph, Barry! How the hell did you do that? How did that little weasel get that much out of you?' Aimee was stunned.

'It seemed like too good an opportunity to miss. I made money from his investment tips before,' Barry retorted defensively.

'Where did you get that much money?'

'Here and there,' he hedged.

'Where?' she snapped.

'I borrowed it,' he muttered.

'You *borrowed* it?' she repeated incredulously. 'You borrowed to invest in shares in a company that hadn't even been floated on the stock exchange? Are you *mad*?'

'It looks like it, doesn't it?' he said sullenly, furious at her derision. He hated it when she went all judgemental and superior. It was bad enough that she was the main breadwinner without her making him feel like a complete and utter loser as well.

'And you weren't going to tell me?' She sat down on the sofa and shook her head.

'I would have told you when the time was right.' He shrugged, completely pissed off.

'And when would that have been?' Aimee said scathingly.

'Aw, shut up, Aimee,' he exploded. 'You're one to talk about telling things. If it hadn't been for Melissa finding the pregnancy-test kit, would you have ever told me about the baby? I think not.'

'That's completely different,' she hissed.

'Really? In what way?' he said nastily. 'I lost us money and you were going to lose our baby. In my eyes, your behaviour was far worse than mine. I was trying to protect you. You didn't give a fuck about me,' he said bitterly.

'Oh, so we're back to that,' she spat. 'Was that why you changed your mind about letting me have the termination? If I'd gone ahead and had it, did you feel I wouldn't be able to say anything to you about your stupendously irresponsible fiscal recklessness? Is that it, Barry? God, I never thought you'd be so devious. So calculating!' She shot up from the sofa and stood in front of him.

'*Aimee!*' He felt he'd been punched in the gut, horrified at her take on things. 'That never crossed my mind, I swear. I'm not that much of a shit. If that's what you think of me, there's not much point in us staying married to each other. Maybe it's time we ended it once and for all. We can't go on like this. I've had enough, Aimee. I can't take it any more. You are such a hard bitch sometimes – most times now, actually, if you want to know the truth. Well, be self-righteous and judgemental all you want. We all make mistakes, Aimee. I was doing it for the best possible reasons. I was doing it for you and Melissa. I was doing it for you to be proud of me. I miscalculated, badly, sure, but not half as badly as many people I know who've lost *everything*. At least I knew I had assets to cover the loan, so I wasn't a *complete* idiot. Who was to know the whole thing would take a dive? Who could foresee the worldwide recession? Not me, for damn sure. So go ahead: be smug and superior, the way you always are, Ms MD. I've had it up to here.' Barry indicated his neckline with a slashing movement of his right hand. 'I'm sick of being emasculated and, Aimee, you do emasculation *so* well.' He was stone-cold sober by now as he stared at his wife in disgust.

The colour drained from her face and she slumped back down on the sofa, taken aback by the force of his anger. 'I'm going to bed, and to prove I'm not a complete heel, I'll sleep in the guest room, even though it should be you that should be discommoded.' He turned and strode out of the lounge, glad he'd had his say. He'd kowtowed to Aimee long enough in the last year, trying to keep her pacified. He was damned if he was going to do it any more. He still had *some* pride left, he fumed, grabbing his pyjamas from under the pillow of their big queen-sized bed and walking down to the small sage-green and cream guest room. Barry flung the fancy lace-edged cream cushions on the floor and undressed in the dark. He was asleep in minutes.

Aimee switched out the lights in the lounge and locked the hall door in a daze. Her head was beginning to pound. She went into the kitchen and poured herself a glass of slim-line Schweppes tonic. It helped her heartburn, for some reason. She really had pushed Barry to the edge; she'd never seen him so angry. Now he was claiming he wanted to end their marriage. And this time she knew he was serious. When she'd told him she wanted to end their marriage once the baby was born after he'd played the dictator when he found out she was pregnant, she'd meant it at the time. Looking back, however, it had been pride, hurt feelings and her hormones talking, and when things had settled down between them she'd been glad not to have to go it alone. Barry had always been her touchstone. Her comfort. Aimee didn't want to lose that.

She slipped out of her Jimmy Choos and padded down the hall to their bedroom. She didn't bother switching on the light but stepped out of her evening dress and left it on the floor where it fell. Normally meticulous about removing her make-up, she went into the en suite, poured some cleansing lotion on to a pad and gave her face a quick wipe. This night had turned into an unmitigated disaster, and yet again they were on the brink of separating.

She pulled her nightdress over her head and got into bed. The sheets were cold and she shivered, wishing she had Barry's body heat to keep her warm. He had been so gutted when she'd accused him of having an agenda for saying he'd stand by whatever choice she made about the termination. That had been below the belt, she admitted as she lay there in the darkness. And then he'd accused her of emasculating him, rubbing his nose in it about her being the main breadwinner. What was it about men and their egos? Was she supposed to have turned down the chance to run her own company and a salary that was higher than his just because it made him feel less manly? Aimee fumed.

Was that why he had taken such a gamble with those shares that Jeremy Farrell had been flogging? A thought struck her. Myles Murphy had taken a big hit with those shares. Lost millions, Roger had told her. That was why he'd pulled out of Hibernian Dreams. That was why the name had sounded familiar. If Myles had invested in SCIP, it had to have been fairly blue-chip, Aimee conceded, somewhat mollified that Barry hadn't been a total prat and lost a fortune on some dodgy company that no one knew anything about.

That was the new house she'd planned to buy in Killiney or Dalkey blown out of the water. That hundred thousand, plus the price they'd have got for the penthouse, would have bought them a fine detached house in a more upmarket area than Dun Laoghaire. It looked like they would be staying put for the time being, or rather, Melissa, the baby and herself would be staying put, if Barry was serious about leaving. Just what she needed . . . to be a single parent with a new baby and an anexoric teenager in a recession.

Maybe it was the drink talking: he'd had a lot to drink at the dinner and he'd been milling into beer all the time they were arguing, Aimee thought wearily, tossing and turning. She'd have to apologize. His manly pride had been dented. His feelings were hurt. What a friggin' tragedy. She moulded a pillow into a more comfortable shape. She'd have to act like a subservient wifey for a while. That might defuse the situation. If it didn't, and he really was serious, she was in big trouble. It wasn't fair. *He'd* lost them a fortune, and she was the one having to apologize and appease. 'Bloody men,' she muttered indignantly into her pillow. 'Bloody, bloody men.' It was almost dawn before she fell into an exhausted sleep, relieved beyond measure that it was Saturday and she didn't have to get up for work.

The smell of sizzling bacon woke her and her stomach growled hungrily. She cast a sleepy eye over at the alarm clock by her bed and saw with a shock that it was almost midday. She had slept deeply when she'd finally fallen asleep and she felt strangely refreshed. She couldn't remember the last time she'd slept in so late. She lay snug in the cocoon of her bed, the softness of the 1000TC Egyptian cotton sheets like a caress to her skin, listening to the movements in the kitchen. He wasn't clattering things around: that was a good sign, she decided. She could hear Marian Finucane's dulcet tones on the radio. If he was intent on divorce, he'd hardly be listening to the radio and cooking breakfast. But was it breakfast for one or breakfast for two? she pondered, running her fingers through her hair. The need to pee drove her reluctantly out of bed. She caught sight of her face in the mirror when she washed her hands, and grimaced at the sight that stared back at her. Dark panda eyes, blotchy skin, clumpy mascaraed lashes where she hadn't cleaned off all her make-up. There was a time when she wouldn't have been seen dead looking like that, and she certainly wouldn't have let

Barry see her looking anything less than desirable. She wrapped her dressing gown around her and walked down the hallway to the kitchen. He had his back to her when she went in, busy buttering brown bread to place on a tray he had already set. She felt a wave of relief. Breakfast for two. Maybe all was not lost. Compromises had to be made, that was what marriage was all about, and in fairness to Barry, he compromised a lot.

Aimee took a deep breath. 'Barry, I'm very sorry about what I said last night. It was' – she searched for a word that would pacify him and make him feel superior – 'um . . . unforgivable and uncalled for.'

'Oh!' He turned to face her. 'I'd never do something like that to you, Aimee,' he said. 'You're my wife, the mother of my child. It hurt that you would think so badly of me.'

Oh get over it, she thought irritably, but then saw the glass of chilled orange juice, with two ice cubes, just the way she liked it, and the napkin folded neatly in the silver napkin holder, and she damped down her irritation and held her arms out to him.

'I'm sorry,' she repeated. 'Please forget it. Let's not fight any more.'

Barry took a step forward and enveloped her in a hug, and she rested her head against his chest, glad their row was over. It was only much later when she thought about it that she realized that her husband had *not* apologized to her for losing a goodly chunk of their money. Her being the subservient wife seemed to give Barry the idea that he was off the hook, and diminished, in his eyes, his errant behaviour. He obviously felt that no reciprocal apology was necessary. Aimee scowled as she examined her own investments and accounts to see exactly how much in savings *she* had, which she was very, very sure Barry wouldn't be getting his hands on . . . *ever!*

CHAPTER TWENTY-THREE

'Oh, it's so good to see you, Jillian.' Judith threw her arms around her best friend and was warmly hugged in return.

'Come in, come in, it's freezing. Have you ever known it so cold?' Jillian led the way into her big country kitchen, where a roaring fire blazed. 'Give me your coat, and sit down there. I have the lunch ready,' her friend invited, and Judith felt the stress of the car journey drift away as her shoulders relaxed and she sat down at the pine table set for two. A jug of red and white carnations and sprays of evergreen rested in the middle.

'Was it hard driving over?' Jillian asked sympathetically when she came back into the kitchen and began ladling steaming, creamy homemade mushroom soup into two bowls before adding crunchy croutons.

'I'm glad I did it. I was dreading it, to be honest. It won't bother me again now,' Judith confessed, buttering a slice of walnut bread.

'You know, I would have driven to Dublin for you,' her friend said, placing one of the bowls in front of her.

'I know that. But I had to do it, Jillian. I had to face it and I've done it and I'm glad.'

'Did memories come flooding back?'

'I felt a bit sick with apprehension the nearer I got to where the crash happened but, just before I got there, a big delivery truck was coming along on the other side of the road and I was keeping an eye on him and, before I knew it, I had driven past. I just got a glimpse of the tree in the rear-view mirror, and that was that. I was fine then and now I'm here, and thanks so much for having me.' She smiled at her friend.

'A pleasure. Eat up now, and I've made a chicken and pasta dish for mains.' Jillian handed her the big pepper mill before pouring two glasses of chilled Chardonnay for them. 'Let's go early go ugly,' she grinned. 'It's not often I can start drinking at four in the afternoon. It's such a treat to have a free house. We can go on the piss, and not get up until late tomorrow and lounge around in our dressing gowns, with no kids looking for lifts to hurling and swimming and no husband looking for grub. I love them all dearly but I need some "me" time. It was perfect timing that Mick and my brother-in-law took the boys to watch Arsenal playing. I don't know who was more excited, the kids or the adults. They arrived safely, and the hotel is fine, and I told Mick they weren't to ring until at least eleven tomorrow morning.' Jillian lifted her glass.' Cheers!' she toasted.

'To Arsenal winning,' Judith laughed, taking a long drink of the refreshing liquid.

'How's Lily?' Jillian asked.

'Good form, delighted with the patio and the new doors. She's waiting until the spring to get the back room done. Tom's going mad at all the money she's spending.' Judith bit into a crouton.

'She's dead right. She might as well spend her money on herself and enjoy it. Especially now that she's really coming out of herself,' Jillian remarked. 'Anything on the house front for yourself?'

'I don't know if I'm being too fussy but I haven't seen anything that I really love.' Judith mopped the last drop of soup from the bowl with a piece of bread. 'That was *gorgeous*.'

'You'll know the house when you find it. You'll walk into it and you'll say, "This is the one." Trust me. Of course it would be no harm for you to light a candle every so often and ask for the right house to become available for you.' Jillian cleared away the dishes and placed a bowl of salad in the middle of the table before serving up the chicken and pasta.

'You're a great woman for the candles.' Judith smiled.

'I love lighting candles. I love the symbolism of opening to the light, of bringing down light to a situation. It just brings another dimension to the problem, or the issue, or the task at hand. And I love when people light a candle for me.'

'Oh, you're so spiritual, Jillian,' Judith sighed. 'You have such faith.'

'Oh, don't say that. I hate people telling me I'm spiritual.' Jillian grimaced. 'It's only opening to another dimension of your life, that's all, Judith. Everyone has the choice of doing it; it's no big deal. *You* know what I'm like, a wagon of the highest order a lot of the time. I just love knowing that there's so much more to all of this life than we think.'

'I guess I've been thinking a little differently since my accident,' Judith admitted. 'Do you think it happened for a reason?'

'Perhaps. Look at the difference in your and Lily's relationship. Sometimes we need a wake-up call to change. There's a whole other aspect that makes you look at things in a different way when you go into that "spiritual" zone, as you call it. It takes the sting out of what appear to be bad things that happen. I like to think that there's a great plan for all our lives, I like to think there is a loving higher energy that is our source but, having said that, you know me as well as anybody, Judith, and you know that I'm no goody-goody and I can curse and swear and rant and rave as good as the next one.' Jillian took a swig of her wine and laughed.

'You would probably have understood all that stuff that Sheeva one was spouting. You know, that anything that's not done with *loff* is no use and that the only people we are responsible for are ourselves. I mean, that's not *realistic*! People would be abandoned to their own devices all over the place if that was the case.' Judith speared a piece of creamy pasta, with venom. She had told her friend of her encounter with Sheeva in an irate phone call when she'd got home from Dun Laoghaire.

'Oh, for God's sake, that kind of stuff drives me mad.' Jillian threw her eyes up to heaven. 'We're only human, we have to learn the lessons we were sent to learn as best we can. All we can do is our best, Judith. And God knows you did your best with Lily. Sheeva might be a very evolved being in her own eyes but belittling what you did and making herself appear superior sounds like she might be on a bit of an ego trip, if you ask me. And the *loff* thing and only being responsible for yourself makes me wonder: is that a bit of a cop-out for not helping out people in her own life? It's a very convenient excuse, if you ask me,' Jillian said derisively. 'Some of these ones are a bit OTT. And some of them think they're "special" because they have "gifts". Give me a break. We're *all* special! We all have our gifts. I make meatloaf to die for.' She grinned again.

'I can vouch for that. Your meatloaf was one of the highlights of my stay in hospital,' Judith enthused, chuckling.

'Honestly, Judith, you just have to be discerning with all of this,' Jillian advised. 'I was reading a website recently and this one, who claims to be the only "authentic" seer and mystic – there's ego for you – was going on about the revelations she'd been given about the world. All doom and gloom of course, although she wasn't specific. Naturally, only she was allowed to know these revelations, her being "special", but she wasn't allowed to tell people what they were in case they were worried and frightened. What's the point of mentioning them if that's the case, and worrying people anyway?' Jillian scoffed. 'All that was about was showing how allegedly "special" she is . . . ego stuff again.'

'Weird,' Judith agreed. 'Do they lose the run of themselves? One of the young ones at work was very upset after someone like that told her that her father was going to pass very quickly after her mother died. She kept expecting to get a phone call with bad news about him and was in a terrible state for months every time the phone rang on her desk. That shouldn't be allowed. People are vulnerable enough after a death without being burdened with fear of another one.'

'My mother always says God decides and no one else, and she's right.' Jillian offered Judith the salad bowl. 'Some of those people are very good at manipulating people. I've seen it happen, and it ruins it for the really gifted healers and mediums who are genuine and want to help people.'

'Sheeva said I chose my accident and my pain.' Judith scowled.

'You know, I think life's hard enough without us being told we choose all the things that happen to us so that we can learn lessons from them. Your life has changed a lot since the accident, true, and so has Lily's, so yes, that has brought new ways of thinking and being into your life, but the pain thing I never understand. Or the cruelty of old age – I cannot for the life of me understand how pain can help anyone evolve or grow spiritually.' Jillian shook her head. 'There are so many different teachings, so many different viewpoints. Some of them are so complicated: "I am what I am not" type of thing. Or we could be "healed in the twinkling of an eye if we believe it to be true". I've tried that one with my migraines, believe me,' she said sarcastically, and Judith laughed heartily.

'Give me simplicity any day.' Jillian spooned another helping of chicken and pasta on to Judith's plate. 'Some of the nicest and most understandable teachings that I've read are in the White Eagle books – they're lovely, Judith. I'll put some of them in your room. Stop fretting about what that Sheeva one said to you. You and Lily love each other, and none of what you did was wasted. And it *was* difficult. You're a great daughter, Judith, and now Lily is coming into her own as a mother, and that's all that matters. Now drink up like a good woman, so you can catch up with me and I won't feel like a right lush,' Jillian ordered, picking up the wine bottle.

Several hours later, Judith made a face as she drained the last drop of Prosecco in her glass. 'God, I haven't been this pissed since I had that one-night stand before my accident,' she said. She was draped along Jillian's comfy sofa while her friend lounged with her legs over the side of an armchair and the fire crackled companionably up the chimney as a howling gale keened around the house.

'I'm afraid the best I can offer you is Johnny Carter in the house two fields across from us. He's about seventy-five, he has all his money under his mattress because he doesn't trust the banks, and he thinks "wimmin" should stick to the home and not be going out to work and taking good jobs off the men. And they shouldn't wear trousers either.' Jillian giggled.

'So if I went over in these jim-jams I wouldn't get a warm reception, then.' Judith stretched out her pink-clad legs and winced as a dart of pain shot up her left leg.

'Is it sore?' Jillian asked sympathetically.

'Probably from the driving. It's the longest one I've done.' Judith yawned widely.

'Deep Throat has nothing on you! Johnny Carter, eat your heart out – you don't know what you're missing,' Jillian wise-cracked and Judith guffawed.

'Spiritual, aren't I?' her friend snorted and they fell around laughing as Jillian poured them another glass of Prosecco.

It was after midnight when Judith slid under the duvet of the big double bed with the white bolster and quilted brown and gold eiderdown. It reminded her of her late grandmother's snug bedroom. The bed was toasty warm from the electric blanket that Jillian had thoughtfully switched on earlier. She was such a dear friend. It was a great comfort to have someone to talk to who knew you inside out and who understood where you were coming from. Maybe she and Jillian had had past lives together and were of the same soul group? That was one of Sheeva de Burca's theories. Some of what she'd been saying did seem to make sense. Judith liked the idea of the soul group, but as for doing everything with *loff* – she gave a tipsy smile – idealistic and all as it sounded, it wasn't realistic. Jillian had confirmed that, and she was far more in touch with reality than Floaty Sheeva, and far more compassionate about human frailties too. Judith snuggled down feeling deliciously woozy and relaxed. It had been the perfect evening, she didn't have to get up in the morning, she was on her holliers for a few days before she went back to work and she was going to make the most of it.

It made such a difference not having to worry about Lily. She had sounded so perky on the phone when Judith had phoned her to tell her she'd arrived safe and sound. She was meeting her friends for an outing the following day and so looking forward to it and that, more than anything, gave Judith enormous pleasure. Her mother had a life again after all these years, and so had she. Judith fell asleep and, for the first time in a long time, slept the whole night through.

CHAPTER TWENTY-FOUR

The creaking and rattling of the pipes as the central heating harrumphed into action woke Lily, as it usually did around six thirty every morning. She could feel the chill in the bedroom and her nose was cold. She remembered still having busy Lizzies and blooming geraniums in her flowerbeds on a few occasions in November, but some heavy frosts had wrought havoc in the garden this year.

She sat up and shivered. She needed to use the bathroom. She found her slippers, in the dark, placed neatly side by side the way she always left them at night and, easing her feet into their soft comfort, made her way to the bathroom. The house was freezing. Judith was always telling her she should keep the heating on low all night, but it felt like overindulgence to Lily. It was far from central heating she'd been brought up. They'd had fires then to heat the house they lived in and, in the winter, an igloo would have been warmer.

Thinking of Judith reminded her that her daughter was spending the weekend with Jillian. She'd forgotten for a moment. Once she would have been petrified to be in the house overnight on her own, but she'd grown used to it during all the weeks Judith was in hospital. Now it hardly bothered her at all. That was a real blessing, a gift from above, Lily thought gratefully as she hurried back into bed and burrowed into the warm spot. She had prayed for her daughter all day yesterday until she'd got the phone call from her to say that she'd arrived safe and sound. It must have been traumatic driving past the place where she'd had the accident. One thing about Judith: she never ran away from the difficult things in life. Jillian had offered to drive over to Dublin from Sligo for her, but Judith had insisted on driving over to The West herself.

It was good that she was taking the few days' break; she'd be back at work soon, back into the humdrum way of life, and Lily would miss her company and their little jaunts to view houses and their lunches out. These past couple of months had been immensely enjoyable. Lily felt a tear trickle down her cheek. All those wasted years when she and Judith could have been the best of friends. But she'd been given a second chance and she'd grasped it eagerly, she comforted herself as the heating took hold and vanquished the chill of the early morning. She was meeting Moira and Joan, her friends and bingo partners, that afternoon and they were going to go to the cinema in Omni. She hadn't been to the cinema in years and she was looking forward to it enormously. And that was something else she could do with Judith and, indeed, Cecily. That would be a nice evening for the three of them. They'd be like a real family. Mother and daughters enjoying each other's company and having fun. The thought cheered her up enormously and she drifted back asleep before the early kiss of dawn had even begun to lighten the eastern sky.

Later that day, she went through her wardrobe, wondering what to wear to the cinema. In her day, going to the pictures was an occasion, one to dress up for, but nowadays it seemed you could wear anything. Smart casual was the effect she was looking for, she decided. She'd read that phrase in an article about some woman who was well known for her charity work. She was most comfortable in 'smart casual', she said, even though she had to wear a lot of ball gowns and could never wear the same one twice. What strange creatures the rich were, Lily mused as she parted the clothes-laden hangers in her wardrobe. She'd recently read about some very rich woman who had six thousand pairs of designer shoes and the cheapest pair was about €400. Many of them were never worn. How did these people sleep well in their beds? she wondered, mystified. People were starving in the world, children dying of malnutrition; she would be riven with guilt to indulge in such excess. And mortified to have the world know of it. She glanced down at her six pairs of shoes, polished and placed neatly on the bottom shelf of her wardrobe. They were more than sufficient for her needs, and her patent-leather pumps for very special occasions were as good as any designer pair, she thought spiritedly.

Her gaze rested on a pair of dark-grey trousers Judith had bought for her a few years ago for Christmas. Lily had been quite vexed with her daughter, she remembered. She never wore trousers, preferring skirts and tops. She'd grown up being told by her rather strict father that trousers were unladylike. And Ted liked her legs anyway, and had told her when he was courting her that she had a very delicate and well-turned pair of ankles.

But everyone wore trousers now. Moira wore them a lot and always looked rather well in them. Even the Queen wore trousers now and again. Lily had seen a picture of her in a tabloid magazine in the doctor's waiting room and been very surprised indeed. Judith would be delighted if Lily told her she'd worn her trousers to the cinema. She picked out the hanger. The label was still on them: 'Marks & Spencer Classics'. She liked that. 'Classics.' It reminded her of Audrey Hepburn, and she had often worn trousers.

She unzipped the side of her skirt and let it fall to her feet. She stepped out of it and picked it up and hung it back in the wardrobe. She cut the tag off the trousers with her nail scissors and held them in front of her. They were very smart, with a little pocket at the side and a discreet design on the waistband. Lily pulled them on and fastened the zip. They fitted perfectly and the sharp crease in the front looked very well. They were rather elegant indeed, and most comfortable. She had a black cashmere jumper, another gift from Judith, that would go very well with them, Lily decided, feeling quite pleased with her new look. And a string of pearls around her neck would finish it off nicely. She had bought the pearls herself. Husbands were not allowed to buy pearls for their wives. It was an old superstition.

'Lily, you look a million dollars,' Moira exclaimed when she knocked on the door to pick her up. Joan waved from the car. 'I never saw you wearing trousers before. You wear them so well. You have the figure, you see. I look like a little dumpling in mine. I've a bottom like a question mark.'

'Moira, don't say that, you always look extremely fashionable.' Lily laughed, but she was delighted with the compliment. 'Judith bought me these ages ago and I thought they'd be ideal for the cinema, in case it's cold.'

'Isn't it bitter?' her friend agreed as she waited for Lily to put on her coat. 'Wrap your scarf around your neck so you don't catch a chill,' she advised.

'And I've got my gloves.' Lily picked up her leather gloves from the hallstand, gave her hair a last pat and set off on her latest new adventure with just the tiniest flurries of nervousness fluttering like butterflies.

Several hours later, as she sat ensconced before the fire sipping hot chocolate and watching an episode of *Emmerdale* that she had taped, she told her daughter gaily, 'I had a terrific time, Judith. The cinema was so modern and the seats were extremely comfortable and very clean. There was even a holder for your drink. 'Twas a great afternoon out, and then we went down to the Regency Hotel and had a bite to eat. I thoroughly enjoyed myself and, Judith, do you know what I wore?'

'What did you wear, Ma?' Lily could sense that her daughter was smiling.

'Do you remember that pair of grey trousers you bought me one Christmas? I decided I'd give them a try and, do you know, they were lovely, and I got great compliments from the girls.

They keep your legs grand and warm. I might get you to come into town with me some day and pick a few more pairs. Would you do that with me?'

'I'd love to do that with you, Ma. I'm *delighted* you wore them. And I bet they looked great on you, because you have a good figure for trousers. I was always hoping you'd start wearing them.'

'Do you think so? Moira said the same thing. I thought they looked smart all right. I took them off when I came home and pressed them. I'm rightly pleased with myself today, Judith. It was a very good day – but I'll be looking forward to seeing you when you get back,' she added hastily, in case Judith felt she wasn't missed.

'And I'll be looking forward to seeing you too, Ma, and I'm so glad that you enjoyed yourself. Jillian sends her love. Sleep well now.'

'The same to you, dear, and my love to Jillian as well.' Lily smiled as she hung up. She was tired, but pleasantly so. She was looking forward to getting into bed tonight. Cecily had invited her to Sunday lunch the next day, and she was actually looking forward to it. Her daughter had suggested an outing to the Newbridge Centre in the afternoon. She was going to start her Christmas shopping and wondered if Lily would like to come. That would be another new experience, Christmas shopping with her younger daughter. She'd be able to buy some pretty gifts for her new friends and perhaps one of the lovely Newbridge pieces of jewellery for Judith, for Christmas. It would be good to have Cecily's opinion; she was a seasoned shopper. Lily would wear her trousers again. Now that she'd worn them so successfully once, there was no stopping her. Lily yawned. She'd have an early night. Life was so exciting now she wanted to have plenty of energy to enjoy it.

'Ma's absolutely buzzing. She wore trousers that I'd bought her ages ago for the first time and she thoroughly enjoyed the cinema. She's off to Cecily's for lunch tomorrow. It's all go. Isn't it fantastic?' Judith sipped from her glass of McGuigan signature Shiraz, one of her favourites, and cut another piece of tender fillet steak, piled soft golden fried onions on to the fork and ate it appreciatively.

'I'm delighted for Lily. After all these years it's great to think she's enjoying life at last. Long may it continue.' Jillian lifted her glass and clinked it against Judith's. 'And here's to my friend enjoying life to the full too,' she added warmly.

'Well, for the first time in decades, I wake up in the morning looking forward to getting up and seeing what the day brings,' Judith said cheerfully.

'Don't say that too soon.' Jillian topped up their glasses. 'We could have the hangover from hell tomorrow.'

'Sure we'll walk it off like we did today. I haven't had such an amount of fresh air in ages. I know I'll sleep like a log. It's such rich air, isn't it?' she remarked, devouring another forkful of steak and onions. They'd gone for a walk up at Rosses Point to see the Metal Man and Oyster Island, wrapped up like two Eskimos in the biting wind, and it had been invigorating and exhilarating. Judith had felt thoroughly refreshed by the time they got back to the house. They'd lolled on the sofas reading the papers, had a snooze and then gone down to support a craft fair in the local village hall. They had coffee and cream cakes in the coffee shop and come home and piled up the fire and gossiped until it was time to cook the dinner.

She hadn't been as relaxed in years, Judith thought that night as she pulled the eiderdown up to her shoulders and turned over to read a few pages of her book before going asleep. Not even the thought of her impending return to work caused her any concern. One thing she had decided in this new phase of her life was that work would not be the be-all and end-all of her life. She would work to live from now on, and she was going to emulate her mother and start living life to the full. Fifty was the new forty: she could moulder away from middle age into old age or she could get off her ass and start anew. Life was short; she'd learned that the hard way. Sheeva would probably have told her that her accident was the Universe giving her a wake-up call. She opened the book and felt her heart constrict as she read, under the heading 'Release Comes With Forgiveness':

> To forgive is often difficult, my children, but with forgiveness comes release to the spirit.

She and Lily had truly forgiven each other for the hurts of the past, and that was all that mattered. She read more of the loving words of calm comfort until her eyes began to droop. *Give me a message, please,* she asked silently, as Jillian had suggested she do when reading the White Eagle books. She closed it, paused, opened it and smiled as she read: *Be Gentle With Yourself.*

After Sheeva de Burca's pronouncements, which had upset her a lot, Judith admitted, White Eagle's compassionate message was balm to her weary spirit. She was sure the other woman hadn't meant to sound judgemental and unkind. Perhaps Sheeva had achieved great spiritual mastery and she was able always to act with love. It was something Judith would aspire to, but for now, starting out on this new path of learning, she would try and take the message she had been given to heart. Having always judged herself rather harshly, it was a very consoling message to receive. Greatly comforted, Judith fell soundly asleep with the precious little book under her pillow.

Chapter Twenty-five

'Good luck now today, and don't overdo it. And if you feel very tired, come home early. I'm sure they won't mind for the first few days if you do.' Lily patted Judith on the back as she walked out into the hall to go to work.

'Thanks, Ma, and thanks for getting up to get me my breakfast, but there's no need for that every day, especially on these cold, dark mornings,' Judith said firmly, knotting a soft pink scarf at the neck of her black woollen coat.

'I know that, but today is a special sort of day.' Lily shivered as a sharp blast of cold air infiltrated the warm hall when Judith opened the front door.

'I'll give you a ring and let you know how it's going.' She waved and hurried to the shelter of the car. Her mother stood wrapped in a green candlewick dressing gown, waving encouragingly as though Judith were a child on her first day at school.

The car was freezing and she'd already poured a kettle of hot water over it to de-ice the windows. The early-morning commute was well under way and dark figures scurried from houses like little voles and made their way by car or by foot along her road. Driving towards the Drumcondra road, as she'd done a myriad of mornings to get to work, her mother's words kept repeating in her head: 'Today is a special sort of day.' And it was, Judith agreed. It was a very singular day in her life. She was going back to work not the old, angry, resentful, unfulfilled Judith of yore but a woman who was at peace with herself after years of deep unhappiness. Having that accident had been a turning point in her life and perhaps her greatest blessing, looking back on it, she mused as she waited patiently to turn right to join the tide of vehicles, headlights like giant, glowing torches, that flowed relentlessly towards the city.

Once she'd finally accepted responsibility for the choices she'd made in regard to her caring of her mother and all that had entailed, peace had come. It had been a gradual process of acceptance, but now she was going back to work, no longer bitter and angry but glad, in the current economic climate, that she had a very good job indeed, and determined to keep work in its place and live life as it should be lived. One thing she was clear about: she was not going to be the dragon she'd been previously at work. Wages and Salaries had survived the loss of Judith Baxter for the last few months, she thought in wry self-mocking, and she was perfectly sure Caitriona Slater had ruled her domain with a very light hand. Judith knew that the staff in her department would not be relishing this morning. And that was to her shame, she thought regretfully. But it was never too late to change, never too late to make amends – she and Lily were the perfect proof of that – and perhaps the big creamy gateau she'd ordered from Thunders with the words 'Thank You' piped across the top in gold icing that was now in the boot of her car would be the first step in détente.

Usually an avid listener to *Morning Ireland* on her commute to work, Judith found the news depressing: the economy, sexual abuse, the property slump, the bank bail-outs and greedy ex-billionaires who had brought the country to its knees, whinging and taking no responsibility. Judith shook her head as she heard the poor regulator being blamed for doing his job – and a very good job he was doing, if he was let get on with it. It really was all about accepting responsibility for your choices and accepting the consequences, as those avaricious men would learn at some stage in their lives. She'd had to face the issues of choice and acceptance of responsibility in a way that was momentous to her. Perhaps it was a lesson everyone had to learn during their lifetime.

She reached out and changed channels, and the soothing strains of a Viennese waltz permeated the car, and not even a Merc hogging a yellow box and holding up the traffic could raise Judith's ire, as it once would have.

'The good times are over, girls,' Sally Ford grimaced as she hung her coat in her locker in the changing room.

'I know, back to no mobile phones and no personal phone calls, and being spied upon from the Eagle's Nest. I wonder *has* the eagle landed yet? She was probably in at seven checking everything. She's got Caitriona up there for the handover of power,' Eilish Reilly sneered.

'Ah, leave her alone, she's had a rough time. Let's give her a chance to settle in before we start giving out,' Orla Ryan remonstrated.

'I told you I met her a few weeks ago and she was actually quite nice.' Debbie touched up her lipstick and set her phone to silent.

'Right, let's go.' Carina snapped her fingers, grinning, and they all trooped down the corridor to the big open-plan office. Judith's office door was open and they could see their boss sitting at her desk engrossed in deep conversation with Caitriona and Janice from HR.

Judith looked up, saw their downcast faces as they walked past and gave a half-smile. Only Debbie and Carina smiled back. 'Good morning, ladies.' Judith came to the door of her glass-fronted office. 'I'm just getting up to speed on things with Caitriona, and when we're finished, perhaps you'd all join us for a cuppa.' She smiled again, noting the double takes and looks of surprise flashing between them. In all the years she'd worked there she'd never invited anyone into her office for a cuppa, let alone her entire section.

'I'll leave you to it then, Judith. Take it easy and go home early.' Janice stood up. 'I'll see you in the canteen later. Thanks, Caitriona, you did a terrific job, I'm sure Judith will agree.' She smiled at the younger woman.

'Indeed.' Judith nodded. 'I knew when I heard who'd been given the acting position that the section was in a pair of very capable hands.'

'Thanks, Judith. But when you take over a section that's extremely well run, it makes it a lot easier,' Caitriona responded graciously. She was a particularly calm, competent young woman, Judith reflected. She'd never really used her to her full potential because she'd been so concerned about keeping 'control' in the office. She'd have to try hard not to let old ways take hold again. She noted that Caitriona had the slats in the blinds lowered halfway. Judith had always had them open flat so that she could see out into the big office and check what was going on. That would be her first change. She would keep them the way Caitriona had them, as a gesture of good faith. A small gesture, but a gesture all the same. From what she could see, the department was running smoothly, and she knew that Caitriona would have been a far more relaxed boss than she had ever been. She should try and emulate her.

'I hope you won't find it too difficult reverting back to your old position, Caitriona. Did you enjoy the experience?' Judith asked when they were on their own.

'It *was* very challenging,' Caitriona responded. 'When you're on the outside looking in it doesn't seem such a big deal, and I never really understood how hard it is to be in charge of a section, especially one like this, so I guess I'll be more appreciative of the demands that are made on you and of the demands you make on us,' she admitted honestly. 'I did feel the weight of responsibility, but yes I did enjoy it, Judith. It was good to push myself. And they are a good bunch out there. One or two did try to take advantage, as you can imagine,' she added. 'So I had to nip that in the bud, but once they saw I wasn't going to take any messing, it was fine.'

'Ms Reilly and Ms McKeon, I'd imagine,' Judith murmured, and Caitriona laughed.

'Spot on.'

'Well, I'm sure they're not jumping up and down that I'm back, but new day, new beginnings,' Judith said dryly. 'Caitriona, it's excellent experience to have on your CV, and of course, should any interviews for promotions come up, this will stand to you and I will of course be giving you the highest references. Thank you. You did a great job. I had every faith in you, as I said, when I heard you'd been made acting.'

'Thanks very much, Judith. If I can be of any help during the next few days, please let me know. Janice is right, you should go home early for the next couple of days.' Caitriona stood up. 'Can I do anything here?'

Judith stood up too and plugged in the kettle she'd filled earlier. Then she took some paper plates, plastic cups, a box of teabags and a jar of coffee from her press. 'I got a "Thank You" cake,' she said lightly, lifting it out of the big square white box. 'I'll let you do the cutting and slicing.'

'Oh, that looks delicious,' Caitriona exclaimed.

'Hmmm, it does,' agreed Judith, licking some cream off her finger. 'Will you call in the girls?'

They crowded into the small space when Caitriona called them in, and Judith could see that they were most taken aback when they saw the cake in all its luscious glory on her desk in front of them.

She took a deep breath. 'Girls, I just wanted to say thank you for all your good wishes and the flowers when I was in hospital, and I particularly wanted to thank Caitriona here. She's done a fine job, I'm sure you'll agree. When I heard she had been given the acting position I knew the section was in good hands—'

A round of applause for Caitriona erupted, led by Debbie and Carina.

'Well deserved.' Judith felt herself relaxing. 'Er . . . just before I get Caitriona to cut the cake for us, I had time to think over the past few months and ... um ... I was wondering what you would think of this suggestion. I was thinking that on the first Friday of every month we could have an informal cuppa here in my office and we could discuss any issues that come up, or any suggestions people might have about our work practices. That might make life easier for all of us.'

A murmur of approval rippled around the office and Judith could feel the edge of tension when they'd first come in begin to trickle away. It would take time for them to relax with her – she had been an authoritarian, there was no denying it, but small steps led to bigger things, and she would do her best to become a nicer boss to work for, she vowed, handing a knife to Caitriona. 'I'll make the tea or coffee as required; you cut the cake and give everyone a decent slice.'

'I will, and I'll give myself the biggest slice of all.' Caitriona laughed as she sliced into the creamy confection and the girls lined up to partake of the tasty treat.

Half an hour later, Judith sat at her desk. It was strange not being able to look out at her staff to see if they were all gainfully employed, as she'd done before her accident. But to open up the blinds would be to go back to the old regime of distrust and control, and she didn't want that, so she bent her head to the figures on her screen and focused her energies on making sure they balanced correctly before signing off on them.

'She must have got a right bang on the head when she had that car accident, or else she's had a personality change,' tittered Edna McKeon.

'Not nice, Edna, don't be such a bitch,' Carina said sharply as she set her lunch tray down on the table in the canteen.

'She has changed, though, you can't deny that,' Sally retorted. 'I was waiting all morning for the blinds to open, and she never touched them.'

'Me too.' Debbie sprinkled Parmesan cheese over her pasta dish. 'It was a bit nerve-racking. But she's obviously had a rethink about the way she was running the office, probably after seeing how smoothly it went when Caitriona was in charge, and she's trying to be less heavy-handed. I think that Friday thing is a good suggestion. It shows she's making an effort.'

'Yeah, but will she take note of our suggestions? I wouldn't think so,' Eilish scoffed.

'Time will tell, but I say we give her a break. She's had a rough time – I saw the state of that car on the news and she was lucky to get out alive,' Carina said firmly.

'I'd agree with that,' Debbie concurred.

'Why? She was absolutely horrible to you. How can you be nice to her now? How can you be such a doormat?' Eilish retorted, flabbergasted.

Debbie glowered at her colleague, disgusted. 'Because I'm not a total bitch, Eilish. I believe in giving people second chances. You don't know this, but I spoke to Judith about her attitude problem towards me and she took it on board. Nor am I a doormat, I can assure you, and the proof of that is: you owe me €20 for the last two office collections and this is my *third* time to remind you, so I really would like it back. In light of what you've just said, I'm sure you'd agree it would be very doormatty of me not to ask you for it.' Eilish Reilly could be a real little troublemaker and Debbie didn't particularly like her. She was the kind of colleague who would smile to your face and stab you in the back five minutes later, and she was a complete skinflint to boot. She could fumble for Ireland when it came time to pay a bill; Debbie had been caught out a couple of times when they had had lunch in the Snackery, a small deli near the office, and Eilish would say, 'I'll leave the tip,' and put a euro coin on the table, leaving Debbie to pay. The last two office collections, Eilish had asked her to put in a €10 note, and had never given the money back. Debbie was damned if she was going to let the other girl get away with calling her a doormat, or get away with being a sponger.

Eilish flushed cherry-red and took out her purse. 'Here's your twenty,' she muttered sourly.

'Thanks, Eilish, third time lucky,' Debbie said with pretended airiness.

'Whatever,' Eilish said coldly. 'Excuse me, I have to go and speak to Peter Walsh about something.' She took her plate of Caesar salad and walked across the canteen to another table.

Carina gave Debbie the thumbs-up. Eilish's mean streak was well known. She'd pulled the tip stunt on most of them and left them to pay the bill with a little derisory smile, knowing she'd got away with it again.

'Probably looking to scrounge the twenty she gave you back,' Sally declared. 'Well done for calling her on that, Debbie. She gets away with murder. Has she left you to foot the lunch bill and paid the tip, by any chance? I got stung with that one recently.'

'That's her favourite stunt.' Debbie shrugged, slipping the €20 into her purse. It would come in handy to get something for the dinner later.

'It was a nice touch bringing in that cake, and Judith clearly wants to make a fresh start, so who wouldn't be in favour of that?' Lourdes Marcos interjected diplomatically, changing the subject.

'It's just such a turnaround. She used to be a total wagon, you can't deny that,' Edna said huffily, still annoyed at Carina's earlier rebuke.

'Maybe a close shave with death *does* change you, Edna,' Carina said briskly. 'All I'm saying is, Judith came back to work extending an olive branch and I for one am going to accept it and give her a chance. That's my position on the matter; you deal with it the way you want to deal with it.'

'It won't last, and you're mad if you think it will. A leopard never changes its spots,' Orla warned portentously. 'Gooey "thank-you" cake or not!'

CHAPTER TWENTY-SIX

'Step on the scales for me, Melissa, please,' Dr Morton said pleasantly, and Melissa's heart began to thud. She had forced herself to eat for the past week so she would be showing an increase in weight for the psychiatrist. Otherwise, Dr Morton had told her, she would be taking her into hospital. She'd wanted to put Melissa's name down for a bed on her first visit to her, but her new patient had promised that she would eat sensibly and managed to convince her that she was being truthful and sincere in her promise. She would be fine as an outpatient, Melissa assured her parents and the consultant. The only problem was that it was becoming harder to keep food down. Melissa *wanted* to eat to keep herself out of hospital but as soon as she put food into her mouth she was almost gagging.

She'd managed to increase her weight by a pound for each of the first two visits to Dr Morton, but she had really struggled in the last week to eat enough to convince the doctor that she was in control of her eating and that hospitalization was not necessary. The previous day had been particularly bad. All she'd managed was a half a Weetabix and a banana.

The doctor glanced down at the small square screen and held a comforting hand under her elbow to guide her off the scales. She sat back down behind her desk. 'Sit down, Melissa,' she invited, writing a note in the file in front of her. She was a tall,

273

slender, dark-haired woman with big brown eyes and a steady gaze. She reminded Melissa of Charlotte in *Sex and the City*.

'Not good, Melissa. I can see you're struggling. I'm going to take you in as soon as we have a bed for you. You *would* like to get this sorted, wouldn't you? You can't do it on your own. You need help, and that's what we can give you,' Dr Morton said firmly.

'I'm fine, Dr Morton, honestly!' Melissa said frantically. 'I had a bit of a tummy bug last week, I think.' She truly did not want to go to hospital, where they would make her eat and she'd get fat again and her life would be an absolute disaster.

'Your parents have told me you've been making yourself sick—'

'Honestly, it was a tummy bug,' Melissa lied. 'It was going around the school.'

'That's as may be, but you haven't gained enough weight over the course of your last two visits to convince me that you can do this on your own. In fact, you've lost weight. We had an agreement that if you could gain sufficient weight and maintain it, we would work together on an outpatient basis, but it's not happening, pet, and I don't want you sliding down any further than you've gone already. I'm just going to call in Mum and Dad.'

Tears of frustration brimmed in Melissa's eyes as the doctor went out to the waiting room. This was, like, so totally unfair. Why couldn't everyone leave her alone?

'I've had a little chat with Melissa, and I think that our next step is to take her into hospital for a couple of weeks to go on our inpatient programme. We've tried the outpatient approach, but it's not working and I don't want her to slip any further. I think she'd make more progress with hospital care. I'll put her on the list for a bed.' Dr Morton directed her words to Aimee and Barry, and Melissa could see the relief on her parents' faces. Obviously there was no point in looking to them to argue against it.

'I don't want to go into hospital. I'm not sick.' She started to cry. She felt very frightened. She'd never been away from her parents except for school tours or sleepovers at friends' houses. She didn't want to be on her own at night in a strange bed, sharing a ward with other people.

'It's the best thing for you, Muffin. We're at our wits' end to know what to do to help you. We have to take the doctor's advice to get you well again.' Barry put his arms around her and she cuddled in against him, sobbing.

'Don't cry, Melissa. Lots of my patients come into hospital for a couple of weeks and do the programme and they sort themselves out. You'll be fine,' Dr Morton said kindly.

'I need you to be well for the baby, Melissa. Remember our talk about you looking forward to being an older sister? If you're not well, you won't be able to look after the baby for me,' her mother pointed out, and to Melissa's shock she could see tears in Aimee's eyes. Her mom *never* cried.

'OK, Mom.' She struggled to swallow the huge lump that was almost strangling her as tears ran down her cheeks and her nose streamed snot from crying. Dr Morton handed her a tissue.

'My secretary will give you a call when a bed becomes free. In the meantime, Melissa, try and follow the eating plan I gave you. We will help you all we can but in the end you have to decide for yourself that you want to get well and be healthy again. OK? It really is *your* decision.'

'OK, Dr Morton,' Melissa said curtly. She *hated* the doctor for interfering in her life and making it a misery.

'It's the best thing for you. I really think that.' Aimee slipped an arm into Melissa's as they walked back to the car, and Melissa felt consumed with guilt. Her mother looked so pale and stressed. She had enough to worry about with the new job and the new baby without having to worry about her. She felt thoroughly scared. She had always thought *she* could control *it*, but more and more *it* was controlling *her*. When she saw food on a plate in front of her she felt actual terror, even though she knew she needed to eat it or she would get very ill.

'I'll see you later, Muffin.' Barry kissed her when they reached Aimee's gleaming new black Lexus. 'I'll be home from work around four – how about we watch a DVD together tonight?' he suggested.

'I'm going down to Drew's stables with Connie. Drew told Connie I could ride Venus whenever I wanted to, and when you said I didn't have to go back to school after this, I arranged it with Connie 'cos she's finishing work at two. I told you that the other day,' Melissa reminded him.

'Sorry, I forgot. Enjoy yourself, and I'll see you when you get home,' Barry said. 'And wrap yourself up warm. It's very cold,' he added as they got into the car. He waved at them and went to cross the road to where his car was parked.

'Are you sure you're up to going horse riding? I'd prefer it if you didn't,' Aimee said as they snapped on their seatbelts.

'I'm fine, Mom,' Melissa said irritably, switching the radio channel to 2FM. 'I just can't wait to see Venus and Frisky and Marino again. I'm always *really* happy when I'm with the horses.'

'OK, OK.' Aimee backed down, as Melissa knew she would. Her parents were always keen to let her do things she wanted to lately, so if she wanted to get her own way about something she always said it would make her *happy*. She hadn't been to the stables for a few weeks because Connie had had to work extra shifts because one of the other nurses had been off work with a broken wrist, and she was longing to see the horses and Miss Hope and Connie.

'You have to eat something before you go to Greystones,' Aimee said when they got home. 'Let's have some soup and a ham sandwich.'

'OK,' Melissa agreed, and her mother gave her a suspicious look. 'Melissa, I have to get back to the office in the next hour. I'm trusting you and asking you to give me your word of honour that you will not make yourself sick after you eat,' her mother said seriously.

'I promise,' Melissa said, making herself sound as earnest and sincere as she could, really glad that her mother had finally moved into her new office.

'You're on trust now,' Aimee warned, taking out a carton of Butler's Pantry leek and potato soup and pouring it into a bowl to heat in the microwave. She buttered four slices of bread, placed some ham, tomatoes and lettuce between them and cut them neatly in eight triangles. She put four on a plate for Melissa and handed them to her.

Melissa carried the plate to the small kitchen table and tried not to think about the amount of fattening butter that her mother had smeared on the bread. There was so much food on the plate she felt a wave of panic smother her at the sight of it. Think of Venus, she urged herself as she nibbled at the soft middle part. She made herself eat the sandwiches, leaving the crusts, and then turned her attention to the soup. Potato and leek had always been her favourite. She could see her mother looking at her, so she lifted her spoon and pretended to eat with relish, longing for the moment when she could get rid of it and feel the comforting, deeply satisfying moment of relief and control. Aimee's mobile rang, giving Melissa a chance to take a welcome break from eating and, seeing that her mother was distracted, she casually stood up and carried the dishes to the dishwasher. She gave the soup bowl a quick rinse under the tap, allowing half the contents to go down the sink in a smooth, swift, practised movement as Aimee retouched her make-up and checked through her briefcase to see she had everything she needed. She took €30 out of her wallet and gave it to Melissa. 'For your Dart ticket – and perhaps you should buy Connie some chocolates or something for going to the trouble of bringing you to the stables,' she suggested.

'Thanks, Mom, you're the best.' Melissa gave Aimee a hug and felt her small round bump sticking in to her. 'Is it kicking?'

'Yes, put your hand on it.' Aimee smiled, placing her hand on top of Melissa's.

'Oh, it's so cool!' Melissa squealed when she felt the hard kick against her palm. 'Do you think it knows my voice?'

'Of course it does. Darling, you have to get well,' Aimee pleaded. 'Your baby sister or brother needs you to be well, and so do Dad and I. OK?'

'OK, Mom.' Melissa sighed, wishing her mother would leave so she could upchuck.

'Have fun today, and do as Dad says and wrap up warm. I have to go. Remember: you're on your honour not to be sick. Promise me.'

'I promise,' Melissa said solemnly, making her eyes big and earnest.

'Good girl. Text me when you get there and enjoy it. Bye.'

'Bye, Mom, see you later, and thanks for letting me off school.'

'We all need a day off now and again.' Aimee grimaced before grabbing her car keys and hurrying out of the apartment.

Melissa walked out to the windy, wraparound balcony and waited until she saw the car drive out of the car park, floors below, before hurrying to the bathroom. This was positively the last time she would make herself sick, she assured herself as she knelt on the floor. But oh, the relief of it, the absolute and utter joy of being in control of something in her life. The high of know-ing she would not put on those pounds they were all determined to make her gain. No one could understand how good it felt, she thought as she got rid of that stodgy white bread and soup. When it was over she sat on the side of the bath breathing deeply, trying to ignore the palpitations that were making her heart race uncomfortably. Her phone vibrated in her pocket and she saw Sarah's name come up on the screen. Her friend must be making a sneaky phone call, she guessed.

'Hi,' she said.

'How did it go?' Sarah whispered.

'OK,' she answered non-committally.

'What was she like? What did she say?'

'I've to have tests done.'

'What kind of tests?' Sarah's voice rose to a squeak.

'Blood tests, ones on my stomach. I might have a viral infection,' Melissa lied.

'Oh!'

'Look, I have to go, I'm going out to Greystones to meet Connie. Mom said I could have the afternoon off. I'm going over to Drew's stables. I'll ring you when I get home, OK?'

'OK,' Sarah said flatly, and Melissa felt a flicker of guilt.

'Thanks for ringing, Sarah, you're a great friend,' she said earnestly. 'I'll talk to you later. Bye.'

'Bye,' her friend said, and hung up. Melissa sighed. She and Sarah were having a hard time again. They had rushed into each other's arms and vowed never to have another row when she had ended up in hospital in September, and for a while things had been OK and they had been as close as ever, but in the last few weeks Sarah had grown edgy and anxious and was always asking her if she was puking up her food because she was getting so thin, and telling her she was crazy to be dieting. No matter how hard Melissa tried to reassure her that she was eating properly and that she was fine, Sarah would not believe it and had grown tense and irritable.

Melissa had eventually confided that she was going to a specialist about her 'tummy problems', as she'd called it and Sarah had made her promise to tell her 'exactly' what the consultant said. Melissa thought the 'viral infection' sounded quite plausible but somehow Sarah's less than friendly tone on the phone led her to think that she didn't quite believe her. Melissa bit her lip; it was hard trying to keep everyone happy. She didn't need Sarah on her case, it was bad enough having her family annoying her. She hurried down the hall to her bedroom and took the weighing scales out from their hiding place in her underwear drawer. When she had first visited Dr Morton, the consultant had, to her great dismay, told her parents to get rid of the scales in the bathroom. Aimee had removed them immediately they'd got home and put them in the bin. Melissa had promptly gone out and bought herself another set of scales and smuggled them into the apartment in her schoolbag.

She stood on the scales and looked down, heart thudding against her ribcage. She knew she had lost weight, and Dr Morton had confirmed it. '6.13' it read. She was under seven stone . . . for the first time ever, she was under seven! Adrenalin surged through her as she gazed at the precious numbers. What a triumph! What an absolutely fantastic achievement! She was ecstatic. She was going to be as thin as Posh and Keira Knightley. And to cap it all, she was going to get to ride Venus at last. It was turning out to be a far, far better day than she'd expected.

Sarah shoved her phone into her uniform pocket and trudged in through the heavy wooden door leading from the small garden into the corridor that ran the length of the school. She made her way towards the wide oak stairs and walked slowly up the dark, polished steps, heavy-hearted and angry. She was glad she had a study period in the library. She didn't want to talk to anyone. No one else in the class knew that Melissa was going to see a doctor today, or that she'd been going to see one since September. And as far as Sarah could see, this doctor was doing her friend absolutely no good whatsoever. Melissa was getting thinner and thinner, and paler and paler, and was losing even more weight instead of gaining it. And she wouldn't talk to Sarah about it, that was the really hurtful thing. Friends were supposed to share their problems. Friends weren't supposed to try and kill themselves with anorexia and leave their other friends worried sick and feeling helpless. Sarah's lip wobbled and tears dripped down her cheeks. She bent her head and hurried along to the toilets, ducking into a cubicle and burying her head into the crook of her elbow, trying to stifle the sobs that shook her body as she grieved for her best friend and hated her at the same time.

Melissa's high lasted all the way out to Greystones. It was a gloriously sunny day. The sun sparkled on the sea so brightly it almost cut her eyes to look at it as the train curved around the coastline and the elegant houses on Sorrento Terrace overlooking the sea gleamed white in the sun. Further along, as the train raced along the tracks, the Wicklow Hills and the Sugar Loaf rose up against the vivid blue sky like a landscape painting etched in the brightest, sharpest colours. To her left the sea surged and shimmered, and the waves, ridden by great white seahorses of foaming surf, crashed along the beach.

6.13. 6.13. 6.13, the train seemed to sing as it *clickity-clacked* along the rails, and Melissa flicked through a magazine with pictures of a magnificently skinny Posh in skintight leather trousers and dreamed of looking just as thin as her.

'So she's waiting for a bed and, to tell you the truth, Connie, it can't come quick enough as far as Aimee and I are concerned. We're at our wits' end. There's no talking to her. No reasoning with her. Whatever twisted idea is in her head, we can't get through to her.' Barry's despair carried along the phone line and Connie's heart went out to him.

'Well, please God, the programme will work for her. It may take time but at least she's in the system and she's under a top-notch psychiatrist and team. The results are good there, so try and keep your spirits up, and Aimee's. I'm sure it's not easy for her, being pregnant and everything,' Connie said sympathetically.

'She's not too bad now that the morning sickness is over and done with and of course she's up to her eyes with the new business. Work's always been Aimee's escape,' Barry said with a hint of irony.

'Well, it's never been mine.' Connie laughed. 'So I'm on the doss now for the afternoon with your daughter. And I'm hoping our daughter will be joining us later, although I haven't said it to Melissa. It's to be a surprise. They can ride home together on the Dart.'

'Connie, you're a brick,' Barry said warmly.

'I like seeing them together. I always feel you and I did something good when I see how close they've become.'

'We did something very special together, Connie,' he said huskily. 'We had Debbie and we stayed friends and there are times – and I want you to know this – that I'm really sorry we split. Really, really sorry,' he added for emphasis.

'There's no point looking back, Barry. We've both moved on and I'm very, very happy with Drew,' Connie said firmly, not going down that road, no matter how much Barry might want to.

'That's good, of course it is,' he said unconvincingly, and she smiled to herself. Barry could not disguise the fact that he was rather put out that she was with someone else after all her years of being single. Tough, it was her time now; she'd been in the doldrums for long enough.

'Anyway, have to go, the Dart's coming into the station. I won't let on you've said anything. If Melissa wants to tell me herself I'll act surprised. Take care and keep me updated. Bye,' Connie said briskly.

'OK, and thanks again.'

'No problem.' She slid the phone into her bag and sighed as the train slid to a halt. Her ex and Aimee were certainly going through the mill. Although she wasn't on the best of terms with the other woman after Debbie's wedding debacle, she still felt a degree of sympathy for her for what she was enduring.

Melissa was in trouble if hospitalization was on the cards, she thought gloomily, and her heart gave a twisted little lurch when she saw the teenager step off the train and saw how much weight she'd lost in the space of mere weeks. Connie wanted to cry when she saw the gaunt, pale, stick-thin creature walking towards her beaming in a black coat that was too big for her, remembering the lovely, healthy, bright-eyed youngster who had first come to visit her before Debbie's wedding. She composed herself and walked towards Melissa, trying hard to hide her dismay.

CHAPTER TWENTY-SEVEN

Hi Mom, have arrived OK. Connie waiting on platform. C U later.
XXXXXX

Aimee read her daughter's text and felt a lump in her throat. She was worried sick about Melissa. Watching her reluctantly make her way into Dr Morton's rooms, hunched up, emaciated and pale-faced, her coat by now far too big for her, she had almost cried aloud and had wanted to go rushing after her. But Dr Morton always insisted on seeing Melissa alone first. Aimee had wanted the doctor to admit Melissa to hospital after that initial visit, and had been shocked to hear that she was not considered an urgent case and that because there were so few beds allocated to eating disorders, a patient had to be very ill to be admitted. Now that Melissa was finally on the list for a bed, she felt terror as well as relief. Her mobile rang and she saw Juliet's name come up on the screen.

'Mum, I was just about to ring you. I'm just back in the office. Melissa's on a waiting list for a bed – at last. Dr Morton decided she needs intervention it's got so bad.' Aimee burst into tears.

'Darling, don't cry. At least she'll be well looked after and in the best of hands. Are you sure you don't want me to ask your father to use his contacts?' Juliet said delicately.

'No, Mum, I don't think it would make any difference, to be honest. I think they have to be at a certain stage before

283

hospitalization, and I think Melissa's reached that level. Don't worry, it's not pride or anything. Believe me, if I thought Dad could help I'd be on my knees to him,' Aimee sniffled.

'I know you would, darling, and he would help, you know that. He might be a bit of a termagant but he would do everything in his power to help Melissa.'

'I know.' Aimee rooted for a tissue in her bag.

'Is Melissa gone back to school, or is she at the apartment? I could go and spend the afternoon with her if she's on her own,' Juliet offered kindly.

'Thanks, Mum. I kept her off for the rest of the day. She's actually gone out to Greystones to meet Connie and go horse riding. It was all she could talk about.'

'Lovely,' said Juliet. 'Just what she needs. And of course she gets on so well with Connie, and she loves that gorgeous little cat Connie has. That will take her mind off things. And how are you, darling? Exhausted, I'd imagine.' Her mother oozed sympathy.

'Not too bad, considering. It's actually a relief to have the new office up and running and to have it to come to. It's my sanctuary, if you could believe that.'

'Oh, I'd believe it. You're more of your father's daughter than you care to admit,' Juliet said dryly.

'*Mum!*'

'*Mum!* indeed! How's Barry?'

'Being supportive and worried sick like I am. It's been a hell of a year. How are you getting on? Are the builders finished the snags yet?'

'Soon. I'll be having the grand unveiling when the painters are finished and I can put my furniture in,' Juliet said cheerfully.

'And how's Dad coping? I'm sorry I haven't been over these past few weeks. It's all a bit manic.'

'I think your father has thrown in the towel. I don't get arguments or slamming doors any more, just the occasional deep, deep, hurricane-strength sigh. I caught him having a sneaky look the other day. I think he's impressed in spite of himself.' Juliet chuckled.

'Well done, you.' Aimee smiled. 'I'm dying to see it.'

'Bring Melissa – I'd love to see you both. Darling, keep in touch and let me know what's happening.'

'I will, Mum, thanks for ringing,' Aimee said gratefully. Juliet was such an undemanding mother – which was just as well, she thought, as Aimee hadn't been over to visit her in ages. She really should make more of an effort, but life was so hectic at the moment. At least Juliet had her refurbishment to keep her occupied, and things with Ken seemed to have settled down. Her point to him that at least Juliet was still living under the same roof as him seemed to have resonated.

Tears blurred her eyes as she swung around in her cream leather chair then stood up and walked over to the big plate-glass corner window in her new office. She stared out at the Liffey hurling itself angrily against the quay walls, white caps frothing and foaming like cappuccinos. There was a sharp easterly breeze blowing up the river even though the sun was a dazzling lemon disc in a clear blue sky. She liked the view from her office windows, which stretched along the river as far up as Butt Bridge and downriver past the graceful new Samuel Beckett Bridge, the O2 and beyond. Roger owned the building, and Hibernian Dreams had river-frontage offices on the third floor. Paying no rent was a huge plus to their overheads, and she had to admit that with the spectacular new conference centre further along the quays and the new concert hall across the river, there was a lively buzz to the area that perfectly suited what Hibernian Dreams was about. Roger O'Leary was a shrewd businessman, and the more she got to know him, the more Aimee had grown to respect him. They were making slow but steady progress and he was adamant that there would be an upsurge of business and that new millionaires and billionaires would rise from the ashes of the Celtic Tiger. He'd been through recession and weathered it before, he'd assured her.

For all his bombast and bluster, she could see that he had never lost his focus or forgotten his roots and that was why he had held on to his wealth and his assets in this current economic tsunami. 'I was wined and dined and offered loans to buy bank shares, pressurized even,' he'd told her over a working lunch one day. 'The sky was the limit, I could have had as much as I wanted – hundreds of millions. I was never tempted, Aimee. Greed is a terrible thing, and it was, and still is, rampant in those circles. I would never put the business I've worked so hard to build up at risk, or the jobs of all my employees on the line, by borrowing reckless amounts of money no bank should ever have lent. It was immoral stuff, Aimee, and I have no sympathy for those greedy bastards who'll never have to pay it back who've brought the country to rack and ruin and put their workforces on the dole queues. I might not be smooth and sophisticated,' – he made a face – 'I worked my way up from living in a small cottage halfway up a mountain to where I am now, but I can pay my way, and pay my workforce, and any loans I have I can cover. They can call me a cute hoor all they want, I still have my millions, Aimee, and I intend to keep them. Eat up – you're looking a bit scrawny in the face,' he'd admonished as he speared a prawn and ate it with relish.

'And I intend to make you a few million more,' she'd smirked at him, biting into a piece of monkfish, and they'd laughed together companionably, quite aware that a hack from one of the more trashy tabloid papers was busy scribbling on a pad as she looked over in their direction from a table at the other end of the well-known restaurant.

> Multimillionaire businessman Roger O'Leary and soignée party planner Aimee Davenport showed no signs of being concerned by the current economic downturn as they lunched in L'Ecrivan last week. The pair have recently set up Hibernian Dreams Events and Catering, with offices on the quays. Rumour has it that O'Leary, who is often seen socializing with model Rosa Taylor, is diversifying in more ways than one. Watch this space . . .

The article had appeared in the gossip column the following Sunday, much to Roger's amusement.

'Great plug for the company,' he'd approved the next morning during the first phone call of the day. Privately, Aimee had been a tad miffed with the derisive 'party planner' tag, but it went with the territory and Roger was right: a free advertisement was not to be sneezed at. She wondered had Ian Kelleher, her ex-boss at Chez Moi, seen it. He hated her guts even more now for head-hunting three of his staff, especially Helen O'Connor, a very capable young woman whom he had earmarked to take over Aimee's department in the long term.

'You have no morals, no ethics,' he'd ranted down the phone at her when three of her ex-staff had resigned from his company to come and work for her, at a much higher salary. 'You're a hard, hard bitch, Aimee Davenport, and you'll get what's coming to you.'

'It's business, Ian, you'll get over it. Now *I* have work to do, if you don't,' she'd said coldly, and hung up.

Right now, though, planning events and parties was the last thing she felt like doing. She couldn't get the image of her daughter sobbing piteously on Barry's shoulder out of her head.

What would Connie make of Melissa when she saw her? It had been a while since Melissa had been to visit her in Greystones. For the first time since the falling-out at the wedding, Aimee wished she were on speaking terms with Barry's ex. How good it would be to have someone to talk to about her daughter's condition. She didn't want to discuss Melissa with the people she socialized with. Having a daughter with an eating disorder would surely reflect on her parenting skills, and she couldn't bear to have people talking about her and Melissa behind her back. But Connie was different. Aimee sighed as she watched a gull swoop down and snatch a crust of bread from the edge of the quay.

The truth was, she had always looked down her nose at Connie. Aimee had felt Barry's ex was a woman of little ambition, a woman content to let herself slide into middle age, a run-of-the-mill sort of woman who wouldn't be noticed in a crowd. She'd always felt triumphantly superior when comparing her sculpted, toned body to Connie's curvaceous, wholesome one. Aimee had been so relieved the first time she'd met her to know that Connie would never be a threat. Connie was ordinary to her own sparky, ambitious vibrancy, she'd reassured herself, wondering what Barry had seen in her. Connie dressed well enough but not with Aimee's sharp, effortless style, Aimee had noted smugly, and she'd been comforted that, in her mental list of comparisons, Connie came second every time. In fact, she didn't rate at all!

What was it about second wives and partners that they felt they had to compare and contrast with the first wife and come out on top? Aimee thought ruefully, remembering her initial impressions of Connie Adams. Was it some sort of inferiority complex that engendered these feelings? Some lack of confidence because of being the interloper? She'd always enjoyed it when, in the early years of their relationship, Barry had spoken dismissively of his first wife. Feeling a cut above Connie had always made her feel good . . . until now. Now she felt mean-spirited. Now she was ashamed, Aimee admitted silently, rereading her daughter's text.

Connie could have frozen Melissa out, just as Aimee had frozen Barry's first family out and been glad of an excuse to do so. But even though things were frosty between Aimee and her, Connie had never let on to Melissa and had treated her with immense kindness. She'd helped Juliet out in Spain and become firm friends with her – no wonder her mother rated her so highly. No wonder Barry did too. And Debbie was just like her mother in that regard. The apple hadn't fallen far from the tree.

Aimee had taken to calling the other woman 'Saint Connie' in a jeering manner when Barry had stood up for his ex; now she was very grateful indeed that Connie was a special part of Melissa's life and that Debbie had finally embraced the role of half-sister. Today Aimee's worst fears had been realized. She had hoped against hope that her daughter would listen to reason and follow the plan Dr Morton had drawn up for her. It was a futile hope. Melissa was very ill. Dr Morton had told them that their daughter was in danger of slipping off the ladder and that her body could no longer sustain the damage she was doing to it. She wasn't at rock bottom by a long shot, she had reassured them, but to make sure she didn't get there, it was now time to intervene.

Aimee had seen the fear in Melissa's eyes and her heart ached for her. Only when her daughter had started to talk about Connie and her cat and going horse riding had her eyes come alive and a little bit of the old Melissa had resurfaced. It was because of Connie and her good nature that Melissa had that modicum of happiness. Aimee might be the smart, stylish, successful career woman but Connie had the bigger heart and the stronger character, Aimee reflected, momentarily shamed by her shallow, prideful, egotistical condescension. She should at least acknowledge that she appreciated what Connie was doing for Melissa, difficult though it would be to make the first move. She'd send Connie a short text to thank her when Melissa got home, she decided. The worst the other woman could do was to ignore it, but at least Aimee could say she'd tried to mend fences.

Feeling somewhat comforted, Aimee sat back down at her bespoke rosewood desk and began to dictate a letter to the chairwoman of a well-known media company who wanted to host an event to promote a glossy new arts magazine, and winced as the baby kicked lustily, reminding her that, soon enough, she would have two children to worry about and not one.

Connie walked along the platform to meet her and Melissa hugged her tightly. 'How is Miss Hope?' she asked eagerly. 'Will we be going to see her?'

'Indeed we will,' Connie assured her. 'We're going to pop in home now to feed her and then we'll carry on to the stables. How about that?'

'Oh, Connie, I can't wait to see Miss Hope and Venus. This is, like, the best afternoon I've had in ages. Here's some Ferrero Rocher, I know they're your favourite.' She thrust the bag with the gold-wrapped chocolates in their shiny box at Connie.

'Ah, you dote, that was kind,' Connie said, touched. 'You shouldn't be spending your money on me though, there's no need for that, but I love these and we'll have one with a cuppa.'

'Well, actually, Mom gave me the money and told me to buy you some chocolates and I knew these were your favourites. I bought you a Euro Millions ticket too, 'cos it's huge on Friday, and if you win you can buy me a horse.' Melissa laughed, pleased at the result of her hastily selected gift purchases en route to the Dart.

'You bet I will. Drew can advise us. That's really kind, pet, thank you.' Connie gave her another hug and Melissa felt a wave of affection for her. Connie was so kind and reassuring. She felt she could tell her anything. Suddenly the urge to confide overwhelmed her. It was so hard keeping it all to herself. She was so weary of it. Connie was the type of person you could say anything to, and she was very knowledgeable about medical stuff, being a nurse. Maybe she might suggest a good tonic, Melissa thought hopefully as they began to walk towards the exit.

'Umm . . . you don't know this' – she glanced sideways up at Connie – 'but the reason I'm off school today is 'cos I had to go and see a consultant. Mom and Dad think I've a bit of an eating problem and they have me going to see this doctor, who wants to bring me into hospital. I'm fine really. Do you think you could tell them they're worrying about nothing, 'cos you're a nurse and they'd listen to you. Maybe I just need a good tonic – could you give me the name of one?' she ventured.

Connie stopped walking and looked straight at her and Melissa couldn't hold her gaze. She saw how sad and serious she looked and felt a sudden knot of fear in her stomach.

'Melissa, I will be very honest with you, because I hope we'll always be honest with each other and you've been honest with me. If this doctor that your parents have brought you to wants you to go into hospital, it's serious, love. And I would be lying if I said I wasn't concerned. You look very pale and anaemic and, as a nurse, I can see you're not well and, as your friend, I want you to know that I'll help you any way I can. But you need to face up to the fact that something's very wrong, Melissa, and we need to get to the bottom of it. A tonic isn't the answer.'

Melissa swallowed hard. Connie wouldn't lie and, somehow or another, she knew there was no point in trying to pull the wool over her eyes like she did with her parents. She knew that Connie could see right through her fibs and wasn't taken in, not in the slightest. Dr Morton was the same. There was no fooling her, as she had found out this morning. No way would Dr Morton take what she said on trust, like Aimee had earlier. In a way, it was a huge relief to come up against someone who *knew*. A relief to have someone to whom she could tell the whole truth. A relief not to have to pretend any more.

'I . . . I . . . thought I could stop . . . but I can't. I thought I could control it. I'm afraid, Connie. I hear voices in my head telling me it's bad to eat food,' she blurted out, looking down at her feet as her heart began to pound.

'That's OK, love.' Connie drew her into a comforting embrace. 'That's OK,' she murmured, rubbing Melissa's back. 'You'll get all the help you need. There's no need to be afraid. It's really good that you've told me that, because now you've admitted it to yourself and that's the first step.'

'Is it?' Melissa was utterly torn, raging with herself for revealing her torment and her secret and relieved beyond measure that she didn't have to carry the burden alone any more. She was so confused in her head about it all. One minute she was desperate to stop what she was doing; the next, desperate to lose more weight. Now Connie was telling her that admitting something was wrong was a big step. 'Is it really?'

'Yes, darling, it is, and once you do that, you've done the hardest thing of all. Trust me. Now come on and let's get to my place, because there's a very hungry little cat who has no problem eating,' Connie teased, and Melissa laughed and felt the tiniest little bit of happiness for the first time in a long, long while that had nothing to do with weight loss.

It had been such a struggle from when *it* had started controlling her. There were times she really *did* want to eat and she couldn't, times when she didn't want to make herself sick. At night in the dark, she would try hard not to admit that she was doing bad things to her body. She would try and not be scared but, mostly, she would listen to the voice in her head that told her food was bad. Now she'd told someone else about it, and Connie hadn't told her she was loopers but had been encouraging, so maybe everything would be all right and she could just go back to being normal, because that was what she wanted more than anything. *Thinly* normal though, she thought hastily, in case God might be listening and grant her wish.

Miss Hope came racing down the garden path as fast as an arrow when Connie parked the car and curled herself around Melissa's ankles, purring loudly, arching her back in ecstasy as Melissa stroked her. 'That cat loves you, Melissa,' Connie grinned as she opened the front door. 'Just as well I'm not the jealous type. I never get a look in when Drew's here either. She just plonks herself on his chest and gazes at him adoringly and I'm completely ignored.'

Melissa laughed. 'Animals love Drew, don't they? They can tell what people are really like. The horses all neigh like mad when they see him coming. Maybe I might train to be a vet after school. I'd like that, although I think Mom would like me to go to college and do business studies.'

'I'm sure when the time comes your Mom will want you to do something you'd really like, and I think you'd make a very good vet.' Connie led the way into the kitchen and filled the kettle. The wood-burning stove sent out a blast of heat as she threw a log in, and it blazed and sparked, filling the room with warmth. Melissa stood in front of it feeling the welcome heat infuse her cold hands as Hope rubbed her head against her leg, meowing loudly. She picked Hope up and buried her face in her soft, black silky fur. 'Oh, you are such a gorgeous little cat,' she exclaimed, feeling her heart bursting with love. Miss Hope always made her feel like that, and her green eyes were amazing. Wise and kind and full of love, her pupils like big black marble orbs that stared right into her soul. Melissa always felt that Hope knew *exactly* what was going on in her head. She fed her a treat of tuna in jelly and sat with her purring on her lap on the small squishy sofa waiting for the kettle to boil while Connie went upstairs to change out of her nurse's uniform.

'I love you, I love you, I love you,' she whispered in the cat's pointed velvety black ear and smiled when Hope licked her cheek with her pink tongue. She felt so safe and happy in Connie's warm kitchen with the cat purring on her knee and the flames flickering merrily in the stove. How wonderful it would be to stay here for ever and not have to go into hospital or school or anywhere at all, she thought wearily, as her tummy rumbled and the familiar ache of hunger assaulted her. Lassitude spread through her, making her want to close her eyes and sleep.

She put on a bright smile when she heard Connie coming downstairs. Maybe when she saw Venus she'd feel better, she thought, making a huge effort to ignore the dizzy tiredness that fogged her brain, and began chatting animatedly.

She thought Drew gave her a strange look when he saw her after they arrived at the stables. He was sitting astride his horse and cantered over to where Connie had parked. Maybe she was mistaken, she decided, as she gazed up in awe at Marino's impressive height and patted the side of his gleaming neck. Drew's boots were mud-spattered and dusty and she suddenly remembered with dismay that she had forgotten to bring her new riding boots with her, she'd been so anxious to make herself sick and then rush out of the apartment to get the Dart and not keep Connie waiting. Barry had treated her to them and she had to admit she loved looking at herself in the mirror with her boots and riding cap on. She hoped Drew would still let her ride. She had her riding cap in her tote bag. He swung his leg over the side of his big horse and dismounted in a lithe, athletic movement that she hoped she'd emulate and master eventually. She was so relieved that her ass was no longer huge. She would have been utterly *mortified* to have him see her tree-trunk thighs and massive buttocks of yore. Thank God she'd stuck to dieting, she thought with a wave of pride. She was no longer a whale, and that could only be a good thing, no matter what they all said.

'Hi Drew. Wow! Marino looks amazing, I can't wait to ride Venus. I'm *so* excited about it,' she burbled. Did she imagine it, or did Drew look over at Connie with that funny look in his eyes? What was wrong with *him*? Why did everything and everyone seem so weird today? she thought irritably, feeling suddenly deflated.

'Hey, Melissa, let's walk over to Venus's stall. I'll just get Triona to unsaddle Marino,' he suggested, giving Connie a kiss. 'Connie, it's very cold to be hanging around. Why don't you go up to the house and have a cup of tea,' he said lightly. 'Melissa and I will manage fine.'

'Sure,' Connie agreed, pulling the two edges of her pink parka tighter around her. 'You won't get any argument from me. It's *freezing.*'

Triona took Marino's reins and led him towards his warm stall while Drew and Melissa headed across the yard to where Venus stood, her head over the half-door of her stall, neighing a welcome.

'Melissa, I have to talk to you first before we tack up,' Drew said quietly, and her heart sank. She just knew he wasn't going to let her ride Venus today, she just *knew* it.

'What about?' She couldn't meet his piercing gaze.

'Have you eaten today?' he asked bluntly. His blue eyes were like laser beams as he studied her intently, raking her from head to toe.

'Of course I have,' she said quickly. 'I had lunch with Mom.'

'Melissa, you need to tell me the truth. I can't let you up on a horse if there's a danger you might faint. And you look as if you could faint to me. You're very, very pale. You could fall and hurt yourself very seriously or you could spook the horse and she could injure herself. You have to be strong and healthy to go horse riding. You have to be able to control your horse. I know I'll be walking her around the paddock with you. I'll be there, but I need to know you're OK to get up on her back.' Drew's face seemed to fade away from her. She could see him frown and look worried. He was saying something to her, but he seemed very far away. And then darkness started to close in like a weaving mist and she felt horribly weird. Melissa didn't remember him catching her just before she hit the ground.

CHAPTER TWENTY-EIGHT

Aimee jumped out of the taxi and raced towards the A&E department, dodging the smokers congregated at the door and a variety of young patients with splints, on crutches, in wheel-chairs, who lined the corridor before she arrived at the information desk. 'My daughter, Melissa Adams, brought in by ambulance,' she panted to the girl behind the desk. A gentle tap on her arm made her turn in confusion and she saw Connie standing beside her.

'Oh God, Connie, is she all right? I didn't want her to go horse riding. I tried to persuade her not to but she was adamant, and it gives her such pleasure I couldn't refuse,' she babbled before bursting into tears.

'She's OK, Aimee. Let's go and sit down,' Connie said sooth-ingly, nodding to the receptionist. She led Aimee to two empty blue plastic seats in the waiting room.

'Let me get you a cup of tea,' Connie said kindly. 'I won't be a sec.'

Aimee swallowed hard and nodded. Her heart was pounding and she felt quite faint from fear and stress. When Connie had phoned her to say that Melissa had fainted and that she had called an ambulance, Aimee had almost fainted herself. All the weeks of pent-up anxiety and dread seemed to coalesce into that one moment and she could hardly hear what the other woman was saying, her heart was pounding so loudly in her ears.

'I'll meet you in the hospital,' she'd said, before taking a few moments to try and gather her wits and her composure. She'd had to get her PA to call a taxi because she'd taken the Dart and Luas to work. Aimee had assured herself that she'd be very calm and collected and she would thank Connie politely for her trouble and tell her she'd take over from there. She'd expected Connie to be frosty, to say the least, considering their past history, and instead she was being kindness itself and Aimee felt completely wrong-footed.

'Are you OK? You're very pale.' Connie handed her a cardboard cup of steaming tea and a little plastic carton of milk and a sachet of sugar.

'Just got a bit of a shock,' Aimee murmured, remembering that the last time she'd spoken to Connie she'd been uttering scathing insults to her on the steps of the church at Debbie's wedding. 'What happened?' she asked, glad of the excuse to busy herself with the milk so that she didn't have to look at the other woman. 'Did she fall off the horse?'

'God no, Aimee! Drew wouldn't let Melissa ride in the state she was in,' Connie exclaimed.

'I didn't mean . . . I was just . . .'

'No, no, it's fine. Drew was asking her if she'd eaten, because he didn't think she was fit to ride, and she collapsed.' Connie sat down beside her and took a sip of her coffee.

'I want to see her right now.' Aimee jumped up agitatedly.

'Yes, of course. I came out because she was using a bedpan so I wanted to give her privacy. They have her on a drip. It's her potassium again. She told me it happened once before.'

'Oh!' Aimee sat down again. 'Sorry, I'm a bit distracted,' she apologized. 'I didn't mean to be sharp.'

'That's OK, Aimee, I guess I'd be frantic myself if it were Debbie, I'm upset enough because it's Melissa. I'm sure you're up to ninety,' Connie acknowledged quietly.

Aimee's face crumpled and she was overwhelmed by a fresh

bout of tears. 'I don't know what to do, Connie. We've tried everything. I don't know why we can't get through to her, I feel such a failure as a parent.'

'Shushh, you're not a failure at all, Melissa is a very lucky child, but these things happen, Aimee, it's no one's fault, and every parent's nightmare.' Connie put a comforting arm around her as she sobbed her heart out, not caring that people were looking at them.

'How can you be so bloody nice – to me?' she sniffled when the tears had subsided.

'Not that hard when you're crying your eyes out over some-one we both love.'

'Oh, you *are* a bloody saint. When Barry sings your praises to me I call you Saint Connie to shut him up,' Aimee said crossly, wiping her eyes and nose.

Connie laughed. 'Trust me, I'm far from saintly, believe me, and you should *never* have to listen to Barry singing my praises. That's just not on.'

'No, it's not, sure it's not.' Aimee managed a watery smile. 'Connie, I was a bitch at the church. I'm very sorry for causing a scene at Debbie's wedding. It was unforgivable.'

'Ah forget it, Aimee, it's water under the bridge now.' Connie shrugged. 'I gave as good as I got,' she added with a rueful smile.

'You did. I was impressed,' Aimee said spiritedly. Their eyes met and they laughed awkwardly.

'I just wanted to thank you for all your kindness to Melissa and to Mum, I really appreciate it. Melissa is mad about you,' she said quietly.

'And I'm mad about her. She's a dote, it's easy to be kind to her,' Connie said warmly. 'And Juliet is such a lovely person. We had a great laugh in Spain.'

'So she told me. I never told her about our row, she would have ticked me off big-time,' Aimee admitted.

'Aimee, let's forget it. We have someone we love in there to focus on, we're connected by family ties, it would be so much nicer and make life so much easier if we got on, don't you agree?' Connie said frankly.

'A bloody saint and right to boot.' Aimee sighed. 'I guess it's time to let bygones be bygones. I'm glad to put it behind us, Connie. Thank you. Barry will be pleased.'

'This is more about you and me, Aimee,' Connie said firmly. 'It would make me really happy to know that you're OK with Melissa coming to visit. I was always worried that it would be a problem for you.'

'Oh Connie, no, I'm so glad she has you. And I'm so glad she's got close to Debbie too. I'll admit I was miffed at the start, after the ... incident ... but when I see how happy it makes Melissa I'd be a real bitch indeed not to encourage it. At the end of the day, as I'm slowly learning, family is all that really matters,' she confessed.

'Yeah, well, family can drive you mad sometimes, as I well know,' Connie grinned, draining her coffee. 'There's one or two that my feelings are far from saintly for, I can assure you. But I'm glad we're sorted, Aimee. And anything I can do to help with Melissa, you only have to ask.' She reached out her hand and Aimee grasped it and squeezed it tight as emotions welled up again and she was unable to speak.

'I think my hormones are in chaos,' she muttered as she wiped her eyes yet again.

'Of course they are, but they'll get back to normal when you've had the baby,' Connie said, waving her hand up and down in front of her face. 'Mine are worse than that bloody Icelandic volcano. I could tell you about eruptions, believe me,' she groaned as a hot flush enveloped her. 'Thank your lucky stars you're only pregnant and not menopausal.'

They were laughing, sharing that moment of womanly solidarity, when Barry arrived, almost doing a double take at the sight.

What an eventful day it had been, for sure, Connie reflected as she sat on the Dart en route to Greystones. Drew was going to pick her up at the station and she was going to get an overnight bag together and stay at his place, seeing as her car was still there.

Melissa had wrapped her arms around her neck when she was leaving and the sight of her thin little face and huge blue eyes had almost brought her to tears. Barry had contacted Dr Morton and the specialist had told him that she would admit her to the unit the following day, directly from A&E, as a bed was due to become vacant.

Connie felt sorry from the bottom of her heart for Barry and Aimee; she knew what a tough journey lay ahead of them. It wouldn't be easy on them or Melissa. Aimee was a changed woman for sure, she mulled as the train glided out of Monkstown and picked up speed. The wan, agitated woman who had rushed into A&E was a far cry from the ice-cool businesswoman Connie had known previously.

She gazed unseeingly out the window, reliving the awful moment when she had seen Melissa fold into Drew's arms, the journey in the ambulance when she had drifted in and out of consciousness and then the encounter with Aimee. It had been inevitable that they would eventually run into each other again, but she hadn't in a million years imagined it would be in the busy waiting room of an A&E department.

Aimee had been magnanimous in her apology, to say the least, thought Connie. And there had been humour when she'd admitted that she'd called her Saint Connie to Barry. If only she knew! Connie had found it difficult to listen to the younger woman thanking her profusely for her kindness to Melissa. How would Aimee have felt if she'd realized that Connie and Barry had had sex just before Debbie's wedding? Connie wouldn't have gotten profuse thanks, for sure. She wished with all her heart that event had never happened now. She hadn't felt too bad about it at the time, when Aimee had been at the height of her powers and given to looking down her nose at Connie. In fairness, she had remonstrated with Barry and told him that he was the married one, and it hadn't bothered him in the slightest. She really should not waste energy on guilt and regrets, she told herself glumly as they cruised into Dun Laoghaire. Connie could see Barry and Aimee's darkened penthouse in the distance.

They had seemed like the couple who had it all. A lovely child, affluence, top-notch careers, good looks, and Connie had envied from afar their luxurious lifestyle, contrasting it with the financial struggle she'd sometimes had bringing up Debbie, who had had none of the advantages her half-sister had. But behind closed doors their life was far from smooth, as Connie had discovered. Marital strains had been rife – hence the one-night stand – and she wouldn't wish what they were enduring now on her worst enemy. She had never thought she would end up feeling sorry for Aimee Davenport, but today, despite her fashionable high-heeled suede boots and her stylish honey-coloured pure-wool coat, she had seen a vulnerable, anxious, tearful Aimee and realized that, under the sophisticated, chic, successful façade, she was a woman with worries and problems just like the rest of them. It hadn't been difficult to comfort her or accept her apology, or to agree to put the past behind them. The hard part was knowing that she had slept with Barry, and Aimee thinking she was 'so bloody nice'. That was something Connie was going to have to deal with. She had to put it behind her and get on with things or she would be no help to Melissa, or Aimee, for that matter, she thought guiltily, feeling the start of a faint headache at her temples.

When she got off the train, Drew leaned over to kiss her. 'How is Melissa? God, I got a hell of a shock when she crumpled up in a heap in front of me,' Drew exclaimed. She'd sent him a text to say what time she was getting in at, and he'd been waiting on the platform for her.

Connie snuggled in against him, resting her cheek on the soft material of his fleece. 'She's on a drip and they're going to transfer her over to the eating disorders unit when there's a bed free tomorrow. That poor kid has a tough road ahead of her.'

'She'll come through. She has good family support – that counts for a lot,' Drew comforted as they walked to where the car was parked. 'Have you eaten?' he asked as they drove from the station to collect her overnight case and feed Miss Hope.

'No, I just had one of those horrible coffees out of a machine. Maybe that's why I've a headache.' She yawned.

'I have a chicken casserole in the oven, why don't you have a quick shower and get into your PJs, and we can eat in front of the fire when we get home,' he suggested.

'Tell me again why I love you?' She smiled, so utterly glad that she wasn't coming home to an empty house and no one to confide in after the day she'd had. How lucky was she? Connie thought gratefully, packing a nightdress and dressing gown and a few other bits and pieces for her stay over. Miss Hope gazed at her sleepily from the middle of the bed where she had been snoozing when Connie had arrived home. 'My other great companion,' she murmured, dropping a kiss on the cat's silky head and getting an appreciative purr in return. She made sure there was plenty of food and water in her dishes and tested the cat flap before finally setting off to her beloved's.

'This is delicious, Drew,' she complimented him less than an hour later as she tucked into a steaming plate of casserole and dipped crusty garlic bread into the gravy. The chicken fell away from the bone, moist and flavoursome. It was the perfect comfort food, washed down with a chilled glass of Chardonnay in front of a blazing fire. They ate in companionable silence, making the odd remark here or there, him ladling more food on to her plate, she topping up their wine glasses and smiling at him in the glow of the candles he had lit just as she had come downstairs after her shower.

The wind shrieked mournfully, hurling itself around the chimneys, and the spatter of rain against the windowpanes brought an end to the dry, cold spell, and the storms forecasted by the weatherman swept in across the Irish Sea. Afterwards, snug in her dressing gown in the heat of Drew's comfortable sitting room, curled up on the big, plump-cushioned terracotta sofa in front of the fire, with Drew's dog Tusker snoring on the floor beside her, Connie felt all the tensions of the day drift away as she listened to him tidying up after their meal. Her eyelids drooped and she never heard him come in and drop a blanket gently over her before picking up his paper to do his crossword under the lamplight at the other end of the sofa.

'It was horrible leaving her, Barry. She was scared. Do you think we should have stayed?' Aimee fretted, as they drove home from the hospital. It was after midnight and she was exhausted.

'They didn't want us to. You could have got a taxi home and I would have stayed, but they were fairly adamant,' Barry said wearily, driving past RTE at speed. He didn't care if he got done for speeding; he just wanted to get home and fall into bed. 'And she was well out of it really; the mild sedation they gave her was taking effect. She's in the best possible place, Aimee, maybe today was all for the best.'

'She swore to me that she wouldn't throw up after lunch, and I believed her,' Aimee said miserably, yawning so widely her jaws ached.

'That's all part of it – the lying, the deviousness about food – I've been reading up on it. Melissa's only doing what they all do. Don't take it personally, Aimee,' her husband counselled, jamming on the brakes at a red light at Foster's Avenue.

'Go easy,' Aimee murmured, 'we don't want to orphan her as well.' She reached over to the dash and switched on Lyric. The soothing strains of 'Greensleeves' wafted into the car, and she lay back against the headrest and closed her eyes, glad she didn't have to drive. The traffic was light and they were home in ten minutes.

'I'm going to have a quick shower. I smell of hospital,' Aimee said, dropping her briefcase in the hall. She should check up on her emails, but she was too frazzled and tired.

'I'm going to make a bacon sandwich, I have to eat something. Do you want anything?' Barry dropped the car keys and his mobile on the hall table.

'I'll get some crackers.' Aimee headed for the bedroom.

Barry carried on down to the kitchen and rooted in the fridge until he found the bacon. He switched on the grilling machine and filled the kettle while it was heating up. Today had been the day from hell, he mused, laying the strips of rashers on the grill and lowering the lid. But at least it was out of their hands now and Dr Morton was in charge. He was impressed with the woman. She had an air of calm authority that was reassuring, to say the least.

One good thing to come out of the whole sorry mess was that Aimee and Connie were back on speaking terms again. That would make life easier all round, he thought, cracking open a bottle of Miller and taking a long swig of the cool, refreshing beer.

'Don't you dare *ever* tell Aimee that we had sex,' Connie had warned him when he'd walked her to the doors of the A&E after she'd refused his offer of a lift to the Dart.

'I won't, and don't feel guilty about it, I don't,' he'd said as they'd taken the lift to the ground floor.

'Well, you should,' she retorted crossly and he'd refrained from any more comment on the matter.

He didn't feel an ounce of guilt, he thought grimly as he lifted the lid of the grill and turned the sizzling bacon. That sex with Connie had been fantastic, and he'd love an opportunity to have another encounter with her, but that would probably never happen now that she was all loved up with this Drew guy, Barry thought regretfully. Aimee and he hadn't had sex in weeks; she was just too tired when she came home from work and there was still a lingering resentment about the SCIP fiasco. Seeing Connie looking fresh and vibrant in her jeans and a periwinkle-blue fleece had put the longing on him again. That colour blue was always gorgeous on her.

He scowled in disgust. What sort of man was he to be lusting after his ex-wife when his daughter was lying in a hospital bed on a drip and drugged up to her eyelids and his pregnant wife was down the hall taking a shower? He took another slug of beer and slathered some butter on two slices of bread. He was a sad and lonely man wishing for some comfort from a woman he loved. What was so awful about that? he asked himself.

He couldn't hear the sound of the power shower any more, nor any noise coming from the bedroom. He walked down to the room and peered in. Aimee was in bed fast asleep, her towel on the floor where she'd dropped it, her clothes draped across the chaise longue at the bottom of the bed rather than put away neatly as they usually were. Sighing deeply, Barry picked up the towel and hung it back on the towel rail in the en suite before going back down to the kitchen, where he opened another bottle of beer and ate his sandwich alone.

Melissa drifted in and out of sleep. All around her the night-time sounds of the hospital made their own symphony. A boy in the next cubicle coughed, a harsh racking sound that impinged on her consciousness momentarily, reminding her of where she was. The cannula on her hand hurt and the drip got tangled, causing it to beep. A nurse gently swished the curtains apart and straightened it all up. 'Everything all right, Melissa? Do you need anything?' she asked.

'I'm fine, thank you,' Melissa slurred. Her tongue felt thick in her mouth.

'Good. Press the bell if you need anything,' the nurse encouraged, but Melissa had drifted back to sleep. She was riding Venus across the big green meadow at the back of Drew's stables and she was so light and exhilarated and free. And she'd never felt happier in her whole life.

CHAPTER TWENTY-NINE

'Any word of Melissa?' Debbie asked her mother, kicking off her shoes and sinking down on to the sofa. Bryan was out in the kitchen making chicken fajitas for their dinner, and the smell was making her mouth water. It had been a busy day at work and she'd only had a sandwich and she was starving.

'She's been transferred over to Dr Morton's unit today, so at least she only had a day and a half in A&E. It's good she's under medical care and hopefully they'll get a handle on why she's spiralled into anorexia,' Connie said.

'I'm glad she's in hospital.'

'Me too.'

'And imagine Aimee apologizing to you! And pigs didn't fly!'

'Don't be mean, she's not the worst,' Connie reproved.

'Stuck-up cow!' Debbie was unimpressed, remembering the other woman's uncalled-for behaviour the day of her wedding.

'Ah, Debbie, she has her own problems too.'

'I suppose. It must be horrible for her watching Melissa starve herself. It's horrible for us, and you're not even blood-related,' Debbie conceded.

'Exactly.'

'Dinner's ready,' Bryan called from the kitchen.

'Have to go, Mum, dinner's on the table. I'll talk to you tomorrow.' Debbie hauled herself up off the sofa.

'Bye, love, have a nice evening and enjoy your meal,' her mother said and hung up.

'I'm ravenous. This smells gorgeous.' Debbie perched on the stool at the kitchen counter, dying to tuck into the steaming wraps her husband was putting in a serving dish. She helped herself to some crispy salad and garlic bread. 'I don't know how Melissa can stop herself from eating. I don't think I could ever go down that road,' she remarked as Bryan filled two glasses with apple juice. They only drank wine at the weekends now and Debbie sighed, thinking of the good times when they didn't have to worry about what they spent on luxuries.

'You have to be very single-minded. The mind is a powerful tool, when you think about it.' Bryan handed her a dish of roasted peppers. 'I did these especially for you because I know they're your favourite.' He gave her that boyish lopsided grin that always melted her heart.

'And it's not even my birthday,' she teased, feeling a rush of unexpected happiness. This was how it should be, she thought contentedly, beginning to relax after the stress of a crazy day at work and the worry of Melissa's collapse. They chatted over their meal, and she mentioned getting an email from a friend who had gone to work in Canada and how much she was enjoying it.

'That's interesting. They rode out the recession in Canada because they have good politicians and good fiscal and banking practices. I never thought of going to Canada,' Bryan said casually, offering her another wrap. 'I . . . er . . . I've been checking things out and talking to Pete Flynn, and he thinks I could get a visa for Oz, no problem. He said we could rent a few rooms from him if we wanted to go over on a holiday visa and suss things out.'

Debbie's heart sank. No wonder she was getting a dinner cooked for her. Bryan was trying to soften her up and she'd given him the perfect opening talking about Rita's email. She could have kicked herself.

'I thought they'd stopped working visas for a whole lot of occupations recently,' she said equably, pretending not to be bothered.

'Oh yeah, hairdressers, plumbers, gardeners and the like,' Bryan said dismissively. 'But he thinks office planning and design is fine. I just need to get my portfolio together.'

'And what about me? What could I work at?'

'Oh, you'd get something once we're there. Do waitressing for a while until we find our feet. You'll land something, no bother,' he said airily.

'And what about the house?'

'Give it back to the bank. They can't *make* us pay them,' he said petulantly.

'I don't want to emigrate.'

'I don't want to stay here.'

'Well, we have a problem then,' Debbie said calmly. Bryan's mobile rang, saving him from making a response, and she ate the rest of her wrap half-heartedly, the meal having been spoilt by their conversation.

'Have to go out for a while, babe,' her husband said, stuffing the last of his wrap into his mouth. 'Martin Scott's trying to put up one of those Lidl satellite dishes before his wife gets home from her night class and he's making a complete bags of it, and if she misses her *Grey's Anatomy* she'll freak,' he said. 'And you know what Michelle's like when she loses it.'

'What's he doing putting up a satellite dish at this hour of the evening, in the dark?' Debbie grumbled.

'Typical Martin, gung-ho for everything. It was one of the special offers this week, and of course he couldn't wait until the weekend to put it up, knowing him. See ya later, babes.' He kissed her, grabbed his car keys off the counter and was gone, leaving her disgruntled and dispirited.

He really wanted to chuck everything up and live abroad. And the thought of leaving her home and family filled her with dread. She didn't want to move to the other side of the world.

And Bryan was living in cloud cuckoo land suggesting they could just hand the keys back to the bank and scarper with no financial repercussions. It didn't even seem to bother him that they would lose a shedload of money in the process.

She tidied up after their meal and went upstairs to gather clothes together for a wash. Bryan hadn't bothered to do it, even though she'd asked him to stick the whites in the machine before she went to work. He had plenty of time to suss out info about emigrating to Australia, and surf the web and do his sudoku, but no time to load the friggin' washing machine, Debbie thought furiously as she began to sort through the clothes in the linen basket. He couldn't even be bothered to take the loose coins out of his jeans, she fumed, as a twenty-cent piece rolled out on to the floor. She stuck her hand into the pocket and took out another coin and some rolled-up papers. She'd asked her husband time and again to empty his pockets before putting his jeans and trousers in the basket. The machine had got broken once because a nail he had in his pocket got stuck in the drum. The last time he'd done a wash a tissue had come apart and left a load of her black knickers and bras and a pair of black tracksuit bottoms covered in a fine white film. He was *hopeless*!

She opened out the creased papers and was about to put them on his bedside locker when she recognized the dreaded yellow heading of a Visa bill. What on earth was Bryan keeping that for? Their credit-card accounts were closed. It wasn't like him to hoard old bills and, besides, she'd thought she had all their Visa bills in their banking file. She scanned down the list of purchases and saw that they were dated for the previous month. Lunch in One Pico. A bill for €40 in O'Brien's . . . They hadn't bought any drink in O'Brien's, she thought, puzzled, reading down to see a bill for €54 for Amazon and another thirty for Play.com.

She checked the name. Bryan Kinsella: it was definitely Bryan's, but how could that be? She hadn't seen any bills coming through their letterbox. Bemused, Debbie glanced down at the amount owed and felt a jolt of shock. It was almost €5,000. She looked at the name again just to make sure and saw with dawning disbelief that it was addressed to him in Walkinstown. His old home address. She sat on the side of the bed, stunned. Bryan had a credit card he'd never told her about!

Her heart started to pound. Had he had this card for years, if the address was his parents', or had he applied for a card and given his parents' address deliberately so as to keep it from her? Whatever the reason, it was just so underhand. So ... so ... *disloyal*. She would never, ever, do something like that to him. She had thought that everything in their marriage was shared, money included. She had often dug deep into her wages over the past weeks before her dad had come to their rescue, to give him the same amount of spending money as she had now they were struggling. And all the while he was buying things for himself – goodies from Amazon, lunches out and God knows what – while she'd made herself packed lunches and thought twice about buying *Vanity Fair* every month. Her heart felt as if Bryan had taken a scalpel to it and cut deep. Debbie was utterly gutted. A wave of sorrow swept over her and she cried like she hadn't cried since her father had walked away from her and Connie when she was a child. Once again a man she loved wholeheartedly had left her devastated.

Eventually Debbie composed herself, having grown cold sitting on the side of the bed. She dumped the clothes back in the linen basket and got undressed. Her head was throbbing and she felt drained and exhausted. She got into bed, switched out the lamp and lay in the darkness. She hadn't closed the curtains, and the orange sodium light of a streetlamp cast an eerie glow into the room, making the bare, skeletal branches of the trees weave strange shadows on the walls. A full moon flaunted its yellow, gouged visage across the rooftops, and she turned on her side, trying not to remember dancing on a beach in Cyprus with Bryan under the light of a full moon, feeling ecstatically happy because he'd just told her he loved her for the first time.

The only person Bryan *really* loved was himself, Debbie finally admitted to herself. And a lot of that was due to the way Brona had reared him. He was her youngest and her favourite, and anything Bryan wanted, Bryan got. He'd never had to share or think of anyone else, and Brona had enabled that behaviour right up to the present. She knew they were in financial difficulties, she knew that Barry had bailed them out with their credit cards, and she obviously knew, seeing as the Visa bills were going to her address, that Bryan had a credit card Debbie probably didn't know about, and she didn't feel it was inappropriate for him to be going behind his wife's back.

Debbie was fighting a losing battle. Moving to Australia wouldn't change things. He was never going to change. She heard the car pull up outside and her stomach lurched and tightened. She had two options: she could pretend she knew nothing about the second card and keep the peace and keep Bryan, or she could confront him and risk rocking their marriage to its very core. It was a stark choice.

Debbie swallowed when she heard her husband call her name, checking in the sitting room before taking the stairs two at a time.

'Hey, Dollface, what are you doing lying in bed in the dark? It's not even ten yet,' he asked, leaning against the doorjamb, a tall, skinny figure silhouetted against the hall light.

Debbie sat up and switched on the lamp.

'What's wrong? Have you got your P's? You look ganky.' Bryan peered at her.

It would be so easy just to say she had a headache, Debbie thought in desperation, knowing this could be the end of them. 'I . . . I . . .' she stopped.

'Do you want a cup of tea and a paracetamol?' he asked kindly, making it harder. 'Have you a headache?'

'Yeah,' she managed, and it wasn't a lie. Her head was pounding. 'Just paracetamol and a glass of water,' she said feebly, shirking the confrontation.

'OK, I'll be up in two minutes,' he said obligingly. She heard his familiar tread on the stairs and anguish overcame her at his duplicity and the nonchalant ease with which he practised it. It clearly didn't bother him one whit that he could treat her and their marriage so dismissively.

'You're a coward,' she accused herself bitterly, switching off the lamp and lying back down as she heard the opening and closing of the press door in the kitchen.

'Now, petal,' Bryan said gently moments later, shaking out two paracetamol into her palm and handing her a glass of water.

'Thanks,' she murmured, glad that the bedroom was in darkness and she didn't have to meet his gaze.

'I'll be up in a while – just going to watch some TV.' He bent down and kissed the top of her head.

Judas! thought Debbie bitterly, lying back down and pulling the duvet up to her ears. Maybe it wasn't fair to compare Judas with her husband, she thought irrationally, having read somewhere that Judas and Jesus were now believed to have been the greatest of friends, and if Judas hadn't betrayed Him, Jesus would not have been able to undertake His great task.

'Sorry, Judas,' she muttered, 'there is no comparison between you and my complete bastard of a husband.' Debbie lay in turmoil as the sound of channels being surfed wafted up the stairs. As angry as she was with Bryan, she was even angrier at her own cowardice. What did it say about her if she let this pass? What did it say about their sham of a marriage?

She pretended to be asleep when he came to bed a few hours later and he didn't bother switching on the light but undressed in the dark, letting his clothes fall where he dropped them. He turned on his side when he got into bed and was asleep in minutes, and she felt like stabbing him as she lay beside him in the dark, desperate for sleep and oblivion from her torment. Sleep was fitful when it came and she woke before seven. Bryan was snoring, sprawled beside her, his hair tousled boyishly as he lay with one arm flung over her. She shrugged it off and got out of bed, heavy-hearted. The thought of going into work was soul-destroying. Even though Judith Baxter was doing her best not to be heavy-handed, it was different to the easygoing atmosphere that had prevailed under Caitriona's reign. Today she didn't want to think about figures and tax bands and pension entitlements and the rest of it. Even the powerful jets of hot water sluicing down over her could not shift her ennui. She could not summon the energy to put on a façade. Tears mingled with the running water. There was no one she could confide in. She wouldn't tell her mother, she didn't want her friends at work to know that her marriage was on the rocks, and Jenna was abroad, and it wasn't the kind of thing you could say on email or even on Skype: *Hi, Jenna, how are you getting on, Bryan's a complete shit and our marriage is a farce! What should I do?*

Her husband never woke as she dressed for work and she stared down at his sleeping form consumed with fury. She wanted to pull his hair and pummel him, rake her nails down his face and chest until she drew blood. She was the one going to work her ass off. He was lying in bed like Lord Muck because today was one of his free days. If anyone should have a secret credit card it should be her. Unable to contain her anger for another second, she poked him hard in the shoulder.

'Hey, hey, what's going on? What did you do that for?' Bryan rolled over on his back, bleary eyed.

'I want to talk to you, you bastard,' Debbie erupted, poking him again, this time in the chest.

'Hey, what the fuck is wrong with you? Cut it out. You're acting like a madwoman,' Bryan snapped indignantly, sitting up and pushing her hand away from him.

'Why, Bryan, *why*?' Debbie cried, grabbing the creased Visa bill off the locker and thrusting it at him.

'What are you talking about? What *is* this?' He threw back the covers and sprang out of bed.

'Your secret Visa bill, Bryan, that's what we're talking about,' she yelled.

A dull, mottled red spread like a maroon wave from his neck

to his forehead. 'What are you doing rooting in my pockets, spying on me?' He grabbed the pages off her. 'How *dare* you, Debbie? That is so low.'

'Don't do that. Don't put it back on me like you always do, Bryan. I *wasn't* rooting, you smart git.' She was incensed at the way he turned it back on her. 'I was getting clothes out of the linen basket for a wash. A wash *you* were supposed to do, and there were coins in your pockets because you didn't empty them like I've asked you to over and over—'

'Ah, for chrissakes, listen to yourself. Nag nag nag. "You didn't empty them like I've asked you,"' he mimicked nastily. 'For crying out loud, even my mother never went on at me the way you do. I'm sick of it.'

'And I'm sick of you,' she shouted. 'Lying, going behind my back, spending money on yourself when I'm scrimping for us, Bryan, for *us*. But with you there is no us, there's only *you*.'

'Well, it's all your fault,' he shouted back, his brown eyes full of loathing. 'You were the one that wanted to get married—'

'You could have backed out. I gave you the chance to get out of it, Bryan, but you didn't take it, so stop blaming me all the time. You made a choice too. For God's sake, be a man and accept some responsibility for where we're at,' she flung at him bitterly.

'Well, I thought marriage was meant to be *fun*, not this on-going crucifixion, day in, day out. God, it's such a drag. We're young; we shouldn't be living like middle-aged frumps. We used to have fun once, Debbie, lots of it. We used to enjoy our life. Now it's a pain in the arse.' He stood, angry and resentful, in front of her and again she had the urge to inflict as much bodily pain as she possibly could. She longed to kick him hard in the goolies, but she controlled the impulse, knowing that if she resorted to physical violence so would he.

'Look, it's not just us, it's everyone. We're all in the same boat whether we like it or not. There's a recession we can't do any-thing about. We've gone from spending money that wasn't ours to spend to owing money we're struggling to pay off, and that's reality, Bryan, whether you like it or not, so yeah, that does take the fun out of it,' she said sarcastically. 'But never, ever, in a million years would I be so mean and sneaky as to have a credit card and not tell you about it – especially if one of your parents had cleared our credit-card debts for us. Bryan, do you know how I've scrimped and saved and shared my money with you so that you'd have the same as me? I've rooted in handbags and coat pockets and down the back of the sofa looking for two-euro coins because I'm skint. How could you do that to me? How could you, Bryan?' she said brokenly, all the fight going out of her.

'Ah, leave me alone, Debbie, I've had it up to here,' he muttered, brushing past her to go downstairs. 'I'm sick and tired of this and, right now, I'm sick and tired of you. This isn't what I signed up for,' he said resentfully, standing at the top of the stairs.

'What did you sign up for, Bryan? Grow up, will you? It's not all about you. The universe doesn't revolve around Bryan Kinsella, believe it or not,' she shouted at him in frustration.

'I've had it, Debbie!' Bryan roared, stung. 'If this is marriage, you can have it. I've had enough of it. I just can't take any more of this nightmare. And I really mean it. This is the end of the road for me. I can't do it any more. I'm cracking up.'

They stared at each other then, knowing a boundary had been crossed. 'I'm going to Oz,' he said, more calmly this time. 'You can have the house and do what you like with it. And I'm moving back to Ma's. I'll be gone when you get home.' He said it with such finality as he turned and walked down the stairs that Debbie knew it was over. Her husband was walking away, just as her father had. In the future, when she looked back on this moment, it wouldn't be the hurt and sadness and anger she would remember; her outstanding memory would be the utter contempt she felt the moment her short, disastrous marriage ended.

'Bryan!' she said, and her tone was so commanding he turned to look up at her, surprised.

'Take this with you. I won't be helping you to pay it off,' she said in disgust, rolling the Visa bill in a ball and throwing it into his face. 'You'll have to run to Mammy like you always do. You're pathetic.' She turned on her heel and walked back into the bedroom to apply her make-up for work.

Her hand was shaking as she held her mascara wand to her eyelashes, and she took some deep, calming breaths. The sooner she composed herself the sooner she could get away, and that was what she wanted more than anything: to put some distance between her and Bryan and the toxic atmosphere that was making her feel faint and sick. Now that it had finally happened, now that the confrontation was over, Debbie felt strangely calm. At least she could look herself in the eye, she thought with a quiet sense of relief as she applied the mascara and traced some lipgloss over her lips. She'd stopped running. She'd stopped trying to make everything better. She'd stopped denying what was patently obvious. She and Bryan had made a huge mistake getting married. Now it was time to deal with that and move on.

She could hear Bryan in the kitchen filling the kettle as she walked down the stairs. 'Bring your dirty washing with you, because I won't be doing it,' she called from the hallway, furious that he could perform such a mundane task when to all intents and purposes he had just ended their marriage. She grabbed the car keys, which, fortunately, he'd dropped on the hall table the previous night. He wasn't getting the car, Debbie thought coldly as she marched out of the house and closed the door on her husband and her marriage.

'What else are you taking, love?' Brona surveyed the array of cases, sports bags and paintings in the hall. 'What about the TV and the stereo system? Don't give her everything. Get what you're entitled to.'

'Yeah, you're right, Ma. To hell with her. Let her buy her own

TV,' Bryan muttered, conveniently forgetting that it was his father-in-law's money that had paid off the large amount owing on both items.

'We'll make two runs then, love. We'll get your clothes and belongings first and then we'll come back for the rest, and when we're finished I'll cook you a lovely rack of lamb and you can relax and unwind after the upset you've had,' Brona said sympathetically, patting her beloved son on the back.

Several hours later his mother poured him a glass of chilled white wine while she put the finishing touches to his welcome-home dinner. 'You're doing the right thing, you know. You've never been happy since the day she inveigled you to put that ring on her finger. Put it all behind you and start afresh,' she advised.

Sound advice, thought Bryan as he sipped the refreshing drink. How good it was to be in a place where he was appreciated. He was glad it was finally over. He could stop struggling and be himself again. He had loved Debbie but, right now, he wasn't sure what his true feelings towards her were, he felt so angry and resentful. All he knew was that he hated being married, hated the way they were making each other miserable and hated the dull and boring vista that seemed to stretch to infinity if they stayed as they were. Someone had to make the decision to change things, and Debbie's discovery of his second Visa card had given him the perfect opportunity to walk. He couldn't help it, he admitted, but he felt an enormous sense of relief. He couldn't have engineered it better if he'd tried.

The past few weeks had been the worst of his life. He'd seriously thought he was going to crack up. Now there was light at the end of the tunnel. Freedom beckoned. Connie would probably think he was the greatest heel ever but, with luck, he'd never have to meet her again. He knew when things had calmed down and he was back on track he'd possibly miss Debbie, but never seeing Connie again would not cause him to lose one second's sleep. Goodbye and good riddance to her and her macho new boyfriend. Bryan would never forget how Drew had made him feel like a naughty five-year-old when he'd chastised him at lunch in Connie's. 'Sonny', he'd called him. Bryan's nostrils flared at the memory. That bogger had some nerve. Sonny indeed. Goodbye and good riddance to the lot of them.

He sipped his wine appreciatively. It was just like old times being the centre of attention and being fussed around, he reflected as his mother lifted the sizzling, spitting rack of lamb out of the oven and the aroma made his mouth water. At the end of the day it had to be said: there was no place like home. And here he would stay until he had everything set up to start his new life on the other side of the world, far away from this godforsaken banana republic of a country. Bryan felt a burden lift from his shoulders and he tucked into his meal with gusto.

Was it all her fault? Debbie wondered, lying in bed weary to her bones. It had been the worst day of her life. Work had been a nightmare. Trying to concentrate, trying to keep up a façade when she just wanted to put her head in her hands and bawl her eyes out had been a nightmare. Just short of six months married and it was over. Bryan couldn't get away quick enough. She had given him the perfect escape route, and he'd taken it running.

And he'd even taken the flatscreen and the stereo system. That had given her an even bigger shock than seeing all his clothes gone from wardrobes and drawers and the blank spaces on the walls from where he'd taken the paintings. That showed cold, serious intent. Anyone could clear clothes and pack bags in the heat of a row, but taking the TV and stereo unit was a clear, pre-meditated action that sent a signal that what had happened that morning was much, much more than a nasty argument.

He'd thought marriage would be fun – well, so had she. She'd been totally committed to their marriage. Bryan had been totally committed to Bryan. And what was new about that? His hurled abuse had hurt, though. And she had to be fair about her contribution to their break-up. Had she nagged too much? She didn't mean to. Most of their arguments had been about money and his lack of help with the household chores. It wasn't unreasonable for her to expect him to help out. Both of them were working; it wasn't as if she was lolling about at home all day, even if that was precisely what he'd been doing twice a week for the past few weeks.

Had her expectations of marriage been too high? When they'd lived together in the apartment before they got married they'd got on great and that *had* been fun, she conceded. If Bryan had been left to his own devices they would never have married. They'd have been better off, she thought sadly. Now they weren't even friends any more. They'd parted with great rancour and all she had to show for their five-year relationship was a house in negative equity and a ton of money worries. At least they'd had no children. Debbie shuddered, thinking how horrendous it would have been if they'd had a child. It would have been history repeating itself, she realized with a dull sense of shock. Connie had faced what she was facing now and she'd had Debbie in tow. No wonder her mother had cried herself to sleep every night for the first year after Barry had walked out on them. What would Connie say when Debbie told her? What would her friends say? All those ordeals had to be faced. As did the ordeal with the bank manager and the worry of what to do with the house and where she was going to live. She'd have to get legal advice. What a nightmare – and a nightmare that was partly of her own making. She had known in her gut from long before her marriage that Bryan was not capable of commitment, but she'd ignored it. Ignored the doubts and disquiet she'd felt when he'd let her down or gone on his drug and drinking benders. She could only blame herself for that and take responsibility for not listening to her instincts. Now she had to deal with the consequences.

The weight of failure pressed heavy on her spirit and Debbie tossed and turned in the big bed, crushed and feeling more alone and scared than she'd ever felt in her life.

'IF WINTER COMES CAN SPRING
BE FAR BEHIND?'

CHAPTER THIRTY

It was appropriate, Debbie thought, that a relentless downpour of sharp, stinging, bitingly cold hailstones should mark her arrival at the solicitor's office where the first steps towards ending her marriage would take place. In the weeks that had passed since the acrimonious row with Bryan she had agonized over their situation, imagining different scenarios, some where she begged him to come back and others where she sent him on his way without even a backward glance, veering constantly from despair and darkness to hope and positivity while doing so. They had not seen each other since. Bryan had suggested meeting for coffee in a neutral place to discuss the best way to resolve their affairs but Debbie had said no. She knew it would end up in a row, she knew she wouldn't be able to contain the bitterness and anger she felt. If she hurled accusations at him he'd fling them right back, and it would be a pointless exercise. At least on the phone when she couldn't see him she was able to stay somewhat composed and focused.

The discussions had been cool, businesslike exchanges as they tried to come to some agreement about the house. They ended up agreeing that he would sign it over to her. In the future there might be money to be made from it by hanging on to it, but for now it was a loss maker. Bryan had asked for and received a respectable redundancy package; he would keep that money to set himself up in Oz. They had no life-insurance policies, never having had the money to pay into them; they had no savings; and there actually wasn't any other money to split between them. Their second-hand car wouldn't get much – a couple of thousand. Bryan magnanimously told her to keep it. Debbie didn't even bother to ask him about repaying the cash Barry had given them. She would try, in the years to come, to do that herself. In all, a half a dozen phone calls had sorted their business and tied up the loose threads. How sad was that? she'd thought after the last one, where they'd agreed a time and date to meet their solicitor.

Bryan had come back several times to collect more of his personal belongings – his passport, tax papers and the like – but always when she was at work, like she'd asked him to, so she wouldn't have to see him. She knew Bryan of old. He hated fighting with her and he would come and be charming and kind and draw her back in, and she'd forget how horrible things were between them and probably end up in bed with him – their make-up sex had always been great – and hate herself afterwards.

The only person she'd confided in was Carina. Her friend hadn't been completely shocked at the news. 'Bryan was always a bit of a free spirit, wasn't he?' she'd said tactfully, too kind to say that Bryan was immature, selfish and irresponsible and she was surprised they hadn't broken up years ago. That first weekend of their parting, Carina had made Debbie stay with her. She'd fed and watered her and listened to her griefstricken outbursts, and when she felt Debbie was receptive, gave helpful and sound advice. She'd walked the legs off her in the Botanic Gardens after forcing her to eat a breakfast and drink two cups of coffee in the coffee shop first. Even in her distress, Debbie had marvelled at the beauty of the gardens, an oasis of peace and tranquillity so close to the capital city. 'It really should be much more prominent, shouldn't it? It's the first time I've been here. They don't promote it enough,' she observed. 'Wouldn't you imagine they'd have big planters full of flowers in that outdoor café area to give some colour? I'd love to design that properly; it's very stark and dull for such a lovely setting.' She studied the area critically.

'You're right, I hadn't noticed,' Carina agreed looking out at the white tables and the off-white slabs of concrete that had no colour to break it up. It was all quite drab and functional.

'I'm sure garden design is a very rewarding career. Much more rewarding than sitting at a desk working out the wages sheet.' Debbie managed a weak grin.

'We could do a course, and give this lot a run for their money. They've shown no imagination at all, and especially when they have such expertise to create a beautiful little haven. We could call ourselves Kinsella and Warner Garden Designs. Diarmuid Gavin, look out.' Carina grinned, pleased that Debbie's spark of interest in her surroundings had taken her out of her distress for a little while. 'Seriously, though, you could always create a peaceful little nirvana on your deck, it would give you something to occupy yourself with until you're in a better place in your heart and head. Bedding plants aren't too expensive, and they last for ages,' she suggested matter-of-factly.

Debbie had given her a hug. 'You're a great friend, Carina. It's so good to have someone to confide in and be in a heap with without having to put on a front.'

Carina had got her through the past weeks for sure, and she'd never be able to thank her enough, Debbie reflected gratefully as the solicitor's office loomed up and she slowed her pace, reluctant to have to go in and face Bryan. Her phone tinkled and she rooted in her coat pocket and saw she had a message from Connie. Debbie sighed as she read that Melissa was now allowed visitors. Her poor half-sister was going through the mill too, but at least she was on the up. Debbie was longing to see her.

Connie was blissfully unaware that her daughter's marriage was over. Debbie just couldn't bring herself to tell her. Connie had suggested postponing the wedding when Bryan had got cold feet but instead Debbie had taken him to Amsterdam on a surprise trip. Now, she wished with all her heart that she'd taken her mother's advice and not been so desperate to formalize their relationship. Parting when you were a couple did not seem quite the failure that parting when you were married did, nor as daunting.

After the signing over of the house today, Debbie would *have* to tell her that Bryan was leaving for Australia at the end of the week. With Christmas less than two weeks away, Connie had been asking her what their plans were for Christmas lunch. Debbie had fobbed her off, saying they hadn't quite decided, that they might go away for a few days, but she couldn't keep the break-up quiet any more. She was going to have to bite the bullet and tell the truth. She hoped Connie hadn't bought Bryan his Christmas present yet.

'Debbie! Debbieeee!' She heard her name called and felt an ache of sadness and grief at the familiar sound of Bryan's voice. She turned and saw him weaving in and out of traffic as he crossed the busy city street. He was wearing a smart black wool overcoat – new, she reckoned, because she had never seen it before – with the collar pulled up to his ears, and was sheltering under a black umbrella. He had a black leather John Rocha bag slung over his shoulder.

'Hi,' she said quietly, shocked at how seeing him made her want to be in his arms, and to wish that this deep, yawning chasm between them would disappear.

'Hi,' he replied awkwardly. And they looked at each other in silence for a moment before he leaned over and kissed her cheek with a touch of uncertainty, as though afraid she might recoil from him.

'You look awful.' He gave a lopsided grin.

'You look like a city slicker,' she said tartly.

'This is terrible, Debbie. I'm sorry the way things have ended up. I'm sorry I hurt you.' He dropped his gaze and studied his shoes and their umbrellas collided.

'Me too,' she said, trying not to cry, untangling her smaller red umbrella from under his. 'We should go in.' She wanted to say, *It doesn't have to be like this. It's all your fault.* She had to struggle hard to stay silent. There was no point in dragging it out. Even if they did reconcile, the fundamental differences between them wouldn't change. Six months down the line, things would be no different. It was as well to get the whole sorry mess over.

'I'm trying to be fair, Debbie. Signing the house over to you is the best I can do,' Bryan offered.

'I know that.'

'I won't look for a penny if you sell it when the market improves and you make a profit,' he said earnestly.

'That won't be any time soon, I guess, the way the country's going down the tubes,' she said with an attempt at humour.

'How are you going to pay the mortgage?'

'Carina's moving in. I'm changing the dining room into a small sitting room for her, and she'll have the back bedroom and the bathroom. I have the en suite in our room. We'll share the kitchen.'

'Oh!' He looked surprised. 'All sorted then. That didn't take long.' He sounded faintly put out.

'Carina suggested it last week. The girl who had the flat downstairs in her house bought a place of her own and moved out, and the landlord let it to a couple who are very noisy and always holding parties. It's driving her mad. It will suit us both. I'm not exactly in the mood for partying these days. And Carina never was the mad party type, although she is great fun on a night out. She told me she's not going to let me veg.'

'Good for Carina. Have you ... er ... told your mum yet?'

'Nope. I wanted to have things sorted before you went away. I'll tell her this week.' Debbie shivered as the onslaught of hailstones continued. 'Let's go in.'

'Eh ... would you like to go for lunch afterwards?' Bryan suggested.

'Maybe coffee,' she demurred as they walked up the steps and rang the doorbell of O'Shaughnessy and Kavanagh Solicitors.

Twenty-five minutes later they sat in Bewley's sipping cappuccinos and eating muffins. 'That wasn't too bad, sure it wasn't?' Bryan said tentatively. The solicitor had been business-like and matter-of-fact as he'd explained what signing the documents would mean to each of them.

'No. A few documents to sign and a hefty fee to pay and everything's done and dusted and life as we know it has changed completely.' She shrugged, holding her cup between her two hands to try and warm her cold fingers. He said nothing, and she could feel the gulf between them as she struggled to think of what to say next to plug the uncomfortable silence.

Outside, the hailstones had turned to great flurries of snow and the Christmas lights strung across Grafton Street twinkled against the drifting snowflakes, giving them an added luminescence. 'This time next week you'll be in the sun. It's summer over there.' She nibbled at a piece of muffin, making pathetic small talk and wishing she were a million miles away. Imagine ending up with nothing to say to your husband and making awkward conversation like they were two strangers. This had to be the nadir of their relationship.

'Sure you don't want to come and give it a bash? It might be easier somewhere new, away from all this recession stuff,' Bryan urged.

Debbie shook her head. 'We want different things, Bryan. I need roots and security; you don't like to be tied down. That's never going to change.'

'You make me sound like a flibbertigibbet,' he griped.

Aren't you? she wanted to say, angry with herself as much as him. She had made the fatal mistake of thinking she could change him. Of thinking that once they were married he would want to settle down like her. It wasn't fair to put all the blame on him, and she wasn't, but he had to accept his share.

'Just one thing,' she said.

'What?'

'Don't put all the blame on me. I gave you a chance to back out and you didn't take it, *and* I would have lived in a poky apartment with a much smaller mortgage anywhere, and it wouldn't have burdened us so heavily.'

'Fair enough,' he agreed. 'But if we hadn't got married at all and stayed renting we wouldn't be in this mess.'

'No, and when the inevitable parting came it would have been much easier.'

'I love you, Debbie.' He leaned across the table and took her hand.

'Don't, Bryan,' she said, pulling her hand away as tears brimmed in her eyes. 'This is very hard. Don't make it any more difficult for me than it is.'

'It's hard on me too,' he protested indignantly.

'It's your decision to go.'

'It's still hard.'

'I have to get back to work. I took time in lieu.' She struggled to compose herself.

'Can I come and see you before I go? I bought you a Christmas present,' Bryan said shakily.

'No! I couldn't hack it. I have to get out of here, Bryan, or I'm going to bawl. The best of luck and safe journey.' She stood up and picked up her bag.

'It can't end like this!' He was shocked. 'Let me come to the house to say goodbye.'

'Don't you mean "Let me come and have a last shag and then I can go off to Australia feeling at least we parted on good terms." I don't think so, Bryan.' Debbie held on to the anger she was feeling, knowing it would get her out of the restaurant at least before she dissolved into tears.

'That's a bit harsh,' he protested.

'But true.' She buttoned her coat. 'I know you, I know the way you think.' She wanted to be really nasty and childish and pathetic and say, *I didn't always come. I faked it sometimes. You're*

not always the great lover you think you are, either. It would have
been satisfying to see the look of horror on his face, but she
wouldn't drag their parting down to that level; she'd regret it at
some point in the future, if not now.

He didn't argue the point, and she knew that her instincts
were spot on. There were times when she could read her
husband like a book and this was one of them.

'Can I email you when I get there?'

'Of course,' she said coolly. 'We'll have to be in contact about
the divorce.'

'The divorce!' He looked shocked. 'Do we need to? That's a bit
dramatic.'

'I do,' she said emphatically. 'I want closure, as they say. It's
the only way to move on and start afresh.'

'Oh.' He looked so crestfallen she almost laughed. Typical
Bryan: he wanted her as a safety net if Australia didn't work out.

She took a deep breath. 'Right, I'm off. Look after yourself,
Bryan. Enjoy Australia,' she said briskly, the risk of tears having
receded a little as she took back control.

'Thanks, eh . . . I'll walk you out and walk a bit of the way with
you.' He jumped to his feet.

'No. Don't do that. I'd prefer to go on my own,' she said
firmly. She leaned across, gave him a peck on the cheek and
walked through the crowded restaurant with her head held
high. *I will not cry,* she told herself. *I will not cry.*

She managed to get halfway up Grafton Street before her
resolve wobbled and tears flooded down her cheeks. She kept
her umbrella low over her eyes, and tears and snowflakes
mingled as she slowed her battle against the oncoming tide of
Christmas shoppers, all of them oblivious to her grief and
sadness.

So that was where it had ended. Over a cup of coffee in
Bewley's. Typical of Bryan to want a last grand farewell scene.
Well, she wasn't having that. And she wasn't going to be stuck
in a legal limbo until it suited him to get a divorce. It was time

she took control of her life again. Today had been the first step along that path. She would not allow herself to sink into negativity and bitterness. She'd gone through too much of that and spent too many years being angry and hostile to fall back into that way of living her life. She would not mourn for Bryan the way she had mourned for Barry when he left. She'd read somewhere that the only things you could control were your thoughts. She would do her very best to stay positive, she vowed, wiping her eyes and striding along again.

Her great intentions faltered at the top of Grafton Street as a choir collecting for charity launched into a rousing rendition of 'Have Yourself A Merry Little Christmas', and Debbie dissolved into another deluge of tears and cursed Bryan for his crap timing.

CHAPTER THIRTY-ONE

'And what about boys, Melissa? Do you have a boyfriend?' Dr Morton asked easily, as they sat chatting in a consultation room during one of their one-on-one sessions.

'Nope.' Melissa shook her head.

'Ever had one?' Dr Morton smiled.

'No.'

'Would you like one?'

'I don't care. This is boring. Can't we talk about something else?' Melissa shifted in her chair. She really liked Dr Morton, but sometimes she kept on and on about things, things that Melissa felt were private and she didn't want to talk about. Dr Morton always said that what they talked about was absolutely confidential but still Melissa felt guilty when she talked about family stuff. She'd felt really bad when she told the doctor that she had always hated that her mom had often been late to collect her at the crèche and she'd been the last child there and afraid that Aimee wasn't going to come. Or that Aimee often had to cancel a planned 'girls' night' if something came up at work. 'I just feel I'm being pushed off the ladder,' she said crossly, the day that particular discussion took place.

Dr Morton was very good at winkling things out of her. Melissa would often find herself telling her something that surprised her when she thought about it later, like how grumpy her granddad Davenport was, and how she didn't like the way he spoke to her mother sometimes. Sometimes, though, like now, she just didn't feel like talking. And sometimes Dr Morton would keep at her, asking her was she still making herself sick after her meals, and why, and somehow or another she always knew if Melissa was lying to her.

'Do you go to discos?' Dr Morton smiled at her.

'Sometimes.' What was she going on about this kind of stuff for? Melissa wondered, much preferring when she could have a little moan about her mom working so hard and her dad playing golf and her being a latchkey kid. Then she didn't feel so bad for being in here. After all, it wasn't her fault.

'Do you enjoy them?'

'I like dancing with my friends. Well, when I was fat I couldn't help looking at what they were wearing and wishing I could wear cool clothes like them so sometimes I'd be, like, a bit stressed,' Melissa admitted.

'Do you like dancing with boys?'

'Um . . . it's OK.'

'Just OK . . . not fun?'

'Yeah.' She sighed. Sometimes the sessions with Dr Morton were great but sometimes, when she was in one of her real probing humours, they were hard going, like this one. It was much easier to talk to her counsellor Bernadette. Sometimes, when she got upset, Bernadette would get them coffee and tell her everything would be OK, but the doctor would just give her tissues and keep going.

'Did a boy ever do anything that you didn't like or found inappropriate?' The question came out of the blue and caught her completely off guard.

'Ah . . . er . . .' Melissa stuttered, coming back to reality with a bang. How did she know? Dr Morton knew *everything*. It was scary.

'What happened?'

'Em . . . nothing.'

'Tell me about it.'

'Nothing happened, like, totally nothing, Dr Morton, honestly.'

'Melissa, talk to me.'

'Well, once this boy . . . um . . . it was New Year and it was at friends' of my parents, and they have a son called Thomas and we were playing snooker while our parents were talking and having a drink in the other room, and the next minute . . . the next minute he pushed me against the wall and . . .' She started to cry, remembering that horrible episode that had shocked her to her core.

'It's OK, Melissa, take your time,' Dr Morton said kindly, handing her a tissue.

Melissa wiped her eyes and blew her nose.

'Tell me about it, and don't forget: nothing you say to me leaves this room. It's totally confidential,' the doctor reminded her reassuringly.

'Well, it wasn't anything too bad, I suppose, not like a rape or anything,' Melissa sniffled.

'What did he do?'

'He stuck his tongue down my neck and stuck his fingers into . . . up . . . my privates . . . and . . . and . . .' She started to cry again.

'He sexually assaulted you.'

Melissa's jaw dropped. 'Oh! Well . . . I just thought it was, like . . . groping. And he was pissed too.'

'No, Melissa, that boy touched you without your permission, against your will – that constitutes a sexual assault. Did anything else happen? Did he expose himself?'

'No . . . no . . . he just kept rubbing himself against me.' She grimaced at the memory of that ghastly morning.

'How did it make you feel?'

'I just felt . . . um . . . I felt really, really dirty and sort of scared,' Melissa murmured.

'Did you tell your parents?'

'No.'

'Why not?'

'I . . . I didn't want to worry them . . . I didn't want to cause an upset.'

'Did you tell anyone?'

'Just my friend Sarah.'

'And what did she say?'

'She thought it was, like, totally gross.'

'And did you think this assault was your fault?'

'Um . . . not really, but I kinda figured that I was still fat when it happened and so when I started dieting I hoped that if I was really skinny, boys wouldn't do those kind of things to me.'

'Have other boys done those kind of things?'

'Well, you know, when we're at the discos they rub themselves against you and kiss you when they're dancing with you, even though they don't know you. They do it to *all* the girls,' Melissa said impatiently.

'Why don't you walk away and tell them that is not appropriate behaviour?'

'You'd get slagged.'

'Would that not be better than being assaulted? Being touched up and used by boys you don't know? You body belongs to you, and you alone, Melissa. It is entirely appropriate to respect yourself and demand respect from others. When that boy assaulted you in his parents' house at New Year you had nothing to feel dirty or guilty about. Absolutely nothing. He crossed a boundary and imposed himself on you without your permission. You did nothing that should make you feel bad. He is the one who should feel bad. Do you understand what I'm saying, Melissa?'

'I guess so,' Melissa said slowly, as the guilt she'd carried deep down about that awful morning when she'd suddenly and unwillingly been brought to the realization that she wasn't a child any more and that she was stepping into the adult world very much against her will began to unravel. It wasn't her fault. She wasn't dirty and cheap and a slag who'd allowed a boy to finger her. She'd done nothing to invite it. He was just a revolting boy who took advantage of her and ... assaulted her. Melissa shuddered. She couldn't even begin to use the 's' word.

'When that girl at your sister's wedding called you names, that was her bad behaviour.' Dr Morton intruded on her thoughts. 'It was nothing to do with you. Don't take on others' bad behaviour. You are responsible for *your* behaviour, Melissa. And yours alone. Remember that. And it's very, very important that you understand that you do not have to protect your parents and worry about them being upset. They are adults, Melissa, you are still a child; they should know what's happening in your life. Having met both of them, I know they would *want* to know. It is their job to protect you as best they can, and if you don't tell them when bad things happen they can't take care of you. Do you understand?'

'Yeah, Dr Morton. I guess I didn't think of it like that,' Melissa said tiredly. It was easy for the doctor to tell her to tell her parents, but at the time she had been so mortified and horrified at what had happened she just wanted to forget all about it as fast as she could. She gave an involuntary yawn.

'Now, I think that's enough for the moment. You're tired.' The doctor capped her pen and closed her notebook. 'You've done great work this morning. We'll talk about it again when I see you later in the week. Well done, Melissa. I'm very pleased with your progress. You should be too. It would be good if you could talk to Bernadette about this.' Dr Morton stood up and smiled at her. 'You've got art after your snack, haven't you? Go and enjoy it. And enjoy your visitors, but make sure you space them out. We don't want you getting exhausted, and sometimes having visitors can be quite tiring if you have too many.'

'OK, thanks, Dr Morton,' Melissa said, relieved that the session was over. It had been a hard one but she felt lighter and more at ease with herself. Dr Morton was very firm about what she should take responsibility for, such as making herself sick and abusing her body, but she was also very firm about what wasn't her fault, and hearing an adult say that she wasn't responsible for that disgusting thing that had happened was such a relief, she mused as she walked out of the consultation room and down the corridor to the relaxation area of the unit.

'Melissa, time for your snack.' Jason, one of her favourite nurses, said, lifting his head from a chart.

'Food, food, food, that's all you ever think about in this place.' She pretended to be cross, and he laughed and told her to go to the dining room and he'd get her meal-support person to come.

She still couldn't get used to having someone supervise her eating, sitting with her until she finished the food in front of her. They were extremely strict in the unit. Her phone had been taken off her until she had put on enough weight to get it back. Every privilege was hard earned. She was looking forward to the time when she would be off bed rest and allowed to leave the unit to have coffee in one of the coffee shops in the main hospital.

One of the other patients, an older girl called Tess who was in her unit, came up to the desk. 'I want to go off the ward,' she demanded.

'Sorry, Tess, you're back on bed rest,' Jason said firmly.

'Well, I'm making a complaint,' Tess scowled. 'And I want to see Morton.'

'*Dr* Morton has a session scheduled with you tomorrow, Tess. She'll see you then.' Jason said calmly.

'Pig!' muttered Tess and stalked off.

Tess had earned the privilege of going for coffee off the ward but had been caught jogging in the hospital grounds and had had her privileges rescinded. She was flaming with anger and Melissa felt sorry for her. She could perfectly understand why Tess would want to go jogging. Eating three meals and two snacks a day was *horrendous*. She wouldn't mind going for a jog herself, she thought sympathetically.

Melissa sighed as she headed for the dining room. Some people had been in here for months. She didn't want that to happen to her. One of her big fears was that she would be kept back a year at school. It would be dreadful to have to start second year again with a new class and not be with her friends. Bernadette had been very understanding about her fear and had told her to keep visualizing the goal of staying in her own class and getting back to school as soon as possible when she was eating her food.

Sometimes she badly wanted to be back at school but other times, like when she was doing her art and having fun with the nurses, she didn't want to leave the unit. She felt very safe and protected here. It had taken her a while to get used to it. The first few days and nights had been very scary and she'd felt like a prisoner, but she'd slept a lot, and gradually, as her days took on a routine and she got to know the staff and other patients, she'd settled in.

She walked past one of the wards which had a window out on to the corridor so that the nurses could keep an eye on the patients. She'd been in that ward for a week and hated it. There was no privacy at all. She'd felt the eyes of the world were upon her. It had been such a relief to move to a two-bed ward you couldn't see into from the corridor. It was a step up the ladder to recovery, she'd been told, and she felt quite pleased with herself. It was still hard going though. All the food she had to eat made her want to cry and she still made herself sick every so often, but not as much as before she'd come in. Melissa could hear a girl crying in another ward. She was being force-fed through a tube. At least that hadn't happened to her, and she truly hoped it wouldn't. It was a pitiful sound, and she wanted to put her hands over her ears to block it out. She hurried past, and another patient, Wendy, who was coming in the opposite direction, whispered, 'Poor Shelly.'

'Yeah, what a bummer,' she whispered back. 'Just going for my snack.' Wendy made a face and threw her eyes up to heaven, and passed on.

Her phone vibrated in her fleece pocket and Melissa smiled in delight when she read the message. Debbie had sent her a text to say she would be in later. Now that was really something to look forward to. All in all, today was quite a good day, Melissa decided, as she sat down to eat the yogurt and banana that was placed in front of her.

Ken Davenport stood looking critically at a selection of teddy bears, wondering which one his granddaughter would like the best. The white one would be a bit impractical, he decided. It might get grubby. The black one was too big, but there was a nice honey-coloured one that was a good size but could be cuddled comfortably as well. He wished Juliet was with him. She'd know which one to choose. He dithered for another few moments, looking at a pink one and a multicoloured one before returning to the honey one.

'I'll take that one,' he said to the woman behind the counter.

'One of our most popular,' she assured him, wrapping it in cream tissue paper and placing it in a large carrier bag. He thanked her and strode out of the shop over to the newsagent's and spent five minutes selecting a pretty get-well card with a little black cat on it. He knew Melissa was partial to cats. There was no point in buying chocolates, he supposed, when he saw the big selection on the shelf behind the counter as he went to pay for the card. Maybe she might fancy a few Maltesers, he thought. They were light and not too calorie-inducing. He was very fond of them himself. 'I'll take that large box of Maltesers too, please.' He pointed to the chocolates and took out his wallet to pay.

Ken sighed as he walked to the car park. When Juliet had told him that Melissa had collapsed and been hospitalized for anorexia he'd been stunned. 'Why am I only being told this now? Why didn't Aimee get in touch? I'm a consultant, for God's sake. I could have spoken to colleagues and got help before it came to this.'

'Oh, don't be so overbearing, Ken,' Juliet had retorted irritably. 'That's precisely *why* your children don't go to you with their problems.'

'Well, that's very unfair!' he'd said, wounded.

'Look, Ken, you gave Aimee a difficult time when she was growing up. You kept on at her to do science subjects when she had no aptitude for them, you belittled her career even though she's done better than any of them. Don't expect her to go running to you when she's in trouble. She didn't want me to tell you about Melissa's problems because she was afraid you wouldn't be sympathetic and you might say something that would be unhelpful. You have to be very careful what you say to young people with eating disorders.'

'Well . . . well . . . I didn't mean to upset her. I was only thinking of her own good,' he'd said indignantly, wondering had he done *anything* right in his life. 'I . . . I . . . wouldn't say anything untoward to Melissa. I don't understand the illness, I admit, and I don't know enough about it to offer advice, but I could have asked people who work in the field.' He'd been tempted to stomp off in a huff like he used to before Juliet had staged her rebellion, but his huffs didn't work with her any more so he'd merely said stiffly, 'Will you keep me apprised of what's going on?'

'Of course I will,' his wife had said calmly, and had gone off to look at curtain material and blinds for her new 'apartment', as she'd taken to calling it.

This morning, she'd phoned him after his clinic to tell him that the news from Aimee was good – Melissa was sufficiently improved to have visitors other than her parents – and that she'd be going in to see her the following day. She had added that she'd cooked a lasagne and asked if he'd like her to leave a portion in the fridge for him for his dinner later. He'd accepted the offer graciously. His wife's lasagnes were exceedingly tasty.

He'd sat at his desk after hanging up, remembering what she'd said about his treatment of Aimee. It was true; he'd been very disappointed that she hadn't followed him into the medical profession, that none of his children had followed him. He'd taken it as a personal insult. Many of his colleagues had sons and daughters who had become doctors and consultants. Was it because they'd felt pressurized, he wondered, or because they really wanted to? It was a sad indication of his parenting abilities, he'd reflected, that his only daughter couldn't come and tell him that his granddaughter was suffering from a scourge of an illness like anorexia. He had to start trying to make amends with Aimee, or else he would end up unloved and a very lonely old man indeed.

After he'd done his rounds in the clinic he'd driven over to the Blackrock Shopping Centre with the specific intention of buying a gift for Melissa. He would be seeing patients in the hospital where she was being treated later in the afternoon, he could pop in with it, he decided.

He sincerely hoped she liked the teddy bear he'd chosen for her. Ken glanced at his watch. His stomach growled. He'd nip home, have a quick cuppa and a sandwich and head off early so that he could call into Melissa before seeing his patients in the main hospital. Juliet's car was gone, he noted with a pang of disappointment. He'd been looking forward to showing her the teddy bear. That would surely give him a few Brownie points, he thought wryly as he made a cheese and ham sandwich for himself. He ate it standing up, looking out at the swirling snow drifting down into the garden and dressing the bare trees in a white covering.

After he'd drunk a second cup of tea he took the get-well card out of the brown paper bag and sat at the kitchen table pondering what to write.

After thinking about it for a while, he wrote, with a flourish:

> *To my dear granddaughter, Melissa.*
> *Get well soon,*
> *Your loving granddad.*

He studied it and then added two big 'xx's.

Pleased with his endeavours, Ken tidied up after himself and set off, hoping that Melissa would be glad to see him. It wasn't far to the hospital; he'd know soon enough.

She was in a part of the hospital that he was not familiar with, and as he waited to be buzzed in, he felt a little apprehensive. What would he say to his granddaughter? He wasn't used to teenagers. His grandchildren were more comfortable talking to their grandmother than to him.

'I'm here to see Melissa Adams. I'm her grandfather,' he said briskly to the young male nurse at the desk. He was about to say, 'Professor Ken Davenport,' but he decided against it. Juliet would just say he was looking for attention and, besides, he wasn't visiting in his capacity as a consultant, he was visiting as a grandparent.

'She's in her room. Number eight,' the young man said, pointing to the corridor on the left-hand side of the unit.

'Er . . . I bought a few chocolates as well. Is that allowed?' he asked, uncharacteristically uncertain.

'That's fine.' The nurse smiled.

Ken took a deep breath and walked across to the door marked 'No. 8' and knocked. 'Come in,' he heard his granddaughter call. He didn't know which of them got the bigger shock. Her eyes widened, as did his, and he felt he'd been kicked in the solar plexus when he saw her pale, thin face, covered with an eruption of spots, and her skinny little frame, so different from that of the slightly chubby, bright, healthy child she'd been. He was so shocked he couldn't speak for a moment.

'Granddad, what are you doing here?' Melissa took off her iPod and eased herself off the bed, wrapping her arms around herself protectively. He could see she was very embarrassed and that tore at his heart strings.

'I came to see how you were doing,' Ken said gruffly. 'Your gran told me you were allowed visitors. I've brought you a present.' He thrust the carrier bag at her, trying to hide his dismay.

'For me?' Melissa's eyes lit up as she took the bag. 'You're my first visitor, apart from Mom and Dad. I've not been allowed any until now,' she explained hesitantly. 'They didn't want me to be overwhelmed with visitors.'

'I see. That's understandable. Well, I'm very glad I'm the first one, Melissa. I hope you like the gift.' The poor, poor child, what had she been through – and his poor daughter as well? And to think Aimee hadn't been able to come to him and ask for his help. That was appalling. He would have to phone her and apologize, Ken thought miserably, acknowledging his utter failure as a father.

He watched with pleasure, though, as Melissa impatiently unwrapped the layers of tissue paper and gave a squeal of delight. 'Oh, Granddad, he's *gorgeous*! Oh thank you, so much.'

'Maybe you could give your old grandfather a hug?' he suggested awkwardly, and was almost sorry when she threw her arms around him and he felt the sharpness of her shoulderblades and the protruding ribcage. 'I have a card for you as well, and there's something else in the bag.' He patted her on the back, afraid to hug too tightly in case anything cracked, she seemed so fragile.

'Oh, Granddad, I love Maltesers.'

'Me too.' Ken smiled. 'I wasn't sure if you'd eat them.'

'Let's have one.' She tore open the wrapping and handed the box to him, and he took two. She popped one into her mouth and closed her eyes in ecstasy.

'Did you enjoy that?' he asked, sitting on the side of the bed.

'It was lovely!' She sighed. 'I could eat the whole box.'

'And will you make yourself sick after eating them?' He couldn't contain his curiosity, wondering why on earth she had gone down the road of anorexia. 'Forgive me for asking,' he said hastily, seeing the expression on her face, 'it's just that I don't know a lot about eating disorders. They're not my speciality.'

'That's OK, Granddad,' she said with another deep sigh. 'Normally I would make myself sick, but I'm getting counselling now and trying to view food and stuff differently, and myself too,' she said matter-of-factly.

'Oh! I see. And are they good to you here? How do you find it?'

'Oh, they're lovely, Granddad. Very strict though. But Dr Morton, my consultant, is great and I've a brilliant counsellor called Bernadette. I can tell her anything, and she's very good at explaining stuff.'

'Well, that's good. Where's your roommate?' he asked, looking around the bright, airy room, which had two beds in it.

'She's allowed off the ward so she's gone to have coffee with her mother.'

'And are you allowed off the ward?' Ken asked.

'No. You have to earn that privilege by gaining enough weight so they feel they can trust you.'

'Oh! Right. Well, I'm sure you won't be long earning the privilege and then maybe you and I could have coffee and you could tell me a bit more about this anorexia thing. It would be good for me to know – as a consultant, of course. I do know one thing though,' he said, popping another Malteser into his mouth.

'What's that?'

'I know that it can weaken the heart muscles and cause heart failure, and that's when I'd be called in, and we don't want anything like that to happen to you now, do we?'

'No, Granddad.'

'Good, because I won't be around for ever and we don't want anything to happen to that precious heart if I'm not here to mend it, now do we?' Ken pointed to her chest.

'No, Granddad.'

'So have we a date, then?' Ken smiled at her. 'It will be a great help to me to hear what you have to say.'

'Really?' Melissa looked at him, and he could see she was wondering if he was serious.

'Really, Melissa. I have to keep up to date, and patients have the most knowledge about their illnesses, believe it or not. So the minute you've earned your privilege you can let me know, and I'll treat you to coffee and you can tell me what you think I should know. Deal?'

'Deal,' his granddaughter said, and he held out his arms to her and hugged her tenderly.

'Well, I'd better be off. I've to see patients over in the hospital. 'Is it OK if I pop in again?'

'That would be lovely, Granddad, and thank you so much for the gorgeous teddy and ... oohhh ... a little black cat.' She opened the card and read it. 'I love cats. When Mom's had the baby we might be able to get one.'

'That would be great, my dear.' Ken smiled down at her. 'Eat up those Maltesers – and no upchucking, if you can manage it. And I hope you don't mind me saying that,' he added hastily, wondering if he should skirt the issue.

'OK.' Melissa grimaced. 'It's a bit hard sometimes,' she confided.

'I know, just do your best,' Ken said gently, thinking how vulnerable she looked and how awful it was that she wasn't at home enjoying a carefree life at her young age. She offered him the box once more. He took two and gave her the thumbs-up before closing the door behind him. He was in turmoil as he left the unit and walked along the corridor that linked up to the main hospital. His poor little grandchild. He had wanted to cry at the sight of the gaunt little waif he'd found in Room 8. When he'd held her he had thought he *was* going to cry.

He saw the sign for the Oratory and took a left instead of heading across the main concourse to the lifts. He needed a few moments to compose himself. He let himself in through the big wooden door and felt the noise and hustle and bustle of the busy hospital recede when the door closed. A welcome peace descended and he sat on one of the chairs, glad that there was no one but himself there. The soft light of the stained-glass windows shone pale pinks, blue and golds, spilling a kaleidoscope of colour on to the gold carpet. A red votive lamp flickered brightly under the picture of the Sacred Heart and a big vase of lilies scented the air.

'Oh Sacred Heart of Jesus, protect that dear child. Heal her, comfort her in her hour of need and let me help her and her mother in any way that I can.' Ken knelt and bowed his head and prayed fervently, urgently, for his precious granddaughter.

CHAPTER THIRTY-TWO

'I'm very sorry, Judith, but the insurance company is insisting on a medical with their doctor. They've got very strict since the recession and, unfortunately, I can't sanction the loan until the medical referee has passed you,' the bank manager said regretfully. 'They'll contact you to make an appointment. We'll talk again when you've had your medical.'

'Oh! Right. Thanks for the call, Mr Long,' Judith said calmly, although she felt like crying.

'Again, I'm sorry about this, Judith. Frustrating, I know. Difficult times all round. Give my regards to your mother.'

'I will. Thank you,' she sighed, and hung up, uncoiling the cord from where she'd been twiddling it agitatedly around her index finger.

Couldn't she have any luck? she thought crabbily, utterly disappointed at this setback. She'd been so excited that, finally, after months of looking, she'd come by chance on a delightful little cottage in a small square off North Strand. She'd been bringing Lily to get a pair of furry, lined slippers that were like little booties and kept Lily's feet very warm in Murray's Medical Suppliers on Talbot Street one Saturday after they had bought two pairs of trousers each in Marks. After her mother had tried on the slippers, had had a poke around the big medical suppliers and treated Judith to a jar of Manuka honey, they had had a bite to eat in Clerys before going back to the car park. Judith had driven through the orange light at the Five Lamps but had had to stop further on and had idly glanced down a small narrow sidestreet on the other side of the road and seen a row of cottages, one of which had a 'For Sale' sign. Impulsively, she'd swung right and driven down to have a look.

'Look, there's another road down there, you'd never think it, sure you wouldn't? It's like a quiet little backwater,' Lily exclaimed when Judith told her why she'd taken the detour. They came upon a small square of neat, well-kept cottages and saw another 'For Sale' sign on one at the end of a terrace which had climbing roses still in bloom, despite the fact it was nearly December.

'Well, this is a find,' Lily declared. 'Isn't it pretty? Why don't you phone the number on the sign and make an appointment? They might be showing it today.'

As it happened, the estate agents were holding a viewing between two and four, and they only had ten minutes to wait. As soon as she walked into the cottage, Judith knew it was special. It had been remodelled, modernized and extended. The bright, airy open-plan living room and kitchen were decorated in shades of pale lemon and cream with touches of eggshell blue. It was, thought Judith, like a sorbet to the spirit, as she stood in the centre of the living room absorbing the lovely light energy the house gave off. She had, having seen many houses and apartments, come to the conclusion that every dwelling place had its own particular energy. Some of them had been depressing, heavy places that you'd be glad to leave, places she'd known instantly weren't for her. And others had lifted her spirit and made her think: *this might be the one*. None of them, though, had wrapped themselves around her like this one. This one was calling to her and she could see that Lily was also very impressed.

Big glass doors led out on to a small, plant-filled courtyard garden enclosed by high walls. The bedroom, in tones of deep burgundy and pale lilac, was rather womblike and also led out on to the courtyard garden. An array of ferns, bamboo and tall grasses and a large statue of a peaceful-looking Buddha created a very Zen space. A water feature added to the restful air and Judith thought what a lovely place it would be to relax in, to sit reading, or even eat her dinner after a hard day's work. The bedroom had a small en suite with power shower, and the bathroom off the hallway was small but beautifully appointed in shades of gold and beige.

An upstairs dormer bedroom with two Velux windows ran the width of the house. It would be perfect if Jillian came for a visit, Judith thought with mounting excitement. The price was well within her range. It was meant to be, definitely, she thought, remembering how her friend had told her that she'd know that the house was right for her as soon as she walked into it.

'It's just perfect for you, Judith, make your offer,' Lily whispered, watching a stout man with a gold signet ring and a flashy watch inspecting the place thoroughly, opening doors and pulling out drawers as though he owned the place. 'I bet he's one of those investor types buying when the prices are low and selling them for a massive profit down the line. I've read about them buying up properties; they shouldn't get away with it.' Lily had fixed him with a glare, which he hadn't even noticed, Judith thought in amusement.

She'd offered the asking price, subject to contract and loan approval, and the following week the estate agents had phoned to say that the offer had been accepted and it was hers. In an uncharacteristic tizzy of excitement, Judith had paid an architect to do the survey and then, when he'd given her his written report saying that it had no faults or structural defects, she'd made an appointment to see Francis Long at the bank to seek her loan.

And now this! Problems because of her accident. Judith was gutted. If the insurance company wouldn't give her mortgage-protection insurance she wouldn't get a loan. The banks were looking for any excuse not to lend; it was frequently in the news.

What bad timing for her to be looking for a loan. Just this once, couldn't the gods be with her? She walked over to the window and gazed out at the bleak grey sky and the snow-covered roofs and church spires of the city spread out below her. That courtyard garden would be beautiful in the snow.

She turned and saw Debbie Kinsella pass her door in a hurry, and so she might hurry, Judith thought crossly. She was late back to work, having taken the morning off. Something to do with a solicitor's visit. The old Judith would have dished out a cold and cutting rebuke but she had been trying hard since her return to work to keep a good atmosphere in the workplace and had, so far, been quite successful. It would be nice to have someone to vent on though, after her disappointing news. She could feel herself becoming tetchy and crabby like the Judith of yore, wanting someone to blame for her misfortune. The mantle of martyrdom she'd worn for such a long time began to settle, snow-like, upon her and she sat at her desk feeling extremely sorry for herself and hard done by. The afternoon dragged interminably. It had started to snow again, darkening the office and muting the sound of the traffic below to a subdued murmur.

She saw Madame McKeon gossiping with Eilish Reilly at the water cooler. Judith stood up and walked to the door of her office. 'Eilish, a word, please,' she called sharply. If those ladies thought they were at the end of their day's work twenty minutes before they were due to go home, they were sadly mistaken.

Eilish looked startled and blushed as she made her way over to her boss. 'Eilish, your calculations for two of the employees on sick leave are incorrect. I suggest you stop gossiping with Ms McKeon over there and calculate them properly before you leave,' she said coldly.

'Yes, Judith,' Eilish replied sullenly, making her way back to her desk. Judith left the door ajar and returned to her seat. She'd have to tell Lily the news when she got home. Her mother would be so disappointed for her. It had all been too good to be true, a fantasy that she'd end up having a place of her own. She sat doodling, unable to concentrate, before turning her attention to the file she'd been working on, a file Caitriona Slater had sent detailing the Christmas bonuses to be paid to the staff in the department. Caitriona had done an excellent job. She really was a most capable employee, Judith thought, sending her young colleague a brief laudatory email.

She called up a maternity leave file that Debbie had emailed across to sign off on and scanned it briefly. And scanned it again more closely, noting a glaring discrepancy when the net pay was calculated. It wasn't the first time in the past week or so that Debbie had made an error, and Judith's heart sank at the thought of reprimanding her. After all that had passed between them, she didn't want the younger girl thinking that she was picking on her again.

She glanced at her watch and saw that it was just five thirty. Hopefully, Debbie hadn't logged off yet. Her fingers flew over the keyboard as she sent an email requesting that Debbie step into the office before going home, for a quick word. It was better than calling her in and drawing attention to them.

She could see, by tilting her head sideways and looking up through the slats of the slanted blind, that Debbie was still at her desk. Some of the girls started to head home, a few of them calling out 'Goodbye' or 'Have a nice weekend' to her as they left. Before her accident they would never have done that. The first Friday cuppa at the beginning of December had gone well. One of the suggestions made was that if people took a short lunch hour, they could leave earlier in the evening. Judith had been amenable, saying that was fine as long as there were at least two staff on the floor to man the phones. She had given Caitriona the task of supervising it and also the task of organizing the extra two hours staff got every year to do their Christmas shopping. Miss Reilly and Miss McKeon had giggled and whispered together like two silly schoolgirls, but Judith had ignored them and talked to the others, really making an effort to find common ground with them. Because they could see that she was trying hard, they in turn reciprocated, and that was why she didn't want to come the heavy on Debbie. But something was definitely wrong with her concentration. Judith wondered was she pregnant?

A sharp knock on the door brought her back to the present and then Debbie was standing in front of her, pale and exhausted-looking. Judith stared at her in surprise. 'Close the door, Debbie,' she said calmly.

Debbie kicked it closed with her heel and took a deep breath. 'Look, please don't start, Judith. I've had the day from hell and it's not going to get any better. If you're going to bawl me out about something, just get it over with,' she said truculently.

'Sit down, please.' Judith kept her temper in check. Debbie's attitude was unacceptably aggressive.

The younger woman slumped down on to the chair in front of her. Judith looked down at the few notes she'd written on a pad to remind herself of the points she had to make. She looked across the desk at her young colleague, ready to launch into a diatribe, but paused as she met Debbie's tormented gaze. Seeing how miserable she looked, Judith felt her anger fizz away. Something was clearly radically wrong. Instead of going on the offensive, she said quietly, 'Debbie, what on earth is going on to make you so careless with your work?'

To Judith's horror, Debbie's lip wobbled and then she was sobbing, in torrents of tears as though her heart would break. For a brief moment Judith was reminded of how she too had once broken down and cried brokenly months ago when she was in hospital, and it was that reminder that prompted her to stand up, walk around the side of the desk and draw up another chair beside Debbie and put her hand hesitantly on Debbie's arm.

'What is it? Is it something you can talk about? Do you want me to make an appointment for you to talk to someone in HR?' she asked, feeling an empathy that she would never have been capable of until she'd had her own nervous breakdown.

'No, no, it's OK, it's OK. Sorry, sorry.' Debbie was gulping, trying to regain her composure. Judith handed her a tissue.

'Let me make you a cup of tea,' she offered, feeling she had to do something. She busied herself with the kettle and Debbie's crying became less anguished, and by the time she had made the tea and taken a packet of Club Milks out of her drawer, Debbie was sitting, hunched, but more composed, wiping her eyes.

'I'm very sorry, Judith,' she apologized, and Judith could see that she was mortified.

'I'm going to make it nice and sweet, it's good for . . . for distress.' Judith spooned in two heaped spoonfuls of sugar, added milk and slid the mug across the desk before pouring a mug for herself. 'Drink it,' she said, picking up her own mug. Debbie sipped her tea, and Judith could see that she was utterly exhausted. 'Are you feeling better? Would you like me to ring your husband and get him to collect you?' She thought that might be helpful and was horrified when Debbie shakily put her mug down and burst into fresh tears.

'But that's why I'm in bits, Judith, Bryan's going to Australia, we're separating. We're going to get divorced.' She wept bitterly.

'Oh Lord!' Judith was stunned. What was it – under six months since they'd married? And now they were splitting up? And this was the girl she'd been so jealous of. Who knew what went on in other people's lives? How long had she been miserable? Certainly when Judith had come back to work the previous month she'd thought Debbie looked somewhat lack-lustre, but she'd been trying so hard to get used to being back at work herself, trying to ignore the aches and pains of her hip and shoulder, which seemed worse in the cold of winter, that she hadn't noticed that one of her staff was struggling to the extent Debbie had been.

'I'm very sorry to hear that, Debbie. Is that why you were at the solicitors today?'

Debbie nodded. 'He signed the house over to me earlier. He's going next Saturday.'

'Are you going to keep it?'

'I have to.' Debbie wiped her eyes. 'If we sell it now we're in negative equity and we'll lose a fortune.'

'And will you be able to afford it?' Judith asked, thinking it was no wonder that the girl was close to a breakdown.

'Carina's moving in with me.'

'That's good.' Judith came around and sat beside her again. 'At least you won't be on your own. At least you've got a house, Debbie,' she said, trying to offer some comfort. 'I've just found a place I'd love to buy but I have to have a medical because of the accident and I'm not sure if I'll pass it.'

'Oh!' Debbie looked at her through tear-stained eyes. 'That's tough.'

'Please, keep that to yourself,' Judith said hastily, wondering what had possessed her to reveal such personal details.

'Of course, Judith,' Debbie said, before blowing her nose again. 'Look, I'm sorry. I'll make more of an effort with my work, I've just been a bit distracted this week.'

'Why don't you go home and have an early night? Could I give you a lift to the Dart?' Judith offered, thinking how lonely it must be to be going home to an empty house after the trauma of splitting with her husband. 'Is anyone staying with you tonight?'

'No. I haven't told anyone yet, just Carina and, well, now you, obviously.' Debbie twisted her tissue around and around and Judith remembered doing the exact same thing at one of the sessions with her psychiatrist. 'Carina offered to stay, but I've to go and visit my sister. She's in hospital.'

'Oh! The young girl that was with you the day I bumped into you.' Judith remembered how curious the teenager had been about her coma experience.

'Oh, yeah, I forget you met her.' Debbie took another sip of tea.

'What's wrong? Nothing too serious, I hope?' Judith said delicately, offering her a Club Milk.

'She's got anorexia, quite badly actually,' Debbie sighed, shaking her head in refusal.

'Oh dear, how awful, Debbie. She was a lovely young girl. I'm very sorry to hear that. My God, you're getting a hammering, aren't you?' Judith felt truly sorry for the young woman sitting in front of her.

'I guess so. You took a bit of a hammering yourself.' Debbie gave a small smile. 'I'd better go, Judith, if you don't need me for anything else. Melissa's expecting me. It's the first time she's been allowed visitors other than Dad and her mum, and I'm dying to see her.'

'Of course you are. Please give her my regards,' Judith said, feeling a little helpless that she couldn't be of any more assistance. 'Would you like to take a few days off work, sick leave, anything like that?'

'I'd prefer to be here, there's too much time to think at home on my own,' Debbie said.

'True. It's probably better for you to be occupied, but if you need time off, take it. And if I can be of any help, please don't hesitate to come to me, Debbie,' Judith invited kindly.

'Thank you so much for your kindness, Judith,' Debbie said, standing up shakily.

'Debbie, I *owe* you any kindness I can give you. I treated you very badly before I had my accident. It's something I'm ashamed of and I would like you to know that. I was in a very bad place in my life. I was very unhappy and I took it out on my staff and you in particular. I've wanted to say it to you for a long time and I'm sorry it took until now.' Judith could feel the tremor in her voice and the deep-red blush that flooded her face, but she kept her gaze steady.

'Oh! Oh . . . thank you.' Debbie looked taken aback and embarrassed but she looked Judith straight in the eye. 'It was hard, Judith. I used to feel sick coming into work every day, I didn't understand why you were so against me. I'm . . . I'm glad it's different now.'

'I truly am ashamed, Debbie. It was appalling of me and it really wasn't anything personal.' Judith lowered her eyes, horrified to hear that Debbie used to feel sick coming into work because of her. 'You're very magnanimous.'

Debbie took a deep breath. 'I read something once that helped me forgive my dad for leaving my mum and me when I was young. It was: *That was then ... and this is now.* So let's put it behind us,' she said with a weak smile.

Judith managed a smile too. 'Good advice, Debbie. Well done you for taking it. I once read somewhere that Abraham Lincoln said, "When I do good I feel good; when I do bad I feel bad. That is my religion." I'm trying to follow his religion these days, Debbie. Once again, my heartfelt apologies and please ... be as kind to yourself as you can. A hard thing to do, as I've discovered, but necessary.' Judith held open the door. 'I hope you find Melissa recovering well.'

'Me too. Thanks, Judith.'

Judith closed the door behind her, relieved to be on her own. What a day it had been. First the news from Francis Long, and then this. In a million years she'd never have dreamed of having a conversation such as she'd had with Debbie Kinsella. She had wanted to apologize to her, true, but had never been able to pluck up the nerve. And today this opportunity had come, and at least she'd taken it. Debbie had a level of maturity she had never expected and the graciousness to accept the apology in the spirit it was given. She could teach Judith lessons in living with *loff* and forgiveness, she thought, as shame flooded through her at the memory of how she had stopped the other girl's increment and reprimanded her in front of her colleagues. She had been a horrible person, Judith thought guiltily, tears coursing down her cheeks. She was only getting her just deserts by not getting the house of her dreams. She cried for Debbie and she cried for herself, sitting in her small office while, outside, the snow continued to fall silently, unceasingly, on the city.

Eventually, she wiped her eyes. She was very tired and she had a difficult journey home on icy roads, but Lily would have the fire lit and dinner on the table awaiting her. She had a lot more to go home to than Debbie Kinsella had, Judith realized, rinsing the mugs in the small bathroom adjoining her office. She tidied her desk and logged off before switching out the light and making her way to the lift. Tonight was surely a night to be in by the fire with someone you loved, she felt, as the snow swirled around the car when she emerged from the car park and took her place in the slow-flowing traffic heading out of the city.

'Thank goodness you're home safe and sound. It's a terrible night. I've been watching the news reports about the blizzard.' Lily held open the front door, very relieved that Judith was home at last. *Thank you, St Michael and St Joseph.* She sent up a silent prayer as she closed the door on the snowstorm that swirled and whirled outside.

'The house is lovely and warm, Ma,' Judith said gratefully, shrugging out of her coat and grimacing at the pain in her shoulder.

'Is your shoulder at you?' Lily asked in sympathy. 'Why don't you go in and sit beside the fire? I thought we might have our dinner on trays on our laps. I made a pot of braised steak stew with mash because I didn't know what time you'd get home at with the state of the roads.'

'That sounds lovely, it's been a hard day,' Judith said tiredly. She looked pale, Lily thought. Stressed.

'Go in and sit down, and you can tell me all about it when we're having our dinner,' Lily instructed. This weather would stress anyone, she thought as she ladled out two servings of stew over creamy mash and placed the plates on the trays she'd already set. Driving was very difficult in the current conditions and Judith was still rather nervous. She should have an Epsom salts bath after dinner to try and get some relief for her aching shoulder.

Her daughter ate her meal in silence, lost in her own thoughts, but Lily was pleased to see that she cleared her plate and polished off the bread and butter pudding Lily had made for desert. 'Tea?' she offered as she went to gather the trays.

'No, Ma, you sit down, I'll make the tea and fill the dish-washer,' Judith insisted. 'That was a lovely dinner, thank you so much. It warmed the cockles of my heart. I was frozen when I got home.'

'You're very welcome, dear,' Lily smiled, inordinately pleased when Judith bent down and gave her a peck on the cheek. She added another log to the fire when Judith had removed the trays and sat looking at the sparking flames thinking how companion-able a fire was. Central heating was a great invention but you couldn't sit looking at it, toasting yourself.

'Tell me about your hard day,' she said to Judith when they had settled with their tea and biscuits beside the fire.

Judith made a face. 'I got a call from Francis Long. The insurance company wants me to go before their medical referee before I get loan approval. Once they hear that I'm due to have that decompression surgery on my shoulder I bet they'll fail me. They're just looking for any excuse these days.'

'Well, I'm disgusted.' Lily sat up straight. She couldn't believe her ears. 'I'm getting on to Francis Long first thing in the morn-ing and I'm telling him we'll take our business elsewhere if you don't get that loan. The cheek of him. I expected much more from him, I'm . . . I'm livid.' No wonder poor Judith had looked so downcast when she came home.

'It's not really his fault. The banks don't want to lend now. Having an anaesthetic is seen as risky by the mortgage-protection company. It's just my bad luck.'

'Why do you have to pay that blinking thing, anyway?' Lily demanded. 'It's not as if you've anyone that's going to be stuck paying back the mortgage if anything happens to you and you die. Let the banks take the house back. It's all a racket, Judith. A money-making racket, and we're the eejits that put up with it. I was just saying to Moira, what can we expect when we're shovelling out billions hand over fist to rescue the banks whether we like it or not, and to the politicians for their pensions and allowances? Imagine – they have cars and drivers travelling the length and breadth of the country on their own business and we have to pay for them, and they hardly show up for work at all. Yes, Judith, eejits, that's what we are, and the likes of you and me that technically own the banks can't get a loan.' Lily was so annoyed she spluttered her tea and got a coughing fit.

'Well, at least I'm not in debt or in negative equity.' Judith licked the melted chocolate off a mini-Twirl and dunked it in her tea again. 'There's a poor girl at work in a terrible state . . .'

Lily listened with interest to her daughter telling her about the recently married young woman whose husband was leaving her, and thought how lovely it was to be having such a pleasant evening. Before her accident they had rarely spent evenings together. Judith would go up to her room after dinner and watch TV or read. She would miss these evenings when her daughter moved into a place of her own.

'I was just thinking, Ma, you know that lovely angel you gave me when I was in hospital? One of those might be a nice gift each for Debbie and her sister,' Judith said thoughtfully when she'd finished her tale.

'It would be just the thing, Judith. Isn't it an awful thing to starve yourself? Young girls have so much pressure on them these days. I wouldn't like to be growing up now. And imagine that poor girl having to pay a mortgage by herself and her husband skedaddling off to Australia. She'd have been better off single! At least you don't have those sort of problems. We're not too badly off compared to those poor unfortunates.'

'You're right, Ma,' Judith agreed. 'We're not too badly off at all. Where did you get the angel? I never go anywhere without mine.' She smiled, taking her little round angel out of her pocket and holding it in the palm of her hand. It was a small cream figure enclosed in a glass casing, and Lily had pressed it into her hand when she was in the coma. Lily had been extremely gratified when Judith had told her one day that she would always cherish it.

'I got them in the angel shop in Finglas. Angels of Ireland, I think it's called. When the weather improves we could go and have a look. They've lovely things in it. I could get a few bits and pieces for the grandchildren while I'm at it, for Christmas, to go with the money I'm giving them.'

'And I could get something angelic for Jillian to go with the Jo Malone stuff I got her.' Judith brightened.

'And I could treat you to lunch in the Autobahn. Moira and I had lunch there recently and it was very tasty. Pubs have changed a lot since my day,' Lily remarked.

'Well, Mother, no one can't say we haven't become ladies who lunch, that's for sure,' Judith declared. And they smiled at each other in the flickering firelight as the snow continued to fall.

Chapter Thirty-three

'You went in to see Melissa?' Aimee said, astonished.

'Of course I did, once I knew she was in hospital,' Ken exclaimed. 'Why didn't you tell me earlier that there was something up? I could have got help from Richard Ellis, or he could have steered me to someone and we might have been able to prevent Melissa from going downhill so rapidly.' He stood in her kitchen, tall, imposing and stern-faced.

'Dad, I feel a complete failure of a mother as it is, without you adding to it,' said Aimee wearily. 'We made our appointments with the GP and Dr Morton, who Melissa likes very much and trusts—'

'No, no, no, you misunderstand,' Ken said hastily, remembering the reason he was here. 'I'm just so sorry that you didn't feel you could come to me for advice. I'm the one who is a complete failure as a parent . . .' He tailed off.

'Oh!' Aimee stood looking at him, mystified. When he'd phoned her and asked if he could call in on his way home from work, she'd thought there was something wrong, or that he was agitated about Juliet's new accommodation arrangements. She certainly hadn't expected this.

'You should be able to come to me when you're in trouble, Aimee. Your mother says I gave you a hard time growing up, especially with regard to your schooling, but it was only because

I wanted the best for you,' her father said earnestly. 'And you've done very, very well for yourself. People, patients and colleagues have spoken to me about events they've been at that you've organized and they give you high praise.'

'Really?'

'Yes indeed. I'm very proud of you, Aimee,' he said awkwardly.

'Thank you,' she said quietly, thinking of all the times she'd longed for him to say it – times when it would have meant something. Now it was too little too late; she didn't care whether he was proud of her or not, if she was completely honest, she'd grown so far apart from him, but at least he was making the effort.

'So how did you think Melissa looked?' She poured tea for both of them and handed him the milk jug and sugar bowl.

'I thought she looked ... er ... shook.' He spooned in a heaped teaspoon, added milk and stirred vigorously. 'She's very thin.'

'She's actually put on five pounds since she went in. She's allowed to have her mobile phone now and, from today, visitors other than family, so at least she's making progress.'

'And how are you? You look peaky – scans all right?' Ken took a slug of tea and helped himself to a lemon puff from the plate of biscuits she'd put in front of him.

'I'm fine, apart from being very tired. It's a bit exhausting traipsing in and out to the hospital after work night after night, but at least she's being very well looked after, so that's a relief.'

'Well, try not to overdo it,' he advised. 'There'll be even more demands on your time when the baby is born.'

'Easier said than done. Christmas is a busy time. Not that I'm complaining – we're delighted to get the business – but we are a new company, and word of mouth and recommendations are very important, so our standards have to be extra high.' Aimee took a sip of tea and wished she could lie down, but time was getting on and she wanted to get over to the hospital and get home to have an early night. She'd promised herself one every night this week and so far it hadn't happened.

'Your mother's not hosting our annual New Year's Eve party this year, she tells me. Nor is she having the neighbours in for drinks on Christmas morning. I might have to employ you myself.' He gave a crooked smile.

'It's hard work, Dad. She's done it every year as far back as I can remember,' Aimee murmured. 'And then turned to and done the Christmas dinner. She's not as young as she used to be either.' Typical Ken, she thought irritably: me me me. Take it all for granted with not a thought for Juliet.

'I know. It's just slightly embarrassing, that's all. I don't know what to say to people about what's going on with us. I've been invited to a few dos and I've said we may be going to Spain for Christmas this year. It was all I could think to say,' he confessed, somewhat abashed.

'Well, that's perfectly reasonable,' Aimee said, feeling a flicker of sympathy for him. It couldn't be easy, having to cope with so many modifications to his relationship with Juliet and their day-to-day living arrangements. What sort of a slant exactly could you put on it to the outside world?

'It's just going to be very odd, her in those new rooms of hers and me in the rest of the house, having separate dinners on Christmas Day. Or is she going to you?' He eyed her keenly, and she knew he was expecting her to say yes.

'Actually, Dad, we haven't discussed it, to be honest. Christmas has been the least of my worries. I'm just hoping Melissa will be allowed home for a couple of days, otherwise Barry and I would probably go into the hospital.'

'Oh . . . of course. I just wondered.'

'You could always invite her to dinner? Have you thought of that? You could do the cooking.'

'*Me!* Cook a Christmas dinner?' If she'd suggested he fly to Mars he couldn't have been more astounded.

'You know, it was being taken for granted so much that was

one of the factors that made Mum reassess her life. I think if you wooed her again and made a fuss of her she'd be more amenable to going to those social things with you and sharing the odd meal,' Aimee suggested, pouring more tea for him.

'Do you think so? I can cook a steak and chops and a few potatoes, but I wouldn't be confident about that whole Christmas palaver.' This doleful expression made her want to laugh. He was pathetic sometimes, like a big baby if he had to go out of his comfort zone.

'Look, invite her first, and if she says yes, leave the food to me. I'll get you the best of fine dining, all prepared and ready to go with explicit instructions on timing and so on. How about that?' she offered, thinking more of her mother than of him.

'Right. Right, I'll ask her tonight and let you know.' Ken brightened. 'I'll go home now and do it. I expect you want to get over to the hospital.'

'I do, Dad, but thanks for calling and thanks for going in to see Melissa. I'm sure she'll tell me all about it tonight.'

'Do me a favour, Aimee, if you're ever in difficulties again, give your old pa a ring in case he might be able to help out,' he said, getting to his feet.

He'd aged in the last year, she noticed. His once finely chiselled face was puffy and tired-looking and the lines around his eyes were grooved deep. He was almost totally white now, with only the odd streak of grey in his mane of thick hair. He seemed, she thought, somehow deflated, his bombast and vibrancy beginning to wane.

'I will, Dad,' she assured him, knowing it wasn't something she could ever see herself doing. They didn't have that kind of relationship and never would. It was sad, but true, un-fortunately, that her predominant emotion for her father throughout most of her life had been one of dislike. His concern for Melissa now, however, made up for some of what he had put her through when she was growing up, and she leaned up and gave him a peck on the cheek, the first since her childhood days.

'I'm sorry, Aimee, if I caused you upset, I didn't mean to,' he said once more as he pulled on his overcoat. 'As I said, it was never my intention to hurt you.'

She didn't say, 'That's OK, Dad.' Aimee would never let him off the hook for the years of angst he'd caused her, so she merely said, 'Let me know if you want me to organize that dinner for you sooner rather than later, won't you?'

'Will do,' he said briskly. 'Let me know if there's anything I can do for Melissa.'

'I will, don't worry. Bye, Dad.'

'Bye, Aimee. Give my regards to Barry,' he said as he jabbed at the lift button with his thumb and stepped between the doors with an imperious wave.

Her father was something else, she thought, glancing at her watch in exasperation as she closed the front door of the penthouse. He'd obviously felt guilty when he saw Melissa, and had decided that he hadn't been a good parent himself and felt the need to apologize. And now, as far as he was concerned, everything was hunky-dory between them. If she were to live to be a hundred, her father would never be her confidant or someone she would turn to in her hour of need. It was far, far too late for that, but at least they could be civil and put up a façade of having some sort of relationship. That would do her fine, but as far as getting to know and understand Ken better, she had neither the time nor the inclination, and she had no intention of feeling one bit guilty about it either. She touched up her make-up, picked up her bag and set off to go and visit Melissa.

He was too old to go a-wooing, Ken thought tiredly, driving out of his daughter's apartment block into the steady stream of traffic on Crofton Road. But if wooing was what Juliet desired then needs must. It was becoming awkward when their friends wondered where she was or invited them to dinner parties. 'Busy with renovations, trying to get everything done before Christmas,' was his current standard excuse. 'Busy with Aimee's baby' would be his excuse when his new grandchild was born in the New Year. But you could only give excuses for so long. If Juliet would accompany him to one or two functions it would keep the gossips at bay.

Aimee had seemed weary to her bones, unable to summon up much enthusiasm for his heartfelt apology. He'd hoped she'd be touched, keen to make a fresh start, but he'd felt a distinct lack of interest on her part. It had been hard for him to come and try to make reparation; he wasn't used to making apologies. But she didn't seem to understand. She was a strange girl, his daughter, very cool and self-contained. Very touch-me-not. But at least he'd tried.

Juliet's car was in the drive when he got home and he parked beside it, shivering as a gust of cold air hit him when he got out of the Merc. It had stopped snowing and his feet crunched on the white, crispy, packed snow under his feet. He'd ask his wife to get their handyman to clear the drive; the last thing he needed was to slip and break a leg, or worse.

He let himself into the house, glad of its enveloping warmth, and took his hat, coat and scarf off and hung them on the mirrored mahogany hallstand. Before her departure to her new quarters Juliet would always have had a vase of flowers in the hall. Now, the Waterford crystal vase stood sparkling in the lamplight, as empty as their marriage.

Ken took a deep breath and walked along the richly carpeted hall to the door of what had once been the family room. He raised his hand and knocked. His heart began to beat quicker than normal. What if she turned him down? He might end up eating alone on Christmas Day. He felt uncharacteristically nervous as he heard her walk briskly along the wooden floor-boards to the door.

'Ah . . . ah . . . could I talk to you for a moment?' Ken asked, feeling faintly ridiculous to be looking for permission to speak to his own wife.

'Of course, come in,' Juliet said graciously, opening the door wider. He followed her into her new domain and thought how cosy it looked with the wood-burning stove alight with blazing logs. She had been reading, her book spread open on the deep, wide, lemon sofa. A cup of tea sat on the low coffee table and classical music played softly in the background. Lamps dotted around the room gave a calm, soft, diffused light, which gave a gentler, more relaxing aura than the chandeliers he favoured in his sitting room. The cream and lemon curtains were fresh and springlike and gave the room a snug, finished look. It was such an airy, light space compared to the dark colours and heavy drapes he liked.

'You have the place very nice,' he complimented, stepping in.

'Thank you, Ken. I love it. I find it very relaxing,' Juliet said calmly. 'Would you like a cup of tea? I'm just having one.'

'Er . . . well, I haven't had my dinner yet. I called in to see Aimee, and I visited Melissa today, so that's why I'm late.'

'Oh, right. How was Melissa?' Juliet asked eagerly.

'I was shocked, Juliet. I couldn't believe my eyes when I saw her.' Ken sighed deeply and shook his head.

'Oh Lord, was she that bad? I haven't seen her for a while. This is terrible, the poor little dote. Were you talking to any of the medical staff?'

'No, I didn't go there in my capacity as a consultant, I went there as her grandfather—'

'Ken, I'm being very thoughtless, you haven't eaten yet. I've left lasagne in the fridge for you . . . um . . . if you like, you could bring it down here and I could put it in the microwave and toast some garlic bread under the grill and you could update me,' she suggested, anxious to hear the news.

'That would be just the thing, I'm a bit peckish, I can tell you. I just had a sandwich at lunchtime and I've had a busy afternoon.' Ken perked up.

'Would you care for a glass of wine with it? I have a bottle of Gran Feudo, you always liked that in Spain,' his wife invited. 'Would you join me in a glass? It would be . . . companionable.'

'Of course I will. I prefer to drink with someone than on my own. It's never quite the same on your own, sure it isn't.'

'No, it can be quite lonely, actually.' Ken had certainly found that to be true in the last couple of months.

'Right, go and get the lasagne, and I'll heat up the grill and let the wine breathe,' Juliet said briskly, heading towards her little kitchenette.

It was, thought Ken, a bit like a very surreal date. He wished he had flowers or some of those Belgian chocolates she liked. What were they called? he pondered as he opened the fridge for the plate of lasagne Juliet had placed there earlier. Leonidas – that's what they were, he thought triumphantly, glad that his wits were still sharp. He would make it his business to buy some to have in case there was another invitation to the inner sanctum.

'Isn't it a gorgeous teddy, Mom? Granddad was very, very kind, and he bought me Maltesers. Would you like one?' Melissa was more animated than she'd been in a long time and Aimee felt a wave of relief sweep through her. There was a spark of the old Melissa showing tonight, not the subdued, defeated, sullen teenager she had been visiting for the past few weeks. Maybe she was on the up at last.

'So how did your session with Dr Morton go today?' she asked conversationally, not wanting Melissa to think she was prying. Her daughter could be touchy in that regard since she'd started on the programme.

'Fine, OK.' Melissa offered her the box of chocolates and Aimee was about to refuse automatically – she rarely ate chocolate – but thought the better of it: it might send out the wrong signals.

'Did you feel you made any progress?' she ventured.

'Yep, we had a good talk.' Melissa put the chocolates back without taking one herself, much to her mother's disappointment.

'Did you go to art today?' Aimee changed the subject, seeing she was getting nowhere fast.

'Yeah – look what I did.' Melissa took her sketchpad out of her locker and flicked through the pages before stopping on a drawing of a black cat. 'I drew Miss Hope. Good, isn't it?'

'It's excellent, Melissa. You really are quite talented at art. You could do lessons if you'd like to,' Aimee suggested, impressed with the drawing in front of her.

'Umm,' Melissa said dreamily, 'I'd really like that. I think I'd like to be—' A knock at the door interrupted their conversation, and they looked at each other expectantly.

The door opened and Aimee saw a smile of pure happiness break across her daughter's thin face as she spied Debbie framed in the doorway. She hopped off the bed, arms outstretched, and ran into her half-sister's embrace. Aimee watched in bewilderment as they wrapped their arms around each other and hugged each other tightly.

They really love each other! she thought, astonished, having never seen them together since they had become close. She could see tears glittering in Debbie's eyes as she hugged Melissa's skinny frame, and Aimee's eyes locked with her stepdaughter's over Melissa's shoulder and for the first time in their acquaintance there was no hostility in either one's gaze.

'Hey, sis,' Melissa laughed as they drew apart. 'Thanks for coming in.'

'Thanks for letting me know I could visit.' Debbie smiled at her. 'I'm sorry I intruded on your visit,' she said politely to Aimee. 'I won't stay long.'

'Please stay, Debbie. I know Melissa's been really looking forward to seeing you, and she's fed up seeing my boring old face, night in, night out—'

'Mom, don't say that,' Melissa protested.

'Only teasing. Actually, I wouldn't mind having a cup of tea, I didn't have time to have one at home,' she fibbed. 'I might just wander down to the coffee shop for a cuppa and let you two catch up.' Aimee stood up and picked up her bag. 'See you in a while.'

'Bye, Mom.' Melissa didn't offer any objection and took the gift-wrapped parcel Debbie gave her and tore off the paper. 'Oh, these are, like, so *cute!*' she squealed, holding up a pair of pink polka dot pyjamas with kittens dotted here and there as Aimee let herself out, feeling like the proverbial hot potato. She made her way down the long corridor to the main hospital and bought a cup of tea even though she wasn't particularly interested in drinking it. It was just an excuse to leave Debbie and Melissa alone.

She truly had been taken aback at their obvious affection for each other, and only a misery-guts could fail to have been moved by the sight of their embrace. She could finally understand why Barry was so anxious for his daughters to have a good relationship with one another. A loving bond between sisters was a big bonus in life, he'd argued when she'd said he was forcing them into an association that, at the time, it seemed neither wanted.

Aimee had no sister, just two brothers, and had never enjoyed a sisterly type relationship with anyone, being more of a man's woman than a girly girl. Seeing Melissa and Debbie together a few minutes ago made her realize just how much she had missed out.

Melissa was dearly loved by both Connie and Debbie, and that could only be a great gift. For the first time since she had entered into her relationship with Barry, Aimee finally let go of her antipathy towards his first family and was grateful they were in Melissa's life, and that he was the father he was to their daughter. Melissa knew her father loved her. They were friends as well as everything else. Melissa and Barry had a far, far different relationship than she and Ken had, and it had taken her until now to realize how important that was for her daughter.

This year had been a huge and very difficult learning curve, she reflected, holding her cup in both her hands and staring into space. She had never given much thought to her family's dynamics, being too consumed with her career. If she compared herself to her mother, she was actually very lucky. Barry was the complete opposite to Ken. He worked at their relationship. Her feelings were very much his concern, except for the blip over her pregnancy. He did try, she would give him that. And he adored their daughter. Aimee had a lot going for her, and she had taken it very much for granted. Maybe she *was* more her father's daughter than she cared to admit, she thought guiltily. It had taken Melissa's serious illness to get her to appreciate the gifts she had in her life and to finally accept that work was not the be-all and end-all. A good hard kick made her gasp. *And I'm here too.* It was as if her baby was saying to her: *Don't forget me.*

Aimee slid her hand down over her bump and gave it a little rub. She would be glad when the baby was born so she could get back into shape. Barry could have a vasectomy, because this was definitely her last child. By this time next year, Aimee fully intended to be her usual size ten. She hoped it would be a girl and that some day she and Melissa would hug each other with as much love and joy as Debbie and Melissa had a few minutes ago. And maybe this child would help his or her older sister make a full recovery from the blight of anorexia and life would be good for all of them again.

CHAPTER THIRTY-FOUR

'So how are you doing?' Debbie asked, perching on the bed beside Melissa. 'It must have been the pits not being allowed your phone. I was sending loads of texts until Dad told me you weren't allowed it. I think I'd have freaked if they took my phone off me.'

'I *did* freak. I had a mickey fit and screamed my head off and threw my dinner at one of the nurses when I was on bed rest, and they just sedated me and told me that I'd get my phone back when I put some weight on, and the sooner I accepted that the quicker I'd get it back. Mom doesn't know I threw my dinner at a nurse. She'd be mad if she knew that, I'm just telling you,' Melissa said hastily.

'What goes on in the ward stays in the ward.' Debbie smiled at her. 'Are you still pukin' up your food?'

'*Debbieeee!*' Melissa protested, embarrassed.

'Well, are you?' demanded her half-sister.

'Sometimes, but not as much. I need to get out of here to get back to school, that's one of my goals, so when I'm eating my dinner I say that to myself over and over. It's just they feed you so much in here.'

'Look, get yourself sorted as quick as you can, 'cos I need you, and that baby's going to need you, and Sarah and Connie and Drew and your mom and our dad need you,' Debbie urged.

'There's loads of great films on that we could be going to, and a friend of mine bought gorgeous jewellery in the market in Howth; we could take the Dart to that some Sunday morning, and have lunch over there, and we could do lots of stuff like that.'

'I'll do my best.' Melissa sighed. 'People just have no idea that it's very hard to get well even though I want to.'

'I'm sure it is tough, Mellie, and I'm sure it's easy for all of us to talk, but just keep trying.' Debbie gave her a cuddle and Melissa rested her head against her shoulder and felt exhilarated and daunted at the same time.

Debbie could see Aimee hunched over her tea, working her BlackBerry, as she drew nearer the coffee shop just to the left of the corridor she was walking along towards the exit. She supposed it would be good manners to tell her stepmother that Barry had arrived and that she was leaving. Aimee looked elegant, as always, in a tailored trouser suit, but she was pale and washed-out looking. And her bump was quite big now. It must be exhausting lugging that around all day, especially when you hadn't planned on having a child, Debbie mused, thinking that the other woman was having quite a rough time of it these days.

'Umm . . . Aimee, I'm off. Dad's there now as well.' She stood, feeling ill at ease, beside Aimee's chair.

'Oh . . . Oh fine. Thanks for telling me.' Aimee looked up in surprise.

'No problem. See you, Aimee,' Debbie responded politely.

'Wait, please sit down a moment, Debbie,' Aimee asked.

Debbie gave a silent inward sigh. She could do without this today of all days. She sat ramrod straight across the table from the woman she'd once sarcastically called a 'twiglet' to her face.

Aimee gave a sheepish little smile. 'We should get the awkward stuff out of the way, I guess.'

Debbie managed a weak smile too. 'That could take a while.'

'I'm sorry I was a bitch the day of your wedding, I've apologized to Connie and she very graciously accepted. I hope you can do the same.'

'There's no point holding grudges, I suppose.' Debbie fiddled with the sugar bowl. 'I'm sorry for all the times I was rude before the wedding, especially the day we bumped into you, Dad and Melissa in Roly's.'

'Long forgotten about,' Aimee said crisply. 'Look, Debbie, Melissa loves you, loves being with you. She's so glad to have a sister and I want to thank you for that from the bottom of my heart. This has been such a tough time for her—' Her voice faltered and her lip wobbled. 'Sorry,' she murmured as tears welled up in her eyes.

'Ah, Aimee, don't cry. She's going to be OK,' Debbie said in dismay, as a lump rose to her own throat.

'I'm so worried about her, Debbie. What if she doesn't get well? It scares me. It's a dreadful illness; I've read up on it and I'm afraid for her.' Aimee gulped.

'We'll just have to keep encouraging her, keep telling her she's doing great. I'll do anything I can to help, you only have to ask,' Debbie said fervently.

'I know you will. And just being there for her is a *huge* help. Did you see the way her face lit up when she saw you? She was thrilled. I'd never get a reaction like that.' She wiped her eyes and smiled wryly.

'You don't need to get a reaction like that. You're her shelter, her rock, you're her mother,' Debbie pointed out.

'I know. I just feel helpless. It's very hard to know what to say or do sometimes. I wish there was a support group so I could ask other parents who've been through this what their advice would be.'

'Just keep talking to her doctor and counsellor, I suppose. She seems to really like and connect with the girl she called Bernadette. She trusts her a lot, from what she was telling me.'

'Yeah, but she doesn't trust us,' Aimee said wearily. 'God,

the lies she told us, bare-faced, Debbie. It's all part of it of course but so difficult to deal with.' Tears coursed down her cheeks again.

'Look, we're all there for you, all behind Melissa. She *will* get through it, Aimee. We must believe that, it's the only way for all of us to get through this.' Debbie's eyes blurred and she searched in her bag for a tissue. When she'd seen Melissa, as white as a ghost, lost in a pair of PJs that were too big for her and her shoulders as thin as a coat hanger, she'd almost burst into tears in front of her. She could well understand Aimee's fear; she felt fearful herself.

'I can't thank you and your mother enough for your kindness to her. Sorry about this,' Aimee apologized again, clearing her throat. 'I didn't mean to make you cry as well. My hormones are all over the place.'

'Why would we not cry? Why would we not worry about her? It *is* frightening, Aimee, I'd hate to be going through what you and Dad are going through,' Debbie said sombrely, all enmity towards the other woman disappearing in a wave of sympathy.

'I wouldn't wish it on my worst enemy, Debbie, and that's the truth. I wouldn't wish this affliction on anyone. It's hell on earth.'

'I know.'

They sat in silence for a moment, composing themselves.

'Well, at least we've cleared the air. It's a relief to be able to move forward and not dread bumping into you, Debbie. I hope you can feel the same about me.' Aimee stood up and held out her hand.

Debbie stood up and took it without hesitation. 'Onwards and upwards.' She smiled. 'And . . . er . . . thank you, for this, Aimee. As you say, it was good to clear the air.'

'You know this much about me, Debbie: I'm a straight talker, a bit like yourself.'

'No arguments there,' agreed Debbie and they laughed and

went their separate ways, relieved that a hurdle they had both thought insurmountable had been so easy to cross when it finally came to it.

'Before I go, Juliet, I was wondering what are your plans for Christmas lunch?' Ken stood up from the table and looked down at his wife.

'I haven't actually made any. I know I could go to any of the children if I wanted to, but it would seem a bit strange going alone, so I was going to stay here,' Juliet admitted.

'I was wondering would you come to . . . ah . . . my part of the house for lunch? I'd cook us something, you wouldn't have to do anything.'

Juliet started to laugh. 'Ah Ken, you'd give yourself a heart attack trying to cook Christmas lunch.'

'I wouldn't,' he blustered. 'I'm quite capable.'

'Ken, I hear you down in the kitchen sometimes, and it's not for the faint-hearted,' she said, amused at the notion of him cooking a three-course meal for two.

'Aimee told me she'd see me right, and all I'd have to do is stick the damn things in the oven. I'd like to do lunch for you, Juliet. God knows you cooked enough of them for us in our time. I'd like to try and give you as pleasant a meal as you've given me tonight. I enjoyed it very much, my dear,' he said huskily.

'And so did I, Ken. It was nice to talk about the family and about our concerns for Melissa.' Juliet began to clear away the detritus of his meal.

'Yes, I've missed our chats,' Ken agreed.

'They'd become few and far between in the last few years,' Juliet pointed out, carrying the dirty dishes into her kitchenette and loading them into the dishwasher. Ken followed with the condiments.

'Yes, we drifted apart, didn't we?' he said regretfully. 'I never meant to hurt you, you know.'

'I know.'

'Would you do me the great honour of coming to lunch on Christmas Day?'

'I will.'

'Excellent.'

'I'll bring the wine.'

'Goodnight, Juliet, sleep well,' her husband said as they walked towards to the door.'

'You too, Ken.'

They stood looking at each other and then he leaned down and kissed her gently on the cheek. 'Goodnight, and thanks for dinner.'

'You're welcome,' she said.

Juliet closed her door behind him and smiled. It was good to be on speaking terms with her husband again, especially with Melissa being in hospital, and tonight had been unexpectedly agreeable. There was nothing to say that they couldn't dine together once or twice a week, and how wonderful it would be not to have to cook a Christmas lunch, with all the trimmings. Aimee would supply only the best of fare, and even Ken was capable of sticking prepared cartons of food into the oven and following the timing instructions. She would sit back and let him wait on her and not take over for once in her life. And then they could go to their respective sofas and have a snooze before paying a visit to Aimee, or having her come to visit them. The boys always visited on Christmas Eve, living too far from the city to travel on Christmas Day. Aimee was the only child they had living in Dublin.

Christmas would be different this year for sure, but who was to say different wasn't better? Juliet reflected, pouring herself the tail end of the wine and stretching out on her sofa with her book.

'I can't believe I'm actually in bed before eleven.' Aimee yawned and wriggled her toes under the duvet, wishing she could sleep on her tummy, her favourite position to go asleep.

'You should try and get to bed early for the next couple of

weeks.' Barry loosened the knot of his tie and unbuttoned his shirt.

'I know. Roger has been giving out about me working so hard. He wants me to work from home more now that I have all the team in place. He's a very decent boss to work for. I was lucky to find him.'

'He was lucky to find you,' Barry called from the en suite, where he had gone to wash his teeth.

'Do you want to put your light on? I'm turning mine off, I'm whacked,' he said when he got into bed beside her.

'I'm too tired to read.' Aimee gave another enormous yawn.

'I thought Melissa was in much better form tonight, did you?' Barry asked as they lay side by side in the dark.

'Much better – a little bit like the old Melissa. She was definitely more positive and engaged. Barry, you weren't there when Debbie arrived but you should have seen how Melissa lit up when she saw her. You were so right about getting them together. It was lovely to watch.' She reached down and took his hand. 'You might like to know that Debbie and I have made our peace. We had a chat in the coffee shop. Actually, she was very understanding and supportive. She's got a good heart.' Aimee smiled when her husband squeezed her hand back.

'Well done, Aimee, I'm delighted, *really* delighted. When all is said and done, family are what get you through the hard times.' He turned and kissed her.

'Yeah, and we have a good family, you and me.' Aimee stroked the side of Barry's face tenderly before kissing him back, feeling that maybe, just maybe, there was light at the end of the tunnel and that all would be well.

Barry lay beside his sleeping wife and, for the first time in months, felt a modicum of peace descend on his weary spirit. He and Aimee had made tender, gentle love, different from their usual passionate, forceful couplings, and he'd felt as though the bond between them had become renewed and strengthened after their rocky phase, which had seriously threatened to derail them.

If only Melissa could surmount her anorexia, they could all make a fresh start. He was so *proud* of Debbie. She'd come up trumps, even Aimee had to acknowledge that, and it gave Barry a great sense of fatherly pride. He'd been delighted when he'd arrived at the unit to see the two sisters laughing at a private joke. Debbie had looked terribly pale and tired. Perhaps she had her period. He hadn't commented, but he'd phone her tomorrow, he decided, and make sure everything was OK with her. His eyes, heavy with tiredness, began to close and Barry fell into a deep sleep, with his arm around his pregnant wife.

The bed was so cold and lonely. Debbie shivered as she crawled under the bedclothes and turned on the electric blanket on her side, cursing herself for not thinking of it earlier. She switched off the bedside lamp and lay in the dark, arms tight by her sides to keep her warm as slowly the cold chill of the sheets began to give way to an almost imperceptible at first but slowly strengthening welcome heat as the electric blanket kicked in.

What a day it had been. A day of lows with two unexpected, redemptive highs. Bryan signing over the house, resolute about emigrating even though it almost certainly signalled the end of their marriage. That sudden unanticipated jolt at seeing him, looking so handsome in his expensive new coat. Sharing coffee with him afterwards and struggling to make polite conversation. That had been the pits.

Then Judith's fervent apology and understanding sympathy. Her boss had completely taken the wind out of her sails with her compassion, when Debbie had been expecting a tongue-lashing.

And Aimee's tears, something Debbie had been thoroughly unprepared for and which made Barry's second wife appear much more human than the edgy, sophisticated career woman Debbie had known up until then. And their exchange of apologies, so sincerely felt on either side. When Aimee had broken down in front of her, their frosty past had evaporated to nothingness. Perhaps her own secret heartbreak was making her empathetic. No one really knew what another person went through behind their façades, Debbie reflected, having seen Aimee Davenport in a completely different light.

And the shock of seeing Melissa, so vulnerable and fragile in the hospital had been a blow in the solar plexus that had made her feel fearful for her young sibling. Debbie took a pillow and placed it alongside her on Bryan's side so that the bed didn't seem so huge and empty. Even though she'd been sleeping in it alone for a while now, tonight seemed especially lonely and she felt utterly bereft. A memory of long ago when she was a young child, of lying listening to Connie crying softly in her bedroom late at night, making Debbie feel very frightened, came back to her in the dark and it triggered a tsunami of grief that coursed through her, soaking her pillow with tears, until she finally fell into an exhausted sleep.

CHAPTER THIRTY-FIVE

'Oh look, Judith, aren't these gorgeous? I think I'll get them for the girls, I could put them with their gift vouchers,' Lily exclaimed, holding out a little crystal angel with a birthstone in her hands to show her daughter.

'They're lovely, Ma, I'd say they'd go down a treat,' Judith agreed, smiling at Lily's enthusiasm. Her mother was going on a spending spree in Angels of Ireland, the angel shop in Finglas, and had bought a selection of gifts for Moira and her bingo companions. She'd also bought an angel for Cecily. 'I suppose I should buy something for Tom.' She raised an eyebrow. 'It wouldn't be fair to leave him out.'

'You could buy him a St Christopher medal for his car, or a car prayer,' Judith suggested.

'Sure I could buy both,' Lily said chirpily, adding them to the pile already on the counter.

'And I'll get these,' Judith said, picking up two little glass angel worry stones. The owner of the shop, a small, slender, dark-haired woman with huge, kind eyes, smiled at her, and behind Lily's back Judith pointed to a set of mother-of-pearl rosary beads and put a finger to her lips. The woman understood immediately and gave an imperceptible nod. 'I'd like some incense and some candles as well,' Judith pointed to some scented candles for Jillian, 'when you've finished with my mother.'

'Certainly,' said the owner as she wrapped up Lily's purchases. The shop was busy with people doing Christmas shopping and Judith was delighted that Lily had found stocking fillers for her granddaughters that would be extra special.

'Well, that was a good afternoon's work,' Lily remarked as they made their way back through slushy snow to the car. There had been a slight thaw in the weather and the roads, thankfully, were clear although snow remained piled up in gardens and on footpaths. 'Wasn't it great that you could take time off to do that bit of shopping with me?'

'Yes, I took my Christmas-shopping leave with my lunch hour, so it was perfect.' Judith grabbed her mother's arm as Lily slid on an icy patch.

'This weather is the bane of my life,' grumbled Lily, clutching her tightly.

'Well, at least you can go to bingo tonight, now that the roads are clear.'

'And I'm looking forward to it. I might even win us a turkey.' Lily chuckled, enjoying walking arm in arm with her daughter. 'What time are you going to your party at?'

'I'll head off around seven. It's a buffet, thank God, rather than a formal dinner, so I'll make my appearance, do the rounds and get it over and done with.'

'Ah, try and enjoy it, Judith. It might be fun,' chided her mother.

'It might,' agreed Judith, just to pacify her. At first she wasn't going to bother going to the company do, but management liked senior staff to make an appearance, and because it was a buffet, and she could slip off after a couple of hours and not be noticed, she had decided to go. Also, if poor Debbie Kinsella could put on a brave face and go, so could she, Judith had argued with herself when Caitriona had come around the office looking for the names of those who were going to attend. Poor Debbie hadn't been given a chance to refuse. Judith had overheard Carina Buckley saying, 'You're going and that's it,

Debbie. I'm not letting you moulder away in that house because of *him*.'

Sound advice, Carina, well done, Judith had silently cheered and put her own name on the list when Caitriona poked her head in the door and asked if she was going.

Several hours later, as Lily prepared for her bingo outing, Judith was beginning to regret her decision to attend as she studied the contents of her wardrobe critically. She had several dresses that looked very well on her and she finally selected a black, softly draped cocktail dress which showed off her supple figure and shapely legs to their best advantage. She was lucky, she reflected, as she studied her image in the mirror, that she had never had a weight problem, even though she wasn't particularly fussy about what she ate. She'd recently had her hair coloured honey-blond and her eyebrows and eyelashes shaped and tinted, and she'd applied her make-up with extra care, using a slightly darker foundation than she wore to work. She adjusted a diamante cross at her cleavage, inserted two small silver earrings and studied herself. She had good cheekbones, she noted, and her green eyes were bright and healthy again, emphasized by the fan of dark lashes and the now perfectly shaped wing-tipped brows. She looked rather elegant, she decided, and was very pleased when her mother declared upon seeing her, 'Oh Judith, you look as though you've just stepped out of a magazine. You look lovely. Now go and enjoy yourself, for goodness' sake.'

'I will, Mother, I will.' Judith felt a tad irritable as the taxi she had treated herself to tooted outside the door. She wasn't a seven-year-old going to a friend's party, she was a middle-aged woman who had no one in her life to companion her, and she didn't want to go to her work party but felt she had to. She should have had a drink, she thought as the taxi took off at speed before she even had her seatbelt on.

'Do you mind? I nearly died in one car crash, I don't want to die in another,' she said tartly. No tip for him, Judith decided as he muttered an apology and slowed briefly before taking off again to scorch through orange lights. A great start to the night, she scowled, feeling like the grumpy old Judith of yore.

Now stop it! She gave herself a stern silent talking to as they drove past the Bishop's Palace: *Ma is right, try and enjoy the night. If she can change her whole attitude to life so can you.* Fifteen minutes later, she arrived at her destination and paid the surly young foreign driver the exact amount, much to his disgust. She was walking up the steps of the hotel when she heard her name called and turned to see Anthony Larkin coming up behind her. Anthony, one of the section managers, was in his late fifties and had lost his wife to breast cancer when Judith was in hospital that summer. It was the first time she'd seen him since his bereavement.

'Anthony, how are you?' she said, pausing to wait for him.

'Ah, putting one foot in front of the other.' He sprinted up the steps.

'I'm very sorry for your loss, Anthony. I would have gone to Vera's funeral if I hadn't been in hospital,' she said apologetically.

'I know you would, Judith, and I just wanted to thank you for the Mass bouquet you sent. I heard you were in a bad way and it was much appreciated. I'm hoping to get around to sending out the acknowledgements when I have the few days off at Christmas.' He smiled at her.

'There's so much to do, isn't there, when someone dies? It's very exhausting. Don't push yourself too hard,' she advised. 'You should try and rest over the holidays, you've had a tough few years.'

'I know, but she'd want it done. She was a stickler for doing things properly. She probably wouldn't be too impressed with me coming to this thing tonight, but I thought I'd just show my face, have a quick drink with my crowd and slip away. My lot were very decent to me this past year,' he said appreciatively.

'So were mine: that's why I came. I won't be staying for too long either, I don't want to cramp their style.' Judith laughed.

'After you.' He held open the door for her and they walked upstairs together to the suite where the function was being held.

'Best foot forward,' Anthony murmured seeing the MD standing at the entrance ready to greet them and hearing the sound of Dean Martin singing 'Baby, It's Cold Outside' floating out the door.

'Please, Carina, I don't want to go,' Debbie moaned, sitting on the side of her bed in her underwear.

'Tough, you're going.' Carina paused from blow-drying her hair to glare at her.

'But I'm not in the humour for partying. Bryan's going tomorrow and I just want to stay in and—'

'And feel sorry for yourself and sit here on your own. No, Debs. I'm not letting you do that, just as you wouldn't let me do it if the positions were reversed, would you?'

'I wouldn't make you do what you didn't want to do,' Debbie said sourly.

'Just come for an hour or two, just to get you out of the house and then you can come home,' Carina wheedled.

'Carina, my marriage has broken up, I'm in bits, do you not understand that?' Debbie started to cry.

'Oh I do . . . I do. Please don't cry, Debbie.' Carina dropped the dryer and hurried over to sit on the bed beside her friend and put an arm around her shoulder. 'I was only trying to help, I didn't mean to bully you. Stay at home if that's what you want. Honestly, just do what you're comfortable with.' Carina's authoritative air crumpled as she comforted her sobbing friend.

'Sorry, I know I'm pathetic,' Debbie sniffled.

'No you're not. I'm just an insensitive wagon,' Carina countered.

'No you're not, you're a great friend. I don't know what I'd have done without you. You're right. I might as well come in for an hour or two, even if it's just to see what Eilish will turn up in this year.' She gave a watery grin.

'Well, if it's anything like last year's get-up, she might as well not wear anything. Honestly, that one's got more fingerprints on her arse than there are in Dublin Castle, she's such a slapper,' Carina scoffed.

Debbie snorted, laughing. 'Carina, you're awful.'

'Well, she *is* a slapper. She's got no self-respect. Remember last year when she was fiddling with Ritchie Kelleher's unmentionables under the table—'

'Eeuchh! Will you stop!! I've tried to erase that image from memory. It was so horrendous it put me off my dinner.' Debbie made a face. 'It was enough to put you off sex for life, and he thought it was great, the big eejit. Everyone at the table could see them. She thinks she's Samantha from *Sex and the City*.'

'A little trollop from Tipperary is more like it,' Carina jeered and the two of them guffawed. 'Do you think I'll get off with anyone tonight?' She cupped one boob and slid one hand down to her crotch. 'For these are my mountains and this is my GLENNNNNN!!!!! It's been such a long time since a man's been in THEMMMMM!!!!' she sang irrepressibly at the top of her voice, and Debbie creased up laughing as her friend danced around the bedroom shaking her ass. 'Come on, let's party,' Carina grinned, handing Debbie the champagne-coloured dress with the deep-slashed V at the back that she'd picked out to wear. Debbie slid it over her head, settled it around her shoulders and hips and took the flute of Cava her friend proffered.

'Bottoms up,' toasted Carina and they drank the fizzy golden liquid to get them in merrymaking mode.

The party was in full swing when they got there, and Carina grabbed them two glasses of red wine from the drinks table. 'Get that into you,' she ordered.

The Cava she'd drunk at home had taken the edge off Debbie's taut nerves and she relaxed as they began to mingle and were greeted with cries of welcome by their friends. 'Look at Judith – doesn't she look great?' Rosa Ingrassia nudged Debbie in the ribs and Debbie turned and saw her boss, in a most elegant, figure-hugging dress, talking to Frank Hughes from IT. She looked so different out of her work clothes in her flattering cocktail dress, very feminine and classy, Debbie thought with a little shock.

'Holy Mother, would you look at Eilish,' Carina muttered. Tonight their colleague was wearing a very short tunic-type dress slashed to the navel. She really didn't have the cleavage to carry it off either, being rather flat-chested. 'I don't think Elizabeth Hurley need worry unduly,' Carina observed humorously.

'Not a good look,' giggled Rosa. 'Ritchie has been following her around hoping to get a repeat of last year's episode. No one wants to sit beside them.'

'I think she'll have to down a few more vodkas before Ritchie's in danger of getting a thrill. You couldn't molest him sober,' Carina retorted caustically and they hooted with laughter.

For a while Debbie managed to enjoy the party, but as the night wore on and the music got louder and the drink flowed her thoughts turned to Bryan and she wondered how he was spending his last night in Ireland. She'd checked her mobile phone a few times and there was no message.

'Are you OK?' Carina, ever watchful, came up to her as she stood at the buffet nibbling on a chicken wing dipped in a garlic and cucumber dip.

'Would you mind if I went home?' Debbie shouted as the music pounded.

'Of course not. Will I come with you? You did great.'

'It was fun.' Debbie grinned. 'But I don't really want to get pissed out of my skull, it's not the night for it – and don't you even think of leaving. I'm OK.'

'Look, if I end up with someone I'll go back to my place and if I don't I'll come back to yours, I have the spare key. How about that?' Carina said.

'Fine, I won't lock the door. Enjoy the rest of the evening and make sure you stay sober enough to get all the gossip.'

'You betcha. Eilish has already told Stephen Courtney he's talking a load of crap. She just can't hold her drink, that girl.' Stephen Courtney was the MD, and a rather stiff, reserved, poker-faced MD at that.

'OMG! What did SC say?'

'He just looked down his nose at her through his bifocals and said in that toffee-nosed voice of his, 'Perhaps you should have some coffee, young lady.'

'Young lady! She's *forty* if she's a day!' Debbie snorted, watching the 'young lady' dancing energetically with Tim Carroll, a weedy little actuary, while Ritchie Kelleher tried in vain to catch her eye, and Harry Quinn, a lardy telephonist who thought he was God's gift to women, did his best John Travolta impression.

'Look at HQ strutting his considerable stuff. Someone should tell him those chinos are a size too small. He thinks he's such a hunk. I wouldn't touch him if he was the last man on the planet. Why can't there be a few fine things working in the company?' Carina moaned, helping herself to a cold cocktail sausage. 'If I'd any sense I'd go home with you. Are you sure you don't want to have one last boogie?'

Debbie had shot her bolt and had no desire to return to the dance floor. 'Nope, I'm off. Talk to you tomorrow, and thanks for everything.'

'If I play my cards right and shake my bootilicious, do you think I could snaffle Ritchie from under her nose?' Carina smirked.

'And Tim too, now that *would* cause a scene.' Debbie finished her wing, wiped her hands on a napkin and watched as her friend sashayed back across to the dance floor, turning to wink at her as she began to boogie.

She was heading towards her table to get her bag when Judith called her name. 'Debbie, could I just have a word before I go,' she said, coming to stand alongside her.

'Sure. I'm about to leave too. I'll just get my bag, won't be a sec.' Everyone from her table was up dancing which made it easier for Debbie to leave without having to give any explanation as to why she was going early. She took her evening bag off her chair and made her way back to Judith.

'Let's just step outside for a moment, it's so noisy,' her boss suggested, leading the way through the throngs of partygoers clustered near the door.

'Debbie, I . . . um . . . I have something small here for you and your sister. My mother bought me one when I was in hospital and I thought both of you might get some little comfort from them.' She opened her bag and took out two little gift-wrapped parcels. 'It's just a tiny token to let you know I'm thinking of you,' she said, embarrassed.

'Judith, that's very kind.' Debbie was completely taken aback as she took the unexpected gifts. 'Can I open mine?'

'If you like. As I say, it's only something small, but I thought they were nice,' Judith murmured as Debbie tore open the paper and opened the small envelope.

'Oh Judith, it's lovely.' Debbie's face lit up as she saw the little glass worry stone angel. 'Melissa will love hers too. How kind – thank you *so* much.'

'How is she?'

'Not too bad, we're all hoping she might get home for a few days over Christmas. She's making progress.'

'And how are you?' Judith asked delicately.

Debbie's face crumpled and she turned away to hide her tears.

'I'm sorry, Debbie, I didn't mean to upset you,' Judith said hastily.

'No, it's . . . it's OK, Judith.' She swallowed. Judith took a packet of tissues out of her bag and handed them to her. 'Thanks. It's very hard, I won't lie. I didn't really want to come tonight but Carina made me. And we did have fun, but my heart's not really in it. Bryan's leaving tomorrow.' She bit her lip to stop herself from breaking down again. 'I'll be so glad when Christmas is over.'

'Me too,' Judith said sympathetically. 'I'm leaving now. We could go out together if you'd like and walk over to the rank on the Green or get a taxi outside the Westbury. Shall we get our coats?'

'Sure.' Debbie glanced at her watch. 'Twenty to twelve, we'll be home before midnight. Two little Cinderellas,' she joked with an attempt at humour.

'You did very well to come at all, Debbie, especially as you've told me that Carina's the only one who knows your circumstances. No one would guess at your distress. I hope you won't be spending tomorrow alone,' Judith said quietly as they handed in their tickets at the cloakroom.

'Carina may stay tonight. I'm not sure, but either way I think I might go and see my mum and tell her what's going on, I can't really put it off much longer.' Debbie sighed as they walked out into the chill night air.

'That's a good idea, Debbie. I've found out myself this year that no one loves you quite like your mother.' Judith smiled at her as they tucked up their collars and wrapped their scarves around them. It was still reasonably early for a Friday night and there was a taxi idling outside the Westbury when they walked past five minutes later.

'You take it, Debbie,' Judith said firmly. 'There'll be another one along in a minute.'

'Are you sure?' Debbie protested.

'Perfectly. Off home with you, that's an order.'

'Thanks so much for my angel, and for Melissa's.'

'You're welcome, Debbie. I hope it helps a little. I know it's a very hard time for you both right now. And if you're not up to it on Monday, don't come in.' Judith held the door open for her.

'Oh! Thanks, Judith. I'll fill in an annual leave form,' Debbie promised.

'You will not. You're perfectly entitled to sick leave. Annual leave is for taking when you're going on holidays or doing something pleasurable, not when you're going through trauma. Take two days if you need them. You won't need a cert. I'm your line manager, and I'm giving you permission.' Debbie looked at her, astonished. Was this Judith Baxter telling her to take a *sickie*?

'I've only had a couple of glasses of wine, Debbie, I'll remember *exactly* what I've said to you on Monday morning when you ring me to tell me you won't be in,' Judith said dryly with a little twinkle in her eye as Debbie sat into the cab. 'I hope tomorrow's not too difficult,' she added, before closing the door.

Am I dreaming? thought Debbie as the taxi drove off and she gave the driver her address. But the little round glass angel that she took out of her bag and held tightly in her hand told her otherwise.

Judith sat back in her taxi and let out a huge sigh. Tonight had been her biggest test since the accident and she'd passed with flying colours, she thought with relief as she watched the Christmas lights sprinkle their magic over the city streets. She'd stayed much longer than she'd planned and actually enjoyed herself more than she'd expected, and it had been a lifesaver walking in with Anthony Larkin and not having to face the throng on her own.

She'd had a couple of drinks, but not too many, remembering a few episodes after parties when she'd behaved none too wisely. All had been going well and she'd ended up chatting to a colleague in the pensions department, Ian Kennedy, an attractive married man in his late fifties who had given her several admiring glances over the course of the evening.

'We could slip off and have a quiet drink – it's so noisy here I can hardly hear myself speak,' he'd suggested, dropping a casual arm around her waist. His eyes glittered in the low, dim lights of the bar in the function room and Judith knew he wanted to have sex with her. He'd already told her that he, his wife and teenage children were spending Christmas in their holiday home in West Cork and that his family had left Dublin the previous day and he would join them on Christmas Eve.

How nice it would be to lie in a man's arms again and have him make love to her, Judith thought longingly, delighted that a good-looking, interesting man found her attractive. How exquisite to be touched and caressed and reminded that she was still a desirable woman who wasn't written off yet. She was, for a fleeting moment, almost tempted. It had been a long time since she'd had sex, but she remembered how low and sordid she'd felt having had previous one-night stands, the last one in a squalid kip when she'd been pissed out of her head and had woken up remembering little or nothing of the previous night.

'Thanks, but I'm going to head off home soon. I just need to speak to one of my colleagues,' she'd said lightly, slipping out of his grasp.

'No problem,' Ian said coolly, and turned away to go and find someone else to try it on with. Judith watched him go, and knew at least that she'd wake up the following morning with her self-esteem intact. But the interlude made her feel lonely and that was when she'd spotted Debbie and made her way over to speak to her before slipping out to get her coat.

How ironic that both of them would be going home with lonely hearts to empty beds. Once, Judith would have given anything to swap places with Debbie Kinsella. Debbie was going home to an empty house as well as an empty bed. At least Judith would have Lily to go home to. Another irony, she thought. To think she had once hated returning home to her mother's company. But tonight she would look forward to knowing that Lily was in the room along the landing from her, perhaps awake to call out goodnight and hear how she'd got on.

Perhaps things would be different this time next year. Who was to know what lay ahead? This was by far the most momentous year in her life since her father had died and, despite her horrific accident, one of the best, Judith decided as the taxi drove through the city centre towards home, and the sound of Bing Crosby singing 'White Christmas' came across the airways and a flurry of snowflakes began their merry dance outside the cosy warmth of the taxi.

'I don't know what's going on with the pair of them, Drew. It's very hurtful, as well as bad manners, that Debbie won't tell me if they're coming to me for Christmas lunch or not. I certainly haven't been invited to *their* house for Christmas. I'm going to tell her tomorrow that I need to know one way or another so that we can make *our* plans. I mean, for God's sake, there's just over a week to go. You'd think they'd know by now what they're doing. It's probably that pup Bryan's fault,' Connie said irritably as she lay cuddled in against him.

'Well, why don't we decide what we're doing and just tell them if they want to join us, that's fine, and if not, that's fine too,' Drew said sleepily. Connie had been giving out for the last ten minutes about Debbie and Bryan and he wanted to go asleep. It was after midnight and he'd been up since six.

'I suppose so,' she said grumpily. 'But you'd think she might have *wondered* what I was doing. I *am* her mother, and we've spent the last twenty-five Christmases together. For all she knows I could be having lunch here on my own on Christmas Day. It hurts, Drew. And I know it's all because of him.'

'So you've said.' He stifled a yawn.

'Well, if you don't want to listen to me, go to sleep,' she snapped tetchily.

'Right, goodnight,' Drew said equably and turned on his side. He was asleep in less than a minute.

Men! They were all the same, Connie thought crossly as he began to snore. How was it that they could go to sleep in *seconds*? She lay fuming in the dark, thoroughly disgruntled, and gave him a dig to stop him snoring. She'd listened often enough to *his* tales of woe – the least he could do was listen to *hers*. She was going to phone Debbie tomorrow and give her a piece of her mind, she decided as she turned to Drew, snuggled in against his back and put her arm around him. It was wonderful to have him, especially on a freezing-cold night like tonight, even if she was in a snit with him, Connie thought with a hint of a smile. She rested her cheek against him, listening to his now deep, even breathing until she fell asleep herself.

CHAPTER THIRTY-SIX

Debbie hadn't answered the text he'd sent her the previous evening and she had her phone switched off, because it had gone straight to her voicemail. He would have liked to say goodbye, Bryan thought dolefully as he stood in the queue waiting to board the plane that was to bring him to Hong Kong, on the second leg of his trip to Australia. He'd taken the first Aer Lingus flight out of Dublin to make his connecting flight to the Orient, and when he'd changed terminals at Heathrow he'd phoned her to let her know that he was on his way and to say goodbye. Maybe she just didn't want to take his call. Bryan opened his passport to present it with his boarding card. There was no need for Debbie to be bitchy about it. He'd pleaded with her to come with him, and she wouldn't. He could have told her she had to buy him out of his share of the house, but he hadn't. He'd signed it over lock, stock and barrel, and he had no further legal claim on it. In ten years' time, when house prices rose and the recession was long forgotten about, his estranged wife would be doing OK for herself.

His phone rang and Bryan's heart lifted. He *knew* Debbie wouldn't let him travel halfway around the world without saying goodbye. She was a real old softy, he thought affectionately, taking the phone out of the little pocket in his travel bag. 'Hi,' he said light-heartedly, not even bothering to check the number. 'I knew you'd ring.'

'Ah did you, son? I just wanted to make sure you got to Heathrow and the right terminal OK. I'm missing you terribly already.' Brona stifled a little sob and Bryan's face fell. He had been so sure it was Debbie. Not that he didn't want to talk to his mother; she'd been a real brick throughout his separation. And she'd given him €1,000 as a going-away present, even though her wages in the hair salon she worked in had been cut. It was just that she was inclined to be very, very weepy about him going and had shed a river of tears as she'd stood at the front door in the early hours watching him get into the taxi. Bryan had, despite her vehement protestations, insisted on getting a taxi to the airport for that very reason. Under no circumstances did he want Brona weeping and wailing in Departures.

'I got here fine, Ma, I'm just queuing to board. I'll phone you from Hong Kong,' he promised.

'Mind yourself, son,' she blubbed.

'I will. I have to go now, I'm nearly at the front of the queue,' he murmured. 'Bye, and thanks for everything,' he added gratefully before hanging up. Bryan kept his phone switched on until the massive Airbus rolled away from the jetway and lumbered ponderously along to join the queue to take off, just in case Debbie phoned or texted. How very mean of her, he thought when he finally turned off his iPhone, to ignore his texts and phone message. He'd expected a lot more from her. He'd been magnanimous to make contact and she'd behaved like a spoilt child. For the second time that morning he felt a sharp ache of loneliness. The first had been when he'd looked out of the plane window and seen the lights of Dublin and the flashing lights on the iconic twin ESB chimneystacks fade away behind him. It had surprised him to feel that way. He'd imagined that he'd be delighted to shake away the dust of the city that had brought him so low. If Debbie were with him now it would be so different. It would be an adventure. Well, it was still an adventure, he told himself determinedly. *His* adventure.

Bryan settled back in his seat and located the inflight magazine to see what movies were showing on the outward journey. He was on his way to a new life. Debbie could frig off; he wasn't going to let her ruin it for him.

*

The insistent ringing of a phone penetrated Debbie's deep sleep and she came to in a daze, struggling to clear her brain of the cottonwool fog induced by the sleeping tablet she'd taken the previous night. It was the landline ringing and she stretched over to the bedside locker to answer it. 'Hello,' she muttered groggily.

'Oh, did I wake you? I thought you'd be up.' Connie sounded as though she'd been up for hours.

'What time is it?' Debbie yawned, sitting up and glancing over at her alarm clock.

'Nearly half twelve,' her mother informed her.

'God, is it?'

'Were you out late last night?'

'I had my work party.'

'Ah . . . so you're suffering.' She didn't sound particularly sympathetic, thought Debbie, suddenly realizing that, by now, Bryan was probably on the way to Hong Kong. Carina had procured a few tablets for her, having raided her mother's medicine cabinet when Debbie moaned that she wasn't sleeping since Bryan had left. She'd taken a sleeping tablet the previous night in an effort to get a decent night's sleep so she wouldn't be lying awake tormenting herself and it had worked, even if she felt a bit out of it now.

'Only to be taken on special occasions,' Carina had warned. 'You don't want to turn into a druggie and get addicted to the yokes.'

'Was it a late night?' Connie asked.

'No, I was home just after midnight,' Debbie murmured.

'Listen, Debbie, do you think you could tell me if you and Bryan are coming to me or *what's* happening for Christmas lunch? Will you be here, or away, or over at Brona's? I'd like to know so I can make my own plans.' Connie sounded a tad irritable.

Debbie knew there was no point in telling any more lies. She was going to have to tell her mother what was going on at some stage, and it being Christmas she could understand Connie's tetchiness at not knowing whether she and Bryan were going to her for lunch or not on Christmas Day. She took a deep breath. 'I suppose it's time I told you, Mum. Bryan's given up his job and gone to Australia. He flew out this morning.'

'He *what*?'

'He flew out to Australia this morning.' Debbie lay back against the pillow, twisting her wedding ring agitatedly.

'For how long?' Connie demanded.

'I don't know.'

'He left you alone for Christmas? Your first Christmas as a married couple?' Connie couldn't hide her shock.

'Mum, could I come over this afternoon, or are you doing something with Drew? I need to talk to you.'

'Sure, love, I won't be seeing Drew until later. Is everything OK?' There was real concern in her mother's voice.

'Not really, Mum.' Debbie had to struggle not to burst into tears.

'Come over now, get on a Dart and I'll collect you from the station. I'll do brunch for us. How about that?' Connie urged.

'Thanks, Mum, that would be good,' Debbie said, longing to see Connie and get a hug from her. 'I'll see you in an hour and a half or so.'

'Ring me when you're leaving Bray, and I'll hop in the car,' Connie said. 'Would you like a fry-up, or smoked salmon and scrambled eggs, or some bagels and cream cheese?'

'Whatever you feel like, Mum, I'm not fussy,' Debbie said wearily. Right now food was the last thing on her mind.

'OK, just get up and dressed and get on the train,' Connie instructed before hanging up.

Debbie threw back the duvet, got out of bed and opened the

curtains. It was a lovely crisp winter's morning. The sky was clear except for little white marshmallow clouds that blew across the sun's path every so often.

Where was her husband now? she wondered despondently. He hadn't even phoned to say goodbye. She poked in her bag for her mobile and saw with dismay that it was dead. She'd checked it once or twice at the party and then when she got home she'd taken her sleeping tablet straight away, determined to block out her torment by avoiding the dreaded dark night of the soul, and had fallen asleep much quicker than she'd expected. She hadn't checked her phone beforehand and hadn't noticed that the battery had died. She found her charger, plugged it in and switched it on. Two unread messages and a voicemail notification flashed on the screen.

The first text message was from the previous night:

Hi Debs hope ur ok. Just having a farewell drink with Kev and the gang. Ring if u get this, babe. B xxx

Oh, you were having drinks with Kev and the gang, were you? she thought furiously, scrolling down to the next one, which had been sent just after 7 a.m. this morning:

Hi Debs, just about to board my flight from Dublin Airport. Wanted to say goodbye but 2 early 2 wake you. Will ring u from Heathrow. Bxxx

She punched in 171 and heard her husband's familiar voice: 'Hi, Debbie, it's me. I'm just heading for Terminal 5 to catch my flight to Hong Kong and I'd hoped to be able to talk to you, to tell you I love you and to say goodbye. Babes, I hope you might change your mind and join me in Oz. We could have a great time. Start afresh. Have to go, Dollface, I'll make contact when I'm settled in. Love ya.'

Debbie flung the phone away from her in disgust.

Start what afresh? They were only six months married and he couldn't hack *that*. What *exactly* did he want to start afresh? And even if she did go to Oz, nothing was going to change for them financially – they'd still be scrimping and he wouldn't be able to cope with that. He was such a bloody ostrich. He'd probably spent a fortune on his night out with the gang too, knowing him.

She grabbed the phone off the bed and keyed in a text, fingers flying furiously over the keys:

Sorry missed ur texts and call. Was at my xmas party. Brill night!
Safe journey and best of luck in Oz. D

'Stick that up your billabong,' she muttered, not knowing exactly what a billabong was, pulled off her nightshirt and stepped into the shower. Let him see that she wasn't missing him that much. He wasn't the only one out on the tear the previous night. She certainly didn't want him to think she'd been moping. And the 'safe journey and best of luck' bit was casually offhand, as though they were mere acquaintances.

Her anger got her up and running. Debbie showered, dried her hair, left a note for Carina, who was snoring in the guest room, and thirty-five minutes later was standing on the platform waiting for the Dart to Greystones.

'And did she say what happened between them or why he's gone?' Drew asked.

'No, just that that little turd has flown out to Australia this morning. I knew the first time I met that Bryan Kinsella he was no good. I knew that marriage wouldn't last. I wanted her to postpone the wedding, and she wouldn't listen to me, and now look at the mess she's in. If I could get my hands on that selfish, vain, sly little bastard I'd make him sorry,' Connie ranted.

'Calm down, Connie. Maybe it's not as bad as you think. Maybe it's something they've both agreed on,' Drew countered patiently.

'No, if it was something they'd agreed on Debbie would have told me about it before now. Trust me, Drew, this is not good. I'll call you later and let you know what's happening.'

'OK, just don't fly off the handle or say things like "I told you so but you wouldn't listen." This isn't the day for it,' he advised.

'I won't,' she sighed.

'Chin up. I'll see you later,' Drew said comfortingly, and Connie hung up, feeling very glad that she had someone she could share her troubles with. Her poor, poor daughter. Connie almost felt sick for her. Debbie had sounded *so* forlorn. To be left alone the week before Christmas and they not even six months married was incredible. What was that moron thinking?

If she could have ten minutes with Bryan Kinsella he would be a very, very sorry young man. Stressed and agitated, she took some mushrooms out of the fridge and began to slice them, wishing she were slicing her son-in-law's most precious possession instead. Eunuch Kinsella! That would suit him very well, Connie thought viciously as she gave the last mushroom a particularly violent chop, and felt the better for it.

'Your mother did what?' Drew demanded.

'She booked tickets for myself and Katy to come home for New Year's Eve. We're staying for four days. It was our Christmas present,' his eldest daughter repeated.

'But I won't be here on New Year's Eve, Erin. Connie and I are going to Spain for four days. I told Marianna that.'

'Aw, Dad!' She couldn't hide her disappointment.

'When are you flying in?' he asked, trying to keep the anger out of his voice.

'New Year's Eve morning, with Aer Lingus,' Erin said.

'Right, I'll collect you from the airport,' he said firmly.

'I can't believe you're going abroad and leaving the stables, Dad. This must be serious,' his daughter teased.

'It is, actually, Connie's a woman in a million.' Drew smiled. 'You'll get to meet her. We're not flying out until the evening.'

'Katy and I will be giving her a good going-over. Nothing but the best for our dad; if she doesn't pass muster she's outta there big time,' Erin warned.

'She'll pass, but will you? Be on your best behaviour, Miss,' Drew joked, and his daughter made a face at him before blowing a kiss.

'See ya, Dad. Great talking to ya. I love you so much.'

'And I love you too, pet. Enjoy your day.'

'I will. Steve's just gone out to get fresh bagels and then we're going to go out and buy a tree and decorate the apartment. That will be fun. I'll email you some pictures when we have it done. Give Marino and Tusker a big kiss for me.'

'I will. Bye.' Drew blew her a kiss and hung up. Skype was such a wonderful invention, he thought gratefully, thinking how much it enhanced his twice-weekly phone conversations with his daughters.

He couldn't believe how conniving Marianna was. She was something else, he thought, disgusted, and he felt he knew her pretty well. His ex knew he was going away with Connie, because she'd invited him to a small gathering at her mother's house on New Year's Eve. They weren't really celebrating Christmas, she'd told him. She and Edward were flying over from the States on Christmas Eve and he was flying back three days later. It would be all very low key. She would stay with Dorothy until after the New Year. The three of them were going to have Christmas lunch in the Ritz Carlton in Enniskerry, and he was more than welcome to join them. Dorothy would be most pleased if he could, Marianna assured him.

He couldn't imagine anything he'd hate more!

He had plans made, he'd told her, even though he and Connie didn't know yet exactly what they were doing because she'd been waiting on a response from Debbie. Even then, Marianna hadn't given up. Her mother was hosting a small soiree on New Year's Eve for family and friends, who had been very kind to them after their bereavement, and it really would be good manners for him to come for a while, she had persisted.

'Sorry, can't. Won't be in the country, Marianna,' he'd said cheerfully, knowing that not even she could argue with that.

'Why, where will you be?' she'd demanded, most put out.

'Connie and I are taking a few days away. We're flying out on the thirty-first. We want to celebrate our first New Year's Eve together,' he'd informed her briskly, and before she could ask anything else he'd ended their conversation. 'Sorry, have to go, the vet's just arrived,' he'd fibbed. 'Have as good a Christmas and New Year as you can under the circumstances.' He'd hung up, delighted at having a great excuse not to attend any damn soiree she'd be at. Sooner or later his ex-wife would have to take the hint that he had no desire *whatsoever* to be in her company.

And now this! Marianna had deliberately bought airline tickets for the girls on New Year's Eve, when she could have bought them for Christmas or any of the days in between. Both his daughters had told him they wouldn't be home this Christmas and had invited him to come to them, but he'd refused. He'd been to New York the previous Christmas and his manager, Dermot, had looked after the stables; he wanted Dermot to have Christmas off this year so he could spend it with his wife and young children. He'd look after the place for the four days Connie and Drew were away.

Marianna was so sly, so conniving, knowing how torn Drew would be because his girls were home and he wasn't there to spend time with them. She knew exactly how to ruin his break with Connie. He wanted to phone her and tell her just what he thought of her. His ex-wife was a bitch of the highest order and he would tell her so in no uncertain terms.

He glanced at his watch and saw it was just after two. He wondered had Debbie arrived at Connie's yet. He dialled Connie's number and knew she was driving and on the Bluetooth when she answered the phone.

'Are you free to talk?' he said, hoping she was so he could vent.

'Yep, just on my way to the station to pick Debbie up. You sound a bit fraught, what's up?'

'Guess what my witch of an ex-wife did behind my back?'

'What?' He could hear the note of apprehension in Connie's voice.

'She booked airline tickets for the girls to fly in on New Year's Eve for four days.'

'Aw, Drew!' she exclaimed. 'We'll cancel Spain. I can do it today,' she said immediately.

'No we will *not*, Connie! That's exactly what that little she-devil wants me to do,' he said forcefully. 'She's not going to manipulate me like that, now or ever again. She did plenty of it over the years. I've just about had enough of her, and I'm going to ring her right now and tell her exactly what I think of her,' he raged.

'No ... no, don't do that, don't react hastily,' Connie cautioned. 'That's precisely what she wants you to do. She wants to get a response from you. Don't play into her hands. Do nothing. Say nothing. That will drive her mad. Trust me, I know these things, I'm a woman,' she added grimly.

'Oh . . . Right. Yeah, I guess that's a pretty good strategy. That *would* drive her bananas,' Drew said with some degree of satisfaction as he saw the sense of her advice.

'We'll talk about it later, but honestly, if you want to stay in Ireland that's fine. I wouldn't want to deprive you of time with your girls,' Connie insisted.

'Connie, you're the best,' Drew said gratefully. 'But you know, we need to start as we mean to go on. Our relationship is as important as anyone or anything in our lives, and I'm not going to let Marianna or anybody else think otherwise. Our children are very, very important to us and we'll always be there for them – you and I both know that – but this is our time, dearest. We deserve it, God knows, and I hope you feel the same way.'

'I do, Drew. You know that. I love you very much and you're right, and thanks for saying it.'

'I'm only saying what's the truth, Connie. I love you very much too,' Drew said emphatically. 'Go meet Debbie and we'll talk later, and I promise Marianna won't hear a peep from me until she gets the postcard from Spain telling her I'm having a wonderful time.' He smiled and was rewarded by a chortle of laughter from his beloved down the line.

*

What a mean-spirited wagon Marianna Delahunt was, Connie thought, parking the car at Greystones Dart station. To do that to Drew after all his kindness to her when her father had died was the lowest of the low. He loved his girls and spoke so highly of them. They were his Achilles' heel, and that bitch knew it. Their first time away would be tinged with sadness. He'd be missing his girls, she'd be worrying about Debbie. Second relationships had a lot of obstacles to overcome. At least Debbie liked Drew – what if *his* daughters didn't like *her*?

But Drew was right about one thing. They had to honour their commitment to each other by putting each other first, hard as it would be. Watching Debbie's pale, miserable face as she made her way along the platform after the train pulled in, Connie knew for the first time what it was to be torn. If she was away in Spain, what was Debbie going to do on New Year's Eve, the loneliest night of the year?

'Hi, Mum,' her daughter said, before bursting into tears as Connie wrapped her arms around her.

'Come on, let's get you home,' she said tenderly. 'I've got the fire lit and an apple tart in the oven for afters. Tell me what's going on and we'll have a good chat about everything.'

'Thanks, Mum. You're the best.' Debbie rubbed the tears away with the back of her hand, and it caught at Connie's heartstrings, remembering how many times her daughter had done the same thing when she was a little girl and something had upset her. Bryan Kinsella had a lot to answer for, she thought bitterly, remembering how she had felt when Barry walked away from them. Because Connie was under no illusion: her son-in-law had walked and wouldn't be coming back any time soon and her daughter was in for a very, very hard time indeed.

'You were talking to Drew?' Marianna's fingers curled in her palms. 'Did you tell him you were coming home for New Year?' She tried to keep her tone neutral.

'Yeah, Mom, but he said he won't be in Ireland, he said you knew that,' Erin said crossly.

'I didn't realize he was going away on New Year's *Eve*, I thought it was New Year's *Day*,' Marianna lied. 'That was why I booked your tickets. I thought he'd be able to make it to Mamma's little family gathering.'

'Aw, it's such a shame, Mom. I'd love to have spent time with him. He's collecting us from the airport.'

'I'll come with him. I can't wait to see you next week – I'm looking forward to coming up to NY for our girls' lunch before I leave for Ireland. Talk soon, sweetheart,' Marianna trilled gaily. She replaced the receiver and began to anticipate Drew's furious phone call, which should be coming *any* time soon.

She'd teach him to give her the cold shoulder and dismiss her invites as though they were of no consequence. She had seen nothing of her ex-husband in the weeks since her father's funeral, despite her best efforts, not even when she'd phoned him to tell him that she was returning to the States. 'Safe journey,' was the best he could do, she thought bitterly.

If he was running off abroad with his new floozy she'd damn well throw a spanner in the works. She wouldn't be in the slightest bit surprised if that little jaunt was cancelled. The girls were number one in Drew's life; Marianna had found that out years ago and used it very successfully against him. That Connie woman would very shortly be discovering that fact for herself.

She loved getting Drew mad; it was better than his infuriating disinterest. She would *relish* his phone call, and he *would* phone her, Marianna smiled to herself. Drew had always risen to her bait, just as he would now.

CHAPTER THIRTY-SEVEN

'Do you think I'm being unreasonable, Mum? It would be crazy to give the house back to the bank, wouldn't it?' Debbie said tiredly, picking at the smoked salmon, scrambled eggs and mushrooms her mother had cooked for them.

'Absolutely bonkers,' Connie agreed vehemently. 'If you can manage to keep paying the mortgage, that's the way to keep going.'

'And we *were* managing, once Dad gave us the money to pay off the credit cards. Bryan just didn't want to stick it out. He couldn't cope with being tied down. He felt trapped, he told me.'

Where had she heard that before, Connie thought with a sinking feeling of déjà vu. But she said nothing, just allowing her daughter to get it all off her chest.

'It was very unfortunate the downturn happened when it did. It was terrible timing for you,' she said sympathetically when Debbie finished talking. She was finding it difficult to restrain herself from calling her son-in-law all the names under the sun and having a go at him, but she would not criticize Bryan to Debbie, remembering how difficult she had found it when her mother had criticized Barry to her when he'd abandoned them.

'At least you've got Carina coming to share with you. It's someone you know, and you don't have to advertise and have some stranger coming into your home.' She tried to put a positive slant on things. She couldn't believe that Bryan had left Debbie with a big mortgage to manage on her own, even if he had signed the house over to her. Right now that meant zero.

'I guess he didn't love me enough to be with me in the hard times.' Debbie's bottom lip wobbled.

'It happens, love. Look at me and Barry – but we ended up friends in spite of everything.' Connie's heart went out to her daughter. 'And you know I'll help you in any way I can.'

'I know that, Mum. I'll have to tell Dad too. I missed a call from him the other day. At least Melissa's getting treatment. And with all that's going on, I forgot to tell you that I met Aimee in the hospital and she apologized to me. Actually, I felt very sorry for her, she's in bits over Melissa.' Debbie forked up some of her eggs and ate them, much to Connie's satisfaction. Her daughter needed to look after herself right now, and good, wholesome, nutritious food would keep her body going at least.

'That's so good to hear, Debbie. In tough times, it really *is* family that pull you through. I'm glad that both sides of the family are talking, it makes life so much easier and Melissa will benefit hugely. Well done, pet. But like you say, Aimee is having a very hard time. I couldn't hold the past against her and I'm glad you couldn't either. It's best this way.'

'Wait until she hears about Bryan. Oh Mum, it's going to be *mortifying* telling everyone.' Debbie buried her head in her hands.

'Aimee's not the tough cookie she used to be, she might be more understanding than you think, and you don't have to tell people that your marriage is over, you can always say that Bryan's got a job opportunity in Australia and he's sussing it out with a view to you both going. That will give you a bit of space,' Connie suggested.

'Oh! That's a good idea.' Debbie brightened. 'I'll tell Karen and Jenna, of course. I can't wait to see Jenna, it seems like she's been gone ages. That's something to look forward to. Mum, look what Judith Baxter gave me at the party. I was gobsmacked. She gave me one for Melissa as well – aren't they lovely?' Debbie reached into her bag and took out the little glass angel worry stone.

'Aahhh, it's gorgeous. A patient of mine held one in her hand when she was dying. It gave her great comfort. That was kind of your boss. She seems to have calmed down a bit since her accident, I never hear you giving out about her as much now,' Connie observed.

'She really has changed. She's quite nice when you get to know her a bit better. She actually told me to take a sickie on Monday and Tuesday when I told her about Bryan. Can you believe it? I was making mistakes in my calculations and she called me in and I thought I was for it, but she was very understanding.'

'Well, take the two days off. Come over to me if you want to. Stay tonight too, if you like. Be kind to yourself, Debbie. This is a very tough time for you.' Connie leaned across the table and squeezed her hand.

'Thanks, Mum,' she said gratefully, 'but Carina and I are going to start packing her stuff in cardboard boxes later on, and we're doing a declutter first, so that will keep my mind occupied, I can tell you.' She gave a wry smile. 'And I might paint her bedroom. I like painting, it's very therapeutic.'

'I was like that when your dad went,' Connie reminisced. 'Couldn't stop. In fact, I painted the whole house from top to bottom.'

'I'll never forget that.' Debbie made a face. 'Do you not remember, I stepped backwards into the paint tray and ruined my shoes?'

'Oh yeah.' Connie laughed. 'I'd forgotten that.'

'Well, I've never forgotten it, so I'll be very careful where I step. One trauma is enough to be going on with,' Debbie joked as Connie cut into the steaming apple tart and gave her a very generous slice topped with double cream.

*

'He left her with the mortgage to pay and signed the house over to her, and *skedaddled*?' Barry couldn't believe his ears.

'Yep, he headed for Australia this morning,' Connie replied, and he could sense her anger down the line.

'No wonder she looked stressed and under the weather when she was in with Melissa. I thought she had a bad period or something. I didn't like to ask her what was wrong in case it was woman stuff. How long has this been going on?' he said despondently.

'Months, I gather. Seemingly it got worse when he was put on the three-day week.'

'I can't say I'm totally surprised. Once I heard he wanted to go to Australia I felt a bit uneasy. I know you always had your doubts about him.'

'Well, there's nothing we can do about it now. I just wanted to let you know, although she did say she was going to tell you herself,' Connie said.

'OK, Connie, I appreciate the call. Talk soon,' Barry replied, and hung up. For the first time in a long while he wasn't anxious to get into conversation with his ex-wife. He was too consumed with guilt. Although she'd said absolutely nothing, it was like the elephant in the room between himself and Connie. Bryan had left Debbie in the lurch just as he had left Connie. His poor daughter had been abandoned twice in her life, by the two men she'd loved the most, and even after all these years and their very welcome rapprochement Barry felt as guilty as hell knowing that Debbie was going through a terrible ordeal for the second time in her life and there was nothing he could do about it.

At least her mother knew, Debbie thought with relief as she sat on the swaying northbound train. Connie had been so kind and concerned and, in fairness, she hadn't been too critical of Bryan, or not to Debbie's face. But then again, her mother had been through the tribulation of abandonment and a marriage break-up herself. Although Debbie had told Connie most of the saga, she had kept the details of finding the second credit card to herself. That was too shaming. She'd let Bryan get away with so much because she was afraid he would leave her; she'd never, ever, accept bad behaviour from a man again, Debbie vowed as the train slowed into Sandymount and she stood up to get off. She *would* keep her home, and she would make a good life for herself, and if she ever got involved with a man again it would be on equal terms. Bryan Kinsella had taught her a very valuable life lesson. Relationships were about receiving as well as giving. The next time, she would not do all the giving. The next time, her expectations would be far higher, and that could only be a good thing.

Still, it was very strange going home knowing that Bryan was thousands of miles away starting on a new life without her. Did he miss her at all? she wondered, walking out of the station. Or did he feel free of her? Free and unencumbered, like a drowning man suddenly surfacing to sunlight and air. Had she been as much of a millstone around his neck as their mortgage?

Stop it! Don't think like that! Don't be a victim as well as a doormat, for God's sake! Debbie silently chastised herself, walking up the garden path to what was now her home rather than theirs.

'Hi, hon, I have the kettle on. We'll have a quick cuppa before we go to mine,' Carina shouted out from the kitchen when Debbie opened her front door. 'Come on in until I tell you all the news, scandal and gossip,' her friend invited, smirking, when Debbie walked into the kitchen. 'Eilish got plastered last night and started dancing on the table, and eventually had to be poured into a taxi after puking in the fern urn, and Ritchie got off with Una Flannery—'

'She's *married*!' Debbie exclaimed, taking off her coat and producing half her mother's tart in a Tupperware container from her tote bag.

'I know, but they were snogging the face off each other behind the curtains.' Carina poured out two mugs of tea for them. 'And wait until I tell you about Magdalena and Johnny—'

'OMG! Magdalena and *Johnny*, are you serious?' Debbie was agog. Living with Carina was going to be fun. She'd never be bored, that was for sure, and at least she wouldn't be coming home to an empty house, Debbie comforted herself as she cut the tart into pieces, knowing how lucky she was to have such a great friend to help her through her trials and tribulations.

'I'll have the raw scallops with ginger jelly and dill sour cream, and the Wagyu beef, please.' Bryan placed his order with the attentive waiter.

'Certainly, sir,' the waiter said politely, gliding away as another waiter placed a basket of rolls on the table. 'The apricot and squid ink are very popular,' he said helpfully, and Bryan's mouth watered at the gastronomic treat that was in store.

He gazed around at the spectacular view that greeted him. He was sitting at a window table in Le 188°, the stunning rooftop restaurant of the five-star Harbour Grand Hotel where he was staying. Surrounded by floor-to-ceiling windows on three sides, the restaurant and lounge offered a 188-degree view across the magnificent panorama of Victoria Harbour. Far beneath him he could see several enormous luxury cruise liners as big as Croke Park tied up at their berths, and a plethora of Chinese junks plying their trade in the busy waterway. It was all so exotic, so exciting, so different, he thought as he gazed around the busy, plush restaurant, which was humming with the sound of con-versation and laughter and the clink of cutlery on china. He could have gone to a two- or three-star hotel and saved money but, hell, it was his first time in Hong Kong and he wanted to enjoy the experience. He'd had enough of scrimping and saving to do him a lifetime. This was the life he was born to, Bryan felt, as another diligent waiter handed him the wine list.

He felt a sudden ache of loneliness and wished that Debbie was here to share it all. They could have ordered champagne as they always used to with their first meal whenever they travelled abroad. How she would have enjoyed walking into the breathtaking lobby. It had the most enormous chandeliers he had ever seen. The bedroom, with its king-sized double bed, had a huge painting of a Chinese junk as a focal point. The good-sized room, decorated in soothing pastels of cream and beige with touches of blue to give a splash of colour, looked out on to the eastern side of the harbour from its own floor-to-ceiling windows. The vista was unbelievable. By far the best he'd ever had from a hotel window.

The Harbour Grand was an ideal location to explore the city from, only metres from the shopping areas and underground MTR. That was one of the reasons he'd chosen it, apart from the views. He and Debbie could have had the most wonderful stopover and made exquisite love in that big comfortable bed if she hadn't been such a stick-in-the-mud.

He tried to put her out of his head when the food arrived. If she had been with him it would have been the most perfect meal he had ever eaten. The food was utterly different from anything he'd ever tasted before. The scallops were superb with their flavour-enhancing accompaniments. The Wagyu beef had a grilled, crusty outer layer which complemented the raw and tender texture inside – it was exactly the way he liked his meat cooked. The mango sorbet he ended the meal with was frozen in a spherical shell and had whipped cream, tonka beans and biscotti inside it. Debbie would have adored it. She had such a sweet tooth, he thought fondly. This could have been the most magnificent evening of their marriage, and instead he was experiencing this amazing city alone, and feeling surprisingly lonely. He'd looked forward so much to this escape, planned it meticulously for weeks, and yet, now that he was well on his journey, it all felt rather hollow. Bryan gazed out at the remarkable vista in front of him: the skyscrapers piercing the sky; Victoria Peak on one side and the Tsim Sha Tsui shoreline on the other. The barges, junks, tugs and container ships were on the go constantly, sailing up and down. There was so much to see, so much to look at in this ever-moving tapestry. Bryan saw a Star ferry on its way to Kowloon and decided he would take one of their famous harbour cruises. He had obtained another credit card with no problem, once Debbie's dad's loan had cleared the debt on their other ones. He intended treating himself while he was in Hong Kong, he mused, sipping a brandy and wondering was his wife as lonely as he was as he watched the world go by.

Drew hadn't phoned, emailed or texted her. Marianna would have frowned if the Botox had allowed it. What was going on with her ex-husband? It showed almost midnight on her digital alarm clock, which meant it was 5 a.m. at home. She had waited all day for the explosive phone call, or even a furious email or sharply worded text, and nothing, nada, zilch.

What did it mean? Was he going to cancel his trip with this Connie woman to spend time with his daughters or not? She felt an edge of panic. Drew had dated women in the past, the girls had told her about one or two of them, but somehow this was different. This was serious. If he went away with this woman and chose her over his family Marianna had definitely lost any power she'd ever had over him for good. Both she and Drew knew this wasn't about the girls alone, this was a test of how far she could manipulate him with emotional blackmail. He'd succumbed when her father had died and she'd known he still found it hard to refuse her pleas for help when the chips were down. But to go away when their daughters were home from America, that was a biggie. That would be a defining moment in what was left of their relationship.

When he had told her he was going away for the New Year with Connie, Marianna had felt a rush of irrational jealousy. How could he abandon her when she was still grieving her father? This first Christmas was going to be so devastating; surely, he who had lost his own parents would understand that. Had he no feelings for her at all? she'd wondered bleakly. That was when she'd come up with the plan to bring the girls over for four days, her treat. Well, rather, Edward's, if she wanted to nit-pick. Drew might abandon her but, she'd figured, he'd never abandon the girls. Now she was not so sure. Maybe her plan wasn't going to work. If Drew went away with this new woman of his, Marianna knew that she had lost him for good. The final tie would be cut and she would never be able to emotionally blackmail her ex-husband again. He would be utterly and completely lost to her, and all her fanciful notions of getting back together would be confirmed as a pipe dream. It had never had a chance of working out, if she was truly honest with herself.

For the first time ever, Drew had not played the game. He had not responded as she'd expected. Now he was the one pulling the strings and she didn't like it one little bit.

CHAPTER THIRTY-EIGHT

'And then,' said Juliet, to her two favourite luncheon guests, 'I asked Ken did he want to put up the big Christmas tree in his sitting room, and he said he'd like that, so he got it in from the garage where we keep all the decorations and we started to decorate it together, and we finished off the bottle of wine and . . . um . . . had a brandy, and we were a bit tipsy, and he really loosened up and one thing led to another . . .' Juliet looked a little abashed. 'Ken and I . . . um . . . resumed conjugal relations.'

'You Jezebel!' laughed Karen.

'Ah that's great, Juliet,' Connie exclaimed, ever the romantic.

'It was very nice, granted, but now it doesn't mean things are back to normal, or anything like it,' Juliet declared feistily. 'I'm keeping my bedroom and he can have his. This is my haven, and he can woo me, and we can have dinner dates, but I'm not going back to the way things were. I've told Ken that and he's getting his head around it, as they say. But at least we're not at logger-heads any more.'

'That's great news, Juliet,' Karen said warmly.

'Long may it last. It's all working out quite well, really, isn't it? Perhaps it's a blessing in disguise that you weren't able to buy the apartment in Blackrock,' Connie remarked, taking a sip of coffee and biting into one of Juliet's delectable mince pies. She and Karen were thoroughly enjoying their unexpected lunch at

Juliet's. She'd phoned them wondering if they were free; she had, she'd teased, 'a bit of news' for them.

'Any excuse for a girls' lunch,' Connie agreed, a sentiment enthusiastically approved by her sister-in-law. Karen was on her Christmas leave and was more or less a free agent, and Connie had been on the early shift and had changed out of her uniform in Mrs Mansfield's and come straight from work.

Juliet had put up the Christmas decorations in her new sitting room with her usual elegant style. A perfectly shaped four-foot-high real tree sent out the most enticing scent of pine. She had dressed it with red bows and red and silver baubles and tiny white fairy lights. Vases of red-berried holly and red and white carnations sat on her coffee and side tables, and a cluster of red, green and white candles flickered cheerily atop her coffee table. The stove was ablaze with flaming logs and the whole room was cosy and Christmassy. It was raining outside, great deluges spilling down, keeping the skies grey and leaden, and making the room seem even more inviting.

'Guess what Marianna did?' Connie grimaced.

'What?' echoed her friends, knowing it was something untoward.

Connie divulged the other woman's latest stunt.

'What a bitch,' declared Karen, disgusted.

'That's low. Are you going to go away or will you stay?' Juliet poured more coffee for them.

'I offered to cancel, but Drew was insistent that we go, but I know he'll be torn. To be honest, I'm going to be a bit torn myself with Debbie being on her own—'

'She won't be on her own, she can come to us,' Karen insisted. 'You go on that holiday, madam. The apartment is all ready and waiting for you.'

'You'd think when they get older that you won't have to worry about your children, but it never ends, does it?' Juliet ruminated. 'And then the grandchildren come and you worry about them. When I saw the state of Melissa I couldn't believe it.

But at least she's gaining weight—' Her mobile rang and she excused herself to answer it.

'Call in of course, Aimee. I'd love to see her. Connie and Karen and I have just had lunch ... oh right, right, I'll say nothing,' they heard Juliet say. 'See you shortly.'

'Speak of the devil, that was Aimee. Melissa's on day release for a few hours and they were going to call in for half an hour or so. Do you mind, girls?' Juliet asked. 'They're in the Blackrock shopping centre doing some Christmas shopping.'

'Not at all, I'd love to see Melissa,' Connie exclaimed. 'I was going to visit her this week anyway.'

'Me too,' said Karen. 'I did try, but aunts weren't allowed at the time, just Barry and Aimee.'

'The only thing is, Aimee said not to offer her anything to eat, because she's on an eating plan and she gets stressed if she feels she has to eat outside it. It's a big worry for her, seemingly.' Juliet frowned.

'Why don't we clear away the dishes? We're finished anyway,' Connie suggested diplomatically and Juliet shot her a grateful look.

'Good idea.' She stood up and began to stack the plates while Karen and Connie removed the condiments and table mats. Twenty minutes later, Juliet heard Aimee's key in the front door and stood up and hurried out to the hall. 'Hi, Gran,' they heard Melissa say happily, and moments later she followed her grandmother into the room and flung herself into her aunt and Connie's warm embrace.

'Gran, your room is like sooooo cool,' she squealed after the hugs of welcome were over. 'It's so totally different. You should do house makeovers. Does Granddad like it?' She bubbled, delighted to be out of hospital.

'He does.' Juliet hugged her tightly again.

'I love the Christmas decorations,' Aimee approved. 'Very simple and effective.'

'Me and Mom are going to decorate when we go home. I'm

allowed out until seven,' Melissa said giddily, going over to smell the Christmas tree. 'I love real trees; ours is artificial.' She wrinkled her nose. She looked pale and fragile, but there was a sparkle in her eyes and her face had lost the gaunt, hollow look.

'Will you be able to reach the tree, Aimee?' Connie smiled. 'You're all bump now.'

'I know,' groaned the other woman. 'I seem to have ballooned all of a sudden.'

'She's ginormous,' giggled Melissa, rubbing her mother's bulging tummy. 'We're Little and Large,' she joked, and Aimee made a face at her.

'Poor darling,' said Juliet compassionately. 'I always hated the last month. I hated not being able to see my feet and waddling around like a penguin.'

'Me too,' Karen agreed. 'For God's sake, Aimee, rest as much as you can now. Let Barry do Christmas while you put your feet up,' she advised her sister-in-law.

'Don't worry, I will. It's a busy time at work now though, unfortunately. We have two weddings and three big events between Christmas Day and New Year. Thank God I've an experienced team,' Aimee said wearily. She looked exhausted, Connie thought sympathetically, not envying the other woman the sleepless nights that were most certainly coming her way.

'The good thing about being in the business is that I can order in the food all prepared and ready to go and frozen meals that we only have to defrost and heat up. I won't be entertaining this year.'

'You're dead right,' Karen responded. 'Thank God Jenna's going to be home. She's always a great help in the kitchen.'

'Will Debbie go to you?' Juliet asked Connie.

'Yes, I'll do lunch for Drew and myself and herself. She's going to stay with me Christmas Eve and Christmas night.'

'And what about Bryan?' Melissa looked perplexed.

Juliet looked startled and glanced over at Connie.

'Bryan's gone to Australia to see about getting work – you know he was on a three-day week,' Connie said smoothly.

'Poor Debbie, she must be so lonely,' Melissa said innocently. 'But she won't be going to Australia too, will she?' she exclaimed in sudden horror.

'No, no. Not for the moment, anyway.'

'You and she must come and see us during the holidays, Connie. I didn't mean family when I said I wasn't entertaining,' Aimee interjected amiably. '*Family* are always welcome.' She put extra emphasis on 'family'.

'Thanks, Aimee,' Connie said warmly, truly glad that all the hostilities were finally behind them. 'Will you be out of hospital for Christmas, pet?' she asked Melissa, who had come and tucked herself in beside her on the sofa.

'I really hope so, that's why I'm getting out today, it's sort of a practice run,' she explained. 'If I am, do you think I might be able to visit Miss Hope and Frisky? Drew sent me a get-well card with a horse on the front and some photos of Frisky and Venus.'

'Did he? That was kind, and of course you must come for a visit if you're up to it.' Connie felt a little glow when she heard of her beloved's thoughtfulness. Drew's heart was in the right place for sure. Marianna was a fool to have ever let him go, she thought, still furious with the other woman for causing him such trouble.

'Oh I will, but I might not eat anything, if you don't mind. I have to stick to my eating plan,' Melissa said a touch anxiously.

'That's no problem at all, darling, don't even give it a thought,' Connie said reassuringly.

'Speaking of plans, we should make a move if we're going to do the decorating and wrap the Christmas presents we bought today and get our tea,' Aimee said, hauling herself up off the sofa. She gave a little gasp and went pale. 'Ooohhh!' she groaned softly.

'Are you OK?' Connie frowned. Aimee was rather flushed-looking all of a sudden.

'Just got a crampy pain. I just need to go to the loo,' she murmured. 'Won't be a minute.'

'Why don't I come to Dun Laoghaire with you to give Melissa a hand decorating?' Juliet suggested. 'You wouldn't mind, girls, would you?' She turned to Connie and Karen.

'Not at all. I need to go home and give my house a good clean,' Karen exclaimed.

'Me too.' Connie stood up. 'And I should bake a few mince pies.'

'Great, Mum. Get your coat, won't be a minute,' Aimee said and gasped as another cramp caught her by surprise. She hurried down the hall to the downstairs loo.

'I wonder did she eat something that upset her stomach?' Juliet fretted.

'I'll just check on her,' Connie said calmly, and made her way down the hall. 'Aimee, are you OK in there?' she called.

'Oh Jesus no, Connie, I think my waters just broke,' Aimee exclaimed in panic, and gave another louder groan as Connie knocked and opened the door.

'Indeed they have, Aimee,' she said steadily, surveying the puddle on the floor and the white-faced woman in front of her, almost doubled up. 'Let's get you to the hospital.'

'I don't think we've time. I think the baby's coming,' Aimee panted again as another spasm hit, panic written all over her face.

'Let's get you lying down and have a look,' Connie instructed, trying not to let her anxiety show. It was a few years since she'd last worked in a maternity hospital. 'Karen,' she called her sister-in-law, who came sprinting down the hall.

'Aimee thinks the baby's coming. I want to have a look to see if we've time to get to the—'

'Aaaagggggg!' uttered Aimee, and this time it was almost a yell.

'There isn't even a minute between the contractions. Let's get her upstairs.'

Juliet and Melissa rushed out to the hall. 'Mom,' screamed Melissa. 'Are you OK? I'm scared.'

'Don't be one bit scared, Melissa,' Connie said authoritatively. 'The baby might be coming and, if it does, there's nothing to worry about, I've delivered dozens of babies, it's a cinch. I'm just going to have a look at your mom upstairs. OK?'

'OK,' Melissa whimpered, holding Juliet's hand tightly.

'Go into my . . . your old room, Aimee,' Juliet said, white as snow.

'OK,' she muttered, leaning heavily on Connie's shoulder as they made it slowly up the stairs.

'A few towels and a basin of hot water just in case,' Connie threw over her shoulder as Aimee once more groaned in excruciating pain. 'And ring an ambulance.'

'You put on the kettle, Melissa, and I'll get towels from the hot press.' Juliet bit back her panic. Upstairs, Connie and Karen helped ease Aimee on to the bed. Connie began to remove the younger woman's sodden tights and underwear.

'I'm so sorry about this. I'm mortified,' Aimee whispered, sweat pouring down her flushed face.

'Don't be ridiculous, Aimee, I'm a nurse,' Connie said briskly. 'I'm just going to give my hands a quick wash in the en suite.' She put the drenched clothes in the small bin and gave her hands a thorough wash. A minute later she pushed Aimee's maternity dress up around her waist. 'Pretend your legs are in the stirrups until I have a look. Karen, hold her hand and get her to do her breathing exercises.' Connie bent her head to examine her new patient.

'Aimee, you're dead right,' she said a moment later. 'This baby's coming fast, it's crowning. Stop pushing. Don't push again until I tell you. Pant. Keep panting, good girl,' she soothed as Aimee went purple in the face trying to suppress the urge to push.

'Oh God!' exclaimed Juliet, entering the room with an armful of towels as Aimee gave a strangled yell.

'Juliet, did you ring the ambulance? There's no need to panic at all, the baba's coming. You keep Melissa calm, just bring me some hot water in a basin and a plastic bag,' she said urgently.

'*Connieee!*' yelled Aimee, eyes bulging. Karen looked as though she might faint in terror. 'Oh Connie, I'm afraid. Something's going to be wrong with the baby and it will be all my fault. I didn't want it, and now look what's happening. It will be all my fault if it dies. God is punishing me.' Aimee burst into hysterical tears.

'Stop that right now, Aimee. There's nothing to be afraid of. You're doing fine. The baby's going to be fine. Now you have to help it and me by doing what I tell you. Are you *listening*, Aimee?' Connie said sternly. 'Stop crying and wearing yourself out and push when I tell you. Karen, you keep your eyes on Aimee and take deep breaths too.' She placed Juliet's soft towels underneath Aimee as she spoke. 'Breathe, now push, whoooo, whooo, whooo,' she instructed. 'Breathe and push.' She repeated the mantra.

'I can't,' whimpered Aimee, snot and tears streaming down her face, her hair tumbling out of its chignon.

'You can.' Karen recovered her wits and grasped her sister-in-law's hand. 'Push, Aimee, *push*. I can see the head's out. Come on, you're nearly there.'

'Oh Jesus, Jesus, Jesus!' moaned Aimee, in agony.

'Come on, Aimee, the shoulders are almost out. One last push,' Connie urged, utterly relieved that there was no cord around the baby's neck and its colour was good.

'Come on, come on, *push!*' extolled Karen, wiping Aimee's face with a damp cloth. 'It's nearly over.'

Aimee took a deep breath and pushed with all her might and the baby slid into Connie's waiting hands. She made sure the airways were clear and breathed a sigh of relief as the baby gave a wail.

'It's a little girl, Aimee. It's a little girl and she's fine.' Connie beamed, wiping the tiny newborn infant tenderly before wrapping her in a soft towel and placing her on Aimee's tummy.

'I won't cut the cord until the ambulance people take over. I just need to preserve the afterbirth for the hospital – can you give another little push?' she encouraged gently as Aimee raised her head and looked at her new daughter before bursting into fresh tears.

The sound of an ambulance siren rent the air. 'Perfect timing,' Connie said, placing the towel containing the afterbirth into the plastic bag Juliet had procured for her. 'I'm just going to wash my hands and I'll be back in a sec.' When she came back, she made Aimee presentable before the ambulance personnel arrived. 'You did fantastic, Aimee. Well done, and congratulations,' she said proudly, as Karen sniffled beside her.

'Thanks so much, Connie, Karen . . .' Aimee choked up as she stroked her baby's cheek, unable to take her eyes off her.

'Don't cry, pet, it was an honour. She's a gorgeous little thing. Look at the head of hair on her.' Connie smiled down at her, feeling immense relief that it had all gone well and there were no complications. 'Let's get Melissa and your mum in to have a look before you're whisked off in the ambulance.'

Melissa was crying out on the landing as Juliet opened the front door to the ambulance crew. 'Darling, don't cry, you have a new baby sister. Come in and say hello to her.' Connie put her arms around the weeping teenager.

'Is Mom OK?'

'Your mom's fine, honestly. Wait until you see the baby, she has a mop of black hair,' Connie said comfortingly, leading her into the room.

'Oh Mom.' Melissa burst into fresh tears as she hurried over to the bed.

Aimee reached out a hand and took hers. 'I'm OK, sweetheart, everything's OK. Look at your baby sister.'

'Ooohhh, Mom, she's tiny,' Melissa squealed. 'And her face is all pink and scrunched up. Oh! My! *God!* Mom, she *smiled* at me. She opened her eyes and smiled at me. Do you think she recognized my voice?' Melissa was enchanted.

'I bet she did,' Aimee said, as two ambulance men came into the room carrying a stretcher, followed by Juliet.

'You're too late, lads,' laughed Karen, a tad hysterically. The colour had come back into her cheeks.

'A little premmie, a month early. It's a girl. I haven't cut the cord and I have the afterbirth for you. I'm a nurse,' Connie explained.

'Excellent,' said the paramedic. 'And how's Mother?' he asked kindly, looking down at Aimee as he prepared to take her blood pressure.

'Glad it's over, but I'm a bit worried about the baby, she's four weeks early.'

'We'll have you in hospital in a jiffy. You'll be having your tea and toast before you know it and Missy here will be snug and asleep in her incubator. Let's get you on to the stretcher.'

'You'd better ring Barry. He'll have to bring Melissa back,' Aimee said in a panic. 'And tell him to bring in some night-clothes and stuff.'

'Aimee, Karen and I can bring Melissa back, Barry can go straight to you, and we can pack for you. We know what you need, we've been there. You won't mind coming with us, Melissa, sure you won't?' Connie looked at her.

'No, you just get the baby to the hospital, Mom,' Melissa said anxiously.

'May I go with my daughter in the ambulance?' Juliet asked.

'Yes, of course,' the ambulance man said helpfully. 'What's your name, love?' he asked Aimee.

'Aimee,' she said tiredly, cuddling her new daughter.

'Let's get you sorted. If you ladies would leave – apart from yourself,' he said to Connie, 'we'll get you fixed up and off we go.'

Ten minutes later, the ambulance drove out of sight and Melissa clung to Connie in tears.

'Will everything be all right? Will the baby be OK? She's so small.'

'I've seen much smaller than her. She looks at least four pounds to me. I've seen two-pound babies. She'll be fine. Come on, pet, do you want to go home to your place?'

'Yeah, Sarah said she'd come over. I can't wait to see her.' Melissa swallowed. 'I just need to go to the loo.'

'We all need a good strong cup of tea,' Karen grinned. 'I felt a bit iffy for a minute or two.'

'You looked a bit iffy,' Connie remarked. 'A bit green around the gills. The last thing I needed was you going off in a faint. That baby came quickly. Aimee was lucky to have such a short labour, even if it was intense. Just let me run up and gather those towels and stick them into the washing machine. You mop up the floor in the downstairs loo and we'll head off.'

'Well, that was quite an afternoon,' Karen murmured, keeping an ear out for Melissa. 'How lucky was Aimee to have her labour over in twenty minutes? Typical.'

'Ah, she's not as bad as she used to be,' Connie chided. 'She's having a rough enough time.'

'Well, she won't be able to look down her snooty nose at the two of us any more . . . we've seen her bush!' Karen sniffed.

'Stop, Karen,' giggled Connie. 'Don't be such a cow.'

'Well, she is lucky. Not a grey hair in sight down there, and she doesn't have the friggin' menopause. I swear to God, global warming has nothing on me. I can't see beyond my nose, I can't hear, I can't remember my own name, my nerves are shot every time I drive on the M50 and Juliet's in better nick than I am and boasting about having sex,' Karen grumbled as they went to do their respective chores.

'I'd better ring Barry,' Connie said, as they were about to leave the house.

'Can I tell him?' Melissa appealed.

'You sure can, love. Tell my dear brother he's now the proud poppa of three lovely girls,' Karen said cheerily, closing the door behind them as Melissa dialled her father's number.

CHAPTER THIRTY-NINE

FYI: That little runt Farrell is home. Was spotted skulking around the Merrion Centre. Thought you might like to know the little fucker is still alive. Not for long if I see him! Happy holidays! Al.

Barry shook his head as he read his friend's email. Al was still livid at losing 500,000 big ones thanks to Jeremy Farrell's hot tip. He was going to have a serious go at the 'financial guru', as he sneeringly called him, if and when he ever bumped into him. At this stage of the game, thought Barry, it wouldn't make any difference, apart from giving Al the satisfaction of venting his feelings. The money was long gone and there was no chance of any of the investors getting their cash back. His friend was as well off howling at the moon. Barry wasn't going to waste his time on the little snake; he had far more pressing things to worry about.

His mobile rang and he saw Melissa's name come up. She and Aimee were shopping and the plan was that he would leave the office when they were finishing up so he could get home and spend the rest of the afternoon with her before taking her back to the hospital. They must be heading home now, he reasoned, pressing the green button. 'Hi, Muffin, have you spent all your money?' he teased. 'How are you feeling?'

'Dad, Dad, Mom's had the baby. It's a girl. She had it in Gran's, they've just gone to hospital in an ambulance.'

427

Melissa was talking so fast he could hardly make out the words.

'Whoa! She's had the baby?' he repeated, stunned.

'Yeah, Dad, a baby girl. It all happened really fast, Connie was brill, she just took charge.'

'Connie!'

'And Karen was there too. Dad, she's tiny, and you should see her hair. You have to go to the hospital *immediately*! Connie and Karen are going to bring me back to the unit.'

'Is your mother all right?' Barry felt a flash of apprehension. She wasn't due for another month at least.

'Yeah, do you want to speak to Connie?'

'Thanks.' He gave up a silent prayer that his ex-wife was there with Melissa.

'Everything's fine, Barry.' He heard her reassuring voice down the line. 'Aimee went into labour in Juliet's, and Karen and I delivered the baby. As far as I could tell, she's OK and Aimee's grand too. They've taken them to Holles Street. It all went very smoothly, if rather quickly. Congratulations, Barry. You got an early Christmas present.'

'Well done, big brother,' Karen chipped in in the background.

'But . . . but . . . what . . .'

'Barry, just get yourself to the hospital and don't worry about anything else. We have everything under control,' Connie ordered. 'And don't buy flowers – they're not allowed in most maternity hospitals, as far as I know.'

'Right . . . right. I'm off.' He hung up and grabbed his jacket and car keys. 'Aimee's had the baby. Have to go. Won't be back today,' he told his startled PA, racing through the office, desperate to see his wife and child. He had wanted badly to be at the birth, to support Aimee as much as he could and to hold their newborn baby as soon as it was born. He'd worried all along that the vibes of Aimee's unhappiness and antipathy about being pregnant would be absorbed by their baby and he'd wanted so much to make sure that it felt loved and cherished from the moment it was born.

Who would have thought, he mused, reversing the car out of his parking space at speed, that Connie, of all people, would be at the birth of his third child? What a strange, strange irony.

It seemed to take an age to get to the maternity hospital, and he had to circle around Merrion Square twice before he got parking. He was panting as he stood at reception in the Front Hall enquiring about Aimee's whereabouts. 'Baby Adams has been admitted to the NICU and your wife is in the Merrion Wing. Mr Adams, we have a strict visiting policy—'

'I'll get all the info when I'm leaving, I need to see my wife, she was brought in by ambulance,' Barry said urgently, and headed for the lift. The lift was full so he climbed the old, creaking stairs, pausing to let pregnant women come past him on the way down, thanking God privately that he was a man and would never have to endure the indignities, traumas and pain that women had to.

Aimee was lying in bed in a hospital gown with her eyes closed when he slipped between the curtains of her cubicle. She heard him and opened her eyes and stretched out her hand to take his. 'So much for trying to be in control all the time.' She gave a weak grin. 'Madam was coming, come hell or high water. Thank God I wasn't in the office.'

'I heard you did great – are you OK?' Barry leaned down and kissed her tenderly.

'Well, apart from feeling as if I've been run over by a steamroller.'

'And the baby?' he asked anxiously, pulling up a chair to sit beside her.

'She's fine. She's in the NICU. She'll have to stay there for a few days until she gains a little more weight, but she's doing well,' Aimee assured him. 'They have to do the heel test and all the other ones they do but they're not concerned about her. Oh, Barry, I'm so, so glad it's a little girl. Melissa's *thrilled*. You should have seen her face when she saw her. This will give her something to get better for.' Tears slid down her cheeks. 'Sorry,' she murmured. 'It's my hormones, they're all over the place.'

'Of course they are. God, I don't know how you did it, Aimee. I would have been petrified if I was there.' Barry gripped her hand tightly.

'I was a bit, and then Connie got stern when I threw a wobbly. She was absolutely brilliant, Barry – you're dead right, she is a saint,' Aimee declared. 'I was absolutely mortified, but she wasn't having any of it. She was really, really kind and so . . . so *confident*. I thought poor Karen was going to faint, but Connie wouldn't let her and then she was great when the baby was coming out. I was so lucky to have them. Imagine if I'd been having a meeting with a client or Roger! It doesn't bear thinking about.'

'Well, it's all over now, relax and take it easy—'

'And you're having the snip. I am never *ever* going through anything like that again,' Aimee decreed emphatically.

'Fair enough,' Barry agreed. 'I owe you that much.'

'You do,' she said. 'But, in fairness, you were right about one thing. It's wonderful that Melissa has another sister. Do you think that the hospital would give her a bit of leeway so she could come in for a few minutes before she goes back tonight so we could make a bit of a fuss of her? I don't want her thinking that we've dropped her like a hot potato just because the baby's here.'

'Good thinking, Aimee, I'll get on to them about it. We still have a couple of hours. We'll have to be vigilant that she doesn't feel left out or sidelined in any way.' Barry took out his phone. 'I'll just send her a quick text to say you and the baby are fine.'

'Would you like to come and see the baby? Let's ask if we can go and visit her. I'd love to see her again,' Aimee said. 'She *is* gorgeous.'

'Just like her mother.' Barry smiled, his heart lifting at her words.

All his fears that Aimee would reject their child began to recede and, for the first time since he had found out that she was pregnant, he finally allowed himself to feel all the joy he'd been suppressing at the prospect of being a new father all over again.

'Wow, I'd have been scared out of my wits. How cool was that?' Sarah said, sitting at the kitchen counter in the penthouse sipping a cappuccino with Melissa. 'And did you see it coming out?' she asked, making a face.

'Oh . . . no . . . I could just hear Mom, like, groaning really loudly and Connie and Karen telling her to push. I didn't get to see the baby until it was all over. Oh Sarah, she's, like, totally awesome. Wait until you see her. I'm so excited. I can't wait to get home. The baby won't be allowed home for another few weeks. I'm going to try really hard to get out of hospital,' she vowed.

'Is it awful?' her friend asked sympathetically.

'Sometimes. But they're very kind to me. Swear to God you won't say this to anyone . . .' Melissa gazed earnestly at her best friend.

'Swear on my life, pinkie promise.' Sarah hooked her little finger around Melissa's.

'Well, I have to talk to a . . . a psychiatrist—'

'Why – are you, like, *loopers*?' Sarah looked startled.

'Don't be silly.' Melissa giggled. 'No . . . I just, like, have issues I have to address. That's what Dr Morton says.'

'Like what?' Sarah couldn't hide her curiosity.

'Well,' Melissa sighed, 'like that bitch at the wedding calling me a little fat tart – and remember I told you that horrible thing that that Thomas pig did last New Year? Remember when Mom and Dad and I went to visit on New Year's morning?'

'Oh yeah, that was, like, totally gross,' Sarah grimaced.

'Well, Dr Morton – that's the psychiatrist – said that, subconsciously, because that happened when I felt fat, I felt that it wouldn't happen if I was skinny, and that sometimes girls are afraid to grow up and they develop anorexia. That's what I've got. Anorexia. I can say it now, and that's good, because before I was in denial,' Melissa confided.

'I could have told you that and, like, saved you a whole load of hassle,' Sarah retorted with a grin, and the two of them chortled happily, delighted to be in each other's company.

'I've loads to tell you about school. Antonia Carroll had to leave and go to an ordinary school 'cos her father's gone bankrupt and can't pay the fees—'

'OMG! She was such a snob—'

'And their SUV and Merc were repossessed and their house is up for sale and . . .'

This was one of the best days of her life, Melissa thought happily as Sarah regaled her with all the goings-on she'd missed for the past few weeks. And the best thing of all, her dad had phoned to say that she could have an extension until eight thirty and he was coming home to bring her in to see her mom and the baby before he took her back to the hospital. She nibbled at her ham sandwich and was so interested in what Sarah was telling her she even forgot she was eating.

'Thanks a million, Connie, I . . . *we* all owe you big-time.' Barry hugged his ex-wife tightly and was warmly hugged in return.

'Don't give it a thought, I'm just so glad Aimee and the baby are well,' Connie said good-naturedly. 'Melissa and I have a case packed for her, and the baby. Aimee had clothes bought already; she was very organized.'

'That's Aimee – but not even Aimee could dictate to our new arrival. She's a real little sprite, isn't she?' Barry couldn't hide his pride.

'She is. She's a dote,' Connie agreed.

'And how's our other dote doing? Any word from that fella?' Barry scowled.

'I'm just going to have a bite of supper with her now before I go home. He sent a couple of texts, from what I can gather. He seemed to be having a ball in Hong Kong, and why wouldn't he?' Connie said tartly. 'Her boss told her she could take today and tomorrow off, which was kind. I was trying to persuade her to come and stay with me for the week, but she said no. You know Debbie: she can be stubborn.'

'I know,' he said dryly. 'Give her my love and get her to ring me. Perhaps she might come and have dinner or lunch with me and Melissa if she's given another day release.'

'I'll say it to her. Give Aimee my best. I won't come in and visit, tell her, I know how strict they are about visitors, but I'll see her over the Christmas.'

'You take care, Connie, you're the best in the world.' Barry leaned over and kissed her cheek.

'It took you a long time to realize it,' she said drolly, and sashayed into the kitchen to say goodbye to Melissa.

Aimee lay drowsing as the painkillers kicked in and the exhaustion of the last weeks took their toll. She couldn't believe that she had given birth and that she had a new baby girl on the floor above. Intense though it was, to have gone through the whole process in a matter of half an hour was hard to believe. She knew second labours often didn't take half as long as first ones – she'd been in labour with Melissa for fifteen hours – but she hadn't expected anything like this, or a premature baby. Thank God she was fine, and she'd seemed quite contented when Aimee had given her her feed. Now she had a night's sleep to look forward to, Aimee hoped. She blessed Connie's cop on. As well as all her nightclothes and toiletries, Connie had packed a large supply of STs, breast pads and a box of earplugs. It would have been wonderful to have a private room, but they were in short supply and in great demand so she hadn't a hope. The semi-private ward she was in, though bright and airy, was noisy with the to-ing and fro-ing of staff and visitors.

Melissa had told her that, if she got out of hospital on Christmas Eve, more than anything else she was looking forward to getting into her own bed, in her own room and not having to share. Aimee could empathize. The woman in the next bed was snoring loudly, and Aimee hastily inserted her earplugs and turned off her reading light.

Connie and Karen had been very good to her today, and once she'd got over her total embarrassment of having them see her lower half naked, she had felt most reassured by Connie's complete self-assurance. She was the consummate professional at her job, Aimee acknowledged, remembering, with shame, how she had looked down her nose because Connie had never done much to further her career. Connie Adams had a much more balanced life than she had, Aimee admitted. And she had friends, good friends to share her ups and downs with. Aimee had left all her friends behind in her stampede to the top of her career ladder. She had a social circle that she and Barry mixed with but no close women friends any more. Juliet, Karen and Connie had seemed so relaxed and were having such fun at lunch, she thought enviously. She should try and not see her work as the be-all and end-all of her life. She had a good, supportive husband and, now, two beautiful daughters. She would try and devote much more time to her family than she'd done before because, as had been proved to her today, yet again, family was all that really mattered when the chips were down. Aimee's eyes closed and she drifted into a restless sleep, only woken by the rattle of the breakfast trolley at an indecent hour the following morning.

CHAPTER FORTY

CHRISTMAS DAY

Melissa woke to unaccustomed darkness, not sure where she was, with no light from the corridor spilling in under her door and no red emergency light casting its eerie glow. And then she remembered, with a burst of excitement: it was Christmas morning, she was in her own bed *and* she had a new baby sister. She stretched out and luxuriated in the softness of her Egyptian cotton sheets, the comfort of all her cuddly toys around her and the silence, the absolute, glorious silence, with no hospital sounds and coughing, sneezing, snoring roommate to disturb her sleep. She turned over on her tummy and snuggled down into the warm hollow of her own bed. Her hand touched something hard and round and her fingers closed around the little angel Debbie's boss had given her. She slept with it under her pillow now and she just loved it. It was very comforting having her own personal little angel. And very helpful too. The night she had gone back to hospital after her day release, when the baby had been born, she had stood in the loo, very tempted to make herself sick. She had held the small, round angel tightly and thought of her new baby sister and getting to be at home again and, eventually, the big, scary knot in her tummy had eased and the urge to upchuck her food had diminished and she'd gone to bed quite proud of herself. Dr Morton had told her she was very pleased with her progress when she had given her permission to spend three days at home for Christmas. Instead of making herself sick two or three times a day, she had cut it down to once every other day. Soon, Melissa hoped, it would be once a week, and then never.

She'd probably have to make herself sick today, there'd be so much food and goodies to eat, so today didn't count, Melissa assured herself. No one could stick to an eating plan on Christmas Day, and both Dr Morton and Bernadette had told her there'd be setbacks, that was the way it went, and just to pick herself up and start again, but tomorrow she'd be really good, she promised herself.

Melissa lay in the dark thinking how great it was that there were no breakfast trolleys trundling noisily down the corridor and no one to sit watching her eat her meals. Best of all, she didn't have to get up early and go to consultations and classes and therapy. She could lie in as long as she liked, her mom and dad had told her, because they were lying in too and, after breakfast, when they opened their presents, they were going to visit her gran and granddad for lunch. Then they were going to Holles Street to see the new baby. She had got special permission to go and visit her. Her mom wanted to call the baby Angelina, and her dad wanted to call her Caroline, but they didn't quite suit, Melissa felt. She lay racking her brains, remembering that scrunched-up little pink face and the way she had opened her eyes wide and looked at Melissa as if to say, *Here I am, sis. You'd better get well quick.*

And she *would* get *well*, she promised herself, feeling happier than she'd been in ages. It was, thought Melissa gladly, going to be the best Christmas ever.

Debbie lay in bed in her old bedroom in Connie's staring up at the ceiling. It was still dark, although her clock told her it was gone seven forty. How she would love to stay in bed all day and pretend this day wasn't happening. She was sure, if she hadn't been here, Drew would have stayed over with her mother. She felt like a complete gooseberry and an absolute and utter failure. Her mobile phone vibrated and she picked it up off the floor. She'd put it on silent in case she got any texts from Bryan in the early hours. Sydney was eleven hours ahead of Dublin, and she knew that if her estranged husband was out partying, there was nothing to stop him from making drunken phone calls. She didn't want Connie's lie-in being ruined.

It wasn't a text, as she'd thought. It was a phone call, and she dithered, watching the light on the screen flashing her husband's name before pulling the duvet over her head and whispering, 'Hello.'

'Babes, it's me. I just wanted to wish you a Happy Christmas.' Bryan's familiar tone came over the airwaves.

Don't be ridiculous, she wanted to snap. *How can you possibly wish me a Happy Christmas when it's one of the worst Christmases of my life, definitely on a par with the first Christmas when Dad left us and went to America?* But she stayed mute, not wanting to give him the satisfaction of knowing how gutted she was, especially as he sounded laidback and happy.

'Babes, it's me, can you hear me? I'm at Pete's Christmas Day barbie on Bondi Beach, and I wish you were here with me. I miss you.' She knew he was pissed, or worse, by his tone of voice. The slight slurring of his words, the careful enunciation so that she would think he was sober. She knew her husband of old.

'I hear you,' she said in a low voice. 'I'm staying at Mum's and I don't want to wake her up.'

'Oh! Right, what time is it at home?'

'Nearly quarter to eight.'

'Sorry, did I wake you? I just want you to be here, Debs. You'd love it, babe, it's mega,' he enthused, and she could hear him take a swig of a drink. 'I'm going to another barbie tomorrow, we're having Boxing-Day lunch on the beach – why don't you book a ticket and fly over?' he said expansively. 'Have fun, live a little. Don't be such a stick-in-the-mud, babes.'

'Look, have a good Christmas, Bryan. Don't get sunburnt,' she said flatly and hung up, not knowing which was the worst, the rage and anger she felt or the sadness. A few minutes later he phoned her again, but she didn't answer. He was pissed or coked up or smoking a joint. There was no point in talking to him. He hadn't changed one bit. Things were still the same.

Well, that wasn't quite true, Debbie reflected as a pale lemon light tinted the eastern sky. *She* had changed. She wasn't putting up with his bad behaviour any more. Christmas might be miserable but at least she was solvent and had a roof over her head and a job that paid well. If that was being a stick-in-the-mud, she was happy with that, Debbie thought defiantly as the phone continued to ring. She gave it the two fingers. 'I don't jump when you tell me to any more, mate!' she muttered, proud of herself that she was ignoring his call. The old Debbie would have given in and answered it. It rang out and two minutes later started vibrating again. In the end she turned the phone off completely and threw it back on the floor. Before the sun had made its appearance over the horizon Debbie was fast asleep again, oblivious to the fact that Bryan was sprawled on the sands of Bondi Beach muttering to himself about what a selfish, mean-spirited cow he was married to as he smoked another spliff and downed yet another can of beer.

Connie lay in bed wishing she could get her hands on Bryan Kinsella. She had heard the muffled sounds of conversation and guessed that he had phoned Debbie to wish her Happy Christmas.

Not only had he ruined her daughter's life and made her miserable, he was ruining *her* Christmas and making *her* miserable!

She and Drew had planned on going to midnight Mass together before going back to his house to have mulled wine and mince pies on Christmas Eve. They had decided to sleep at his place because he had to be up early to take care of the horses. Then, after exchanging gifts and having breakfast together, she was going to go home and prepare the Christmas lunch. And then Debbie had dropped her bombshell about Bryan's departure.

There was no question that her daughter would come and spend Christmas with Connie, but it had meant a complete change of plan, especially in regards to their sleeping arrangements. It had been awkward all round. She would have felt uncomfortable sleeping with Drew knowing that Debbie was next door. It would have been just as weird for Debbie, she figured. Drew knew that and had diplomatically decided to go back home after supper. She'd nearly been in tears kissing him goodbye.

'This should have been our first Christmas together. Are you sure you won't stay?' she cajoled, bitterly disappointed, as they sat in front of the fire together. Debbie had gone to bed soon after they came home from Mass.

'The last thing she needs is to see us being so happy and lovey-dovey when she's devastated and lonely. It's a bit like rubbing salt in the wound,' Drew said gently. 'We'll have other Christmases.'

'I was so looking forward to this one.' She'd rested her head on his shoulder.

'We have New Year all to ourselves.'

'Yes, but you'll be fretting about being away from your girls.'

'It can't be helped, Connie. This is what happens when you get into second relationships and you have children, even if they are grown up, allegedly.' He traced a finger along the side of her face and bent and kissed her and she never wanted to let him go. 'I'm going to give you your present now, and I hope you like it,' he said, pulling away from her and going out to the hall where his parka was hanging.

Connie got up and rooted under the Christmas tree they had decorated together and found her gift to him, a small painting of a beautiful chestnut horse in a field, with the Wicklow hills and the Sugarloaf as a backdrop. It was beautifully executed, and the perspective had made her feel she was almost in the field herself. She'd seen it in a gallery window on the town's main street weeks previously and knew instantly it was what she would give Drew for Christmas. She'd also got him a soft new wine-coloured fleece and a packet of mini-Crunchies, their absolute favourite.

'Here you go,' Drew said awkwardly, thrusting a small gift-wrapped parcel into her hand, and she knew that he was embarrassed.

'Are you morto,' she teased, 'giving your mot a prezzie?'

'I just hope you like it, Connie. I'm a bit out of practice buying presents for a beautiful woman,' he said bashfully.

'Well, I'm not used to buying presents for gorgeous men either, so I hope you like mine.' She handed him his gift. He tore the Christmas paper off eagerly, ripping it, while she was more contained, unwrapping the gift-wrap carefully.

'Ohhh!' she exclaimed. 'It's beautiful, Drew.'

'Oh, *very* nice, Connie,' he approved.

They spoke almost together as she stared at the exquisite necklace and matching earrings he'd bought her.

'They're handmade, by a designer called Tina Ashmore. I thought her jewellery was very classy and unique – just like you,' he said quietly as she gazed at the delicate crystals that sparkled like raindrops and snowflakes in the beautiful pendant necklace and drop earrings.

Tears came to her eyes at his words and she buried her face in his chest, gutted that they weren't spending the night together. It could have been such a perfect night, the best of her life, but she felt terribly guilty being happy when Debbie was in such a distressed state upstairs.

'Don't cry, it's supposed to make you happy.' He held her tightly, resting his cheek in her hair.

'It does, I am. Very,' she gulped. 'I just wish we could be together.'

'You won't be saying that at six in the morning when I'm getting up,' he teased, wiping her tears with his fingers. 'Now have a Crunchie with me and cheer up, and try on the necklace and let me study my painting.' He smiled down at her, took the necklace from her and placed it around her neck, where it sparkled and shimmered in the lamplight, as bright as the tears that glittered in her eyes.

What sort of a selfish mother was she? Connie thought, torn between guilt and resentment, wishing that Drew was alongside her now as the morning dawned, bitterly cold and threatening snow, as she lay alone on her side of the double bed. All she could focus on was her own sense of disappointment. Drew was much more thoughtful regarding Debbie's feelings. Even if he had stayed over Connie wouldn't have been able to have sex with him. That would have been *too* peculiar. What was it about parents and children and sex? She would have hated to know that Bryan and Debbie were at it in the next room, had that scenario ever occurred. The walls were too thin, and she was too old to jump over that particular hurdle!

All was silent in Debbie's bedroom. Connie hoped that she had fallen back asleep. She wanted her to have a good lie-in. She looked exhausted, with big dark circles around her lacklustre eyes. Connie sighed deeply. She knew well what her only child was going through. The sadness, the grief, the loneliness, the self-recrimination, the anger, the bitterness and resentment. She'd tasted every one of them. There was no escaping from it. Debbie would get over her husband's rejection of her in time, just as Connie had got over Barry's leaving. And hopefully her daughter wouldn't have to wait as long as she'd had to before a really good man would come along and be her companion through life.

She glanced at her clock and saw that it was almost eight. Drew would be over for breakfast shortly. She felt the now familiar prickling at the top of her head and waited for the rush of heat to engulf her. 'Bloody flushes,' she muttered grumpily as she was enveloped in a scorching rush, then she grabbed her

441

dressing gown and went down to the kitchen to be greeted by a purring Miss Hope, stretched out in her padded nest in front of the stove. Connie smiled as her cat wrapped herself around her leg. 'You couldn't stay in a bad humour for long with a welcome like that, could you, Miss Hope?' she murmured, lifting her up and kissing her silky black head. The purring revved even louder and Connie kissed her again before filling her food dish.

She set the table and sliced the brown bread before making a pot of creamy porridge with honey, berries and bananas, just the way Drew liked it, and when he strode in the back door and placed his freezing cold hands on her ass Connie squealed in protest and was promptly silenced with a very satisfying Christmas kiss.

'If we cook the dinner in the big kitchen, we could have it at your table, in your room,' Ken suggested as he and Juliet strolled back from church together, calling greetings to friends and acquaintances.

'Right, that's a good idea,' his wife agreed, privately enjoying his use of the plural: *If we cooked dinner.* That was a first in forty-five years of marriage.

'Christmas isn't working out quite how we expected.' Her husband took her arm as she slid on an icy patch on the pavement. There had been another blizzard overnight and the country was having a white Christmas.

'Isn't it wonderful to have a baby in the family again?' Juliet declared. 'And one that was born in our house, Ken. What a gift.'

'Indeed. Aimee was very lucky that your friend was there.'

'She was, because I would have panicked. When it's your own child it's different, isn't it?'

'I might have panicked myself,' Ken admitted. 'Almost as much as I was panicking about cooking Christmas lunch for you,' he said sheepishly. 'I have to admit I'm very glad not to be doing the meal on my own, even though it's all prepared. I was having palpitations at the thought of it. I wouldn't have been half as worried doing a VAD implant,' he confessed.

Juliet laughed. 'You needn't think you're getting away with it. You can do it next year. Still, it will be nice to have Aimee, Melissa and Barry for lunch. It means Aimee can relax. She's a bit shattered after all the drama.'

'At least she's home from hospital for Christmas.' Ken opened the gate for his wife. 'Now what about Melissa, how do we handle her problem at lunch? Will she eat *anything*?'

'I don't know.' Juliet sighed. 'It is a worry, isn't it? You just don't know what to say or do. Aimee told me not to tell her that she's looking well. That's a big no-no, seemingly. Why don't we just let her help herself to whatever she wants and not refer to it at all? We won't offer her anything, we'll just say, "Melissa, help yourself to whatever you want," and leave it at that.'

'Right! That's a good plan,' Ken agreed, opening the front door. 'Let's have a cup of coffee and a mince pie to keep us going. Your place or mine?' He cocked his head at her.

'Let's have it in mine. The snow looks wonderful in the garden and you can't see it so well from your room. And I've got the stove lit,' Juliet said lightly, very pleased that her husband was *finally* getting sense.

'No one's coming, I told you, but you wouldn't listen to me.' Doris Farrell's voice had a hint of hysteria in it as she surveyed the trays of canapés and the flutes awaiting the chilled, sparkling Dom Pérignon placed on the side tables in their elegantly appointed lounge.

'They will come. Relax, will you?' growled Jeremy, stopping in mid-pace to glower at his wife. The doorbell jangled. 'See!' He flashed her a triumphant look. 'I told you they'd come.' He felt relief wash over him. When Doris had told him categorically that she was fed up in Portugal and wanted to spend Christmas at home he'd reluctantly agreed to return to Dublin. They had arrived home two weeks before Christmas, and he'd kept a low profile. He'd decided impulsively, despite his wife's protests, to host a small drinks and canapés party as per usual, on Christmas morning. There was a time when they would have sent out eighty or more invites, but having trawled through his address book he'd decided to invite twenty carefully selected guests who he thought might possibly come, even though most of them would have lost some money on their investments. He'd decided not to invite any of the investors who'd been stung in the SCIP fiasco. There was no point in rubbing their noses in it and inviting opprobrium.

Now the ringing doorbell vindicated his strategy, he thought smugly, hurrying out to the hall to open the door.

''Tis yourself, Jeremy,' his elderly neighbour – not on the invite list and a SCIP investor – said, handing him an envelope. 'This came in through our letterbox yesterday; it must have been one of those temporary postmen they take on for Christmas who mustn't have known you.'

'Ah ... William ... thank you ... er ... would you like a Christmas drink? I've invited a few friends and family for canapés and champagne,' Jeremy said smoothly, caught between a rock and a hard place as he saw the Clearys pulling up. Up until now, his neighbours had always been invited in on Christmas morning.

'Isn't it well for you to be able to afford champagne?' William retorted acerbically. 'Thanks to you, Patsy and myself will be doing well to have a bottle of Lucozade! It was a sorry day that I let you persuade me to invest our life savings in that damn company. We've known you twenty-five years, we welcomed you and Doris to the road when you moved in, we showed you friendship and loyalty, and you've shown us neither. You pushed and you pushed and you pushed until you got your hands on our money and now I hope you're satisfied that we don't sleep easy in our bed at night because of worry.'

He stomped off down the drive leaving Jeremy doubly mortified that his guests had heard the exchange, although out of politeness they pretended not to have.

Six out of the twenty invited guests arrived subsequently, and they only came out of nosiness, wailed Doris two hours later when she closed the door on their retreating backs. Their children had left to go to visit their in-laws and he and Doris were on their own. Jeremy slumped down in his favourite arm-chair and surveyed the limp canapés. They'd have to do him for his dinner, his wife wept, because she was going to bed for the rest of the day. He could go to one of their children if he wanted feeding, she told him bitterly. He heard her moving around upstairs and then silence.

To hell with them all! He grabbed a bottle of Dom and poured himself a glass. Just because he hadn't been a fool and borrowed to make a killing like that prat Barry Adams and some of his golfing buddies had, or invested all his readies in one basket like William had. Adams had sent a couple of virulent emails and texts, lambasting him. He'd called him a devious, two-faced little skunk who had no integrity or business ethics. Jeremy scowled, remembering how, of all the ones he'd received, that particular text had stung. Just because he'd been astute enough to read the markets and see what was coming and move to keep most of his Smarties, he was being *vilified*. None of them could deal with it. Tough! Jeremy blanked from his memory the un-deniable fact that, even when SCIP's shares were on the slide, he had urged William, Barry and others to invest. He had no intention of taking any responsibility for the losses they had incurred.

He swigged the champers angrily. He was fed up being treated like a pariah, skulking behind his four walls. Jeremy Farrell was not going to hide like a fugitive one more day, he decided, and if the idiots who'd lost money didn't like it, they could lump it; he didn't give one fig!

'Will we save opening the rest of our gifts for when we get home and are settled in for the night?' Lily suggested when she and Judith got home from Christmas Mass.

'That would be nice, Ma. We won't stay too late in Cecily's –

there's more snow forecast and we don't want to be stuck in a blizzard in Meath.' Judith peered out the window at the leaden sky.

'Would you like me to ring up and cancel, and I could cook us a steak out of the freezer?' Lily pursed her lips. 'I don't want you to be driving on those roads if you don't want to.'

'Ah no, Ma, I'm sure Cecily's gone to trouble for us, I wouldn't like to let her down. We've to be there for one thirty; we'll leave in the next half-hour and try and be home before dark.'

'Grand,' agreed her mother. 'I'm going to record the Queen's speech to watch it later. Isn't she a great woman for her age?' Lily said admiringly. 'A life of duty though; I'm sure she gets browned off having to get dressed up and pretend to be interested when she'd rather put her feet up and watch the racing on TV.' Lily perched her glasses on her nose as she went in search of the *RTE Guide*.

'It's on the chair at the end of the table, I was reading it earlier,' Judith said helpfully. 'There're some good films and shows on later.' She filled the kettle to make them a cuppa.

'Excellent.' Lily clapped her hands. 'Judith, I love the new TV you've bought me. It's like being at the cinema.' Judith had bought Lily a flatscreen TV for Christmas and given it to her the previous week, and Lily was delighted with it. It certainly was a vast improvement on the clunky old TV whose colour tubes had been on the blink and had given a faintly green hue to the screen. Watching TV had become a much more pleasurable experience and Lily was enjoying being snug and warm in her front parlour, sitting in front of the TV in the afternoons with the fire lit and the dusk encroaching, watching *Come Dine With Me* – one of her favourites – knowing that Judith would be home from work and they would eat from trays on their knees and watch the news together and discuss the topics of the day. She had never been so contented with her life since her darling Ted had died, Lily reflected, thinking how much she'd been looking forward to this

Christmas because of her renewed closeness with both her daughters.

They had been invited to Cecily's for Christmas lunch, and when Judith had agreed to go, Lily had been extremely pleased. Her youngest daughter was making more of an effort since Judith had had her accident, and the three of them had had a most enjoyable lunch and shopping expedition in the Newbridge Centre. Lily had been like a child in a sweet factory with all the gorgeous gifts they stocked. She had bought Judith a beautiful necklace and matching earring set from their Hollywood Collection, and a less expensive but very pretty pendant and earrings for Cecily. Judith had loved the jewellery when she'd unwrapped it earlier at breakfast and had promptly put it on to go to church. And she herself had loved the mother-of-pearl rosary beads Judith had given her, telling Lily they were for her sitting room, so she wouldn't have to climb upstairs in the afternoon to get her brown ones on her bedside locker. It was such a thoughtful gift, and she had hugged Judith tightly when she'd opened them.

The sky was heavy with huge, dark banks of snow-burdened clouds which threatened to blanket the city when they left Drumcondra. Judith found the driving conditions nerve-racking after they drove off the motorway on to the frozen, winding country roads of County Meath. Lily had been tense in the passenger seat after the car skidded slightly on one icy hill. It had been a relief to get to Cecily's, and the aromatic smells wafting out of the kitchen were a welcome sign that lunch was well under way. Judith didn't want to be rude, just eating and running.

For the first time in years, she didn't feel like a guest in her sister's home. Her offer of help in the kitchen was not turned down, as it usually was. In fact, Cecily seemed pleased to have an extra pair of hands, while her husband Ben wrestled with a set of lights that had gone on the blink on the Christmas tree.

'What is it about men and Christmas tree lights?' She threw

her eyes up to heaven. 'Would you mash the spuds, Judith, while I carve this beast?' Cecily asked, wiping a spot of perspiration off her forehead. She was looking a little frazzled, although elegant as always in a deep-burgundy velvet V-neck dress, with a rope of pearls to accessorize it.

'Mummy, don't forget: no turkey and ham or sprouts for me. I hope you made my macaroni cheese.' Alice, Cecily's fifteen-year-old daughter pranced into the kitchen in a pair of impossibly high stilettos, more like stilts, Judith thought in amusement, and a skirt that barely covered her skinny little bum.

'Yes, I made your macaroni cheese, now would you make sure that there's water in the jug on the table and tell your brother to stop playing his music so loud, and make sure your gran doesn't need anything,' Cecily said in exasperation.

'Gran's fine, Mummy, she's watching *Mary Poppins* with Millie,' Alice said airily, sashaying out of the kitchen.

'Paris Hilton, eat your heart out,' Cecily wisecracked and Judith laughed as she added a good dollop of butter to the potatoes. 'She's turned vegetarian recently, and it's such a bloody nuisance,' Cecily grumbled. 'I'd eat macaroni cheese no problem, but if I gave a plate of it to her father he'd look at me as if I'd lost my reason. He's a real meat, spuds and two veg man. I hate having to cook separate meals. I hope it's just a fad.'

'Ma and I have similar tastes, so at least I don't have that prob-lem, but I don't envy you trying to come up with different menus.' Judith wielded the masher vigorously.

'Mam's looking fantastic, Judith, how did you ever persuade her to wear trousers? They're fabulous on her.' Cecily paused from carving the turkey to take a sip of wine. She'd offered Judith a glass, but she'd refused, not wanting to have her wits impaired by even one glass for the drive home.

'I'd bought her a pair ages ago, and when I was over at Jillian's before I went back to work, she went to the pictures with her friend Moira, and decided to wear them to the cinema and *loved* them. So we went shopping for a few more. They really do suit her and they keep her warm too.'

'She talks about that woman a lot; isn't it great she's got a friend? Did you ever think Ma would be going out and about, going to the cinema and bingo and coming Christmas shopping with us after all the years she took to the bed for?' Cecily spooned the stuffing out of the turkey.

'I know, it's great. She's a different woman.' Judith leaned over and had a pick. She loved stuffing.

'So are you, Judith, if you don't mind my saying so.' Cecily offered her a taste of the turkey.

'Nothing like a serious car crash to make you look at life differently,' Judith said, licking her fingers before taking the fork of succulent meat from her sister.

'Ma was saying you've been looking at houses.'

'Yeah, but I've run into problems with the insurance companies because of having to have a medical after the accident. It's a bit of a bummer,' Judith said despondently.

'Oh! That's tough.'

'It's this bloody recession. The banks are just looking for excuses not to lend money, the lousy shaggers.' Judith added a sprinkling of salt and pepper to the potatoes and garnished them with a dash of parsley.

'Maybe everything will improve in the New Year,' her sister comforted. 'It can't last for ever.'

'No, it can't,' Judith agreed as Cecily yelled at her family to go and sit at the table.

Lunch was enjoyable, with plenty of lively banter from the teenagers, and Judith and Lily found themselves laughing at their antics, especially when the crackers were pulled and the jokes were read out, but by three thirty, as the snow began to fall, Lily said apologetically, 'Cecily, do you mind if we make a move? I don't want Judith to be driving in bad weather in the dark.'

'Of course not,' Cecily agreed. 'What a shame, though. I hope you enjoyed your lunch.'

'It was lovely, most enjoyable,' Judith said warmly, 'but I would like to get home before it freezes any harder. Poor Mam's nerves deserve some consideration.'

'That went well,' Lily remarked approvingly ten minutes later as she waved regally like the Queen and they drove away from Cecily's, with a goody bag of turkey and ham and stuffing to have cold for their dinner the following day. 'And we had a good excuse to make a quick getaway.' She settled herself in more comfortably as the heating kicked in, banishing the chill. 'We can have a little snooze in front of the fire at home – I don't know about you but I'm as full as an egg.' She yawned delicately behind her hand.

'Me too,' Judith said, switching the wipers on to full to try and clear away the whirling snowflakes.

'Don't worry, St Michael will get us home safe, I had a word with him,' Lily said confidently as Judith inched her way out of the drive before increasing her speed and heading south.

An hour later they were home safe and sound and ensconced before the fire. The blizzard intensified but they didn't care now, and they settled down to a refreshing snooze after the rich lunch they'd enjoyed. As Lily made herself comfortable with her feet on her footstool, she glanced over at Judith tucked up on the sofa under a throw with a thriller her nieces and nephews had given her. Their eyes met and they smiled at each other and Lily sent up a little prayer of heartfelt thanks for the most enjoyable Christmas she'd had in years.

'I think we should call her Holly,' Melissa declared, thrilled at the way her baby sister was grasping her little finger tightly with her tiny fingers. 'She was born at Christmastime, and Gran had loads of holly in the vases in the house she was born in and I think it just suits her.'

'Do you know, I think you're absolutely right, darling,' Aimee said slowly. 'Holly Adams.' She rolled it around her tongue to get a flavour of it. 'Holly Adams – what do you think, Barry?' She smiled at her husband as he stood looking at his family with immense pleasure.

'Perfect,' Barry exclaimed, delighted. 'Melissa, you're a genius. Holly Adams it is.'

'Debbie and Melissa and Holly. The Adams sisters,' Melissa enunciated experimentally, smiling tenderly at the baby, who opened her eyes and gazed up at her before falling fast asleep, her little rosebud mouth curved in a smile.

CHAPTER FORTY-ONE

'Marianna, cut it out, *I'm* collecting the girls from the airport, and that's final,' Drew snapped down the phone at his ex-wife. 'You can go to the airport if you want to, but you go in your own car. Erin and Katy are coming home here to me for breakfast, and we've arranged to meet Connie and her daughter before I drop them over to you. You'll have them all to yourself for the next few days.'

'Don't talk to me like *that*, Drew. I'm not a child! I can't help it if you booked a holiday with your girlfriend and won't be here to be with them.'

'Marianna, I'm going to bed. Goodnight.'

'You know something, Drew, you're mean and childish and unforgiving,' his ex-wife said spitefully.

'Fine, yes, I'm all those things if that's what you want. Deal with it.'

'I've had the worst Christmas of my life, I'm grieving for my father and you can't even be civil. All you think about is yourself.'

'We won't get into the kettle, pot argument, if you don't mind, it's getting late. Suit yourself about tomorrow. Once again, Marianna, goodnight.' This time he hung up.

'Bastard,' Marianna swore, slamming the phone into its cradle. When she'd realized that Drew was not going to cancel his holiday to be with the girls, she'd known she'd lost her last tenuous hold on him. Anger had taken over. He'd rejected her and their children, she'd told herself, conveniently forgetting that she was the one who had walked out on him. She knew she'd irritate him by suggesting she go to collect the girls with him, and she was right, she thought triumphantly, wandering out to the kitchen to pour herself a brandy.

She was glad she'd sent Drew to bed in a bad humour. Marianna hoped he didn't sleep a wink. This time tomorrow he'd be in Spain with his trollop, while she was hosting a family gathering with her mother and daughters, grieving and in need of the support which he was selfishly withholding because he was a hard, cruel and callous man. That Connie one was welcome to him, Marianna thought bitterly, downing the brandy and pouring herself another to bring to bed. Maybe it would help her get some sort of a decent night's sleep, because she didn't want to lie awake tormenting herself with thoughts of her fit, toned and still very sexy ex-husband lying with his arms around a woman who meant more to him than Marianna cared to imagine.

'She's something else, Connie. Why does she keep bugging me?' Drew unbuckled his belt and unzipped his jeans.

'Because you're not playing her game any more. She can't hack it that you're just not that into her, as they say,' Connie said lightly.

'Is that it?' He smiled down at her. 'You women have all the answers.'

'Afraid so.' She held the duvet back for him. 'Now get your gorgeous ass in here, buster, and let's start our holidays early.'

'I've to get up before dawn to get to the airport,' he protested as he finished undressing before getting into bed beside her.

'Turn out the light and don't be such a wussie,' Connie commanded. 'You'll have plenty of time to sleep in Spain.'

'I'm exchanging one tyrant for another,' he retorted, turning to draw her to him.

'Well, I think Master William is rather pleased to see me,' she said smugly, pressing herself against him and feeling his body respond.

Drew started to laugh. 'Connie, let's face it, I don't think you or I are going to be getting *any* sleep in Spain.'

'Mmmmm, how wonderful,' she murmured, before he silenced her with a kiss.

'Dad, Dad!' Katy Sullivan raced past the barrier in Arrivals and threw herself into Drew's arms, leaving a trolley of luggage abandoned on the concourse. Drew swung her off her feet, bear-hugging her before turning his attention to his eldest daughter, who stood laughing at them.

'Erin.' He put an arm around her and embraced her, still holding on to Katy, who was kissing his cheek yet again.

'Well, women, let's get you to Wicklow for some proper grub – the pair of you look as if you could do with it.' He eyed them up and down, noting their slender figures and thin faces.

'Dad, don't, I always put on half a stone after one of your breakfasts,' Katy giggled.

'I'm starving! I could eat a horse.' Erin tucked her arm in his as he grabbed hold of the trolley and steered it in the direction of the exit.

'So you're off to Spain this evening?' Katy glanced up at him as he dropped a couple of euros into the cash machine to pay the parking fee.

'I am,' he said equably.

'This woman must be special.' She eyeballed him.

'She is.' He eyeballed her back.

'I'm jealous. She's got no right taking you away from us,' Katy pouted, looking just like her mother. She was small, petite and blond, with her mother's colouring and flirty manner, while Erin was more like him, dark-haired, tall and blue-eyed and rather direct in her manner.

'Go for it, Dad,' Erin smiled. 'You sure as hell deserve it.'

'You think so?' He grinned at her.

'You bet I do,' his eldest daughter declared, glaring at her sibling, who made a face right back at her. Her mobile phone rang and she scrabbled for it in her bag. 'Hi Mom, we're down and heading for Wicklow. Dad's doing breakfast for us; we'll see you and Grandmamma after lunch. Say hello to Katy.' She passed the phone over to her sister.

'Hi Mommy, we made it and Dad was waiting for us,' her younger daughter chirruped. 'We had a bummer of a flight; my stomach was flipping over coming in to land. It was like tornado alley! You'd have been in hysterics. See ya soon, Mommy dearest! What? He didn't want you to come and that's why you weren't here?' She glanced over at her father, whose mouth thinned into a grim line. 'But you didn't need to be here, we only saw you last week, and you, like, *never* get up early!' Katy pointed out cheekily. 'Go back to sleep and we'll see you later.' She handed the phone back to her sister. 'Mom's being a drama queen.' She threw her eyes up to heaven. 'Saying you forbade her to come to the airport, Dad,' she added.

'As if I could forbid your mother to do anything,' Drew retorted, disgusted that Marianna would air their argument to their daughters within minutes of their arrival home.

'Precisely,' smirked Katy, 'although you're probably the only one who actually *could* make her do something. You're pretty awesome when you do your stern act.'

'Me? I'm a pussycat,' Drew drawled, and the girls laughed, delighted to be with him, even if it was only for a few hours.

What would his daughters be like? Connie wondered. Would they be very American? Would they be like Drew, or Marianna? She felt unaccountably nervous at the thought of meeting the loves of his life. She and Debbie were meeting them in the Romany Stone for a light lunch, after which Drew would drop them to their grandmother's house before coming back to Greystones to collect her to go to the airport. Debbie was meeting up with her cousin Jenna after lunch, to go and spend New Year's Eve with Karen, so at least she didn't have to worry that her daughter would be alone for New Year's Eve. She glanced over at her Debbie, who was deep in thought as they drove through the snow-quilted countryside en route to their lunch date. She had spent a lot of time sleeping over the holidays, and she was subdued and uncommunicative. Connie had told her it was fine if she preferred not to come to lunch to meet Drew's daughters but she'd said firmly, 'I'm not letting you do that on your own, Mum. I remember the first time I met Aimee – I was like a briar to her. I was sooo rude. They might be the same to you.'

'I hope not, but if they don't like me, I'm not going to lose any sleep over it. I won't be seeing much of them with them living in America.' Connie shrugged, giving thanks privately that Debbie had liked Drew very much when she met him.

They arrived at the chic restaurant and upmarket lifestyle shop on the N11 twenty minutes before they were due to meet Drew and the girls. Connie wanted to be in situ before they arrived, and had reserved the table in front of the fire, as it was more private and cosy than the general seating area. She didn't want them all to be sitting on the high stools at the long communal benches in the main section, to share this first encounter with other diners. The restaurant was buzzing, but the table she wanted had her reserved card and the fire in front of it was blazing up the chimney, throwing out welcome heat. Two expensive leather sofas sat on either side, and there was more than enough room for the five of them to eat in comfort.

'I'll go and order us two small coffees to keep us going,' Connie suggested, feeling somewhat tense at the prospect of meeting Drew's daughters. He adored them and, more for his sake than her own, she hoped that they would all hit it off. The freshly brewed coffee gave her a welcome hit and she began to relax in the warmth and convivial atmosphere of the restaurant. Then her heart flip-flopped as she saw Drew arriving with his girls in tow, dead on time.

His face lit up when he saw her, and he smiled, his blue eyes crinkling up the way she loved. Would he kiss her in front of the girls? Connie wondered, and soon found out when he put his arms around her and kissed her swiftly before turning to make the introductions. There were a lot of cross-over handshakes and polite how do you do's and Connie indicated the sofa opposite her and invited her guests to sit down.

'This is lovely,' Erin exclaimed, glancing around her. 'Has it been here long?'

'A few years now. It used to be the Tap pub before it was converted,' Connie explained, thinking that the way they were seated, Drew and his daughters on one sofa, Connie and Debbie opposite them, made it seem a bit of a them-and-us scenario.

'Ah yes, I remember it now. They've done a terrific job. Are all these sofas and tables for sale?' She was friendly, making an effort, and Connie liked her immediately.

'Yes, if you can afford them,' Connie said, indicating the hefty price tag, and Erin laughed. Katy was less friendly, watchful, more like her mother, Connie thought, and undoubtedly viewed Connie and Debbie as interlopers, and rivals for her precious father's affection.

'Would you like to go up to the menu board and choose what you'd like to eat, then come back and tell me and I'll order everything together?' Connie suggested.

'Honestly, Dad did one of his bumper breakfasts, I'm still stuffed to the gills. I'll just have a regular coffee and a cookie,' Erin exclaimed.

'Me too.' Katy shrugged.

'Drew?' Connie arched an eyebrow at him, hoping that he'd choose something substantial so that she and Debbie could order a proper lunch. Erin and Katy might be stuffed to the gills, but she was starving.

'I'll have one of those chicken-wrap things that I had the last time we were here.' He gave her the tiniest wink, and it gave her heart. He understood that this was difficult for all of them.

'And I'll have the New Yorker,' Debbie said, and Connie knew she was making a huge effort for her.

It took a while for their order to be processed and they were in the middle of eating when Erin's phone rang. 'We won't be long, Mom, we're just having our coffee in the restaurant so we should be with you in less than an hour?' She looked questioningly at Drew, who nodded. 'See you soon then.'

'That was Mom. She was just wondering when we were coming,' Erin said lightly.

'We should have invited her.' Katy took a sip of coffee and gave Connie a faintly hostile stare.

'Maybe she wouldn't be in the humour for socializing after her bereavement,' Debbie interjected coolly.

'Isn't it so unusual to have snow here? It was like a winter wonderland flying in this morning.' Erin changed the subject diplomatically and the tension eased perceptibly.

'It's twenty degrees in Marbella. I checked, so I guess we'll be slathering on the protection factor.' Connie smiled across the table at Drew, who had just finished wolfing down his wrap.

'Speaking of which, we really should be getting a move on shortly if we want to make it to the airport on time.' He glanced at his watch.

'I'm finished.' Katy drained her cup and stood up. She was a rude little madam, Connie thought.

'Why don't you go on with the girls, and we'll finish up here? And I'll be all ready when you collect me. I'm packed to go,' she said evenly.

'Are you sure? It's not very good manners to leave when you and Debbie are still eating,' he added pointedly, for Katy's benefit.

'Don't worry about that. We're all a bit pressed for time and I'm sure Marianna's dying to see the girls.' Connie stood up and held out her hand to Erin. 'It was lovely to meet you,' she said warmly. 'Drew's told me so much about you and I can see why he's so proud of you.'

'Thank you, Connie, have a lovely time in Spain, and thank you so much for lunch.' Erin gave her a good firm handshake and a ready smile before reaching across the table to shake hands with Debbie.

'Lovely to meet you too, Katy.' Connie turned to the younger girl.

'Mind our dad for us,' she said archly, giving Connie a brief, limp handshake.

'I certainly will. Enjoy your stay.' Connie smiled, determined not to let Drew's younger daughter rile her. It helped that she could understand the young woman's antagonism. By going to Spain with Connie, Katy could well say that he had chosen to be with her rather than his children.

'Debbie, take care of yourself.' Drew gave her a hug and was hugged back affectionately in return, much to Katy's disapproval. 'Connie, I'll see you when I see you. Drive carefully.' He kissed her cheek and gave her hand a squeeze before following his daughters out to the Range Rover.

'I liked the elder one; the other one is a little wagon,' Debbie said bluntly, dipping a bread stick into a small ramekin of pesto sauce, when they were alone.

'Hmmm, a touch hostile,' agreed Connie, 'but I guess that's to be expected. Erin's more like Drew, I'd say. Isn't she a lovely-looking girl?'

'She could be a model,' Debbie remarked. 'Anyway, the main thing is: you've met them. That's the worst part. So that ordeal's over. It won't be so difficult the next time.'

'And there speaks the voice of experience,' Connie said ruefully. 'Are you sure you'll be OK when I'm away?'

'I'll be fine, Mum. It's only for four days, and you're not going to Timbuktu. You have a great time with Drew, you deserve it. Jenna and Carina and I are going to chill in my house tomorrow night and then I'll be back at work the day after and it will be all over, thank God. And it will be a new year and a fresh start for all of us, and that can only be a good thing,' Debbie said firmly, leaning over to plant an affectionate kiss on her mother's cheek.

'But you *must* come in, Drew. You can't just drive up, unload the girls and drive off. It's rude! Mama will be offended,' Marianna rebuked, as Drew sat with the engine running and the girls got out of the car.

'Sorry, Marianna, I have a flight to catch and time's not on my side. Have as good a New Year as you can under the circumstances. Girls, enjoy yourselves.' He leaned out the window to kiss them.

'Thanks for the gorgeous bracelet, Dad. Enjoy yourself.' Erin hugged him tightly.

'I'm glad you like them – they're handmade, like I told you.' Drew smiled at her. He'd bought his daughters a Tina Ashmore bracelet each and, not wanting to leave her out, he'd bought Debbie a delicate pair of drop earrings. He'd decided it would be totally hypocritical to buy Marianna a gift, so he'd given Erin a bottle of champagne for his ex and her mother to toast the New Year.

'Dad, I wish you weren't going,' Katy said tearfully.

'It's unfortunate timing but that's the way of it,' Drew said brusquely, aware that Marianna was enjoying his discomfort.

'Dad, you just go and get yourself off to the sun, you so deserve it,' Erin ordered, glaring at her sister.

'Will do, love,' he said gratefully, and waved as he drove off, leaving Marianna scowling ferociously in his wake.

'A new year, and a fresh start for all of us.' Debbie's words came back to Connie that night as she stood barefoot in the sand watching a silver moon cast silver streamers of light over the calm, rippling sea that washed up gently on the shore. On the horizon, the lights of Africa twinkled faintly and further up the coast they could see fireworks dancing in the sky as Marbella celebrated the arrival of the New Year.

She and Drew had eaten a light meal and enjoyed a few drinks at Max's beachside restaurant and were strolling back to Karen's apartment across the moonlit beach when they'd stopped to enjoy the view. 'Are you glad you came?' she asked. Drew, who was standing with his arm loosely around her waist looking out to sea, turned to face her. 'Very,' he said, smiling at her. 'Are you?'

'Very,' she echoed vigorously. 'Very, very, very glad.'

'I want to give you something,' he said with a bashful grin.

'What are you up to now?' She laughed, entertained that he still got embarrassed giving her a gift. He took a small box out of his pocket, and she looked at him, perplexed. 'What is it?'

'Open it?'

Connie's heart flipped when she saw the platinum ring with the sparkling solitaire nestled inside. 'Drew!' she exclaimed, almost speechless at this totally unexpected turn of events.

'Shush!' He put a finger to her lips. 'Don't panic! We don't have to change anything. I just want to give you this ring as a sign of the *commitment* I want to make to you. I know it's been difficult this Christmas because of circumstances, and our kids needing us, but I want you to know how important you are to me, Connie. Let's call it a commitment ring. I will try my very best to always put you first,' he said, sliding it on to the third finger of her left hand. 'I commit myself to you for as long as we live and hope with all my heart that you feel the same about committing to me,' he said, lovingly cupping her face in his hands.

'Oh I do, I do, I do, I do, with all my heart, Drew, and I will do my very best to put you first too and – you know what would be good? If we commit as long as we both shall *love*, rather than live. It's much nicer to be with someone because you *want* to be with them, not because you *have* to be.' Connie wrapped her arms around him and held him tight, knowing that they would be together for the rest of their lives.

CHAPTER FORTY-TWO

'And you have the ten chauffeur-driven cars booked for the two days, two nannies for the children and a selection of the most recent films, including *Shrek*, for the youngest, a nurse and wheelchair on standby for the elderly grandmother, the harpist and quartet for the music?' Aimee raised her head from her checklist to confirm that her deputy was keeping up.

'Everything is sorted, Aimee. Please go home,' Helen said calmly.

'I just want to have a look at the dining room,' Aimee said. 'Then I'll go.' She walked down the hallway of the exclusive boutique hotel Hibernian Dreams had rented out for a very wealthy businessman friend of Roger's to celebrate a two-day birthday bash for his octogenarian mother. Aimee was making sure that *nothing* had been overlooked.

She stood at the entrance to the dining room and surveyed the round tables dressed with the finest cream linen tablecloths, laid with sparkling glassware, delicate fine bone china and gleaming silver cutlery. A pine bough entwined with crystal fairy lights and adorned with clusters of red- and yellow-berried holly draped the Victorian fireplace, scenting the air with a fresh pine scent. Elegant tapered red and cream candles in a centrepiece of red and cream roses decorated every table, coordinating with the expensive cream and red crackers at every place setting. Understated but very elegant, Aimee approved, noting the sparkling mirrors and highly polished chairs. Her phone rang, and she saw Roger's name flash up. 'Roger. Happy New Year. What can I do for you?' she asked.

'You can get home this minute and rest yourself,' her boss ordered.

'How do you know I'm not at home?' she enquired.

'Because, seeing as I want this to run very, very smoothly, Jim Daly being a good friend of mine, I rang Helen to see if everything was going to plan and did she need any back-up for this birthday gig, and she told me you were inspecting the dining room. You've just had a baby, woman. Go home, I'm telling you.'

'I'm fine. Anyway, Holly is nearly two weeks old. I'm hoping to have her home in another day or so; she got a bit chesty, so they wouldn't discharge her,' Aimee said. 'And it's because the client is a friend of yours that I want everything to be perfect. Well, actually, I like *all* my events to be perfect, FYI, Roger,' Aimee added humorously. 'Honestly, it was doing my head in being stuck at home and being waited on hand and foot. Barry's treating me like a piece of porcelain. So I escaped for an hour. Listen, Roger, I've a favour to ask you.'

'Shoot,' her boss said.

'The thing is, I'm not completely happy with our accounting system. It's a drag having to deal with your company accountants for day-to-day stuff. They're over on Stephen's Green, but I'd prefer to have an inhouse person working a couple of hours a week who could do basic accounting for me – debit and credit ledgers, costings, etc. – and do the books at the end of the year to be signed off by one of your lot. I want to keep a strict eye on my operating budget too. I have someone in mind.'

'I'm listening.'

'It's nepotism,' Aimee said briskly.

'That doesn't bother me if they're up to the job,' Roger said affably. 'Hire your part-timer – you're the boss in Hibernian Dreams, Aimee. All I care about is that you keep everything above board and make a profit and, praise where praise is due, you're playing a blinder, like I knew you would. '

'Thanks, Roger. It helps that I've got a great boss. This is going to be a good year for us.'

'You know, Aimee, I think you're right. Now go home. Everyone else I know is still in their bed.'

'Yes sir,' she said, and hung up. She glanced at her watch. Eight fifteen on New Year's morning: Roger was probably right – who else would be mad enough to be up working when it wasn't strictly necessary? She'd left Barry and Melissa fast asleep at home.

'It's all yours, Helen. Good luck with it.' She caught up with her deputy, who was making sure the small cut-glass candle-holders in the entrance hall had new nightlights in them. A florist working on a flower arrangement in the foyer yawned her head off. 'Make sure she's not around, yawning, if Jim Daly calls in to check up on things,' she murmured.

'No prob. I'll tell you how it all goes tomorrow. Happy New Year, Aimee, enjoy the rest of your day.' Her very efficient deputy walked her to the door.

'I will,' Aimee said, thinking how different the role of MD was. This time last year, she was the one who would have been hands on like Helen, overseeing the entire event. Sometimes Aimee found it difficult letting go of that aspect of the job. Delegating was the hardest thing to do sometimes, she reflected, making her way to the car.

Ten minutes later, she found parking directly outside Holles Street and strode along the slushy footpath to the entrance, look-ing forward to feeding her daughter. Holly had developed a minor chest infection and had been kept in hospital for a few extra days, much to all their disappointment.

Who would have thought that she would bond so well with her child, the child that had been so unwanted, the child she had wanted to get rid of? Aimee sighed deeply as she took the lift to the unit. She had been so petrified that she'd have no feelings for her baby, that they wouldn't bond when she was born, but in those frightening minutes when she'd gone into premature labour and had thought her baby might not survive, Aimee had realized that she did indeed want her. When Connie had placed her on her tummy, she'd felt a primal surge of overwhelming, protective love that she hadn't realized she was capable of. That had been a revelation, and it hadn't gone away either as she'd feared it might once her hormones began to settle and life got back to normal.

Holly Adams had brought Aimee's family closer than she had ever thought possible. Melissa and Barry were besotted by her, as were Juliet and Ken. But the most besotted of all was herself, Aimee acknowledged, waving at the unit nurse, who gave her the thumbs-up.

'Hello, Holly.' Aimee smiled, looking down at her baby daughter. Holly's blue eyes widened, and she turned at the sound of her mother's voice.

'How is my very precious girl?' Aimee said, lifting her up and cuddling her gently. Holly gave a little gurgle and waved her tiny hands.

'You are *so* beautiful,' Aimee told her. 'I *can't* wait to have you home,' she added, tenderly kissing her gorgeous downy little head.

Judith was glad it was all over, glad that she didn't have to pretend that she wasn't heart-wrenchingly, gut-achingly lonely. There was something about Christmas and New Year's Eve that always magnified the loneliness of not having a companion in life, and in previous years she'd often drunk brandy in the solitude of her bedroom to get her to sleep in a woozy stupor. But this year had been different. It hadn't been the worst Christmas and New Year's Eve of her life by any means, lonely and all as she was, she decided, as she lay drowsily in bed watching the snow dancing playfully against the windowpane, blotting out the spindly branches of the horse chestnut next door and the line of leylandii at the end of the garden.

She had been due to spend a few days with Jillian, but the weather conditions had been so bad, the country almost ground to a halt by blizzards, they'd had to postpone it. The blizzards had been a blessing in disguise in one way, enabling herself and Lily to cut short duty visits to Lily's sister and cousin on the other side of the city because of the road conditions. And when Judith and Lily had invited their relatives to visit in return, later in the week, the weather had been so bad they'd had to cancel, leaving Lily and Judith to watch a movie about the golden days of Hollywood which Judith had enjoyed as much as her mother.

She and Lily had had a very lazy, relaxing Christmas all in all, which had suited Judith down to the ground. She'd found her return to work more tiring than she'd anticipated, and the disappointment of not getting loan approval in time to buy the cottage had hit hard. When Judith had gone back to the estate agent and told him that she had to have a medical, he had come back later that day to say that a couple had put in an offer, and they *had* loan approval and the vendor was going to go with them. She'd been so disappointed she'd cried, sitting in a traffic jam in Fairview.

'Never mind,' Lily had said comfortingly when Judith told her about it. 'What's for you won't pass you by. A better house will come your way.'

Judith wasn't too sure, but she knew she couldn't let herself sink into depression about it. She had to fight her life-long tendency to be pessimistic. Just because she'd had a setback didn't mean she was never going to find a place.

'Morning, dear, I brought you a cup of tea,' Lily called from the landing.

'Come in, Ma. Happy New Year.' Judith struggled into a sitting position.

'And to you too, Judith. I hope it's the best one you ever have,' Lily said fervently, setting the steaming cup on its china saucer on Judith's bedside locker. 'Would you like me to bring you up a slice of toast or some cereal?'

'It's me that should be bringing you up your breakfast,' Judith said, reaching out for her tea.

'I wanted to get up early today. I want to bake some fresh mince pies for Moira and Joan. Moira always goes to trouble when I visit, I want to reciprocate,' Lily said. Her two friends were coming for lunch later on, and she was looking forward to their visit immensely.

Judith had planned to drive over to the Botanic Gardens to go for a walk and leave her mother to entertain her friends, but it was so cold and miserable, and the paths were still quite lethal in places, so she thought she'd stay put and read her book in her room.

'How about I make one of my apple strudels?' she suggested helpfully.

'Would you, dear? They're so tasty, and Moira has a terrible sweet tooth, and you have such a light touch with pastry. And it's much nicer to serve homemade pastries rather than shop-bought. Thank you, Judith, I'll look forward to a piece of it myself.' Lily beamed, bustling off to get dressed and begin her baking.

Judith sipped her tea and picked up her book. She was re-reading *The Twelve Caesars*, and had just started on Augustus, one of her favourites. She would enjoy reading about him while Lily was entertaining. The card she was using as a bookmark fell out and she picked it up and smiled. It was a thank-you card from Debbie's young sister for the angel Judith had bought her. It had been a nice surprise to find the thank-you note on her desk before the office closed for the holidays. She certainly hadn't expected it.

Melissa had excellent writing, she noted, rereading it:

Dear Judith,

Thank you very much for the angel you sent me. It's lovely and I keep it under my pillow. You might like to know that having it is helping me a lot and I'm very grateful to you for thinking of me. I have to go to my session with my doctor now. I am working through my issues with her. She is very good.

I hope you are feeling better too.
Yours sincerely,
Melissa Adams

The poor child, she thought sympathetically, working on her 'issues' at that age. It had taken her until her late forties to address hers, Judith thought glumly. She hoped that Melissa would get herself sorted so that she could have a happy and carefree teens. *She*'d been happy enough in her teens, Judith remembered. Her problems hadn't really started until her father had died, even though she'd often had to run the house if Lily was going through a bad phase with her nerves. Her dad would be so delighted to see how well Lily was doing, Judith reflected, swinging her legs gingerly out of bed to go and shower and get dressed.

She was dipping the pastry brush in beaten egg to spread on her pastry before putting it in the oven when the phone rang. 'I'll get it,' she called to Lily, who was giving her front parlour a quick polish.

'Hello,' she said, tucking the phone under her cheek.

'Howya, Judith, I just rang to wish you and Ma a Happy New Year. What's the weather like?' Tom asked. He and Glenda and the children had spent Christmas in their place in Spain. He was obviously making his New Year's Day duty call.

'Happy New Year. It's not as bad as it's been. There's supposed to be a thaw coming, and not before time. Is it nice in Spain?'

'Lovely, although it gets a bit chilly at night. Is Ma there?'

'Hang on, I'll get her,' Judith said coolly. Her brother clearly had no desire to make polite conversation with her.

'Ma, it's Tom,' she called.

'I'm here.' Lily appeared at the kitchen door, duster and polish under her arm.

'Hello, Tom, Happy New Year,' she said, giving Judith a little wink.

Judith chuckled, returning to her pastry duties.

'I had a lovely Christmas, thank you. Judith and Cecily were very kind to me. And how are Glenda and the children? Good. Give them my regards. When will you be back? Oh, right, well, enjoy yourself, and safe journey when you're coming home. God bless, son,' Lily said kindly and hung up.

'Your brother's not the chattiest on the phone but at least he rang to wish us a Happy New Year,' she observed, putting her polish and duster away.

'He hardly had two words to say to me.' Judith slid the baking tray into the oven.

'He's a terrible lad for holding a grudge, he always was, and it's not a good thing.' Lily sighed. 'Poor Tom. He's only concerned with what goes on in *his* life, and that's not a good thing either. He's his own worst enemy. Try not to let him get under your skin, dear. Life's too short to be on bad terms,' Lily advised, banging the window at her sworn enemy, the marmalade tabby from next door, who was sharpening his claws against the bark of Lily's much-loved lilac tree. 'Get back into your own garden, ye little gurrier,' she shouted crossly, and Judith hid a smile. Lily and the tabby had waged war on each other for years and, in Judith's considered opinion, it was a battle her mother was never going to win.

'How is your mother?' Glenda Baxter stretched out on her lounger, enjoying every second of the glorious heat of the Spanish midday sun. It was perfect weather, balmy and warm, much nicer than the scorching heat of a Spanish summer, when she wouldn't dare sunbathe until after five o'clock.

'She sounds fine, telling me how good Judith and Cecily were to her. That Cecily one is up to something, changing her tune the way she has. She never had a good word to say about Judith, and she never lifted a finger to help Ma, and now she's bringing her Christmas shopping and encouraging her to get the house done up. She's sly, that's what she is,' Tom complained, shoving his hands in his pockets and staring out at the kids splashing and diving into one of the big pools on the complex.

'Maybe she felt guilty after Judith's accident and is trying to make amends,' Glenda pointed out reasonably.

'Maybe she's after Ma's money the way Judith is,' Tom retorted, unimpressed.

'Tom, will you give it a rest? You're obsessed with your Ma's money.'

'You would be too if you had my bills to pay.' Her husband scowled.

'Ah, you're not doing that bad. Look at the Blaneys, having their penthouse repossessed by the bank.' She took a sip of her G&T, her third that morning.

'By God, the Spanish banks take no prisoners. Two missed mortgage repayments, and you're a goner. And they were such blow holes, always namedropping and going on about their mansion in Howth and being neighbours with Gay Byrne and Moya Doherty. Spoofers of the highest order. I hope I run into him some day – we'll see how much Big Tycoon Blaney spoofs then,' Tom declared, returned to good humour by the idea of looking down his nose at the snobby ex-banker who had come on hard times. 'The kids are down at the pool; do ya fancy a ride while we have a bit of peace?'

'Sure, we're on our holliers,' giggled his wife tipsily. 'Lead me to the bedroom.'

'. . . and did you see them all bending to kiss his ring in their long frocks, and whinging and moaning that they were suffering too? And him enjoying every second of it. And did you hear what he said about women priests? What woman in her right mind would want to be a priest in that boyo's church? The little scut has some nerve, in his fancy, swanky slippers. Designer, I believe—'

'Are you serious, Moira? And to think, Jesus was a carpenter's son. I'm quite sure He's disgusted with the way those poor abuse victims, and women, are treated by that lot.'

'I agree with you wholeheartedly, Joan. And it's very unfair on the good ones. We have a grand chap in our parish—'

'I quite agree, Lily, the rotten apples spoil it for everyone . . .'

The Pope and the hierarchy were getting a going-over big-time, Judith thought in amusement as she placed a plate of sliced apple strudel on the table. Lily and her guests were just finishing their tea and were having a right old natter.

'Judith made the strudel; it's her speciality,' Lily informed them proudly.

'It looks very tempting, Judith, I'll enjoy some of that. We've had a lovely meal,' Moira Meadows said appreciatively. 'The poached salmon was delicious.'

'Yes, a lovely treat after all the turkey and ham. You get fed up of it, don't you?' Joan helped herself to one of Lily's mince pies. 'That was a very tasty salad, I like the little nuts in it.'

'Pine nuts,' supplied Judith helpfully. 'A friend of mine always uses them in her salads.'

'I must try them myself.' Joan spooned a generous dollop of cream on to her mince pie and bit into it with gusto.

Judith's mobile phone rang. 'I'll take it in the parlour, Ma. Excuse me,' she said, seeing Jillian's name flash up. 'How is it going?' she murmured, walking down to her mother's sitting room and curling up on the sofa in front of the fire.

'My mother-in-law is driving me mad,' Jillian whispered. 'She's giving out to the kids for making noise, and she's hogging the TV. How are you doing?'

'Mam's having a lovely time with her friends. They've just

been airing their views on the hierarchy and not pulling any punches. Hold on.' Judith cocked her head and earwigged, hearing her mother's indignant tones:

'. . . and we have to pay for his VIP lounge and his mobile-phone bills and his secretaries and drivers and so on and so forth. What sort of fools are we? We should be down picketing outside his house, Moira, it's an absolute disgrace.'

'Oh, don't get me talking about that fella, Lily. Do you know, he's so shallow he couldn't drown himself.' Gales of laughter erupted from the kitchen, and Judith giggled. 'The politicians are getting it now. It will be the bankers and developers next. We could be here all night.'

'Well, at least it sounds like a bit of fun, I'm ready to explode. Thank God she's going home early because of the weather and I'll have done my duty,' Jillian confided.

'Jillian, you have to do it with *loff* or it's no use,' Judith said solemnly, and her friend snorted laughing.

'Smarty,' she said. 'I'll ring you later.' Judith grinned. Poor Jillian, she was having the day from hell and had phoned several times to have a moan.

She sat for a little while listening to the laughter and chat coming from the kitchen. What a wonderful sound. Those kind women had made such a difference to Lily's existence. She loved their company, loved being able to talk about their generation's common experience. So different from Judith and Jillian's.

The women had been talking about the war earlier on, and rationing, and the blackout, and it was extremely interesting to listen to them reminisce. Joan had told of her mother having to burn her John McCormack gramophone records for heat because there was no fuel one bitterly cold winter due to rationing. They walked or cycled everywhere, Moira added, 'and we were never as healthy.' It was true, Judith reflected: her generation were soft and unhealthy in comparison to their parents at the same age.

Moira poked her head around the door. 'Judith, did I leave my bag there? I want to show Lily some brochures,' she asked, spotting the black leather bag on the floor. 'We're hoping she might agree to come on a Mediterranean cruise in the spring with us. What do you think?'

'Oh Moira, that would be fantastic for her. I don't know if she'd have the nerve, though. She's never flown.' Judith shook her head ruefully.

'Leave her to me,' the elderly woman said firmly, taking a sheaf of colourful brochures out of her bag with a flourish.

Two hours later, when she and Lily were tidying up the kitchen after Moira and Joan had taken their leave to get home before the roads froze, Judith asked, 'Well, are you going to go on the cruise?'

'I'd love to, Judith, but I don't know if I'd be able for it. I'd be a bit nervous about flying,' her mother admitted. 'That's the only thing that's putting me off. The ship looks very luxurious, and the girls were telling me about all the shows, and the restaurants, and how there are shopping and sightseeing tours when you get to all the different ports. Barcelona and Genoa and Nice and Naples – doesn't it sound wonderful?' Lily sighed wistfully.

'You could always take a mild tranquillizer. Or, do you know what we could do, Ma?' Judith exclaimed. 'You and I could fly to Cork for a day as a sort of practice run, and then you wouldn't have to be anxious about it because you'd know what to expect.'

'Judith, that's a *brilliant* idea, I'd never have thought of it,' Lily said excitedly. 'Do you know, I think I will tell Moira I'll go. Because I'd be very sorry if I didn't. It's a wonderful opportunity, isn't it?' Her eyes were sparkling, and her cheeks flushed pink with excitement.

'It is, Ma. And you all get on so well. It will be the trip of a lifetime for you,' Judith said fondly, delighted at her mother's bravery.

'Two trips of a lifetime,' Lily said. 'The first one will be with you to Cork.'

'We'll take a taxi to Patrick Street and have lunch in Brown Thomas. I had lunch there with Jillian two years ago when we had that weekend away. The food was gorgeous,' Judith enthused. 'You'll love it.'

'And I love you, Judith. Thank you so much for all your kindness.' Lily's voice broke. 'I'm sorry I wasn't a better mother to you all.'

'Ah Ma, don't.' Judith put her arm around her. 'I love you too,' she said awkwardly, 'and you had a hard time when Dad died. Don't be sad or look back, there's no point.'

'It's not sadness, dear.' Her mother sniffled. 'I've had a lovely Christmas and I've such a lot to look forward to, I'm having the best time of my life since your father died. I never thought I'd enjoy my life, I was always so nervous and anxious, and look at me' – she gave a teary smile – 'jetting off to Cork and going on a cruise – there'll be no stopping me.'

'Why don't you go in and have a little nap in front of the fire? I'll finish off here,' Judith suggested.

'I think I will, Judith. I'll get my rosaries said, and then we'll watch that film you were telling me about tonight.'

'*The First Wives Club* – it's very funny, Ma, you'll enjoy it,' Judith assured her, looking forward to it herself. She finished loading the dishwasher, put the tea towels into the washing machine and decided to go up to her room and lie on her bed and have a read. The twilight was deepening into night, the rooftops sharply etched against the blue-black sky, but at least it wasn't snowing. Judith yawned. She might have a nap herself, she decided. She'd be back at work tomorrow and wouldn't be able to indulge in such decadent behaviour.

'Ma, I'm just going to have forty winks myself. I'll make us a cup of tea and a sandwich around half six and we can have it in front of the TV if you like.' She closed the kitchen door and walked into the sitting room.

'Yes, you go and have a snooze too, dear, and we'll do that.' Lily settled herself in her chair and picked up the mother-of-pearl rosary beads Judith had given her for Christmas. 'I love these,' she said. 'I'll bring them on the cruise with me.'

'Enjoy your nap,' Judith said, and impulsively bent down and kissed her mother's soft cheek as she placed a soft throw over her.

Lily flushed with pleasure. 'Thank you, dear, I will, and you do too.' She lifted her feet on to her stool and blessed herself, and Judith closed the door softly behind her and left her mother to her prayers.

CHAPTER FORTY-THREE

'So much has gone on since I went away. I never thought you'd give Aimee a second look after your wedding-day episode. Honestly, Debbie, you've been on a roller coaster for sure,' her cousin Jenna remarked as Debbie found a handy parking space close to her father's apartment block. She and Jenna were on their way home to Debbie's house, having spent New Year's Eve with Karen. Her aunt had cooked a big family dinner in celebration of Jenna's return from Bangkok. The riotous good humour in her aunt's household had cushioned Debbie from the desperate loneliness of New Year's Eve. Strangely, the worst moment had been Connie's phone call. Because of the time difference with Australia, Brian's text hadn't come until some time this morning when she'd been fast asleep, and she hadn't responded to his New Year greeting. She should send him a text, she supposed, even though, right now, she hated him. She had veered between hatred, fury and wild optimism over the past few days; Jenna's description was spot on. A roller-coaster ride described exactly how she felt and it was exhausting, to say the least. Still, this had to be the hardest time; next Christmas would be a doddle compared to this one, she assured herself, taking her phone out of her jacket pocket and sending a brief text to her estranged husband before quickening her pace to catch up with her cousin.

They were going to spend the evening unpacking Carina's belongings, and Debbie intended having a relatively early night before going back to work the following morning. She and Jenna were on their way to visit Melissa en route home to Sandymount.

'Will Aimee be here?' Jenna asked as they walked past Meadow's and Byrne.

'I'm not sure. Dad said she was sorting out some work thing this morning before going in to Holles Street to feed the baby. But that was hours ago.'

'You have to give it to her, she's some woman to go,' Jenna remarked. 'At least everyone's talking again.'

'In fairness, she sorted things with Mam and myself, and everyone's rooting for Melissa. And now, with Mam and Karen delivering the baby, it's brought a new closeness. I feel like I've got a real family unit as well as the one I have with Mam. It's nice. And it couldn't come at a better time for me,' Debbie confided, ringing the bell to announce their arrival.

'Welcome, girls. Happy New Year.' Barry greeted them warmly when they stepped out of the lift, kissing each in turn as Melissa emerged from her bedroom, her face splitting into an endearing grin when she saw her half-sister and cousin.

'Hey, guys, it's great to see you. Thanks for calling in. Guess what?'

'What?' Debbie hugged her sister tightly, relieved that she was beginning to look well again. Her eyes were bright and her cheeks had a touch of colour, in contrast to the dull, exhausted, pale and wan mien of the past weeks.

'Dr Morton is so pleased with my progress she's thinking she might discharge me in another week or two and I can do the programme on an outpatient basis.'

'Well done you,' Debbie applauded.

'Way to go, coz.' Jenna gave her a high five.

'Isn't it a great start to the New Year?' Barry ushered them into the lounge, where Aimee was lying on a sofa reading an interior design magazine.

'Hello, girls.' She made to get up.

'Don't get up, Aimee,' Jenna said firmly. 'Get all the rest you can.'

Aimee smiled and lay back against the cushions. 'There's only so much resting you can do. Barry's taken my BlackBerry off me, and I'm feeling very, very weird without it. How's Connie getting on, Debbie?'

'Good, sunbathing in the daytime; it gets a little chilly in the evenings. They should have gone for a week if they'd had any sense. They—'

'They couldn't – Drew couldn't leave the horses that long,' Melissa interjected sagely and Debbie laughed.

'How are *you* doing?' Barry asked, his eyes full of sympathy, as he took her jacket. He'd been so kind to her, ringing and texting after she'd told him about Bryan's departure.

'OK.' She shrugged.

'Why, what's wrong?' Melissa looked at her in concern.

'Nothing, hon, just missing Mum and Bryan.'

'Aw, my poor sis.' Melissa put her arm around her and gave her a hug.

'Will you have a drink – tea, coffee? Something to eat?' Barry offered.

'Oh God, don't mention food,' Jenna groaned. 'Mam's been stuffing me since I got home.'

'I know the feeling,' Melissa said impishly, and they all laughed.

'Brat,' said Aimee affectionately, giving her a cuddle.

They spent a pleasant hour chatting and laughing, and Debbie was surprised at how quickly the time had passed. 'We should make a move,' she said, glancing at her watch. 'My friend Carina is moving in and we're supposed to be helping her unpack. Melissa, when you're home for good you'll have to come over and stay some Friday night and meet her, she's great fun.'

'Brill, but you do know that I'm on an eating plan and I have to stick to it,' she said, a touch anxiously.

'No problem at all, Melissa, that's fine,' Debbie said reassuringly.

'Debbie, just before you go, could I have a word with you? It's about work.' Aimee stood up gracefully, and Debbie marvelled that she looked to have lost any weight she'd put on during her pregnancy and appeared to be her normal slimline, elegant self. She was wearing a superbly cut pair of black trousers and a magenta silk tunic and she looked effortlessly groomed and chic.

'Let's go into the dining room; my computer is there,' Aimee said easily and Barry smiled at her.

'Sure.' Debbie was mystified but she followed the other woman out of the room. Why would Aimee want to talk to her about work?

'Debbie, I'm very sorry for your situation. Barry told me what's happened and I'm sure it's very, very tough. He said you've taken over the whole mortgage and I'm glad to hear that. Having a roof over your head and keeping your independence is *vital*,' Aimee said emphatically.

'I don't really have much choice, to be honest,' Debbie said glumly. 'I'm in negative equity, like a whole lot of other people I know.'

'Sandymount is a good area, and the recession will end. We can see it in our business: people are starting to spend again – and that's what I want to talk to you about.' Aimee sat down at her dining table and motioned to Debbie to do the same.

'I need someone to do a couple of hours' part-time work every week to keep my books for me – basic accounting really, a debit and credit ledger. I want to keep on top of my outgoings, and the company accountants I use are far more concerned with my boss's bigger firms and it's a nuisance dealing with them, to be frank. I want an inhouse person and I was hoping, with your experience of figures, and your bookkeeping qualifications, that you'd consider taking the job. Will you think about it? As I say, it's only a couple of hours a week. You can do it in your own time, either at home or in my office. I just need to have the figures on my desk every Monday morning and the books ready for auditing at the end of the year. I'd be talking about paying €150 a week.' She arched an eyebrow at Debbie.

'Why me? I don't want you to feel sorry for me,' Debbie said bluntly. 'I don't want charity.'

'Trust me, Debbie, I don't do charity,' Aimee said dryly. 'If you don't want to do it, I'll find someone who does. But I will say I'm very, very grateful for your kindness to Melissa. She loves you very much, and that means a lot to both myself and Barry and I would like to help out if I could. I know that we've had our differences but we *are* family, and besides,' she said good-humouredly, 'I owe Connie one. She's been so good to my two daughters, even going to the trouble of delivering one of them, that I owe it to her to help her girl out.'

'I love Melissa, it's been great getting to know her, and I'm really glad about it too, so thanks, Aimee. It sounds like an interesting proposition, I won't lie, and the money would come in very handy. The bloody interest rates are going up.'

'Well, how about a three-month trial? That way we can see if it suits both of us, and no hard feelings if it doesn't. That gives us both a bit of leeway,' Aimee suggested matter-of-factly.

'Right, that sounds good to me,' Debbie agreed.

'OK, why don't you give me a buzz tomorrow, and we'll make an arrangement for you to come over to the office and I'll bring you up to speed?'

'OK, boss,' Debbie grinned, thinking that this was such a surreal moment but a good one, and the extra money would be a lifesaver, a real lifeline. As she followed Aimee back down to the lounge, Debbie slipped her hand into her jeans pocket and rolled the little angel that Judith had given her. Maybe she was a lucky angel, maybe Debbie's luck was on the turn. All she could do was put one foot in front of the other and get on with things as best she could, Debbie decided, as her father dropped his arm around her shoulder and gave her a hug when she walked back into the lounge with Aimee.

*

It was strange to think that New Year's Day was over, Bryan thought, grimacing as he swallowed a couple of painkillers to try and ease his aching head. He had the mother and father of a hangover and the sun, streaming in through a gap in the curtains, hurt his eyes. They were having blizzards at home. He'd caught up with the RTE news on the internet and felt a totally unexpected bolt of homesickness as he sat listening to Bryan Dobson's familiar tones reading the six o'clock news.

He was starting a new job tomorrow, in an office-design company, and the wages were a lot less than he'd hoped for. His mother had told him that there was a hefty credit-card bill waiting at home, and she'd sounded uncharacteristically cross about it and told him she wouldn't be able to give him any more money to pay it off.

Australia wasn't exactly the land of milk and honey he'd expected it to be. Sure life was more laid back, but bills still had to be paid and he needed to get a pad of his own; he couldn't stay in Pete's small box room for ever. He'd met two Irish couples in the past week who were returning home to Ireland because their money had run out. He couldn't let that happen to him. He had to make it here, there was nowhere else to go. His BlackBerry tinkled and he scrolled into his texts eagerly, seeing there was a message from his wife.

All it said was: The same 2 u. Cheers.

Bryan gazed at his phone in disgust. What kind of a message was that to send to your husband for New Year when he was all alone on the other side of the world? It was probably that Connie one influencing her, telling Debbie to forget about him. His Debbie would never send him such a curt text of her own volition, of that he was sure. Or was he? He frowned, wincing as he did so. Did he not vaguely remember Debbie telling him that Connie and that he-man culchie of hers were going away for New Year?

Maybe his wife *had* sent the text off her own bat, Bryan thought apprehensively. Maybe Debbie was moving on and, if that was the case, he was well and truly up the creek without a paddle.

It had been a lovely day, Lily thought sleepily after she'd finished her rosary. The lunch with Joan and Moira had been most enjoyable. Such fun. And now she had the cruise to look forward to. This new year was going to be even better than the last one. What a brainwave it had been on Judith's part to suggest the trip to Cork. That was something she would look forward to immensely. She wouldn't be at all nervous flying if she had Judith with her and it would be a short flight – a hop, skip and a jump – she assured herself as a log settled in the fire and threw up a shower of sparks. It was dark now, and there wasn't a sound in the house. Judith must have fallen asleep. She was ready for her nap herself, Lily thought with a little yawn, snuggling under her soft throw.

Her life had changed so much this year. And it looked as though it was going to change even more in this new one coming. She, who had never looked forward to things, she who had always dreaded events out of the ordinary, was planning on going on a cruise to the Mediterranean. Lily could hardly believe it. She was proud of herself, she decided with a little smile. Ted would be immensely proud of her too. After all these years, she was finally coming into her own.

She must have a touch of indigestion, Lily felt, she was a little uncomfortable under her ribs. It must be the cucumber; she liked it but it didn't like her. Maybe she should get some bread soda, Lily thought, not wanting to stir from her comfortable chair. Goodness, she thought, opening her eyes wide, it was like her husband was standing right beside her, smiling that familiar much-loved smile and holding his hand out to her. 'Ted,' Lily said joyfully, smiling back, and her eyes closed as her rosary beads slipped from her fingers, glinting in the firelight as they fell on the floor.

CHAPTER FORTY-FOUR

'She looks so peaceful, so happy, doesn't she, Judith?' Moira said sadly as they stood beside Lily's coffin in the front parlour.

'Yes, she does. She looks contented,' Judith said quietly.

'Look at the lovely smile on her face. Ted must have come for her,' Moira surmised.

'Oh, Moira, I feel so bad I wasn't there and that she died alone. I was up in bed having a nap. What if she was in pain? What if she called for me and I didn't hear her?' Judith exclaimed, raw with grief.

'No, no, don't think like that. She *wasn't* alone. Someone always comes, Judith, you never have to go on your own. Look at her face: there's no trauma, only serenity. It was her time, Judith, and she died happy. She wouldn't have been able to go if you were there. Ted and Our Lady and all the saints she was so devoted to came and were with her,' Moira said with great authority. 'Your mother had a very peaceful death. And she was very happy these past few months. She told me that herself. So what better way to go, my dear?'

'I can't believe it, I just can't believe it,' Judith whispered, stroking Lily's cold hands. The mother-of-pearl rosary beads Judith had bought Lily for Christmas which she'd been praying on when she died were entwined around her fingers.

Judith had thought Lily was still sleeping when she'd woken

up in the pitch dark and come down the stairs thinking she'd not meant to sleep so long. She'd opened the sitting-room door and seen her mother with her head resting to one side, eyes closed, and a little smile playing around her lips.

'Ma, you should wake up. You won't sleep tonight – it's after seven,' she'd said, shaking her gently. And then Judith had known, known that Lily would never wake up. After the initial indescribable stomach-lurching shock, a strange, unreal peace had descended on her. She knew that she should ring the doctor and the priest, and Cecily and Tom, but once she did that Judith knew her mother would be gone from her. Lily would belong to other people, to ambulance men and doctors and undertakers and mortuary attendants. There'd have to be an autopsy because it was a sudden death and then funeral arrangements would have to be made. She remembered the stress of organizing her father's funeral. Arranging funerals was an exhausting, agitating, worrying task that she'd hoped she'd never be presented with again.

Judith wanted to postpone the inevitable for a little while at least. She wanted her mother's spirit to have some peace in the room she had loved, so she'd gone upstairs to Lily's bedroom and got her crucifix and the two golden candlesticks with the cream candles that she kept in front of the picture of the Sacred Heart that reposed on the chest of drawers. She took Ted's photo and the prayers to the saints that Lily kept in the pages of her missal and brought them all downstairs. She set them on the small coffee table beside her mother, talking all the while to her. 'Now, Ma, I've got your photo of Dad, and your pictures of Jesus and St Joseph and St Michael, and St Anthony, and all the ones you pray to, here with us, and I'm just lighting the candles and we'll have a peaceful little time before I have to make the phone calls,' she said, striking a match. The candles flamed, the light flickering over Lily's face, and Judith felt the merest hint of a cool breeze on her forehead, like a kiss.

She sat on the floor at Lily's feet and took her hand in hers. It was still warm, which was comforting. Judith told her how she would miss her and how proud she was of her, and how she was glad that Lily was with Ted again, and outside the snow began to fall again, softly, silently, as Judith shared those last, most precious moments with her mother.

'What do you mean, she's not bringing her to the church for a removal, what sort of a carry-on is that?' Tom demanded. 'She needn't start dictating what's going to be done. We have to be consulted. Judith has no business taking unilateral decisions.'

'Mam left instructions,' Cecily said.

'What do you mean, she left instructions?' Tom blustered, feeling completely out of control and sideswiped.

'Judith asked Mam ages ago what she'd like to happen when she died and would she write down her wishes, and she did. Judith showed it to me. She wanted to be waked in her parlour and spend her last night at home and go directly to the church. A lot of people are choosing that now rather than having a removal,' Cecily said tiredly, not up to dealing with her brother's belligerence.

'But sure it doesn't make any difference to Ma now. She's gone, we should do things properly. I bet Judith put this notion into her head because she doesn't want the hassle of a removal.' Tom marched up and down next to the departure gate at Malaga airport feeling completely powerless.

'Tom, Judith organized Dad's funeral, and made all the arrangements and never complained, and we had a removal at that. That's very unfair. Ma didn't want to be left alone in a church at night, she wanted to spend her last night at home. Judith and I were there today waiting when they brought her home from the mortuary and I'm really glad it's what she decided. It just feels right for Ma, and you are not to have a go at Judith when you get home later on.'

'Yeah, well, as long as she remembers she's not the only one in the family,' Tom retorted.

'Tom, you listen to me now,' Cecily said crossly. 'To all intents and purposes, for the last twenty years or so she might as well have been the only one as far as Ma was concerned, because we did not step in. We left everything to Judith. We did our duty visits and that was it. We got away with *murder*, Tom. We took no responsibility at all for our mother, because Judith took it on, and we let her because it suited us. We got on with our own lives and we didn't give two hoots about Judith or what she had to give up to take care of Mam—'

'What the hell has got into you, Cecily? Why are you going on like this, like Judith is your best friend or something? Are you hoping she'll share the goodies with you?' he said nastily.

'You know what's wrong with me, Tom? Something that's really horrible to have to deal with and something it's too late to do anything about,' Cecily said quietly. 'It's guilt, Tom, guilt. When I saw Ma lying in her coffin I felt like a complete and utter heel. I abandoned Ma and I abandoned Judith and I feel as guilty as hell, and you should too. Judith is the only one of the three of us that can look herself in the eye when she looks into a mirror and say, "I did my best," because we sure as hell didn't. So don't you dare have a go at her when you get home, because she's in bits and she did love our Ma, which is more than can be said for either of us.' Cecily burst into tears and hung up, leaving her brother staring at his phone in astonishment as his flight's boarding announcement echoed around the departures terminal.

'You bring the kids home, I'll go straight to Mam's in a taxi and then you can come over and collect me later,' Tom said heavily as the plane rolled up to the jetway and the flight attendant prepared the doors for disembarkation.

'OK,' Glenda murmured, relieved that she wasn't expected to accompany her husband to Drumcondra to see his mother lying in her coffin. She wouldn't have gone in to see Lily; she'd have been terrified. Glenda gave a little shudder. Typical of her mother-in-law to die when they had three more days of their holiday left. It had been a nightmare trying to get a flight home; they couldn't get one until two days after Lily had died and then they'd had to pay a fortune to slum it on Ryanair. Coming back to bitterly cold Ireland and with his mother's funeral facing them was a dreadful way to start the new year, and Tom was in a foul humour after his phone call to Cecily. He'd clammed up and hardly spoken except to take the nose off the kids when they'd argued about where they were sitting on the flight home. The flight had been three hours delayed because of yet another French air traffic controllers' strike, which meant they'd had to be rerouted and had a much longer flight time than normal, sitting in those dreadful narrow seats with the glaring yellow headrests that gave her a headache, and all the while her husband had sat staring out the window giving the deepest of sighs, which would have given the tail wind they had a run for its money.

What had got into Cecily to have a go at him like that? Tom ruminated as he took one taxi and his family took another. Was she going to give him the cold shoulder when he got to Drumcondra? Going on about guilt. It was too late for guilt, and besides, he wasn't going to indulge in that kind of nonsense. Judith had had a free roof and lodgings over her head all these years while the rest of them had to pay hefty mortgages and worry about rearing a family and running a business and the rest of it. She hadn't had half the worries he'd had. So Cecily could get over herself saying they'd got away with murder.

He felt strangely apprehensive as the driver took the right turn to drive down Lily's road. There were cars parked along both sides of the street and he could see the glow of lights in the house, upstairs and down. 'Here's fine,' he said gruffly, a few houses away. He needed to gather his equilibrium. He paid the driver, adding a small tip. There was a recession and he wasn't Onassis, he thought, seeing the driver's disdainful expression. Tom took a deep breath and began to walk towards what had once been his home.

His stomach knotted in a twist of anxiety and dread as he knocked on Lily's front door. A neighbour opened it. 'Ah Tom,' she said. 'I'm so sorry for your trouble.' She shook his hand respectfully. The house did not feel at all subdued and sombre. It felt, incongruously, full of life. There was a hum of conversation in the kitchen and dining room, where a buffet was laid out. He could hear his aunt's voice in the background and Jillian, Judith's friend, was there, he noticed, offering plates of sandwiches to the neighbours and relatives. The door to his mother's parlour was partly ajar and he could see part of the coffin, resting under the window. He felt a dull thud of shock at the sight that almost brought him to a standstill. Lily was dead. He would never see his mother alive again. It was unbelievable, surreal, like a dream, he thought wildly as the light oak coffin brought the numbing reality home to him.

There were candles lit on the mantelpiece and Lily's photo of Ted, and a picture of Jesus and a crucifix set between their flickering lights. Judith was sitting in Lily's chair, Cecily on the sofa, which had been pushed against the wall to make space. Some other women were there, and when he came into the room they excused themselves to give him privacy to pay his condolences to his mother.

Judith stood up; she was deathly pale, eyes red-rimmed. 'Hello, Tom,' she said quietly. Their eyes met. There was no hostility in hers, just weariness and sadness, and he felt all his anger fade away. He nodded. He couldn't speak. To his horror, tears blurred his eyes and his mouth shook. Judith took his arm, seeing his distress. 'It was very peaceful for her, Tommy,' she said, calling him by his boyhood name, a name she hadn't used in many, many years. It was his undoing; Tom gulped and took a deep breath. 'Good,' he managed. 'Good,' and then he was sobbing like a child as he looked down at Lily in her coffin, so calm and serene in death, so happy-looking, all stress and anxiety erased from her creamy skin. 'Ah, Ma,' he wept as his heart contracted. 'Ma.'

'Don't cry, Tom, don't cry.' Judith held his arm tightly as she started to cry herself. Cecily, weeping softly, closed the door so that they could grieve their loss in private, coming to stand beside him, and the three of them wept their goodbyes to their mother, standing side by side, looking down at her, Tom's arms around his two sisters' shoulders as the candles radiated their light around them.

It was a beautiful, crisp, cold morning as the mourners streamed out of the church to pay their respects to Lily's children. They stood in a line receiving the condolences of all those who had come to support them.

It had been a lovely, simple funeral, Judith thought gratefully. No over-the-top eulogies that had people shifting in their seats, just the old, familiar hymns that Lily loved and readings she had selected one evening soon after Judith had come home from hospital when they had been discussing what they would each like for their funerals. It had made it all so easy, knowing Lily's wishes, and it brought a balm of its own knowing that every-thing was as her mother would have wanted.

She had shown Tom the handwritten page of instructions in their mother's beautiful script. 'If that's what she wants, we can't argue with her now.' He'd given the ghost of a smile. And her heart had softened even more. Her brother was not an easy man to get on with, but watching him sobbing his heart out as he stood looking down at their mother had taken away all the sharp edges of animosity she'd harboured. She'd remembered him as a boy, casting anxious glances at Lily when she was having one of her bad days, and how he would be glad to scuttle up to his bedroom or out to play with his friends. Poor Tom, he'd spent his life scuttling away from their mother, even as an adult. Not for him the peace of mind Judith had been gifted with in her relationship with Lily.

Cecily had apologized to Judith over and over for not playing her part in helping her to look after their mother, especially after

Lily's breakdown, but it made no difference now, Judith thought, sighing. Nothing could be changed, they just had to move on and try and support one another in the future. And in fairness, Cecily had been a brick these past few days, doing anything Judith asked of her and minding her, urging her to rest.

Now Cecily was talking to their aunt and Tom had a stream of colleagues waiting to talk to him. Then Judith saw Janice, Carina, Debbie and a large group from the office heading in her direction. *How kind,* she thought. They could have just sent a representative, but it looked as though most of her department was here, as well as people from other ones.

'Judith.' Janice took her hand and hugged her, and then they were all around her, shaking her hand, murmuring words of sympathy. Debbie stood in front of her, holding out her hand, tears in her eyes, unable to speak. Judith gripped her hand tightly and Debbie placed her other hand on top of hers. They said nothing; they did not need to. And then she moved on and Carina took her place. Judith shook many hands, the words people spoke a blur, and then she felt her hand taken in a firm grip and she saw Anthony Larkin standing in front of her.

'Ah, Anthony,' she murmured. 'Thank you for coming. I'm sure this is hard for you. It must bring back memories.'

'I just wanted to support you, Judith. I remember the comfort I got from all the friends who stood by me at the funeral, when my wife died,' he said gently. 'You must be kind to yourself in these coming weeks. Rest as much as you can. I remember waves of tiredness coming over me for no reason. I couldn't understand it. It's grief. And try and be careful when you're driving, you lose concentration easily, that was another thing I found, so I just wanted to tell you about these things so you can keep them in mind. And if ever you want to talk about how you're feeling, I'm just on the floor above at work. I found it helped to talk to someone who had been through a recent bereavement. They understood it very well,' Anthony said, and then, after patting her hand gently, he was gone, and someone else had taken his place.

The rest of the day had passed in a daze. Judith had not cried at the graveside. She had felt a great sense of peace as Lily's coffin was lowered beside her husband's. Lily was with her beloved Ted: how could she cry because of that? Something she'd read when her father died came to mind: *We only mourn for ourselves, for they have gained everything.* It was so true.

Afterwards, there had been a meal for the mourners in the Maples. Tom had offered to pay, but Judith had told him that Lily had made provision for it in her will. Their mother wanted to do things 'properly'. Moira Meadows, Joan and Lily's bingo friends had demurred from coming, saying it was for family, but Judith had insisted. 'Moira, my mother had a new lease of life thanks to you and Joan and the women. Please, please, come to the meal,' she'd urged. 'Mam would really want you to. We really want you to.' And Moira, with tears running down her cheeks, and a motherly hug for Judith, had accepted.

When they had said goodbye to the last of their guests, Cecily had offered to come back with Judith and stay the night, but Judith had told her to go home to her own bed and get a good night's sleep. The three of them had stayed up all the previous night watching over Lily, reminiscing and praying, and Cecily was as white as a sheet with exhaustion. Jillian was staying another night, so she'd be fine, Judith told her younger sister, who couldn't hide her relief.

And then, half an hour later, mercifully, she was alone. Judith drew a deep breath, unbelievably thankful for the solitude. Jillian had gone to get petrol for the return trip to Sligo the following morning. The unwelcome shrill of the doorbell rent the silence and Judith groaned. She was spent. She couldn't face another person offering condolence, no matter how kindly it was meant. She just wanted to be alone. Taking a deep breath, she opened the front door and saw her brother standing on the step.

'Tom! I thought you'd gone home,' she said wearily, opening the door wide to allow him in.

'I just wanted to make sure you're OK. There's something on

my mind that I haven't had a chance to say to you,' he said agitatedly.

'It could have waited, I'm sure,' she said mildly, leading the way into the kitchen. 'Would you like a cup of tea?' she offered, wondering, with a sense of dread, had he come to discuss the will. Surely he could have waited. Their mother was barely hours in her grave.

'No thanks, I'm all tea'd out.' He managed a weak smile. 'Judith, I know we haven't got on very well over the years and I'm sorry about it. I was so angry with Ma for being the way she was and I was angry with you because' – he lowered his eyes – 'well, to be honest, I know I left you to it to look after Ma and didn't get involved in any of what that entailed, and it made me feel bad and it was easier to be angry with you than feel the guilt,' he blurted. 'I know she's probably left you the house and I want you to know there'll be no arguments from me. You deserve it. I haven't been much of a brother to you or Cecily, I was a rotten son to Ma, I'm sorry.' To Judith's dismay, Tom burst into tears, his face red and blotchy as he rooted for his hanky.

Tears welled up in her eyes, and she laid a tentative hand on his arm. 'Stop crying, Tommy. I'm just so glad you're not here to fight,' she gulped. 'I wasn't much of a sister—'

'But you *were*,' he exclaimed earnestly. 'You minded Cecily and me so well when we were kids; you cooked our dinners for us and did our homework with us when Ma was having her bad days. You were a very good sister then, Judith, and I never told you that.'

Judith smiled shakily. 'I wasn't a very good cook though, in the beginning. Remember the time I tried to make a steak pie and the pastry sank down and was all gooey and soggy—'

'Yeah, and the dog across the road devoured it.' Tom wiped his eyes.

'And remember the time I put salt instead of sugar into the apple sauce and it made you puke?' Judith chuckled at the memory of her early attempts at cooking.

'I suppose it wasn't all bad, looking back; we got on quite well when we were kids.' Tom blew his nose and looked at her, a touch mortified by his tearful apologies.

'No, it wasn't. You were a good kid brother, and you put up with a lot,' she said quietly.

'Well, I just wanted to . . . to . . . you know, sort of clear the air,' he said slowly. 'I'd better go, there's a chess tournament on tonight in Larry's school that I'm sponsoring, and I told him I'd drop in to it. It makes him proud that his da's giving the prizes,' he said with a shrug.

'Very important to make your son proud.' Judith followed him into the hall. 'Don't be a stranger, Tom,' she said, opening the door.

'I won't, Judith, and if you need anything, or any help with . . . er . . . stuff, let me know.'

They looked at each other and then he gave her an embarrassed hug before hurrying down the path.

Judith waved as he got into the car before closing the door and drawing a deep, shaky breath. Lily was working her miracles already. A new chapter had just opened in Judith's relationship with her brother and there would be no row about the will. For that she was truly grateful, because it had been on her mind. Tom's apology was affirmation of all she had done for their family, even if, as he'd put it, he'd 'left her to it'. She couldn't hold on to her resentment and anger against her siblings any more. It was time to move on.

She dropped a teabag in a mug and brought the water to the boil again as she toasted a slice of bread to have with her tea. She had been so busy making sure everyone was catered for in the hotel, she'd only picked at her roast-beef lunch.

The house was still and quiet after all the company of the past few days but she absorbed the silence gratefully. It was so good not to have to talk or once again give details of Lily's passing to a friend or neighbour. She drank her tea standing at the kitchen sink looking out on to Lily's new patio. Her mother had not got to enjoy it much, she thought regretfully. She saw a robin on a branch of the lilac tree and noticed that the bird feeder was empty. Lily would not be best pleased. Judith smiled, remembering how her mother would replenish the seeds and nuts in the winter and take great pleasure in looking at the flocks of twittering starlings, wrens, robins, blue tits and finches who fed from its bounty. She finished the toast and drained the tea and got out the bag of birdfeed from under the sink.

It was still sunny, bright enough to make her squint against the indigo sky, although the sun was slanting to the west. The early days of January were one of her favourite times of the year, Judith thought as she tipped the feed into the container. It was always so noticeable that the evenings were beginning to lengthen, giving the promise of spring, and the hardship of winter was coming to its end. She hung the feeder back on the branch and gazed around the garden, inhaling the crisp air. The snow had thawed in the heat of the sun, melting back to the shaded part of the garden, freeing the grass and the dark, loamy flowerbed under the lilac tree from its white embrace. Judith glanced down and saw four perfect snowdrops pristine against the dark soil, and the thrusting green shoots of the daffodils pushing up in bright green clumps, their leaves and buds a beacon to the coming season, a true sign that winter's grip was fading and spring was on its way. The thought gave succour to her weary spirit and Judith raised her face to the sun. 'Fly high, Mam, fly high,' she said. 'All is well.'

'Summertime and the
living is easy'

EPILOGUE

Miss Holly Adams was the centre of attention, the place where she most loved to be. Although she did not know it, it was her christening day, and many, many people were smothering her in kisses and cuddles. She gooed and gaahed with gusto, waving her small fists and smiling that infectious melon-slice beam at anyone who looked at her, and that was a lot of smiling. It was tiring though, so she stuck her thumb in her mouth and drifted off to sleep with the sound of laughter and chat wafting around her, as her elder sister, and godmother, held her carefully as they made their way out of the church.

How did Connie do it? Aimee wondered as she watched the tall, lithe, grey-haired man stride around the enclosed field where Melissa was trotting on a horse, sitting proud as Punch while Drew issued instructions.

He was an absolute hunk, there was no denying that, and probably great in the sack as well, she thought enviously. She and Barry hadn't had sex in ages, they were both so tired. Connie was obviously getting plenty: she was glowing and looked so happy, watching from the top of the fence, cheering Melissa on. Aimee turned to her husband. 'Doesn't Melissa look great on the horse?'

'She looks fantastic. I never thought six months ago that we'd be standing here watching her riding a horse and having a barn-dance christening party.' Barry grinned over at her, cuddling his baby daughter, laughing as she pulled his nose.

'Me neither. Everyone's having a good time. I was afraid they'd expect a big, posh do and, in fairness, Roger offered it, but I didn't want that. For once I just wanted family and friends after the year we've had,' she confessed.

'Me too,' Barry said fervently. 'This is *perfect*, Aimee: it's not a corporate event, it's our daughter's christening, on a lovely sunny Sunday. Melissa's having terrific fun with her "country cousins", as she calls them, and we're out in the fresh air. It's a glorious day, the smell of that barbecue is making me ravenous, and I can't think when I've enjoyed myself so much. We're surrounded by love, Aimee. Everyone that's here *wants* to be here and we want them here too, so please enjoy it,' he urged.

It almost was perfect, he thought, except that every time he saw Drew and Connie together he felt a pang of loss. He had to stop thinking like that and focus on what he had in his life and the future he, Aimee, Melissa, Holly and Debbie were making together. Connie was with another man now and that was the end of it. He had to move on.

'You're right,' Aimee said, slipping her arm into his and giving Holly her little finger to grab hold of. 'We've turned the corner in every way, haven't we?'

'Yes, Aimee, we have,' Barry said. 'Our family is finally on the up.'

'I thought Aimee would go for a big flashy do with all her clients and the glitterati – this is so refreshing, full marks to her. I never took her for the country type,' Jenna remarked as she helped herself to some ciabatta bread and salad to accompany the succulent steak the chef had just served on to her plate.

'No, she's not what you'd call a wellies woman.' Debbie helped herself to some spicy beef noodles. 'She and Dad decided they didn't want a big do, they just wanted family and friends, and they

were wondering where to hold it. Melissa said she'd like a barbecue like the one her cousins had a couple of years ago, and Connie
was there when she said it. She mentioned it to Drew, and he
offered them the meadow and his barn for a hooley.'

'He's lovely, you can have a great bit of banter with him,'
Jenna approved.

'He's kind to me too, and not just for Mum's sake, which is
nice. He won't walk out on her, for sure.'

'You're looking better, though,' Jenna observed.

'I feel better, I'm not so depressed and overwhelmed by it all
any more,' Debbie admitted. 'And having that part-time job with
Aimee has taken the pressure off big-time financially, and
Carina's great to live with. She's the best in the world.' She
grinned, watching her friend flap frantically as a bee buzzed her
plate at their table.

'Any word from Bryan lately?' Jenna piled some potato salad
on to her plate.

'He's working and whinging that he hasn't enough money,
and he's living in an eggbox, according to himself, and I'm welcome to come and visit whenever I want.'

'And are you going?'

'Nope,' Debbie said cheerfully, waving at Melissa, who was
heading in their direction. 'I have no intention of going to visit
Bryan now or ever. That ship has sailed and I ain't on it any
more. Hey, Mellie, you looked good on the horse,' she said
proudly.

'Debbie, I just wanted to ask you will you get a photo taken
with me and Holly when you've finished eating? I think it
would be nice to have a photo of the three sisters – what do you
think? We didn't get one at the church with just the three of us
on our own.'

'I think that's a terrific idea, little sissie. Are you going to have
some barbie?' She smiled at her sister.

Melissa hesitated infinitesimally and then said firmly, 'Yes I
am. Can me and Sarah and our cousins sit at your table?'

'You bet, we have the hottest table in town,' Debbie teased, and the two sisters gave each other an elbow in the ribs and burst out laughing.

'Isn't that lovely to see, Ken,' Juliet murmured, watching her grandchildren laugh uproariously as they ate their barbecue with Debbie, Jenna and Carina.

'They've all grown up so much, and look at the clothes on them – they're all half naked with those booby tubes or whatever they call them,' Ken grumbled. Eating out in a field in the middle of the country was not his scene. A proper meal in an elegant well-appointed hotel would be far more to his taste. Burnt ribs and drumsticks was not his idea of fine dining.

'Don't be giving out or I'll leave you to your own resources and go and sit with Connie and Karen. I know what's wrong with you. You're hungry.'

'I don't fancy charred meat and salads,' he moaned.

'Don't be *ridiculous*, Ken, this is Aimee's bash. I can assure you you'll be eating the best of food. Go and sit somewhere and I'll bring you a plateful,' his wife said briskly, making off for the barbecue.

Ken headed over to the dining area, set out on a wooden floor. He noted with surprise that the tables were set with fine linen, china and cutlery. Of course, Juliet was right: Aimee would serve only the best. The food she'd ordered in for him the previous Christmas was extremely delicious, he remembered. His stomach rumbled. Juliet knew him so well. He was cranky because he was hungry. It had been a long time since breakfast.

'Hey, Granddad,' Melissa called as he walked past. 'You should have some of the prawn and crab salad, it's yummy. Mom ordered it specially for you 'cos it's your favourite.'

Ken made his way over to where his grandchildren were seated, tucking into their meal. 'I believe you're going to give us a riding exhibition after lunch?'

'Yes, Granddad,' they chorused.

'Just as well I'm here, I can attend to any injuries that might occur,' he said jocularly. 'I can operate over in the barn. So if you need me, call me.' He leaned over Melissa and stole one of her prawns.

'You're right, they *are* good, my dear. I may go and get a dish of that salad for myself. I must make sure to thank your mother for her thoughtfulness,' he remarked, ambling off to join Juliet at the buffet. 'Is that my plate you've filling up?'

'Yes,' Juliet said, spooning up a small portion of fried onions to go with his steak.

'Give me a bit more than that,' he said indignantly.

'You'll take what you get and don't get upset,' his wife said tartly. 'You don't want to go clogging up your arteries. Now take this and go and sit down and I might allow you to have seconds.'

'Yes, Juliet,' Ken acquiesced, having every intention of going back for more.

'Everything OK?' Aimee came up behind them as they made their way back to the table.

'It's lovely, darling,' Juliet said warmly. 'It's a wonderful day, everyone's having such fun.'

'Yes, well done, Aimee,' Ken congratulated. 'It's very nice to have the whole family together. And I couldn't tell you how good it made me feel to see Melissa tucking into those very tasty prawns.'

'I know, I'm trying not to panic every time she goes to the loo, but by and large she's making a great effort,' Aimee said, pulling out a chair for her mother to sit down.

'She'll be fine,' he said reassuringly. 'You've done a great job with her, and with all of this.' He waved his hand around to the assembled guests, at various stages of their meal, many already going up for seconds.

'Thanks, Dad,' Aimee said graciously and got a wink and a smile from her mother as Ken took a morsel of tender steak and ate it with relish.

*

'Wasn't it very kind of them to invite us to the christening, all the same?' Moira said to Joan and Judith as they sat watching the youngsters showing off their riding skills, assisted by Drew and some of his instructors.

'It was Melissa who suggested it, when her mother asked who she'd like to invite to the christening,' Joan replied, clapping as Melissa's horse jumped over a small fence in the ring.

'Well, Joan, you've done a great job giving her that extra tuition. Her father told me they were very pleased with her progress now that she's back at school.' Moira took a sip of her G&T.

'That was all down to Judith.' Joan smiled over at her. 'Melissa and herself have been writing very encouraging letters to each other these past months, I believe.'

Judith nodded. 'Yes, we are, she's a lovely girl. And I was delighted to be able to help out. Debbie mentioned to me months ago when I asked her how she was getting on that Melissa was desperately worried that she'd have to repeat her year at school, and I thought of you and Moira. A retired maths and English teacher, and a native Irish speaker. Who better to give her a grind?'

'It's all worked out very well.' Joan smiled at Judith, raising her hand to shade her eyes as she watched her young pupil laughing her head off with her best friend.

Judith inhaled deeply, sitting back and raising her face to the sun. It was a beautiful day in early June. The smell of freshly cut grass, the humming of the bees and the trills of birdsong mingled with the sound of laughter and merry chat. A faint breeze hummed in the branches, lifting tendrils of hair off her forehead.

Lily would have loved to have heard all about the christening but, mused Judith, Lily knew all about it anyway. Her mother was only a thought away and Judith had frequent, if one-sided, conversations with her. It was hard to believe that she was five months dead. She had visited the grave this morning and had watered the pots of burgeoning busy Lizzies, salvias and pansies that decorated it so cheerfully.

Judith visited the cemetery every Sunday morning and got great comfort at her parents' grave. Several times she had bumped into Anthony tending his late wife's plot, and they had taken to going for a cup of coffee and a walk in the nearby Botanic Gardens. It was a ritual Judith had come to enjoy. They had much in common, and Anthony's friendship had come to mean a lot to her. He'd laughed this morning when she'd told him that Cecily had said she could tell the banks to 'go and stuff themselves' if another property came up that she wanted to buy. She could sell Lily's house to fund it.

'That would be a sweet moment,' he'd agreed. 'And it will come.'

'Maybe,' she'd said. Judith had not gone looking at properties since her mother's death. She was happy enough for now to stay living at home and feel Lily's energy around her.

'Enjoy your day,' Anthony told her when they had stood at the gates of the vibrant gardens to say their goodbyes.

'Do you ever feel guilty when you find yourself enjoying yourself?' Judith had asked him, wondering was it appropriate to be going off to a social event so soon after her mother's passing.

'Yes, I do, indeed I do, but Judith, Vera and Lily would want us to go out and about. They'd want us to get on with our lives and pick up the pieces and move on. So enjoy your day and make the most of it. And you can tell me all about it this day next week.'

It was good advice, Judith thought gratefully, and she would enjoy telling Anthony about it. That was part of their ritual now. Catching up on the goings-on of each other's week, at work and at home.

Melissa made her way over to her with her friend Sarah. 'Judith, I have something for you that I forgot to give you earlier,' she said, taking a little envelope out of her bag and handing it to her. 'Me and Sarah—'

'Sarah and I,' corrected Joan primly.

'Sarah and I' – Melissa grinned – 'saw it in the angel shop in Dun Laoghaire yesterday, and I bought it because I knew I'd be seeing you today. It's for your car, to keep you safe. I think I'd like to get one for Holly's cot when she's older. I wouldn't give it to her now, she might eat it.' She laughed.

'Oh, Melissa, it's lovely, how *thoughtful*!' Judith exclaimed, very touched when she opened the tissue paper to see a small, sparkling crystal angel to hang on her mirror.

'It's a gorgeous shop. We, like, go into it all the time, you'd totally love it.' Melissa assured her. 'And they've loads of books there too. It's in St Michael's Mall. It was the first angel shop in Ireland.'

'I got an angel candle for my gran, she's very into angels,' Sarah interjected.

'Well, I must certainly go and visit it, so.' Judith smiled up at them. 'Thanks for the info.'

'You're welcome. See you later. Bye Moira, bye Joan.' Melissa blew them a kiss before heading back with Sarah to where the horses were neighing joyfully and feasting on the apples and carrots the guests were feeding them.

Judith laughed; there was something so endearing about Melissa. Her Mass card and letter of condolence the week after Lily had died had been unexpected but utterly welcome, and she had written back to express her thanks. Melissa, back in hospital for the end of her inpatient treatment, had responded and they'd sent several letters back and forth to each other since then. And then Judith had been able to suggest Moira and Joan to Debbie as ideal candidates to give grinds.

Lily would certainly approve of the proposed trip to the angel shop, Judith thought. And she'd approve of her friendship with Anthony. And she'd like him too, Judith knew, as a little white butterfly whispered past her and returned and alighted on her shoulder for the briefest second before flying high, high into the sky.

*

Melissa gave Holly her bottle as Sarah looked on enviously. 'She's gorgeous. You're dead lucky, Melissa.'

'I know, I'm just *crazy* about the *baby*!' Melissa said in a singsong voice as she expertly sat her sister up on her knee and burped her before laying her back in her arms to continue the feed.

The sun had set and the stars were popping out all over the black velvet sky. The band was playing country music and her cousins were dancing enthusiastically to the beat. As soon as she had finished feeding Holly she was going to join them again. She pressed her lips lightly against the top of her sister's downy head. Today had been one of the best days of her life. She had been dreading it a little bit because of the barbecue. But she'd given herself a good talking to and told herself that Holly's christening day would only happen once in her life, and it would be such a waste of a fun day if she was fretting about sticking to her eating plan. She'd made herself act as normal as she could, eating her food at the table with Debbie and Jenna and their cousins, and after the meal was over she'd become much more relaxed and now she was totally looking forward to bopping the night away with her best friend, and watching the stars shoot across the sky.

'You are the best baby in the whole wide world,' Melissa said, and laughed joyfully when her sister grabbed her hair and gave it a good pull with her little fingers, gurgling with laughter as she did so.

Drew laughed as he swung Connie around the floor to a hillbilly dance tune the band was playing.

'Go easy, will you, I'm not a young wan,' she giggled, breathless, bumping into Karen, who gave her the thumbs-up.

'I'll make you fit,' Drew teased, taking her hand and leading her off the wooden floor put down for the occasion when the song ended.

'Where are you going?' Connie wheezed, trying to get her breath back.

'I'm going to snog my bird behind a tree, or maybe she needs the kiss of life from the sound of her.' Drew grinned, dropping his arm around her waist as they strolled away from the riotous hooley, making their way down to Bluebell Field, past the horses' pasture, where they paused to look up at a shooting star streaking magically across the sky.

'Make a wish,' Drew said, drawing her to him.

'I did.' Connie sighed contentedly, resting her head against his chest. 'Did you?'

'I did.'

'What did you wish?' She traced her finger along his cheek.

'I wished we'd always be this happy.'

'That's what I wished,' Connie exclaimed, delighted.

'You see, we know each other inside out.' He smiled down at her, his eyes warm and loving.

'It's a terrific day, isn't it? Everyone's really enjoying themselves. Thanks for giving us the run of the place.'

'Glad to be able to help out. Melissa's chuffed, showing her cousins around. It's great to see her looking so much better, and Debbie's in much better form too. The last six months have made a huge difference,' he observed.

'You've been so good to my family. I love you, Drew.' Connie tightened her arms around him.

'I love you too, Connie,' he said huskily, bending his head to kiss her just as a golden sliver of new moon emerged from behind a wisp of cloud to shine its golden light down on them.

ACKNOWLEDGEMENTS

Earth has no sorrow that Heaven cannot heal

Many things have happened to me in the four years of writing this trilogy – the most life-changing being my mother's passing. But ever constant has been the love, support and guidance poured down upon me, and so it is with much gratitude that I give thanks to Jesus, Our Lady, Mother Meera, St Joseph, St Michael, St Anthony, White Eagle, all my Angels, Saints and Guides and my Beloved Mother who is only a thought away.

Huge thanks also to my precious dad who keeps us all going. To all my Beloveds – family, many dear friends and soulmates, especially:

Fiona and Caitriona Scanlan, who advised me on various aspects of my novel; Alil O'Shaughnessy, who has put up with me (stoically) for the last thirty-seven years; Aidan Storey, who listens to lots of whinges and moans and still comes back for more!; Pam Young (and not forgetting Simon), who sends the most inspiring and comforting emails – your Radiant book, *Hope Street*, will light the way for so many; Claudia Carroll, who is so generous and giving in so many ways and who made our trip to London great fun, and Geraldine Ring, who has such a big heart.

Thanks also to my publisher, Transworld Ireland, and all who have worked so hard on my behalf since I came to Transworld many years ago. Especially to Linda Evans, my very patient and kind editor, Jo Williamson, Vivien Garrett, Kate Tolley, Sarah Day, my proofreaders, and all in editorial, production and the art department who do all the background work to make our books the best they can be. It would take a novella to name you all!

To all at Gill Hess who do massive work for my books here in Ireland. I am very grateful to all of you for your support and kindness over the years.

Thanks also to Sarah, Daisy, Jane, Felicity and all at Lutyens & Rubinstein who work so hard on my behalf. It was great to see you and your fabulous new bookshop, and I feel the urge for another visit sooner rather than later.

Thanks as well to Grainne Fox in New York who keeps the flame burning Stateside.

Enormous gratitude to some very special people who have, with great kindness, improved the quality of my life: Mr Hannan Mullett and Grainne Roche, SSC; Professor Ciaran Bolger and Angela and Michelle; Dr Valerie Pollard and Carol Caul; Ms Deborah McNamara and Joan; Sadie Furlong; Emma, Katherine and Bernadette in D ward, and all in the x-ray department of the Bons; Mr Ray Moran and Val and Lisa.

And finally, and equally importantly, a heartfelt thank you to my steadfast readers who have supported my books and me since I was first published in 1990. I never take you for granted and I am so privileged to have such a loyal following. I hope you enjoy reading *Love And Marriage* as much as I enjoyed writing it. Thank you so much for supporting the trilogy with such enthusiasm and for taking the characters to your hearts.

Patricia Scanlan lives in Dublin. Her books, all number one bestsellers, include *Two for Joy, Double Wedding, Divided Loyalties, Forgive and Forget* and *Coming Home.*

Although Patricia loves writing fiction, she's *really* longing to be asked to research a book on Great Luxury Spas of the World or the Poshest Boutiques in Paris . . . she doesn't mind which!